babylon sisters

and other posthumans

other books by paul di filippo

collections:

The Steampunk Trilogy
Ribofunk
Fractal Paisleys
Lost Pages
Strange Trades
Little Doors

novels:

Ciphers
Joe's Liver
A Mouthful of Tongues
Spondulix (forthcoming)

babylon sisters

and other posthumans

paul di filippo

PRIME BOOKS

babylon sisters
and other posthumans

Published by:

Prime Books, Inc.
PO Box 36503, Canton, OH 44735, USA
www.primebooks.net

Copyright © 2002 by Paul Di Filippo

Cover art copyright © 2002 by Sang Lee
Cover & interior design copyright © 2002 by Garry Nurrish

Publisher's Note:

No portion of this book may be reproduced by any means, mechanical, electronic, or otherwise, without first obtaining the permission of the copyright holder.

For more information, contact Prime Books.

Hardback ISBN: 1-894815-80-7
Trade Paperback ISBN: 1-894815-81-5

table of contents

stone lives 9

a short course in art appreciation 33

phylogenesis 43

a thief in babylon 59

solitons 87

gravitons 101

any major dude 117

mud puppy goes uptown 141

otto and toto in the oort... 159

life sentence 173

angelmakers 195

the reluctant book 215

babylon sisters 235

the scab's progress (with bruce sterling) 283

dedication

This one goes out to the editors, their honored names reflected in the ordering of stories: Ed Ferman, George Zebrowski, Patrick Price, David Pringle, Rudy Rucker and Peter Lamborn Wilson, Jimm Gall, David Garnett, Chris Reed, Scott Edelman, Ellen Datlow, and of course, for his work on this volume, Nick Gevers. Thanks, Chums!

And, as always, to Deborah, my favorite human, post-, pre-, or baseline.

stone lives

ODORS BOIL AROUND the Immigration Offices, a stenchy soup. The sweat of desperate men and women, ripe garbage strewn in the packed street, the spicy scent worn by one of the guards at the outer door. The mix is heady, almost overpowering to anyone born outside the Bungle, but Stone is used to it. The constant smells constitute the only atmosphere he has ever known, his native element, too familiar to be despised.

Noise swells to rival the stench. Harsh voices raised in dispute, whining voices lowered to entreat. "Don't sluff me, you rotty bastard!" "I'd treat you real nice, honey, for a share of that." From the vicinity of the door into Immigration, an artificial voice is reciting the day's job offerings, cycling tirelessly through the rotty choices.

"—to test new aerosol antipersonnel toxins. 4M will contract to provide survivors with a full Citrine rejuve. High-orbit vakheads needed by Mc-Donnell Douglas. Must be willing to be imprinted—"

No one seems eager to rush forward and claim these jobs. No voices beg the guards for entrance. Only those who have incurred impossible debts or enmity inside the Bungle ever take a chance on the Rating-10 assignments, which are Immigration's disdainful handouts. Stone knows for sure that he wants no part of these rigged propositions. Like all the rest, he is here at Immigration simply because it provides a focal point, a gathering place as vital as a Serengeti water hole, where the sneaky sluffs and raw deals that pass for business in the South Bronx FEZ—a.k.a. the Bronx Jungle, a.k.a. the Bungle—can be transacted.

Heat smites the noisy crowd, making them more irritable than usual—a dangerous situation. Hyperalertness parches Stone's throat. He reaches for the scratched-to-his-touch plastic flask at his hip and swigs some stale water. Stale but safe, he thinks, relishing his secret knowledge. It was pure luck that he ever stumbled upon the slow leak in the inter-FEZ pipe down by the river fence that encircles the Bungle. He smelled the clean water like a dog from a distance, and by running his hands along several meters of chilly pipe, he found the drip. Now he has all the manifold cues to its exact location deeply memorized.

Shuffling through the crowd on bare callused feet (amazing what information can he picked up through the soles to keep body and soul intact!), Stone quests for scraps of information that will help him survive another day in the Bungle. Survival is his main—his only—concern. If Stone has any pride left, after enduring what he has endured, it is pride in surviving.

A brassy voice claims, "I booted some tempo, man, and that was the end of *that* fight. Thirty seconds later, all three're dead." A listener whistles admiringly. Stone imagines he latches on somehow to a boot of tempo and sells it for an enormous profit, which he then spends on a dry, safe place to sleep and enough to fill his ever-empty gut. Not damn likely, but a nice dream nonetheless.

Thought of food causes his stomach to churn. Across the rough, encrusted cloth covering his midriff, he rests his right hand with its sharp lance of pain that marks the infected cut. Stone assumes the infection. He has no way of telling for sure until it begins to stink.

Stone's progress through the babble of voices and crush of flesh has brought him fairly close to the entrance to Immigration. He feels a volume of empty air between the crowds and the guards, a quartersphere of respect and fear, its vertical face the wall of the building. The respect is generated by the employed status of the guards; the fear by their weapons.

Someone—a transported felon with a little education—once described the guns to Stone. Long, bulky tubes with a bulge halfway along their length where the wiggler magnets are. Plastic stocks and grips. They emit charged beams of energetic electrons at relativistic speeds. If the scythe of the beam touches you, the kinetic energy imparted blows you apart like a squashed sausage. If the particle beam chances to miss, the accompanying cone of gamma rays produces radiation sickness that is fatal within hours.

Of the explanation—which Stone remembers verbatim—he understands only the description of a horrible death. It is enough.

Stone pauses a moment. A familiar voice—that of Mary, the rat-seller—is speaking conspiratorially of the next shipment of charity clothes. Stone deduces her position as being on the very inner edge of the crowd. She lowers her voice. Stone can't make out her words, which are worth hearing. He edges forward, leery though he is of being trapped inside the clot of people—

A dead silence. No one is speaking or moving. Stone senses displaced air puff from between the guards: someone occupies the door.

"You." A refined woman's voice. "Young man with no shoes, in the—" Her voice hesitates for the adjective hiding beneath the grime. "—red jumpsuit. Come here, please. I want to talk to you."

Stone doesn't know if it is he (red?), until he feels the pressure of all eyes upon him. At once he pivots, swerves, fakes—but it is too late. Dozens of eager claws grab him. He wrenches. Moldy fabric splits, but the hands refasten on his skin. He bites, kicks, pummels. No use. During the struggle he makes no sound. Finally he is dragged forward, still fighting, past that invisible line that marks another world as surely as does the unbreachable fence between the Bungle and the other twenty-two FEZ.

Cinnamon scent envelops him, a guard holds something cold and metallic to the back of his neck. All the cells in his skull seem to flare at once, then darkness comes.

Three people betray their forms and locations to the awakened Stone by the air they displace, their scents, their voices—and by a fourth, subtle component he has always labeled sense-of-life.

Behind him: a bulky man who breathes awkwardly, no doubt because of Stone's ripe odor. This has to be a guard. To his left: a smaller person—the woman?—smelling like flowers. (Once Stone smelled a flower.)

Before him, deskbound: a seated man.

Stone feels no aftereffects from the device used on him—unless the total disorientation that has overtaken him is it. He has no idea why he has been shanghaied, and wishes only to return to the known dangers of the Bungle.

But he knows they are not about to let him.

The woman speaks, her voice the sweetest Stone has ever heard.

"This man will ask you some questions. Once you answer them, I'll have one for you. Is that all right?"

Stone nods, his only choice as he sees it.

"Name?" says the Immigration official.

"Stone."

"That's all?"

"That's all anyone calls me." (Unbearable white-hot pain when they dug out the eyes of the little urchin they caught watching them carve up the corpse. But he never cried, oh, no; and so: Stone.)

"Place of birth?"

"This shitheap, right here. Where else?"

"Parents?"

"What're they?"

"Age?"

A shrug.

"That can be fixed later with a cellscan. I suppose we have enough to issue your card. Hold still now."

Stone feels multiple pencils of warmth scroll over his face; seconds later, a chuntering sound from the desk.

"This is your proof of citizenship and access to the system. Don't lose it."

Stone extends a hand in the direction of the voice, receives a plastic rectangle. He goes to shove it into a pocket, finds them both ripped away in the scuffle, and continues to hold the plastic awkwardly, as if it is a brick of gold about to be snatched away.

"Now my question." The woman's voice is like a distant memory Stone has of love. "Do you want a job?"

Stone's trip wire has been brushed. A job they can't even announce in public? It must be so fracking bad that it's off the common corporate scale.

"No thanks, miz. My life ain't much, but it's all I got." He turns to leave.

"Although I can't give you details until you accept, we'll register a contract right now that stipulates it's a Rating-1 job."

Stone stops dead. It has to be a sick joke. But what if it's true?

"A contract?"

"Officer," the woman commands.

A key is tapped, and the desk recites a contract. To Stone's untutored ears, it sounds straightforward and without traps. A Rating-1 job for an unspecified period, either party able to terminate the contract, job description to be appended later.

Stone hesitates only seconds. Memories of all the frightful nights and painful days in the Bungle swarm in his head, along with the hot central pleasure of having survived. Irrationally, he feels a moment's regret at leaving behind the secret city spring he so cleverly found. But it passes.

"I guess you need this to O.K. it," Stone says, offering up his newly won card.

"I guess we do," the woman says with a laugh.

The quiet, sealed car moves through busy streets. Despite the lack of outside noise, the chauffeur's comments on the traffic and their frequent halts are enough to convey a sense of the bustling city around them.

"Where are we now?" Stone asks for the tenth time. Besides wanting the information, he loves to hear this woman speak. Her voice, he thinks—it's like a spring rain when you're safe inside.

"Madison-Park FEZ, traveling crosstown."

Stone nods appreciatively. She may as well have said, "In orbit, blasting for the moon," for all the fuzzy mental image he gets.

Before they would let Stone leave, Immigration did several things to him. Shaved all his body hair off; deloused him; made him shower for ten minutes with a mildly abrasive soap; disinfected him; ran several instant tests; pumped six shots into him; and issued him underwear, clean coveralls, and shoes (shoes!)

The alien smell of himself only makes the woman's perfume more attractive. In the close confines of the backseat, Stone swims in it. Finally he can contain himself no longer.

"Uh, that perfume—what kind is it?"

"Lily of the valley."

The mellifluous phrase makes Stone feel as if he is in another, kinder century. He swears he will always remember it. And he will.

"Hey!" Consternation. "I don't even know your name."

"June. June Tannhauser."

June. Stone. June and Stone and lilies of the valley. June in June with Stone in the valley with the lilies. It's like a song that won't cease in his head.

"Where are we going?" he asks over the silent song in his head.

"To a doctor," says June.

"I thought that was all taken care of."

"This man's a specialist. An eye specialist."

This is the final jolt, atop so many, knocking even the happy song out of Stone's head. He sits tense for the rest of the ride, unthinking.

"This is a lifesized model of what we're going to implant in you," the doctor says, putting a cool ball in Stone's hand.

Stone squeezes it in disbelief

"The heart of this eye system is CCD's—charge-coupled devices. Every bit of light—each photon—that hits them triggers one or more electrons. These electrons are collected as a continuous signal, which is fed through an interpreter chip to your optic nerves. The result: perfect sight."

Stone grips the model so hard his palm bruises.

"Cosmetically, they're a bit shocking. In a young man like yourself, I'd recommend organic implants. However, I have orders from the person footing the bill that these are what you get. And of course, there are several advantages to them."

When Stone does not ask what they are, the doctor continues anyway.

"By thinking mnemonic keywords that the chip is programmed for, you can perform several functions.

"One: You can store digitalized copies of a particular sight in the chip's RAM, for later display. When you reinvoke it with the keyword, it will seem as if you are seeing the sight again directly, no matter what you are actually looking at. Resumption of realtime vision is another keyword.

"Two: By stepping down the ratio of photons to electrons, you can do such things as stare directly at the sun or at a welder's flame without damage.

"Three: By upping the ratio, you can achieve a fair degree of normal sight in conditions such as a starry, moonless night.

"Four: For enhancement purposes, you can generate false-color images. Black becomes white to your brain, the old rose-colored glasses, whatever.

"And I think that about covers it."

"What's the time frame on this, Doctor?" June asks.

The doctor assumes an academic tone, obviously eager to show professional acumen. "A day for the actual operation, two days, accelerated recovery, a week of training and further healing—say, two weeks, max."

'Very good," June says.

Stone feels her rise from the couch beside him, but remains seated.

"Stone," she says, a hand on his shoulder, "time to go."

But Stone can't get up, because the tears won't stop.

The steel and glass canyons of New York—that proud and flourishing union of Free Enterprise Zones—are a dozen shades of cool blue, stretching away to the north. The streets that run with geometric precision like distant rivers on the canyon floors are an arterial red. To the west and east, snatches of the Hudson River and the East River are visible as lime-green flows. Central Park is a wall of sunflower-yellow halfway up the island. To the northeast of the park, the Bungle is a black wasteland.

Stone savors the view. Vision of any kind, even the foggiest blurs, was an unthinkable treasure only days ago. And what he has actually been gifted with—this marvelous ability to turn the everyday world into a jeweled wonderland—is almost too much to believe. Momentarily sated, Stone wills his gaze back to normal. The city instantly reverts to its traditional color of steel-gray, sky-blue, tree-green. The view is still magnificent.

Stone stands at a bank of windows on the 150th floor of the Citrine Tower, in the Wall Street FEZ. For the past two weeks, this has been his home, from which he has not stirred. His only visitors have been a nurse, a cybertherapist, and June. The isolation and relative lack of human contact do not bother him. After the Bungle, such quiet is bliss. And then, of course, he has been enmeshed in the sensuous web of sight.

The first thing he saw upon waking after the operation set the glorious tone of his visual explorations. The smiling face of a woman hovered above him. Her skin was a pellucid olive, her eyes a radiant brown, her hair a raven cascade framing her face.

"How are you feeling?" June asked.

"Good," Stone said. Then he uttered a phrase he never had a use for before. "Thank you."

June waved a slim hand negligently. "Don't thank me. I didn't pay for it."

And that was when Stone learned that June was not his employer, that she worked for someone else. And although she wouldn't tell him then to whom he was indebted, he soon learned when they moved him from the hospital to the building that bore her name.

Alice Citrine. Even Stone knew of her.

Turning from the windows, Stone stalks across the thick cream-colored rug of his quarters. (How strange to move so confidently, without halting and probing!) He has spent the past fifteen days or so zealously practicing with his new eyes. Everything the doctor promised him is true. The miracle of sight pushed into new dimensions. It's all been thrilling. And the luxury of his situation is undeniable. Any kind of food he wants. (Although he would have been satisfied with frack—processed krill.) Music, holovision, and most prized, the company of June. But all of a sudden today, he is feeling a little irritable. Where and what is this job they hired him for? Why has he not met his employer face to face yet? He begins to wonder if this is all some sort of ultra-elaborate sluff.

Stone stops before a full-length mirror mounted on a closet door. Mirrors still have the power to fascinate him utterly. That totally obedient duplicate imitating one's every move, will-less except for his will. And the secondary world in the background, unattainable and silent. During the years in the Bungle when he still retained his eyes, Stone never saw his reflection in anything but puddles or shards of windows. Now he confronts the immaculate stranger in the mirror, seeking clues in his features to the essential personality beneath.

Stone is short and skinny, traces of malnourishment plain in his stature. But his limbs are straight, his lean muscles hard. His skin where it shows from beneath the sleeveless black one-piece is weather-roughened and scarred. Plyoskin slippers—tough, yet almost as good as barefoot—cover his feet.

His face. All intersecting planes, like that strange picture in his bedroom. (Did June say "Picasso"?) Sharp jaw, thin nose, blond stubble on his skull. And his eyes: faceted dull-black hemispheres: inhuman. But don't take them back, please; I'll do whatever you want.

Behind him the exit door to his suite opens. It's June. Without conscious thought, Stone's impatience spills out in words, which pile one for one atop June's simultaneous sentence, merging completely at the end.

"I want to see—"

"We're going to visit—"

"—Alice Citrine."

Fifty floors above Stone's suite, the view of the city is even more spectacular. Stone has learned from June that the Citrine Tower stands on land that did not even exist a century ago. Pressure to expand motivated a vast landfill in the East River, south of the Brooklyn Bridge. On part of this artificial real estate, the Citrine Tower was built in the Oughts, during the boom period following the Second Constitutional Convention.

Stone boosts the photon-electron ratio of his eyes, and the East River becomes a sheet of white fire. A momentary diversion to ease his nerves.

"Stand here with me," June says, indicating a disk just beyond the elevator door, a few meters from another entrance.

Stone complies. He imagines he can feel the scanning rays on him, although it is probably just the nearness of June, whose elbow touches his. Her scent fills his nostrils, and he fervently hopes that having eyes won't dull his other senses.

Silently the door opens for them.

June guides him through.

Alice Citrine waits inside.

The woman sits in a powered chair behind a horseshoe-shaped bank of screens. Her short hair is corn-yellow, her skin unlined, yet Stone intuits a vast age clinging to her, the same way he used to be able to sense emotions when blind. He studies her aquiline profile, familiar somehow as a face once dreamed is familiar.

She swivels, presenting her full features. June has led them to within a meter of the burnished console.

"Good to see you, Mr. Stone," says Citrine. "I take it you are comfortable, no complaints."

"Yes," Stone says. He tries to summon up the thanks he meant to give, but can't find them anywhere, so disconcerted is he. Instead, he says tentatively, "My job—"

"Naturally you're curious," Citrine says. "It must be something underhanded or loathsome or deadly. Why else would I need to recruit someone from the Bungle? Well, let me at last satisfy you. Your job, Mr. Stone, is to study."

Stone is dumbfounded. "Study?"

"Yes, study. You know the meaning of the word, don't you? Or have I made a mistake? Study, learn, investigate, and whenever you feel you understand something, draft me a report."

Stone's bafflement had passed through amazement to incredulity. "I can't even read or write," he says. "And what the frack am I supposed to study?"

"Your field of study, Mr. Stone, is this contemporary world of ours. I have had a large part, as you may know, in making this world what it is today. And as I reach the limits of my life, I grow more interested in whether what I have built is bad or good. I have plenty of reports from experts, both positive and negative. But what I want now is a fresh view from one of the underdwellers. All I ask is honesty and accuracy.

"As for reading and writing—those outmoded skills of my youth—June will assist you in learning those if you wish. But you have machines to read to you and transcribe your speech. You may start at once."

Stone tries to assimilate this mad request. It seems capricious, a cover for deeper, darker deeds. But what can he do except say yes?

He agrees.

A tiny smile plucks at the woman's lips. "Fine. Then our talk is over. Oh, one last thing. If you need to conduct on-site research, June must accompany you. And you will mention my sponsorship of you to no one. I don't want sycophants."

The conditions are easy—especially having June always close—and Stone nods his acceptance.

Citrine turns her back to them then. Stone is startled by what he sees, almost believing his eyes defective.

Perched on the broad back of her chair is a small animal resembling a lemur or tarsier. Its big, luminous eyes gaze soulfully at them, its long tail arcs in a spiral above its back.

"Her pet," whispers June, and hurries Stone away.

The task is too huge, too complex. Stone considers himself a fool for ever having accepted.

But what else could he have done, if he wanted to keep his eyes?

Stone's cramped and circumscribed life in the Bungle has not prepared him well to fathom the multiplex, extravagant, pulsating world he has been transported to. (At least this is what he initially feels.) Literally and figuratively kept in the dark for so long, he finds the world outside the Citrine Tower a mystifying place.

There are hundreds, thousands of things he has never heard of before. People, cities, objects, events. There are areas of expertise whose names he can hardly pronounce. Areology, chaoticism, fractal modeling, paraneurology. And don't forget history, that bottomless well atop which the present moment is but a scrim of bubbles. Stone is, perhaps, most shocked by his discovery of history. He cannot recall ever having considered life as extending backward in time beyond his birth. The revelation of decades, centuries, millennia nearly pushes him into a mental abyss. How can one hope to comprehend the present without knowing all that has gone before?

Hopeless, insane, suicidal to persist.

Yet Stone persists.

He closets himself with his magic window on the world, a terminal that interfaces with the central computer in the Citrine Tower—itself a vast, unintelligible hive of activity—and through that machine to almost every other in the world. For hours on end, images and words flash by him, like knives thrown by a circus performer—knives that he, the loyal but dumb assistant, must catch to survive.

Stone's memory is excellent, trained in a cruel school, and he assimilates much. But each path he follows has a branch every few steps, and each branch splits at frequent points, and those tertiary branches also sprout new ones, no less rich than the primaries . . .

Once Stone nearly drowned, when a gang left him unconscious in a gutter and it began to rain. He recalls the sensation now.

June brings him three meals faithfully each day. Her presence still thrills him. Each night, as he lies abed, he replays stored images of her to lull him asleep. June bending, sitting, laughing, her Asian eyes aglow. The subtle curves of her breasts and hips. But the knowledge-fever is stronger, and he tends to ignore her as the days go by.

One afternoon Stone notices a pill on his lunch tray. He asks June its nature.

"Its a mnemotropin—promotes the encoding of long-term memories," she replies. "I thought it might help you."

Stone swallows it greedily, and returns to the droning screen.

Each day he finds a pill at lunch. His brain seems to expand to a larger volume soon after he takes them. The effect is potent, allowing him to imagine he can ingest the world. But still, each night when he finally forces himself to stop, he feels he has not done enough.

Weeks pass. He has not prepared a single sentence for Alice Citrine. What does he understand? Nothing. How can he pass judgment on the world? It's hubris, folly. How long will she wait before she kicks his ass out onto the cold street?

Stone drops his head in his hands. The mocking machine before him torments him with a steady diarrhea of useless facts.

A hand falls lightly on his quivering shoulder. Stone imbibes June's sweet scent.

Stone smashes the terminal's power stud with the base of his palm so fiercely it hurts. Blessed silence. He looks up at June.

"I'm no damn good at this. Why'd she pick me? I don't even know where to start."

June sits on a cushion beside him. "Stone, I haven't said anything, because I was ordered not to direct you. But I don't think sharing a little of my experience will count as interference. You've got to limit your topic, Stone. The world's too big. Alice doesn't expect you to comprehend it all, distill it into a masterpiece of concision and sense.

"The world doesn't lend itself to such summations, anyway. I think you unconsciously know what she wants. She gave you a clue when you talked to her."

Stone summons up that day, plays back a view he filed of the stern old woman. Her features occult June's. The visual cue drags along a phrase.

"—whether what I have built is bad or good."

It is as if Stone's eyes have overloaded. Insight floods him with relief. Of course, the vain and powerful woman sees her life as the dominant theme of the modern era, a radiant thread passing through time, with critical nodes of action strung on it like beads. How much easier to understand a single human life than that of the whole world. (Or so he believes at the moment.) That much he thinks he can do. Chart Citrine's personal history, the ramifications of her long career, the ripples spreading from her throne. Who knows? It might indeed prove archetypal.

Stone wraps his arms around June in exultation, gives a wordless shout. She doesn't resist his embrace, and they fall back upon the couch.

Her lips are warm and complaisant under his. Her nipples seem to burn through her shirt and into his chest. His left leg is trapped between her thighs.

Suddenly he pulls back. He has seen himself too vividly: scrawny castoff from the sewer of the city, with eyes not even human.

"No," he says bitterly. "You can't want me."

"Quiet," she says, "quiet." Her hands are on his face; she kisses his neck; his spine melts; and he falls atop her again, too hungry to stop.

"You're so foolish for someone so smart," she murmurs to him afterwards. "Just like Alice."

He does not consider her meaning.

The roof of the Citrine Tower is a landing facility for phaetons, the suborbital vehicles of companies and their executives. He feels he has learned all he can of Alice Citrine's life, while cooped up in the tower. Now he wants the heft and feel of actual places and people to judge her by.

But before they may leave, June tells Stone, they must speak to Jerrold Scarfe.

In a small departure lounge, all soft white corrugated walls and molded chairs, the three meet.

Scarfe is head of security for Citrine Technologies. A compact, wiry man, exhibiting a minimum of facial expressions, he strikes Stone as eminently competent, from the top of his permanently depilated and tattooed skull to his booted feet. On his chest he wears the CT emblem: a red spiral with an arrowhead on its outer terminus, pointing up.

June greets Scarfe with some familiarity, and asks, "Are we cleared?"

Scarfe waggles a sheet of flimsy in the air. "Your flight plan is quite extensive. Is it really necessary, for instance, to visit a place like Mexico City, with Mr. Stone aboard?"

Stone wonders at Scarfe's solicitude for him, an unimportant stranger. June interprets Stone's puzzled look and explains. "Jerrold is one of the few people that know you represent Miz Citrine. Naturally, he's worried that if we run into trouble of some kind, the fallout will descend on Citrine Technologies."

"I'm not looking for trouble, Mr. Scarfe. I just want to do my job."

Scarfe scans Stone as intently as the devices outside Alice Citrine's sanctum. The favorable result is eventually expressed as a mild grunt, and the announcement, "Your pilot's waiting. Go ahead."

Higher off the grasping earth than he has ever been before, his right hand atop June's left knee, feeling wild and rich and free, Stone ruminates over the life of Alice Citrine, and the sense he is beginning to make of it.

Alice Citrine is 159 years old. When she was born, America was still comprised of states, rather than FEZ and ARCadias. Man had barely begun to fly. When she was in her sixties, she headed a firm called Citrine Biotics. This was the time of the Trade Wars, wars as deadly and decisive as military ones, yet fought with tariffs and five-year plans, automated assembly lines and fifth-generation decision making constructs. This was also the time of the Second Constitutional Convention, that revamping of America for the state of war.

During the years when the country was being divided into Free Enterprise Zones—urban, hi-tek, autonomous regions, where the only laws were those imposed by corporations and the only goal was profits and dominance—and Areas of Restrictive Control—rural, mainly agricultural enclaves, where older values were strictly enforced—Citrine Biotics refined and perfected the work of their researchers and others in the field of carbon chips: microbiological assemblies, blood-borne programmed repair units. The final product, marketed by Citrine to those who could afford it, was near-total rejuvenation, the cell-slough—or, simply, the sluff.

Citrine Biotics headed the Fortune 500 within six years.

By then it was Citrine Technologies.

And Alice Citrine sat atop it all.

But not forever.

Entropy will not be cheated. The information-degradation that DNA undergoes with age is not totally reversible. Errors accumulate despite the hardworking carbon chips. The body dutiful gives out in the end.

Alice Citrine is nearing the theoretical close of her extended life. Despite her youthful looks, one day a vital organ will fail, the result of a million bad transcriptions.

She needs Stone, of all people, to justify her existence.

Stone squeezes June's knee and relishes the sense of importance. For the first time in his sad and dingy life, he can make a difference. His words, his perceptions matter. He is determined to do a good job, to tell the truth as he perceives it.

"June," Stone says emphatically, "I have to see everything."

She smiles. "You will, Stone. You will indeed."

And the phaeton comes down—

—in Mexico City, which crashed last year at population 35 million. Citrine Technologies is funding a relief effort there, operating out of their Houston and Dallas locations. Stone is suspicious of the motives behind the campaign. Why didn't they step in before the point of collapse? Can it be that they are worried now only about refugees flooding across the border? Whatever the reasons, though, Stone cannot deny that the CT workers are a force for good, ministering to the sick and hungry, reestablishing electrical power and communications, propping up (acting as?) the city government. He boards the phaeton with his head spinning, and soon finds himself—

—in the Antarctic, where he and June are choppered out from the CT domes to a krill-processing ship, source of so much of the world's protein. June finds the frack stench offensive, but Stone breathes deeply, exhilarated at being afloat in these strange and icy latitudes, watching the capable men and women work. June is happy to be soon aloft, and then—

—in Peking, where CT heuristic specialists are working on the first Artificial Organic Intelligence. Stone listens with amusement to a debate over whether the AOI should be named K'ung Fu-tzu or Mao.

The week is a kaleidoscopic whirl of impressions. Stone feels like a sponge, soaking up the sights and sounds so long denied him. At one point he finds himself leaving a restaurant with June, in a city whose name he has forgotten. In his hand is his ID card, with which he had just paid for their meal. A holoportrait stares up from his palm. The face is cadaverous, filthy, with two empty, crusted sockets for eyes. Stone remembers the warm laser fingers taking his holo in the Immigration Office. Was that really he? The day seems like an event from someone else's life. He pockets his card, unsure whether to have the holo updated or to keep it as a token of where he has come from.

And where he might end up?

(What will she do with him after he reports?)

When Stone asks one day to see orbital installations, June calls a halt. "I think we've done enough for one trip, Stone. Let's get back, so you can start to put it all together."

With her words, a deep boneweariness suddenly overtakes Stone, and his manic high evaporates. He silently assents.

⸺⸺

Stone's bedroom is dark, except for the diffuse lights of the city seeping in through a window. Stone has multiplied his vision, the better to admire the naked glowing form of June beside him. He has found that colors grow muddy in the absence of enough photons, but that a very vivid black-and white image can be had. He feels like a dweller in the past century, watching a primitive film. Except that June is very much alive beneath his hands. June's body is a tracery of lambent lines, like some arcane capillary circuitry in the core of Mao/K'ung Fu-tzu. Following the current craze, she has had a subdermal pattern of microchannels implanted. The channels are filled with synthetic luciferase, the biochemical responsible for the glow of fireflies, which she can now trigger at will. In the afterglow of their lovemaking, she has set herself alight. Her breasts are whorls of cold fire, her shaven pubic mound a spiral galaxy dragging Stone's gaze into illimitable depths.

June is speaking in an abstracted way of her life before Stone, pondering the ceiling while he idly strokes her.

"My mother was the only surviving child of two refugees. Vietnamese. Came to America shortly after the Asian War. Did the only thing they knew how to do, which was fish. They lived in Texas, on the Gulf. My mother went to college on a scholarship. There she met my father, who was another refugee of sorts. He left Germany with his parents after its Reunification. They said the compromise government was neither one thing nor the other, and they couldn't deal with it. I guess my background is some sort of microcosm of a lot of the upheavals of our times."

She catches Stone's hand between her knees and holds it tightly. "But I feel a calmness with you right now, Stone." As she continues to speak of things she has seen, people she has known, her career as Citrine's personal assistant, the oddest feeling creeps over Stone. As her words integrate themselves into his growing picture of the world, he feels the same abysmal tidal suck that he first felt upon learning of history.

Before he can decide consciously if he even wants to know or not, he finds himself saying, "June. How old are you?"

She falls silent. Stone watches her staring blindly at him, unequipped with his damned perceptive eyes.

"Over sixty," she finally says. "Does it matter?"

Stone finds he cannot answer, does not know if her age does matter or not.

Slowly June wills her glowing body dark.

Stone bitterly amuses himself with what he likes to think of as his art.

Perusing the literature on the silicon chip that dwells in his skull, he found that it has one property not mentioned by the doctor. The contents of its RAM can be squirted in a signal to a stand-alone computer. There the images he has collected may be displayed for all to see. What is more, the digitized images may be manipulated, recombined with themselves or with stock graphics, to form entirely lifelike pictures of things that never existed. These, of course, may be printed off.

In effect, Stone is a living camera and his computer a complete studio.

Stone has been working on a series of images of June. The color printouts litter his quarters, hung on walls and underfoot.

June's head on the Sphinx's body. June as *La Belle Dame Sans Merci*. June's face imposed upon the full moon, Stone asleep in a field as Endymion.

The portraits are more disturbing than soothing, and, Stone senses, quite unfair. But Stone feels that he is gaining some therapeutic effect from them, that each day he is inching closer to his true feelings for June.

He still has not spoken to Alice Citrine. That nags him greatly. When will he deliver his report? What will he say?

The problem of when is solved for him that afternoon. Returning from one of the tower's private gyms, he finds his terminal flashing a message.

Citrine will see him in the morning.

Alone this second time, Stone stands on the plate before Alice Citrine's room, allowing his identity to be verified. He hopes the results will be shared with him when the machine finishes, for he has no idea of who he is.

The door slides into the wall, a beckoning cavern mouth.

Avernus, Stone thinks, and enters.

Alice Citrine remains where she sat so many event-congested weeks ago, unchanged, seemingly sempiternal. The screens flicker in epileptic patterns on three sides of her instrumented chair. Now, however, she ignores them, her eyes on Stone, who advances with trepidation.

Stone stops before her, the console an uncrossable moat between them. He notes her features this second time with a mix of disbelief and alarm. They seem to resemble his newly fleshed-out face to an uncanny degree. Has he come to look like this woman simply by working for her? Or does life outside the Bungle stamp the same harsh lines on everyone?

Citrine brushes her hand above her lap, and Stone notices her pet curled in the valley of her brown robe, its preternaturally large eyes catching the colors on the monitors.

"Time for a preliminary report, Mr. Stone," she says. "But your pulse rate is much too high. Relax a bit—everything does not hinge on this one session."

Stone wishes he could. But there is no offer of a seat, and he knows that what he says will be judged.

"So—what do you feel about this world of ours, which bears the impress of myself and others like me?"

The smug superiority in Citrine's voice drives all caution from Stone's thoughts, and he nearly shouts, "It's unfair." He pauses a moment, and then honesty forces him to admit, "Beautiful, gaudy, exciting at times—but basically unfair."

Citrine seems pleased at his outburst. "Very good, Mr. Stone. You have discovered the basic contradiction of life. There are jewels in the dung heap, tears amid the laughter, and how it is all parceled out, no one knows. I'm afraid I cannot shoulder the blame for the world's unfairness, though. It was unfair when I was a child, and remained unfair despite all my actions. In fact, I may have increased the disparity a little. The rich are richer, the poor seemingly poorer by comparison. But still, even the titans are brought down by death in the end."

"But why don't you try harder to change things?" Stone demands. "It has to be within your power. "

For the first time, Citrine laughs, and Stone hears an echo of his own sometimes bitter caw. "Mr. Stone, " she says, "I have all I can do to stay alive. And I do not mean taking care of my body—that is attended to automatically. No, I mean avoiding assassination. Haven't you gleaned the true nature of business in this world of ours?"

Stone fails to see her meaning, and says so.

"Allow me to brief you, then. It might alter a few of your perceptions. You are aware of the intended purpose of the Second Constitutional Convention, are you not? It was couched in high-flown phrases like 'unleash the strength of the American system,' and 'meet foreign competition head-to-head, ensuring a victory for American business that will pave the way for democracy throughout the world.' All very noble-sounding. But the actual outcome was quite different. Business has no stake in any political system *per se*. Business cooperates to the extent that cooperation furthers its own interests. And the primary interest of business is growth and dominance. Once the establishment of the Free Enterprise Zones freed corporations from all constraints, they reverted to a primal struggle, which continues to this day."

Stone attempts to digest all this. He has seen no overt struggles on his journey. Yet he has vaguely sensed undercurrents of tension everywhere. But surely she is overstating the case. Why, she makes the civilized world sound no more than a large-scale version of the anarchy of the Bungle.

As if reading his mind, Citrine says, "Did you ever wonder why the Bungle remains blighted and exploited in the midst of the city, Mr. Stone, its people in misery?"

Suddenly all of Citrine's screens flash with scenes of Bungle life, obedient to her unvoiced command. Stone is taken aback. Here are the sordid details of his youth: urine-reeking alleys with rag-covered forms lying halfway between sleep and death, the chaos around the Immigration Office, the razor-topped fence by the river.

"The Bungle," Citrine continues, "is contested ground. It has been so for over eighty years. The corporations cannot agree over who is to develop it. Any improvement made by one is immediately destroyed by the tactical team of another. This is the kind of stalemate prevalent in much of the world.

"Everyone wanted to be pulled into an earthly paradise by his purse strings, like a Krishna devotee by his pigtail. But this patchwork of fiefdoms is what we got instead."

Stone's conceptions are reeling. He came expecting to be quizzed and to disgorge all he thought he knew. Instead, he has been lectured and provoked, almost as if Citrine is testing whether he is a partner fit to debate. Has he passed or failed?

Citrine settles the question with her next words. "That's enough for today, Mr. Stone. Go back and think some more. We'll talk again."

For three weeks Stone meets nearly every day with Citrine. Together they explore a bewildering array of her concerns. Stone gradually becomes more confident of himself, expressing his opinions and observations in a firmer tone. They do not always mesh with Citrine's, yet on the whole he feels a surprising kinship and affinity with the ancient woman.

Sometimes it almost seems as if she is grooming him, master and apprentice, and is proud of his progress. At other times she holds herself distant and aloof.

The weeks have brought other changes. Although Stone has not slept with June since that fateful night, he no longer sees her as the siren figure of his portraits, and has stopped depicting her in that fashion. They are friends, and Stone visits with her often, enjoys her company, is forever grateful to her for her part in rescuing him from the Bungle.

During his interviews with Citrine, her pet is a constant spectator. Its enigmatic presence disturbs Stone. He has found no trace of sentimental affection in Citrine, and cannot fathom her attention to the creature.

One day Stone finally asks Citrine outright why she keeps it.

Her lips twitch in what passes for her smile. "Aegypt is my touchstone on the true perspective of things, Mr. Stone. Perhaps you do not recognize her breed."

Stone admits ignorance.

"This is *Aegyptopithecus zeuxis*, Mr. Stone. Her kind last flourished several million years ago. Currently she is the only specimen extant, a clone—or rather, a recreation based on dead fossil cells.

"She is your ancestor and mine, Mr. Stone. Before the hominids, she was the representative of mankind on earth. When I pet her, I contemplate how little we have advanced."

Stone turns and stalks off, unaccountably repelled by the antiquity of the beast and the insight into her mistress.

This is the last time he will see Alice Citrine.

Night time.

Stone lies alone in bed, replaying snapshots of his terminal screen, of pre-FEZ history that has eluded him.

History that has eluded him.

Suddenly there is a loud crack like the simultaneous discharge of a thousand gigantic arcs of static electricity. At that exact second, two things happen:

Stone feels an instant of vertigo.

His eyes go dead.

Atop these shocks, an enormous explosion above his head rocks the entire shaft of the Citrine Tower.

Stone shoots to his feet, clad only in briefs, barefoot as in the Bungle. He can't believe he's blind. But he is. Back in the dark world of smell and sound and touch alone.

Alarms are going off everywhere. Stone rushes out into his front room with its useless view of the city. He approaches the front door, but it fails to open. He reaches for the manual control, but hesitates.

What can he do while blind? He'd just stumble around, get in the way. Better to stay here and wait out whatever is happening.

Stone thinks of June then, can almost smell her perfume. Surely she will be down momentarily to tell him what's going on. That's it. He'll wait for June.

Stone paces nervously for three minutes. He can't believe his loss of vision. Yet somehow he's always known it would happen.

The alarms have stopped, allowing Stone to hear near-subliminal footsteps in the hall, advancing on his door. June at last? No, everything's wrong. Stone's sense-of-life denies that the visitor is anyone he knows.

Stone's Bungle instincts take over. He ceases to speculate about what is happening, is all speed and fear.

The curtains in the room are tied back with thin but strong velvet cords. Stone rips one hastily down, takes up a position to the side of the outer door.

The shock wave when the door is hit nearly knocks Stone down. But he regains his balance, tasting blood, just as the man barrels in and past him.

Stone is on the man's burly back in a flash, legs wrapped around his waist, cord around his throat.

The man drops his gun, hurls himself back against the wall. Stone feels ribs give, but he tightens the rope, muscles straining.

The two stagger around the room, smashing furniture and vases, locked in something like an obscene mating posture.

Eventually, after forever, the man keels over, landing heavily atop Stone.

Stone never relents, until he is sure the man has stopped breathing.

His attacker is dead.

Stone lives.

He wriggles painfully out from under the slack mass, shaken and hurt.

As he gets his feet under him, he hears more people approaching, speaking.

Jerrold Scarfe is the first to enter, calling Stone by name. When he spots Stone, Scarfe shouts, "Get that stretcher over here."

Men bundle Stone onto the canvas and begin to carry him off.

Scarfe walks beside him, and conducts a surrealistic conversation.

"They learned who you were, Mr. Stone. That one fracking bastard got by us. We contained the rest in the wreckage of the upper floors. They hit us with a directed electromagnetic pulse that took out all our electronics, including your vision. You might have lost a few brain cells when it burned, but nothing that can't be fixed. After the EMP, they used a missile on Miz Citrine's floor. I'm afraid she died instantly."

Stone feels as if he is being shaken to pieces, both physically and mentally. Why is Scarfe telling him this? And what about June?

Stone croaks her name.

"She's dead, Mr. Stone. When the raiders assigned to bag her had begun to work on her, she killed herself with an implanted toxin-sac."

All the lilies wither when winter draws near.

The stretcher party has reached the medical facilities. Stone is lifted onto a bed, and clean hands begin to attend to his injuries.

"Mr. Stone," Scarfe continues, "I must insist that you listen to this. It's imperative, and it will take only a minute. "

Stone has begun to hate this insistent voice. But he cannot close his ears or lapse into blessed unconsciousness, so he is forced to hear the cassette Scarfe plays.

It is Alice Citrine speaking.

"Blood of my blood," she begins, "closer than a son to me. You are the only one I could ever trust."

Disgust washes over Stone as everything clicks into place and he realizes what he is.

"You are hearing this after my death. This means that what I have built is now yours. All the people have been bought to ensure this. It is now up to you to retain their loyalty. I hope our talks have helped you. If not, you will need even more luck than I wish you now.

"Please forgive your abandonment in the Bungle. It's just that a good education is so important, and I believe you received the best. I was always watching you."

Scarfe shuts off the cassette. "What are your orders, Mr. Stone?"

Stone thinks with agonizing slowness while unseen people minister to him.

"Just clean this mess up, Scarfe. Just clean up this whole goddamn mess."

But he knows as he speaks that this is not Scarfe's job.

It's his.

a short course in art appreciation

WE WERE SO happy, Elena and I, in the Vermeer perceptiverse. Our days and nights were filled with visual epiphanies that seemed to ignite the rest of our senses, producing a conflagration of desire that burned higher and higher, until it finally subsided to the embers of satiation, from which the whole inferno, phoenixlike, could be rekindled at will. There had never been a time when we were so thrilled with life, so enamored of the world and each other—so much in love.

Yet somehow, I knew from the start that our idyll was doomed to end. Such bliss was not for us, could never last. I don't know what it was that implanted such a subliminal worm of doubt in my mind, with its tiny, whispering voice that spoke continually of transience and loss and exhaustion. Perhaps it was the memory of the sheer avidity and almost obscene yearning greed with which Elena had first approached me with the idea of altering our natural perceptiverses.

She entered my apartment that spring day (we were not yet living together then, a symbol, I believe, of our separate identities that irrationally irked her) in a mood like none I had ever witnessed her exhibit. (I try now to picture her unaltered face, as I observed it on that fateful day, but it is so hard, after the dizzying cascade of perceptiverses we have experienced, to clearly visualize anything from that long-ago time. How can I have totally forgotten the mode of seeing that was as natural as breathing to me for thirty-some-odd years? It is as if the natural perceptiverse I was born into is a painting that lies layers deep, below several others, and whose lines can be only imperfectly traced. You will understand, then, if I cannot recreate the scene precisely.)

In any case, I remember our conversation from that day perfectly. (Thank God I resisted the temptation to enter one of the composer perceptiverses, or that memory, too, might be buried, under an avalanche of glorious sound!) I have frequently mentally replayed our words, seeking to learn if there was any way I could have circumvented Elena's unreasoning desires—avoiding both the heaven and hell that lay embryonic in her steely whims—yet still have managed to hold onto her love.

I feel now that, essentially, there was no way. She was simply too strong and determined for me—or perhaps I was too weak—and I could not deny her.

But I still cannot bring myself to blame her.

Crossing the memory-hazed room, Elena said excitedly, "Robert, it's out!"

I laid down my book, making sure to shut it off, and, all unwitting, asked, "Not even a hello or a kiss? It must be something wonderful, then. Well, I'll bite. What's out?"

"Why, just that new neurotropin everyone's been waiting so long for, the one to alter the perceptiverses."

I immediately grew defensive. "Elena, you know I try to steer clear of those designer drugs. They're just not—not natural. I'm not a prig, Elena. I don't mind indulging in a little grass or coke now and then—they're perfectly natural mind-altering substances that mankind's been using for centuries. But these new artificial compounds—they can really screw up your neuropeptides."

Elena grew huffy. "Robert, you're talking nonsense. This isn't one of the regulated substances, you know, like tempo or ziptone. Why, it's not even supposed to be as strong as estheticine. It doesn't get you high or alter your thinking at all. It merely gives you a new perceptiverse."

"And what, if I may ask, is a perceptiverse?"

"Oh Robert," Elena sighed in exasperation, "and you call yourself educated! That's just the kind of question I should have expected from someone whose nose is always buried in a book. The perceptiverse is just the universe as filtered through one's perceptions. It's the only universe any of us can know, of course. In fact, it might be the only universe that exists for any of us, if those physicists you're always quoting know what they're talking about."

"Elena, we've had this discussion before. I keep telling you that you can't apply the rules of quantum physics to the macroscopic world . . ."

"Oh, screw all that anyway! You're just trying to change the subject. Aren't you excited at all?"

"Maybe I would be, if I knew what it was all about. I still don't understand. Is this new drug just another hallucinogen?"

"No, that's just it; it's much more. It alters your visual perceptions in a coherent, consistent manner, without affecting anything else. You don't see anything that's not there; you just see what does exist in a different way. And since sight's our most critical sense, the effect's supposed to be like stepping into another universe."

I considered. "And exactly what kind of universe would one be stepping into?"

Elena fell into my lap with a delighted squeal, as if she had won the battle. "Oh Robert, that's just it! It's not *what* universe, it's *whose*!"

"Whose?"

"Yes, whose! The psychoengineers claim they've distilled the essence of artistic vision."

I suppose I should interject here that Elena was a student of art history. In our bountiful world, where the Net cradled one from birth to death, she was free to spend all her time doing what she enjoyed, which happened to be wandering for hours through museums, galleries, and studios, with me in tow.

"You're saying," I slowly went on, "that this magical pill lets you see like, say, Rembrandt?"

"No," frowned Elena, "not exactly. After all, Rembrandt, to use your example, probably didn't literally see much differently than any of us. That's a fallacy nonartists always fall for. The magic was in how he transmuted his everyday vision, capturing it in the medium of his art. I doubt if any artist, except perhaps those like Van Gogh, who are close to madness, can maintain their unique perspective every minute of their waking hours. No, what the psychoengineers have done is to formalize the stylistic elements of particular artists—more or less the idiosyncratic rules that govern light and shape and texture in an individual perceptiverse—and make them reproducible. By taking this new neurotropin, we'll be enabled to see not *like* Rembrandt, but as if *inhabiting* Rembrandt's canvases!"

"I find that hard to believe..."

"It's true, Robert; it's true! The volunteers all report the most marvelous results!"

"But Elena, would you really want to inhabit a Rembrandt world all day?"

"Of course! Look around you! All these dull plastics and synthetics! Who wouldn't want to! And anyway, it's not Rembrandt they've chosen for the first release. It's Vermeer."

"Vermeer or Rembrandt, Elena, I just don't know if..."

"Robert, you haven't even considered the most important aspect of all this. We'd be doing it together! For the first time in history, two people can be sure they're sharing the same perceptiverse. Our visual perceptions would be absolutely synchronized. I'd never have to wonder if you really understood what I was seeing, nor you me. We'd be totally at one. Just think what it would mean for our love!"

Her face—that visage I can no longer fully summon up without a patina of painterly interpretation—was glowing. I couldn't hold out against her.

"All right," I said. "If it means so much to you..."

She tossed her arms around my neck and hugged me close. "Oh Robert, I knew you'd come around! This is wonderful!" She released me and stood. "I have the pills right here."

I confess to having felt a little alarm right then. "You bought them already, not knowing if I'd even agree..."

"You're not angry, are you, Robert? It's just that I thought we knew each other so well..." She fingered her little plastic pill case nervously.

"No, I'm not angry; it's just... Oh well, forget it. Let's have the damn pill."

She fetched a single glass of water from the tap and dispensed the pills. She swallowed first, then, as if sharing some obscure sacrament, passed me the glass. I downed the pill. It seemed to scorch my throat.

"How long does the effect last?" I asked.

"Why, I thought I made that clear. Until you take another one."

I sat down weakly, Elena resting one haunch on the arm of the chair beside me. We waited for the change, looking curiously around the room.

Subtly at first, then with astonishing force and speed, my perceptiverse—our perceptiverse—began to alter. Initially it was the light pouring in through the curtained windows that began to seem different. It acquired a pristine translucency, tinged with supernal honeyed overtones. This light fell on the wood, the plastic, the fabric in my mundane apartment, utterly transfiguring everything it touched, in what seemed like a chain reaction that raced through the very molecules of my whole perceptiverse.

In minutes the change was complete.

I was inhabiting the Vermeer perceptiverse.

I turned to face Elena.

She looked like the woman in *Young Woman with a Water Jug* at the Met.

I had never seen anything—anyone—so beautiful.

My eyes filled with tears.

I knew Elena was experiencing the same thing as I.

Crying, she said, "Oh Robert, kiss me now."

I did. And then, somehow, we were naked, our oil paint- and brush-stroke-mottled bodies shining as if we had stepped tangibly from the canvas, rolling on the carpet, locked in a frantic lovemaking unlike anything I had ever experienced before that moment.

I felt as though I were fucking Art itself.

Thus began the happiest months of my life.

At first, Elena and I were content merely to stay in the apartment all day, simply staring in amazement at the most commonplace objects, now all transformed into perfect elements in some vast, heretofore-undiscovered masterpiece by Vermeer. Once we had exhausted a particular view, we had only to shift our position to create a completely different composition, which we could study for hours more. To set the table for a meal was to fall enraptured into contemplation of a unique still life each time. The rules of perceptual transformation that the psychoengineers had formulated worked perfectly. Substances and scenes that Vermeer could never have imagined acquired the unmistakable touch of his palette and brush.

Tiring even of such blissful inactivity, we would make love with a frenetic reverence approaching satori. Afterward the wrinkles in the sheets reminded us of thick troughs of paint, impasto against our skin.

After a time, of course, this stage passed. Desirous of new vistas, we set out to explore the Vermeer-veneered world.

We were not alone. Thousands shared the same perceptiverse, and we encountered them everywhere, instant signs of mutual recognition being exchanged. To look into their eyes was to peer into a mental landscape utterly familiar to all us art-trippers.

The sights we saw—I can't encapsulate them in words for you. Perhaps you've shared them, too, and words are unnecessary. The whole world was almost palpably the work of a single hand, a marvel of artistic vision, just as the mystics had always told us.

It was in Nice, I believe, that Elena approached me with her little pill-case in hand. She had gone out unexpectedly without me, while I was still sleeping. I didn't complain, being content to sit on the balcony and watch the eternally changing Mediterranean, although, underneath my rapture, I believe I felt a bit of amazement that she had left without a word.

Now, pill case offered in outstretched hand, Elena, having returned, said without preamble, "Here, Robert; take one."

I took the pill and studied its perfection for a time before I asked, "What is it?"

"Matisse," she said. "We're in his native land now, the source of his vision. It's only right."

"Elena, I don't know. Haven't we been happy with Vermeer? Why change now? We could spoil everything . . . "

Elena swallowed Matisse dry. "I've taken mine, Robert. I need something new. Unless you want to be left behind, you'll do the same."

I couldn't stand the thought of living in a different perceptiverse than Elena. Although the worm of discontent told me not to, I did as Elena asked.

Matisse went down easy.

In no time at all, the sharp, uncompromising realism of Vermeer gave way to the gaudy, exhilarating, heady impressionism of Matisse. The transition was almost too powerful to take.

"Oh my God . . . " I said.

"There," said Elena, "wasn't I right? Take your clothes off now. I have to see you naked."

We inaugurated this new perceptiverse as we had the first.

babylon sisters and other posthumans

Our itinerary in this new perceptiverse duplicated what had gone before. Once we had exhausted the features of our hotel room and stabilized our new sensory input, we set out to ingest the world, wallowing in this latest transformation. If we chanced to revisit a place we had been to while in the Vermeer perceptiverse, we were astonished at the change. What a gift, we said, to be able to see the old world with continually fresh eyes.

Listening to the Boston Symphony outdoors along the Charles one night, their instruments looking like paper cutouts from Matisse's old age, Elena said to me, "Let's drop a Beethoven, Robert."

I refused. She didn't press me, realizing, perhaps, that she had better save her powers of persuasion for what really mattered.

The jungles of Brazil called for Rousseau, of course. I capitulated with hardly a protest, and that marked the beginning of the long, slippery slope.

Vermeer had captivated us for nearly a year.

Matisse kept us enthralled for six months.

Rousseau—that naive genius—could hold our attention for only six weeks.

We were art junkies now, consumers of novel perceptiverses.

Too much was not enough.

The neurotropin industry graciously obliged.

Up till that time, the industry had marketed only soft stuff, perceptiverses not too alien to "reality." But now, as more and more people found themselves in the same fix as Elena and I, the psychoengineers gradually unleashed the hard stuff.

In the next two years, Elena and I, as far as I can reconstruct things, went through the following perceptiverses:

Picasso (blue and cubist), Braque, Klee, Kandinsky, Balthus, Dali, Picabia, Leger, Chagall, Gris, de Kooning, Bacon, Klimt, Delaunay, O'Keefe, Escher, Hockney, Louis, Miro, Ernst, Pollock, Powers, Kline, Bonnard, Redon, van Dongen, Rouault, Munch, Tanguy, de Chirico, Magritte, Lichtenstein, and Johns.

We hit a brief period of realism consisting of Wood, Hopper, Frazetta, and Wyeth, and I tried to collect my senses and decide whether I wanted to get out of this trip or not, and how I could convince Elena to drop out with me.

But before I could make up my mind, we were off into Warhol, and everything hit me with such neon-tinted luminescent significance that I couldn't give it up. This happened aboard a station in high orbit, and the last thing I remember was the full Earth turning pink and airbrushed.

Time passed. I think.

The next time I became aware of myself as an individual, distinct from my beautiful yet imprisoning background, Elena and I were in a neo-expressionist perceptiverse, the one belonging to that Italian, I forget his name.

We were outdoors. I looked around.

The sky was gray-green, with a huge black crack running down the middle of it. Sourceless light diffused down like pus. The landscape looked as if it had been through an atomic war. I searched for Elena, found her reclining on grass that looked like mutant mauve octopus tendrils. Her flesh was ashen and bloody; a puke-yellow aura outlined her form.

I dropped down beside her.

I could *feel* that the grass was composed of tendrils, thick and slimed, like queer succulents. Suddenly I *smelled* alien odors, and I knew the light above spilled out of a novel sun.

The quantum level had overtaken the macroscopic.

Plastic reality, governed by our senses, had mutated.

We were truly in the place we perceived ourselves to be.

"Elena," I begged, "we've got to get out of this perceptiverse. It's just dreadful. Let's go back, back to where it all started, back to Vermeer. Please, if you love me, leave this behind."

A mouth like a sphincter opened in the Elena-thing. "We can't go back, Robert. You can never go back, especially after what we've been through. We can only go forward, and hope for the best . . . "

"I can't take it anymore, Elena. I'll leave you; I swear it . . . "

"Leave, then," she said tonelessly.

So I did.

Finding a dose of Vermeer wasn't easy. He was out of favor now; the world had moved beyond him. Even novices started out on the hard stuff nowadays. But eventually, in a dusty pharmaceutical outlet in a small town, I found a dose of that ancient Dutchman. The expiration date printed on the packet was long past, but I swallowed the pill anyway.

The lovely honeyed light and the perfect clarity returned.

I went looking for Elena.

When I found her, she was as beautiful as on that long-ago day when we first abandoned our native perceptiverses for the shock of the new.

When she saw me, she just screamed.

I left her then, knowing it was over. Besides, there was something else I had to find.

The pill with my original name.

phylogenesis

LIFE IS TENACIOUS, life is ingenious, life is mutable, life is fecund.

Wildflowers spring from vast fields of pillowy black lava barely cool. Bacteria dwell in pockets of oil squeezed between seams and strata, and they proliferate in anaerobic and glacial niches. Nodding fronds and waving worms cluster around hot mineral springs gushing from the floor of the sea, lightless and under immense pressure. Dead staffs, cut in years gone by, planted in good soil, take root and sprout leaves. A subarctic pine thick as a pencil, when examined, reveals seventy annual growth rings. Fish and frogs are immured in mud during years of drought, to reawaken with the first rains. Herman Melville once heard a gnawing sound from within a favorite table and watched an insect bore its way out of the unblemished surface, having gone dormant in the original tree from which the table was made decades ago.

Most hardy, most tenacious of life—if living they can indeed be called—are perhaps the viruses. Classified as obligatory parasites—doomed always to an existence dependent on other organisms—barely more than some nucleic acid in a protein coat, they can lie in wait inanimate—smallpox in a blanket—for a passing host. Given merely an instant's contact, they will plant themselves and flourish.

But all these examples, however diverse, presuppose at least a minimal planetary environment, a nurturing biosphere. Without that—when a planet dies—can life endure?

This was the vital problem the human race found itself facing.

The invaders came to Earth from space without warning, their skins hardened for atmospheric reentry. In blind fulfillment of their life cycle, they sought biomass for conversion to more of their kind. Earth offered all they needed.

Only in the final days of the plague, when the remnants of mankind huddled in a few last redoubts, did anyone admit that extermination of the invaders and reclamation of the planet was impossible. The ecosphere had been fundamentally disrupted, damaged beyond repair.

Then did the chromosartors begin to work feverishly to adapt a new man to the alien conditions. With a snippet from the marsupials, a string from the *Pinnipedia*, incorporating dozens of other genetic components, they refashioned woman and man for the new conditions.

And their overall model, the organism they felt offered the best tactic for survival, was, out of all creatures, the most simple.

Virus.

The host was sick. Here in its adult environment, without predators its own size, capable of a long, long existence, it had succumbed to infection. In the forbidding vastness of circumsolar space it wallowed, out of control, plainly dying.

Stars hung in the limitless vacuum, pinpoints sharp as loss: orange, blue, white, ruby. One blazed only a few Astronomical Units away, correspondingly more dominant. These luminaries were the only watchers. There was no active mind present to care about what was to occur.

Scale was hard to determine in this wilderness, but the stricken creature seemed to occlude a goodly number of stars with its bulk, in its spasmodic progression through the vacuum.

Ripples pulsed across the organism's elastic surface, convulsions engendered by unseen internal disquiet. It was plainly a system out of control.

These wavelike motions picked up speed, acquired a crazy tempo, like that of a fibrillating heart. The host looked like an amniotic sac disrupted by the frantic movements of its strangulating inhabitant.

Suddenly, noiselessly, without warning, the host ruptured. Amorphous fragments and thick sheets of biological substances—along with liquids and gases—blew off and scattered in every direction, the solids pinwheeling and tumbling end over end.

Among these useless fragments were several large flocks of objects that seemed still viable. Small ovoids, complete and self-contained, these were the vesicles. Unlike the object that had expelled them, they were born helpless, without control over their course. They radiated off into the depths of space, limning the surface of a ghostly, expanding sphere.

There happened to be no other hosts in the immediate vicinity. The vesicles were thus doomed to wander indefinitely.

The hosts—the prey of the vesicles—although much larger and more capable than the aimlessly floating parasites, were still insignificant targets, compared to the distances that separated the two.

But time was long, and any likely event must come to pass. Eventually, the vesicles would chance to meet a new host.

There was movement amid the great lifeless night.

A segment of stars was occluded by a tremendous glaucous bulk moving slowly. Its exterior possessed a quasi-organic texture, like a bluish-grey compound of fat and plastic. It had a relatively high albedo, so it was rather bright. Its shape was a featureless ovoid. It resembled nothing so much as a titanic mottled pill-capsule.

In its creeping passage, the host was moving toward something that seemed, at first, a single smaller object with many components. This object was also moving, on a path tangential to the host. As the distance between the two objects narrowed, the latter resolved itself into a flock of discrete entities.

The vesicles' long unconscious seeking was almost at an end. The gravitic memory of their ejection from a common source with identical force and trajectory had kept them together on their uncontrolled flight through the long night, a cluster of small pods that were identical in substance to the host.

Now the foremost portion of the host intersected the flock of vesicles. Some stuck, held not by magnetism or gravity, but by adhesive forces biological in nature. Others—too far away or not tenacious enough—drifted by, losers in the cosmic lottery.

The ones that had clung to the host had a chance to live and reproduce.

The ones that had failed to catch on would, in all likelihood, die. Perhaps they would plunge into this system's sun. Perhaps they would simply wither away, their natural capacities exhausted, their dormancy become final death.

The host emerged from the diminished cloud of vesicles. The two units continued on their separate paths. The sleek uniformity of the host's thick skin was now broken by the scattered forms of the clinging vesicles, like limpets on a rock. But there was no reaction from the host to this change in its condition. It seemed unaware of its doom. No host, in fact, had ever been known to exhibit sentience.

The vesicles, however, sensed the difference in their state, and they emerged from dormancy. Interior cellular mechanisms began to switch on.

Soon, the portion of the vesicles in contact with the host began to secrete a lysis-promoting enzyme. The integument of the host beneath the vesicles began to dissolve. After a short time, the vesicles and the host were immutably fused together. The vesicles continued to eat inward, single-mindedly following a program laid down long ago.

The wounds on the host closed with temporary patches slowly behind the invaders, thwarting the release of the host's interior components into the vacuum of space.

The invasion took place in utter silence, no cries or alarms sounding in the desolation of space, despite the life-or-death nature of the struggle. Success did not lie solely with the invaders. Some defective capsids were stopped by subcutaneous membranes that formed a second line of defense. Their contents were enzymatically absorbed. However, most of the capsids soon penetrated the thick hide of the host completely, gaining access to its interior structure: a labyrinth of cells and arteries, nerves and organs, structural tubules and struts, all lit with exceeding dimness by a yellow-green bioluminescence.

A nonhomogenous environment of wet and dry spaces, some cluttered with pulsing conduits and organs, some home to roving organelles, others like the empty caverns formed in foam.

At the immediate instant of gaining entry to this variegated interior, the vesicles discharged the machinery of subversion, their living blueprints, the carriers of heritage and the template for the formation of more vesicles.

Throughout the interior of the host, falling with liquid plops from the exhausted, dying vesicles, scores of naked neohumans in all stages of maturity landed on their backs and sides and bellies, coughed up pints of fluid, and became instantly aware.

The host had now fully sealed off the holes made by the vesicles, preventing the vacuum from entering, but it was too late to forestall the real damage.

∞∞

6-Licorice opened his brown eyes. He wiped his lips and chin clean of the gelatinous fluid that had until this moment filled his lungs. Already the estivation medium was drying on his body, turning into opaque white flakes that would soon fall off like scales. It felt good to be awake once more—to be alive. It seemed only minutes ago that he had entered his capsid, there to dream uneasily of his short but full life—the past and what might come—but he knew he might in reality have been asleep for years.

6-Licorice lay for a second or two, considering how lucky he was to have survived. Such a short moment of reflection was all he could afford, here in this nurturing yet hostile environment. Then he levered himself up agilely off the warm rubbery floor.

6-Licorice was a fully mature adult neohuman, a fine exemplar of his species in the only form in which it existed now. He stood four feet tall, with limbs rather gracile than muscular. He was completely hairless. His eyes were big, the pupils big within them. His genitals were hidden in a pouch of skin. There was a thick crease or fold of flesh across his otherwise flat stomach.

The first thing 6-Licorice had to do was find out if 3-Peach had made it too.

6-Licorice surveyed his surroundings. He was in one of the drier corridors—roughly cylindrical in cross section—which threaded the flesh of the host immediately beneath its tough skin. (All hosts exhibited an almost manufactured uniformity.) The texture of this corridor was fibrous, almost vegetative. The jaundiced light generated by the host's substance—although dimmer than moonlight—was perfectly adequate for 6-Licorice's large eyes. It was in fact the only form of illumination he had ever known.

Sniffing the moist air, 6-Licorice failed to detect 3-Peach's scent/taste. So he moved to one of the walls, where he found by touch a buried vein, which he bit into with sharp teeth.

One of the many nourishing juices the host provided filled his mouth. 6-Licorice drank it gratefully.

After a few swallows, 3-Peach's taste/scent came to him: her saliva, mixing with the host's fluids, where she too drank upstream. (Had 6-Licorice been upstream of 3-Peach, she would have responded in the same way to his trace.) It was an unmistakable and unique mix of chemicals, being bound up into her very genes, and it possessed a special affinity for all those of 6-Licorice's lineage.

A string consisting of three molecules of allyl cyclohexylcaproate; two of allyl phenoxyacetate; five of cinnamaldehyde: 3-Peach-2-Honey-5-Cinnamon—his mate, his love, the complement to the special cargo of chromosomes that was his share of neohumanity's continued perpetuation.

She was here! She had survived!

6-Licorice left the dribbling wound he had made in the host and began to run up the passage, in the direction from which the liquid had flowed to him.

Luck was with him, for he met no macrophages or lymphocytes or other harmful scavengers on the way. This was as expected, a kind of grace period, it being really too early for the host to have mobilized its defenses yet. Immunologically speaking, the host was still in the primary response stage.

In a short time, 3-Peach's scent/taste filled his nostrils. He picked up his pace.

Attracted by his airborne signature, 3-Peach came running around a corner to meet him.

They collided in an ecstatic embrace and fell to the resilient floor.

In a second, instincts rampant, they were mating.

The sex lasted under a minute.

Still, it was intense, tinged with mortality and separation.

3-Peach and 6-Licorice regained their feet as soon as they were done. There could be no post-coital sleep or restful talk for them. Their world was too relentless.

"Oh, 3-Peach, I'm so glad you made it!"

"And me for you, 6-Lick!"

3-Peach fondly patted 6-Licorice's wet detumescing genitals as they withdrew into their pouch. He stroked her flat, nippleless chest in return.

"That was nice," said 3-Peach. "I'm sure it'll be five healthy ones this time."

"Me too," replied 6-Licorice.

Arm in arm, they set off easily, but with an underlying wariness, to meet briefly with others of their kind.

Out of the large cluster of vesicles, only a bit over two hundred had managed to make contact with the host, the rest sailing off into the cold, destructive darkness. A small percentage of these vesicles had contained children of varying ages. The rest had harbored adults, like 3-Peach and 6-Licorice. And like that couple, the others had quickly mated: with their prior mates, if those individuals had chanced to come aboard the host also, or with new partners whose mates had also failed to be picked up like interplanetary cockleburrs on the back of the host.

Thus, within an hour of the invasion of the host, roughly a hundred pregnancies had been successfully started.

With this all-important task out of the way, the neohumans set about establishing themselves firmly in the host.

Basically, this procedure involved scattering themselves throughout the interior of the gargantuan alien. They could not settle down into a single large community at this stage, unless they wished to chance being completely wiped out in a massive attack by the host's defensive entities and its immune responses. The concentration of so much nonhost antigenic protein would have stimulated an immense marshaling of macrophages and lymphocytes by the host, floods of interferon analogues, which the neohumans would have been hard-pressed to survive.

Therefore, the various couples betook themselves to isolated portions of the host, living for a time like independent frontiersmen of another age. They walked through mazed passages crimson as blood, and rode the sticky turbid currents through large arteries. (These neohumans could go without breathing for as long as twenty minutes, thanks to their seal heritage.) They climbed through honeycombs of spongy lipid-yellow wet tissue just as their remote ancestors had climbed through vines and branches. They burrowed through thin cellular walls when necessary, using their teeth and tough nails.

Some died along the way, by drowning or suffocation or ingestion by the patrolling macrophages: roving jellyglobes as big as the neohumans, motivated by chemotaxis, attraction along chemical gradients. If a couple were threatened together, the male would often sacrifice himself, to ensure the escape of the female and her gestating burden.

Eventually, nearly two hundred neohumans were distributed throughout the entire host.

And exactly thirty days to the minute after their entry into the host—the neohumans monitored the passage of time with unerring precision, thanks to long-ago modifications in the suprachiasmatic nuclei of their brains, which provided them with accurate biological clocks—roughly one hundred women gave birth to their litters.

"Get ready, 6-Lick—they're coming!"

3-Peach rested in one corner of the red-walled, veined humid cavity she and 6-Licorice called home, her legs wide apart, knees drawn up to her ears and gripped tightly. 6-Licorice squatted patiently in front of her, awaiting the births.

Without visible effort, 3-Peach squeezed out the first of her litter. To the eyes of another era, the infant would have looked premature, almost fetal. And in truth, it could not yet survive on its own.

Which was why 6-Licorice took it tenderly and, pulling open the crease of flesh across his abdomen, inserted it gently inside, where it fastened to a hidden nipple.

He did the same with the other four.

Then he and 3-Peach immediately had sex again, to start another batch, moving less frantically than that first time, cautious of the pouched young ones.

When they were finished, 3-Peach—always more optimistic than her mate—said, "They all looked fine, didn't they, 6-Lick?"

6-Licorice softly pressed his abdomen. He had been worried about mutations—induced by cosmic radiations experienced as their vesicles had traveled through space—as much as she.

"Yes, they did. And I'm sure the next four or five litters will be just as strong."

⚭

The neohuman population of the host, after the first birthings, now stood at roughly seven hundred, more than double the number of initial invaders. True, there was not much outward show of this leap yet, since the newest neohumans were all still pouch-bound.

However, at the end of the second month, when all the males were waddling about awkwardly, the first litter came forth, independent, self-mobile, able to feed themselves from the body of the host, not talking yet, but on the verge of speech. They vacated the pouches of the males just in time for the next generation to go in.

(6-Licorice, at the end of each cycle, looked more pregnant with his distended abdomen than 3-Peach ever did.)

The second litter safely pouched, the first afoot, a third litter soon occupied all the neohuman wombs.

By the end of six months, the neohuman population of the host stood at three thousand plus. And the oldest children were half as big as their parents.

At the end of one year, there were six thousand members of the community of invaders who had never known a life outside this present host. The original two hundred settlers, through attrition, were down to one hundred and fifty, 3-Peach and 6-Licorice being among them.

Now the oldest children, aged one year and fully adult, began to breed, along with their still fertile parents.

There were four hundred breeding pairs that month. At the end of thirty days, they gave birth to two thousand children.

And the second-oldest generation, a month behind the first, began to breed. Six hundred and fifty pairs gave birth to 3,250 children.

The next month, nine hundred breeders birthed 4,500.

When the next two hundred and fifty pairs came on-line, the result was

5,750 newborns.

And the next month, and the next month, and the next . . .

By the end of the second year, the neohuman population inside the immense host was nearing one hundred thousand.

And they had barely got going.

⚮

Eldest by a few seconds of 3-Peach's and 6-Licorice's first litter, 2-Honey was now slightly more than a year old, an energetic adult with his mother's optimistic nature.

The male neohuman's full designation was 2-Honey-4-Licorice-9-Clove. His parents' signatures had recombined uniquely in him, as they would in all his siblings.

By these unique families of signatures the neohumans were divided into clans. Clan membership circumscribed mating, the heart giving way—or rather, indulging itself only within certain boundaries—according to an inbuilt determinism. The long-dead chromosartors had limited their progeny in this way for a particular purpose.

Knowing that thenceforth the human race would possess a basically nonmaterial culture, the chromosartors had pondered what faculties, what cargo of knowledge, they could pass on to the neohumans as a legacy of six thousand years of civilization. They had eventually settled on several talents, chief of which was mathematical skill.

The entire corpus of mathematics was literally encoded in, and distributed across, the collective neohuman genome.

2-Honey's clan was the bearer of Riemann integrals. They were born with a predisposition toward solving those abstruse functions in their heads. The circumscribed mating choices insured that the ability would be passed from generation to generation.

2-Honey had taken for his mate a female named/tasted 7-Apple-1-Clove-8-Peach, whom he had met half a host away, while eluding a persistent lymphocyte. Ducking into a fibrous maze too small for the lymphocyte to enter, 2-Honey had stumbled on the home of 7-Apple and her family, distant cousins. It had been love at first scent.

One day shortly after birthing their own first litter, the couple was traveling together to visit 2-Honey's parents. The son and his wife had lately, during a heated session, discovered what they believed to be a new aspect of unbounded Riemann integrals. Now they wanted to confirm with their elders that their discovery was actually original and valid. If such was the case, then the new information would be disseminated as widely as possible among their clan, to insure the survival of this knowledge.

As 2-Honey and 7-Apple loped speedily through the corridors, they fell into speculating on the importance of their discovery.

"If only it's real," said 7-Apple. "It would be such an honor. Why, who knows, it might even lead someday, somehow, to the race returning home, to Earth."

"That's a nice dream, 7-Apple," replied 2-Honey absentmindedly. "Even if it is unlikely. Still, we can always hope . . . " 2-Honey's voice trailed off. He was really in no mood to chatter. The long graceful S-curves of integrals occupied his vision, and he was lost in a numinous realm of abstraction.

7-Apple saw the newly grown patch of acid blisters too late, and 2-Honey never saw them at all. She swerved, but he ran right across them.

The blisters exploded, drenching 2-Honey and just spattering 7-Apple.

When 7-Apple opened her eyes, she saw 2-Honey writhing on the floor. Ignoring her own pain, she moved to touch him.

"No—" gritted 2-Honey through clenched teeth. "You'll burn yourself. Liquid. Wash me—"

2-Honey yowled then, high and long. The sound went right through 7-Apple like a cartilage knife. She ran off, trying to erase the image of 2-Honey's bare white bones showing through his flesh.

When she returned, quickly as possible, with a sac of cool juice pinched from a cluster, 2-Honey's legs, the last part of him visible, were just disappearing into the bulk of a macrophage. His appointed fate, delayed since their initial meeting, had at last overtaken him.

7-Apple threw the sac at the macrophage, where it burst uselessly against its peristalsis-heaving form. Then, stifling her grief, sensible that to lose her own life would be to deprive the neohumans of a possibly important discovery, 7-Apple turned and loped on.

She swore every neohuman would come to know of 2-Honey's bravery and genius. Yes, they would!

2-Honey: from birth to maturity, from nescience to supreme intellectual accomplishment, his life had spanned less than four hundred days.

Mayflies, fast-fading blooms, the little creatures of a short hour. Yet to themselves, their lives still tasted sweet as of old.

More neohumans lived than died. Naturally, the burgeoning population had its effect on the host. This proliferation was the process by which its kind reached their untimely deaths. The neohumans lived off its tissues and byproducts, producing waste products of their own. Such a crowd as now existed was literally devouring it from the inside out, and filling it with metabolic poisons.

The host responded desperately with chemical/biological/physical attacks.

Cell-dissolving enzymes dripped from certain walls and formed pools, which the neohumans warily avoided. Patrols of jelly-globes that would ingest men and women on contact increased. (The neohumans were forced to lick each other regularly from head to toe, in a kind of social grooming designed to remove the chemical tags that allowed the macrophages to zero in on them.) Temperatures in certain areas rocketed to fever levels.

But all these measures were simply too late. The neohumans met the host's offensives with cunning and biological resiliency. The macrophages they simply overwhelmed by numbers, tore apart, and devoured. Eat or be eaten was the only law. The destructive enzymes and other long-chain molecules they countered with biological agents of their own, the neohumans' bodies having been engineered in the distant past precisely to meet such challenges. The walls of living quarters were laved with micturants that had responded to the crisis by altering their composition in a useful manner. Some of the attacks the neohumans were able to shut off by subverting some of the many ganglia possessed by the host.

All was not gloom during these days of increased biological warfare, however. The interior of the host was filled with song. It was the only art form left to the artifact-free neohumans, and they exploited it to its utmost. Intricate choral threnodies for an ancient racial loss, plangent dirges interspersed with bright individual notes celebrating present-day survival, vibrated the tissues of the host with alien stirrings. Plainsong and partsong, madrigals and chorales, these were the supreme weapons in the neohumans' armory of spirit.

At the end of the second year, with the neohuman population approaching half a million, the interior of the host began to appear ineluctably ragged and sick. There were structural failures and organic decay, nauseating stinks and food shortages.

The neohumans were not troubled, for they had expected as much.

They began to prepare for departure.

6-Licorice and 3-Peach stood at a thick transparent portion in the host's outer skin, once intended to admit sunlight on a bank of dimpled blue swellings, for reasons obscure to them, but obviously plain enough to the host. Now the swellings were dead. But the sunlight entered still.

The host had lost its ability to maneuver against solar gravity, by jetting waste gases and liquids, and had been falling for some time down the invisible gravity well into the Sun. It was also rotating slowly without control. However, its own internal gravity remained constant, keeping the feet of the neohuman couple secured firmly to the wet floor, even when that surface had spun one hundred and eighty degrees.

The rotation brought a new sight into the window: a planet and its satellite. The satellite was immemorially grey and dead, with markings that moved the humans strangely, awaking ancestral emotions. The planet, once green and blue, now resembled a white featureless ball, exactly the texture and composition of the host.

3-Peach and 6-Licorice were silent while the planet remained in view. When it had vanished, 3-Peach said, "Do you think they'll ever leave, 6-Lick?"

"Who can tell? Who knows why they even came? We can't even say if they're natural or artificial. Why do we have weight inside them, for instance? And if they did go, what would they leave behind? Bare rock, no life? No, we can't count on it, we can't even dream about it."

A troop of youngsters surged by, laughing and playing tag. 3-Peach said nothing for a time, until they were gone. Then: "I guess you're right, 6-Lick. We just have to make the most of the life we have."

They left the window, holding hands.

In the last month of life aboard the host, no females became pregnant, although the couples continued to engage in sex, for reasons of comfort and pleasure. Metabolisms were changing in anticipation of departure.

At last the day arrived. All signs pointed to the imminent collapse of the weakened host.

Each human sought out a macrophage. There were plenty left for everyone, and their viciousness had decreased in these end-days, almost as if they had internalized chemical messages of defeat. These former enemies were now to become the means of escape for the humans.

Approaching the scavengers one on one, the humans allowed themselves to be ingested.

The encounters were far from fatal. A new secretion produced by the humans overrode the macrophages' instructions. In the ultimate subversion, the defensive eaters became protective vesicles, settling down by the thousands to the floor. The humans inside inhaled the altered cytoplasm of the vesicles and gradually lost awareness.

Watching their fellows become encysted by the score all around them, 3-Peach and 6-Lick paused for a moment before allowing the same necessary fate to overtake themselves.

"It was a sweet couple of years, 6-Lick."

"I can't remember better."

"The kids grew up fine."

"The songs were glorious."

"The math was exciting."

"The sex was marvelous."

"As always."

Silence, save for other soft and private goodbyes. Then 6-Licorice spoke.

"You're the only one for me, 3-Peach."

"And you for me, dear. I can't wait till we're together again."

6-Licorice, not so sanguine as his mate, made no reply but just squeezed 3-Peach's hand.

They went under then, enlarvaed, cocooned.

Only an hour or two passed, so nicely had the humans timed events.

The host exploded silently, its internal pressure rupturing its damaged skin: the end point of the process begun so many human births ago, with the initial pinholes of entry. It looked like a gigantic seed pod distributing its seeds.

Vesicles were scattered in every direction.

Some embarked on a course straight for the Sun; others seemed destined to impact the Moon or burn up in Earth's atmosphere. Chance dictated the course of each, since they lacked maneuvering capabilities.

3-Peach and 6-Licorice were lost amid the thousands. They had been side by side prior to the explosion. Perhaps they would stay together in their long drift. Perhaps not.

But many would live to breed again.

And again.

And again . . .

a thief in babylon

HOW MANY LIGHTYEARS to Babylon?

That's a question members of the Conservancy never fail to ask—and which seldom fails to catch me by surprise. It's so typical of their way of thinking—a way so alien to mine—that no matter how long I tarry wearily among them (on neutral worlds only, of course), I'm always unprepared to answer, much as they seem unready for and shocked by such a simple feature as my spinal plaques, which I take so much for granted.

The fact is, only someone who subscribes to the old notions of Truehome would ask for the distance to Babylon in lights, rather than simply inquire after its relativistic coordinates. Not to mention being repelled by my bodily modifications, while seeing nothing wrong in using a bodyfogger to appear as a disembodied head himself—

But just because I exhibit certain mannerisms and bodymods consistent with the Commensality does not automatically imply that I am rigidly opposed to the Conservancy. That old either-or, bivalent mindset is property of their system solely. It would be wrong to apply it to anyone such as myself.

Truly, although both they and I denote our systems with cees, we are seas apart.

So, I say—facing my hypothetical and stereotypical Conservator interlocutor, whether on moon or planet, ship or station, under suns green, blue, red or white, him usually polite enough to reveal his face by keeping his roiling, gadget-driven optical distortion focused below his neck—your question does not annoy me. I recognize that you have unbent enough to show me your stern face. (I wish—how I wish—that another man in another time and place had unbent as much.) I am pleased to talk with you about Babylon.

Perhaps my composite conversationalist knows the ancient children's rhyme. Conservancy types cherish such things, and it gives me a point of introduction. (I TAPPED the verse once and it stayed with me, so I can relate it now.)

How many miles to Babylon?
Threescore miles and ten.
Can I get there by candlelight?
Yes, and back again.
If your heels are nimble and light,
You may get there by candlelight.

Babylon. Like anyplace else in this infinitely accessible universe, it's just a Heisenberg transition away, so I suppose in a sense you can reach it before a candle's brief flame flickers out. And when you arrive, it helps if your heels—and mind—are nimble and light, as mine once were.

But as for getting back again—

Well—once you invest as much of yourself in Babylon as I and others have, you can never really leave.

Although of course you can always do what our age specializes in.

You can always run away.

Night came down like a hammer.

Certainly, if you know the least little bit about Babylon—and who doesn't?—you must realize I've just lied.

All that really happened was that Babylon shut off the lightstrips that were an integral part of the enormous transparent shell enclosing our city, in accordance with the programmed diurnal cycle.

But what the hell kind of opening line is that? Literalness is such a downer.

No, the story starts much better if I say night came calling. And since some Babylonians—such as myself—who had been born elsewhere still instinctively regarded the phenomenon that way, I think I'll keep it.

Night came down like a hammer.

Outside our shell dirty clouds of methane and nitrogen swirled, banded a dozen shades of smoggy pink, orange and grey, rendered faintly luminous by the radiance of the gas-giant around which our satellite revolved. (Contributing also, of course, was the feeble light from the far-off primary around which the gas-giant in turn revolved, a star somewhere in that part of infinity that the Conservancy insists on calling Gemini, the twins.)

Light bloomed in a thousand tall towers throughout the city, and fell from myriad free-floating globes. The assorted citizens striding the syalon streets seemed to speed up their pace, as if responding to age-old imperatives their rational selves would have denied.

The night quickens. Everyone, everywhere, grows at least a little more alert after dark, wary of the eyes beyond the fire.

I felt hyped up myself. But then again, I had more reason than most to feel so.

Half an hour after mottled darkness fell, I was ready to step from the departure platform on the fiftieth floor of a residential tower, carrying something that didn't belong to me. I was confident that no one had seen me take the item, which was small enough to fit neatly beneath the waistband of my jox. And valuable enough to carry me through half a year of lazy pleasures. Well worth the risk involved, thought I.

With my hand on a brass boss studding my black leather chest-yoke, ready to activate the lift circuitry built into the harness, I was congratulating myself on another job well done. That was when the watchmek's laser nearly clipped my ear off.

I fell flat on the dropledge, having whirled to face the direction of fire. Back in the building, the mek got off another shot that ran a lash of pain along my back.

Biting down on a yell, I pointed my index finger at the officious but stupid thing.

From the small seed that was a solid-state laser embedded under my fingernail sprouted a beam that pierced the mek. It fell over with a dull *clunk*.

I stood, legs shaky, back scorched. (The only good thing about laser wounds is how they self-cauterize.) My harness fell off, neatly severed, leaving me bare except for sandals and thong (and if you count ornaments, however multi-purposed, my carcanet). My first choice for escape was now gone. I wasn't about to step off the platform into mid-air *sans* lift harness, no matter how desperate.

I had two options left. The first was to take the building's slow gravshaft down—at the bottom of which would surely be waiting a nasty crowd of concerned citizens, summoned by Babylon.

The second looked like an even worse choice. I could go up five floors to the roof, send a TAP for a taxi (the platform here was big enough for individuals only) and wait to be immured within the vehicle, which Babylon would surely override and freeze when he realized what was going on.

I raced inside and headed for the roof.

Sometimes a choice looks bad only because you don't know all the angles.

On the roof—fifty-five floors full of chambered sophonts closer to the luminescent killer heavens than where I wanted to be—I issued a TAP for the taxi, just to confuse things, then requested the time.

[20:10:01,] came the response.

The Hanging Gardens were due by in three minutes. I had carefully noted their schedule before I attempted this job.

Searching the gloom, I spotted the floating mass: a twinkling faerie palace overgrown with greenery, set on a wide thick disk bearing aloft several landscaped hectares.

The minutes it took to drift toward me seemed eons. Running one thick finger between torc and neck (a foolish mannerism, I know, but one I couldn't break), I watched the egress to the liftshaft, expecting it to vomit forth meks and men any second.

But no one came. And then the Gardens were overhead.

There were no buildings in Babylon taller than the one I stood on. The Gardens were why.

The polychrome sky was suddenly occulted, and I was in plant-fragrant Shadow; voices drifted down to me. At the same time a creeper brushed my cheek like the antenna of a godhorse. Kicking off my sandals, I tossed my arms up, searching for thicker vines.

Found them.

Swarmed up.

Kids did this on a dare all the time, little caring about the community-service sentence they risked if caught. Once in a while, if they were foolish enough to attempt the climb without a lift harness and lost their hold, they died. Not having grown up here, I had never enjoyed such a thrill before.

Now I was making up for my placid off-world youth.

The Gardens, continuing their slow and stately pavane, left the tower behind. I was halfway up a rubbery liana, hanging a quarter of a kilometer up above the ceramic pavement. I made the mistake of looking down on the carpet of lights, and dizziness blurred my senses. I stopped climbing for a moment until I regained my equilibrium. Then I went as fast as I dared straight to the top.

A leg over the railing, then the other, and I was standing on solid "ground" again. The commingled scents of flowers greeted me.

My arms ached and my legs felt like gelatin. My chest and back were slicked with sweat and possibly blood from my reopened wound. The tension had nurtured a headache that kicked with every pulse.

But beneath my waistband was a fortune waiting to be redeemed.

I looked up in relief. At such a time it would have been good to look upon the stars. (You see, I retained some Conservancy attitudes even after living in Babylon for so long.)

But only a gaudy greasy fog greeted my gaze.

So I moved off.

Avoiding the couples, triplets and quartets ("More than four's a bore," they said in the city that month; next month it would be something altogether different, if not antithetical) gathered in the hidden dim purlieus and bowers, past the dancers adorning a plaza, and to the airbus stand.

If I had known then how soon I'd be back in the Gardens, I might not have hurried so.

Minutes later I was down, and lost in the busy streets.

I still had a lot to do. Meet the fence who'd buy my prize, recharge by induction field the subepidermal capacitor that powered my one-shot laser, then, finally, relax.

Task one took an hour, two a minute of that same hour, and three—

I was in a bar that catered to my kind of pleasure, relaxing with a drink, when I spotted him. He was the most beautiful godhorse I had ever seen.

Conservators, of course, call them mantises, or sometimes even bugs. Funny, then, how they resent being called apes themselves. (Once I TAPPED an ancient novel about humanity warring with a race called Bugs, and wished I never had. Pure Conservancy thinking at its most raw.) But any human in the Commensality will call them by some variation of the old folk etymology, godhorse.

This one was a male, with proud uplifted pyramidal head and finely formed mandibles, shining thorax and strong hind legs. His four folded wings were strong gemmed membranes that stirred slightly as I watched; his forelegs were delicacy and precision incarnate. His color at the moment was a relaxed olive.

I'm a big man, but he was taller, although not half my mass.

I initiated a TAP between us. The godhorses understood human language, but our ears were just not set up to interpret their stridulations. Without Babylon as intermediary, we would have been unable to communicate.

And a TAP was so much more intimate anyway.

[Commensal,] I sent in the familiar way, [your sustenance is mine.]

[And yours mine,] he replied. [Do you wish an encounter?]

[Very much,] I said. [And you?]

[You are a handsome human. I have never seen your color skin before. It is like space itself.]

I knew he was newly arrived then, since I'm hardly the only one in Babylon of this shade. [I take that as a yes,] I sent. [Shall we go to a place I know of?]

[Indeed.]

We left the bar together, and—

I pause here, recalling the reactions I've gotten from Conservators when I've described relations among Commensals before. They always adjust their bodyfoggers to hide their faces in disgust. That's one thing I can't stand. I expect them to listen as fellow sophonts, not as chaoses of optical distortion. Conservators might call all who embrace the Commensality perverts, but they always damn well learn before I'm done that we're perverts with principles.

As I was saying:

—went to a Commensality-supported sensorium.

In our private cube I stripped off my lone pouch of a garment. (I was still barefoot and harnessless). The godhorse wore not so much as a button. He had turned a bright red with excitement.

I laid down on my stomach on the soft warm organiform couch in the twilit room, and he climbed atop me. His chitin was cool, and he weighed nothing in Babylon's light gravity. His mandibles clacked alongside my collared neck, and his forearm spurs bit into my back. (And now you know the reason for my spinal plaques and carcanet: protection from a caress too violent.)

[Now I master you!] he sent.

I felt his intoxicant saliva snail my jaw. (On Truehome they used to believe the brown drool of the little native godhorses would provoke madness.)

The godhorse stridulated wildly, sawing his hindlegs against his wings. Knowing what was next, I got more excited.

Pinning me in a hold I could easily have broken, but chose not to (isn't that the essence of love?), he bit my shoulder, opening up old scars.

His saliva mingled with my blood.

In seconds the world exploded in hallucinatory pleasure, the hot bright fragments shooting off into the void, leaving only pure blackness behind, which swallowed me down and down.

When I came out of it, the godhorse was gone. I flipped over onto my back and let the couch grow a patch for my shoulder. Then I got up, dressed, and left.

What do they get out of it? Good question. The answer lies, I think, in the fact that only the male godhorses indulge, and don't care if their partner is a male or female.

Imagine how you would feel if you could mount someone who absolutely, positively wouldn't bite your head off, as a female or even fellow male godhorse might, in the throes of passion.

The fact that their saliva is synergistic with our biochemistry is just lagniappe for us.

Because they're so beautiful, and humans are so exogamous, we'd lie with them anyway, I'm sure, even if they didn't provide a dose of pure ecstasy.

I was tired and sated and anxious to get home and rest. Night was ending, a full twelve hours of hard work and near-death and the little death of pleasure, and my mind was foggy from it all.

So when the small man with the dead face stepped from an alley outside the sensorium and said, "Hello, Meat," (more about my name later) I didn't react as fast as usual.

Squinting (the light-globe here was dead and lying on the syalon, and the next nearest was three meters off), I said, "Ace? How are you? I heard a bad rumor about you. They said you were brain-cored."

His voice was without affect. "He was."

So then I knew.

I was talking with Babylon.

Let's digress a minute.

The topic?

Governments.

The Conservancy, the Commensality, and the rough, two-backed beast they make up, sprawling across all creation, locked together in a perpetual ritual encounter akin to both sex and cannibalism. (You'll excuse the mixed metaphor, I hope, but food and mating are Commensality preoccupations.)

The trouble is that the two systems (although I might make the point here that the Commensality is really a myriad systems that happen to acknowledge a rather limited set of common principles) are just so damned incompatible.

The Conservancy believes in government by an elite corps of trained professionals, enforcing laws meant to secure the maximum good for the greatest numbers. They desire physical and temporal continuity across the stars, which, you'll pardon my bluntness, is just plain crazy, given the facts of travel by Heisenberg transition. (What can borders possibly demarcate when every point on the space-time continuum is contiguous with every other point?) And they have that completely illogical fetish about an imaginary purity that mankind must adhere to.

That's the Conservancy. I know its principles intimately, from arguments with one of its sharpest proponents, my brother.

His name?

That doesn't matter.

He's dead now.

Anyway. Now what about us? The Commensality.

Our precepts are harder to codify. We don't have an official canon like theirs. But there're a few saints in our hagiography, and one was a pantheistic holy fool from Truehome who claimed, "That government governs best which governs least." We subscribe to that. Also the essential equality of all sophonts, unlike those species chauvinists.

How, you might wonder, does one go about implementing such ideals? Some central coordination is required in any society above a certain level, and once one grants power to any subset of people, it seems they always manage to want more and more. And equality—that's an even more fantastic notion.

The answer to both is Babylon.

Not the city. The AOI beneath it.

Running every large-sized social unit that calls itself part of the Commensality you will find an Artificial Organic Intelligence. Basically a huge biofabbed mass of paraneurons, with an information-carrying capacity that no one has yet effectively delimited, these beings communicate among themselves across space—and with us via TAP. They hold all knowledge in common, dispensing it upon request. (Fair access to information is equality.) They coordinate interpersonal communications by the Tele-Adjunct and Psychoprosthetic which is as much a part of every member of the Commensality as any sensory organ he was born with. And through their agents—mek and human—they do all the managerial scutwork that is so damn boring but necessary.

How can we stand to entrust our welfare to such a "thing?"

How can Conservators stand to entrust their welfare to fallible humans?

That "thing" is literally no more capable of self-aggrandizement than a person is of keeping his pupils dilated if I flash a bright light in his eyes. And for the same reason: built-in biological limits. AOIs are the first truly beneficent "rulers" in history. (Of course you know that word in spoken quotes is all wrong.)

Beneficent, that is, until someone or something threatens them or the Commensality.

Then watch out.

Which brings us to the end of digression—

—and the beginning of panic.

I was talking with Babylon.

The ceramic pavement grew cold beneath my bare feet, although objectively nothing changed. The shadows (not Shadow) around us seemed deep enough to swallow galaxies. I dipped a blunt finger under my torc and rimmed its reassuring solidity. My heart was beating like the core of a sun, and I willed it down to normal.

I knew Ace was going to be a little slower, now that he had been cored—

(Cored? Babylon catches a person who, despite the elastic parameters of life in the Commensality, has qualified as a disruptive rogue, destructive to the freedom of others. ((It's all very scientific, each person building up a life-index sorta like karma in the AOI's banks, and you have to be pretty nasty to qualify for coring. My daily complacency hinged on the belief that I wasn't.)) In a simple operation, the rogue's higher brain components are scooped out, leaving enough of the reptilian brain to handle the autonomic functions. A mass of paraneurons is dumped in, giving the AOI direct control of the body, and *voila*, an agent. Best use of a bad apple. Moral: don't screw with Babylon and your fellows.)

—but I couldn't gamble on taking him out, or outrunning whatever weaponry he had modded in.

Thinking fast, I realized that maybe there was no reason to do either. Perhaps this was strictly a social call, having nothing to do with any of my nefarious deeds.

Although I doubted it, I decided to play it that way.

"Ace—uh, Babylon. Hello. Nice to see you. A simple TAP would have gotten my attention just as well."

The dead man didn't smile. I had heard that Babylon had trouble portraying emotions, and Ace's immobile features tended to confirm this.

"That is exactly the opposite of the truth," said the AOI with the living corpse's unmodulated voice. "You could have denied the TAP. But not this revenant. I find such encounters quite effective."

Babylon stared at me until shivers laddered my dorsal plaques. Then he spoke again.

"Let us walk. We have things to speak of."

What could I say?

We started walking down the nearly empty pre-dawn streets.

Above, it began to rain liquid methane. It sounded like a horde of little clawed animals scrambling atop the dome.

"The Conservancy has made a new move in their war on us," were Babylon's first words after we began to stroll, him in a slightly stiff-legged way.

"War is dead," I parroted.

"Insofar as you mean attack by gross physical means, you merely repeat common knowledge. Neither we nor the Conservancy dare risk antagonizing the other to the point where our opponent would be provoked to, say, translate a few tons of rock directly into the same coordinates as a population center. Being equally vulnerable, we are all equally restrained. But the universe we know is in a constant state of war nonetheless. Our weapon is sheer example. By running an open society, we seduce individuals and worlds constantly away from the Conservancy. Their weapon is propaganda of a most insidious sort."

I stopped short. "They've brought the Chronicle to Babylon."

"Yes. The Conservancy has sent a representative carrying their Chronicle of Mankind. He's just moved into the Gardens, and is already playing it for the curious. I am helpless to stop him. My whole reason for being is the free dissemination of information. But the information he has brought is a virus that will kill this world, or at least transform it into an outpost of the Conservancy. Which is the same as death for you and me. Unless we kill him first."

I started walking again, silent. Babylon followed. We passed a lone axolotl, her neotenic clown's face smiling. I think she wanted to cruise us, but Babylon must have sent some warning TAP. In a second her elastic features grew worried, and she hurried off.

At last I said, "Why are you telling me this? Can't you just handle it yourself? Isn't that your job, to protect our way of life?"

"There can be no official connection between me and the diplomat's death. We dare not risk violent repercussions. So, I need a tool. And you are that tool."

I risked some shuck and jive. I should have known it was useless.

"Me? I don't know anything about such things. I'm a simple hedonist. Why, the very thought—"

Babylon laid a hand on my arm and I shut up.

Then he recited every last crime I'd committed since coming to Babylon.

It was a long list.

"So you see," he finished, "I know you. You are the one I want. Find this Conservator and kill him. If we accomplish nothing else, we'll buy a little time while the Conservancy decides what to do. At best, they might grow discouraged, and pick another target."

I quit pretending. "What's in it for me? Why should I risk myself to help you?"

"You're a member of the Commensality," Babylon reminded me. "As such, you're a *de facto* enemy to the Conservancy. If they win here, and they catch you before you can get out in the mass exodus, they'll scrub your brain. Me, they hate simply because I'm artificial. Mocklife, they call me. But you have two strikes against you. You've dared to modify the sacred human physiological 'norm.' And you practice miscegenation."

"Anti-em," I spat.

"Tagging your opponent with an expletive does not reduce his threat. And you should feel some loyalty toward your commensals. If that is not enough, then consider this. You are about to trip my rogue-trigger. Soon, if you continue your current lifestyle—and I do not predict you will change—you will become a legitimate target for my enmity. If you help me in this, I will wipe the ledger clean, and you will have at least as many years free from my dedicated pursuit as you have yet enjoyed."

I thought about it for a minute. It seemed the type of argument that was kinda impossible to refute.

"Okay," I said. "I'll do it."

Babylon didn't smile, but I sensed an AOI analog to that emotion.

"I thought you would see things my way," he said. Then:

[And I'll be keeping track of you.]

Day was born like a nova.

(Actually: lightstrips, Babylon, literalism, *et cetera*.)

I stood blinking for a second or two. When I was done, the body that had once been my pal Ace was gone. As to the nature of his future errands, I did not care to speculate. Especially since someday his fix might be mine. But I wouldn't be able to worry about it if cored—or would I? What tiny portions of personality and memories were left intact, down there in the coree's brainstem, and what must they feel?

I wasn't anxious to find out.

Sudden fatigue washed over me like a tide of despair. I had gone a day now without sleep—not counting the godhorse-induced trance, which stimulated rather than soothed—and almost that long without food. I had been shot at by a mek, carried aloft on a floating island like Gulliver on Laputa (I remember TAPPING for that particular image), and scared half out of my wits by the civic entity who was supposed to be protecting me.

And the worst of it was that I couldn't stop now. I had to think. Matters were far from settled. Just because I had told Babylon I was going to cooperate didn't mean I would.

There was always the option of flight.

That might have been someone else's first choice. After all, I claimed earlier that this is an age of running away. With interstellar travel so cheap and easy, what else could one expect? Intelligence has always deluded itself into believing that circumstances were the limiting factor, when usually it was intelligence itself that was the source of trouble. And you can't flee yourself so easily.

Now, I'm not knocking escape. After all, I once fled to Babylon, and found a kind of happiness. But there was a good reason why I couldn't just up and run now, except as a last resort, and I don't expect you to see it.

The reason was the TAP.

Conservators are simultaneously to be pitied and envied. More pitied, of course, because they deny themselves all the manifold virtues of a TAP, claiming such devices are intrusions on the human brain. And envied, just a little, because they aren't tied down like us.

Sometimes a TAP goes down deep as a taproot.

Suppose you spent all your life (in the case of someone born into the Commensality) or a good portion of your adult years (my case) relying on this massive auxiliary memory-cum-switchboard-cum-advisor-cum-stimulator. After a while, the AOI, with its individual idiosyncrasies (they do have them) becomes as integral to your sense of self as your bodily feedback. Further suppose you one day decide on a change of scenery. Of course you won't voluntarily pick someplace without TAP facilities. Your destination's bound to be another locus of the Commensality. So you TAP into Babylon and send:

[Please grow a mass of nonsentient paraneurons containing all my personal data, which I may take with me.]

Surprisingly soon a mek or, god forbid, someone like Ace arrives with a little homeostatic container that holds some pretty important stuff. You handle it as nervously as if it were an embryo, which it sorta is.

You arrive at your new home. (Of course, all this applies only for a permanent move. And please notice how neatly the instant transition from the previous orally bounded paragraph to this one mimics the Heisenberg transition itself.) You hand over your container to an agent of the new AOI, who promptly integrates the cells into himself. Now, however, like new lovers, you and the AOI have to accommodate to each other. A rather touchy proposition, and not without its share of urgent uneasiness. And sometimes, like a bad mating, the match never stabilizes.

The net effect of all this is that we in the Commensality tend to be rather sedentary.

And that's why I wasn't going to leave unless forced to.

My stomach rumbled, as I stood there in the rapidly filling streets. The methane rain had stopped, and the sky within the dome was filling with individual fliers and aircars.

I couldn't see too far ahead, but I knew at that moment that I wanted a couple of things.

A meal, and a walk around the Bay.

I set off for a refectory. The movement felt good.

At the refectory portal—just an arched opening without a door; lacking weather there was no reason for doors except privacy, and a refectory was the opposite of private—I passed in. The first room contained the showers.

I stripped and washed up with the others there, then passed into the refectory proper.

Did you ever look up the derivation of "Commensality?" Good, then you'll understand the importance of what went on in the refectory.

Eating binds. Every old human culture locked to the soil of Truehome understood that, on one level or another. Share salt, and an enemy becomes your friend. If you want to forge links with a sophont, try eating with/on/around/against him.

Inside the big, open, high-ceilinged room that was the refectory, there were members of species that employed all those prepositions.

There were humans who ranged from the Conservancy-unmodified norm to those who were altered into the nearly alien. There were godhorses (so beautiful) and axolotls (so comical) and slidewhistles (so noisy). Not to mention a dozen other races I haven't the heart to detail, because I miss them so. All were unclothed and busy eating, from trough and plate and bowl and hopper. The pungent aromas were making my belly sit up and beg.

So I plunged in.

When my hunger was assuaged and my spirits restored, I hit the showers in the room *ante* to the exit. (Some races seem to enjoy wearing their food more than actually eating it.) I picked out a new jox and sandals and liftharness (my standard outfit) from the clothing alcove, and exited onto the streets. (Such necessities are freely disbursed in the Commensality. But there're still plenty of private possessions for me to lift.)

I headed then for the Bayside locks. A quiet place to think was next.

At the locks, I took a quilt from its rack and donned it. The living flesh (no brains, just ganglions) molded itself to my body, sealing my precious hide away from the deadly atmosphere I was about to step into. For a second I was blind and deaf. Then I TAPPED into the feed from a camera mounted in the locker room. I saw myself as I looked now to others: something like an inflated rubber biped balloon.

I switched the TAP to receive the sensory inputs of the quilt. Since it "saw" exclusively by infrared, had no hearing, and "tasted" over its entire surface, you can imagine that the world altered rather radically.

I cycled through the locks and stood on the shore. It tasted like acid and salt beneath my squishy soles.

The surface temperature of our satellite hovers around the triple point of methane: minus 168 degrees Centigrade, the critical temperature at which that compound can exist as solid, liquid or gas.

The shore was solid.

The turbulent sea that stretched away was liquid.

The air was gas (gases, actually, nitrogen supplying the major component.)

Breathing the oxygen suspired by the quilt, I started walking around the curving marge that lay between the city-shell and the lapping sea. It looked like the tide was coming in (courtesy of the primary's gravity), and so I had to be careful not to get isolated on some inaccessible spit. The quilt could stand immersion in the liquid methane, but the damn stuff tasted just like gasoline, and you risked getting swept out into the 400 meter-deep sea. I kept myself oriented by the hottest pointsources of heat within the dome, and the more feeble beacon that was the distant shrouded sun.

Now I could think about my future.

But wouldn't you know, my stubborn brain could only focus on the past.

I remembered my youth.

Did you ever realize that the Heisenberg drive promotes specialization? When transport is cheap, it makes sense to import what you can't produce efficiently. And if there's a big market for whatever you do best, then you tend to do it more and more, until pretty soon almost your whole world's doing it. (This applies, of course, to Conservancy and neutral worlds, the worker ants, and not us lazy Commensality grasshoppers, who traffic more in intangibles.)

I was born and grew up in a grain field. The whole damn world was hairy with wheat and oats and other assorted hybrids. There was no such thing as a city. The one other family on the world occupied the antipodes. On clear days you couldn't see forever, but only about as far as the next stalk. It was boring as a stint in a sense-dep tank.

So I said to my brother one day (over the master combine's radio, for he was a thousand miles away), "Buddy, I'm leaving this world when I hit sixteen."

"Yeah, sure," he staticked back. "And where're you going and what're you gonna do?"

Even then, I was developing "peculiar" (by the lights of Buddy) tastes. For instance, I used to study the native locusts for hours, and was sorry when we had to kill them, lest they eat our crop.

"The Commensality," I said, yanking on the steering bars to avoid an eroded spot. I squinted against the newly angled sunlight, as the big machine responded sluggishly and I wished for illegal mind/machine interface.

"Yuk," Buddy said. "Those exteelovers. What a creepy idea. You wouldn't really go there, would you?"

"Yes. I'm serious. What's the sense of living on a neutral world if you can't choose one side or the other? And I choose the Commensality."

"You're crazy. The Conservancy is the only way to go."

I said nothing in reply; I was too stunned. It had never occurred to me that Buddy would object. We had never really argued before. Oh, sure, some sibling spats that sprang up and blew over like our world's circumpolar storms; hell, there weren't even *any girls* on the whole planet to fight over! But I could sense that this topic, this tone, was deadly serious, the source of potential great dissension. So, with untypical wisdom, I hid my adolescent certitude with a bland comment.

But Buddy wouldn't let it go. I guess I had really shocked him. After work that day, as we sported in our favorite shady swimming-hole, half a world away from home, he kept pressing me on it, until I finally asserted myself, saying that I wasn't joking about my desire to join, or at least investigate, the Commensality when I was old enough.

That was when, amid harsh words that stopped just short of blows, he quit talking to me, and I, perforce, to him.

There was one last time before I left, when I knew Buddy still cared for me.

I was overseeing a force of meks who were sowing half a continent with winter wheat, up in the northernmost latitudes amenable to cultivation. I was about a klick from my ship when a sudden unseasonable blizzard blew in, white-ing out the kilometers of flatness into featureless oblivion. At first I didn't worry. I was dressed for a certain level of exposure, and my ship had a homing beacon.

Which I soon learned I had neglected to flip on.

I started trudging through the howling snow-inferno, heading toward where I thought my ship lay. After covering about five klicks I knew I had guessed wrong. I started tromping in a circle. When I couldn't do that any more, I lay down to die.

I woke up to find Buddy bending over me. (I later learned he had made the instant transition from home to low orbit over my assigned territory, zoomed in on my near-corpse with infrared sensors, then split the atmosphere with a quick descent.)

Through frost-crusted lips I murmured, "Thanks."

And do you know—that lifesaving bastard wouldn't unbend enough even to say, "You're welcome"?

So attaining my majority (age, not size; I still had plenty of growth beyond the two-meter mark I stood at then) I took off, with no goodbyes.

At the spaceport, I pondered travel as our age knew it.

First: why spaceships?

The Heisenberg drive works by transferring all an object's inherent dispersed quantum uncertainty into its spatial dimension, at which time it becomes possible to impose new relativistic coordinates on it. Great. So now we can flit directly from the surface of one world to that of another.

Not quite. Unless you want to risk occupying the same coordinates as something/someone else, and make the biggest possible bang for your mass. Better pick some vacuum close to your destination.

Which means space. Which means a way to get down from space. Which means spaceships.

But no extravagant takeoffs. Landings, yes. But takeoff consists merely of disappearance and the clap of inrushing air.

Maybe it's pretty extravagant at that.

So at the field I bought my ticket and took my chances.

And found myself entering the portside lock of Babylon, dazed, confused, and utterly bewildered. (The ancients thought jetlag was something!)

When I trod accidentally on the paw of a human-sized feline (I was still wearing my loamy shitkickers), she turned hissing, teeth bare, and said, "Watch it, meat."

I backed off, muttering apologies. The first thing I did was unvelcro my boots and ditch them.

But I kept the semi-derogatory, semi-joshing name. I was sick of my old one anyway, and felt I was embarking on a new life. And it proved a fortuitous choice. No one expects much subtlety from a giant named Meat—which pays off when you are trying to separate them from their valuables.

(And now I've kept my promise to you about explaining my name!)

I called us lazy grasshoppers earlier, and I suppose, compared to others, we are. You can exist in the Commensality without working, thanks to the bounty from the labor of mek units directed by your AOI. But sophonts being sophonts, there is still plenty of enterprise in the Commensality, people providing services and products that others want, so as to raise themselves above the lowest common denominator (all in a Commensally aware manner, of course; no rapacious merchant princes need apply).

But such an existence wasn't for me. I had worked harder than these people for all my life. Now I wanted to take it easy. But I wanted to do it in style. So I became a thief. Which turned out to be work too, but also fun. I surprised myself with my talents in this area. For years now, I had been content and happy.

But then Babylon had made me think.

I came walking upon the shore to a delicate spray of frozen methane that looked like the bridge to Asgard. I kicked it to flinders, without deriving even the satisfaction of feeling it through the quilt.

What did I owe the Commensality? I had fitted into this peculiar *polis* like a hand into a glove. They had saved me from a life of boring drudgery, providing a matrix in which I could become me. And what had I contributed in turn? Oh, sure, I had made individuals happy (and some no doubt sad). Anyone can do that. But what had I given to the Commensality as a whole? What were my community responsibilities? Did they involve killing another sophont?

Damn that Babylon! I wanted to cleave the thick roof of his hidden cavern beneath the city and let this frigid sea flow in on him.

I stopped walking, and turned. I was far away from the city now, out on a promontory slapped by the hydrocarbon waves. The thick atmosphere hid the dome from me. The next moment, though, an eddy in the gases developed. (We called these windows mooneyes.) Through the mooneye shone the lights of Babylon, various heat-tones of red, orange, yellow, white and blue, like Captain Nemo's undersea city.

So exotic, so fragile, so mine.

I decided to do what Babylon wanted.

So three days later, why was I still hesitating?

(My nerves were strung so tight that every time I happened to step into Shadow—or Shadow swept over me—I flinched.)

I had passed the time in various pursuits, none of which served to truly allay the nervousness I was feeling.

I conducted a scam or two—nothing too extravagant, just something to keep my hand in, and pass the time while I decided how to take out the Conservancy's envoy. One deal had some interesting facets. It involved the infamous Babylon Sisters—

But that's another story altogether.

In any case, my growing credit balance did nothing to soothe my apprehensions. So I turned to sex.

I picked up this stegasoid in the refectory outshowers, and we spent a fun three hours together. But of course, with the way my luck was running, there had to be repercussions. It turned out she was just in from offplanet, somewhere less fastidious than Babylon, and had a bad case of scale mites. You've never known irritation until you've had those active little critters under your overlapping spinal plaques. Took an hour in the infirmary to make 'em surrender.

When I got out of the ward, I went to a bar to waste a few idle hours in muzzy rumination.

In the dimness of the bar (haven't really changed in centuries, I understand), I got a TAP from Babylon.

[I called to see how matters were progressing,] he sent.

I jolted up in my seat when his words filled my brain. [Oh, fine, fine, Babylon. I'm planning my strategy right this minute.]

[Good. I suggest you pay more attention to the mental condition of your commensals while you procrastinate. Perhaps their malaise may help motivate you.]

I didn't know what the hell he was talking about, but pretended I did.

[Sure. I'll check it out.]

There was silence then, and I thought Babylon had broken the connection. But he came back with a request.

[Meat, I have a thing I wish you to read. Will you?]

I sent back acceptance, and Babylon squirted me a book.

It took a couple of seconds to absorb and store it, but since it was only a few megabytes of information, I soon had it integrated.

The nature of the information took me by surprise. I had expected something that would help me with my goal. Instead, I got a book of poetry.

It was titled *Crimes Embedded in a Matrix of Semi-serious Poems.*

And it was all about me.

[Babylon, I—What's this all about? Who wrote this?]

[I did. But I am not releasing it for general consumption. It would be too likely to incite similar behavior.]

[But why? And why me?]

Babylon sent something wordless akin to a shrug. [I write a lot of poetry in my spare time, and your life seemed dramatically interesting. Not many people talk directly to me, you know, and I have to do something. Also, believe it or not, I actually like you, and would be sorry to have to scoop out your cortex. So I thought I'd share my work with you. I will not hide the fact that I also calculated the action would provoke a slightly higher allegiance from you.]

[Well, thanks, Babylon. I'm touched.] And I was.

[Please think nothing of it. Goodbye, and remember what I said about your compatriots.]

[Goodbye.]

I told you our "rulers" were idiosyncratic, didn't I?

I got up and left the bar. Serendipity dictated that I would step out into Shadow.

Wincing, I looked up, onto the underside of the Gardens: a flat grey disk marked with colorful graffiti and bordered by dangling plants. I hooked a finger beneath my carcanet and glared at the Gardens, trying to will the whole thing away. I wished I were Prospero, and could vanish this particular gorgeous palace into the baseless, uncertain fabric that was the spacetime continuum.

Up there, in a rented palace suite, the Conservancy envoy was dispensing his poison, in the form of the Chronicle of Mankind, and Babylon claimed it was generating some sort of psychic illness among the populace.

I set off to find out what he meant.

And this was what I learned.

There was a split growing between the human and the non-human citizens of Babylon. Whereas members of all species had always existed in complete harmony, now everyone seemed to be acquiring jagged edges that grated and rasped on each other. I saw it on the streets and in the refectories, in the concert halls and null-gee natatoriums.

The humans were exhibiting traits such as arrogance and impatience and coerciveness. The non-humans were responding with disdain and stubbornness and frigidity. Godhorses drooped (so dispirited), axolotls frowned (so sad), and slidewhistles scurried by (so silent). I actually saw a fight or three that seemed to have nothing at their bases other than prejudice. (You must understand that there were fights now and then in Babylon during normal times. We're not talking about Utopia, after all, and any sentients might come to blows about certain disagreements. But over negligible physical details—no, never that.)

I knew what the Conservancy planned. Babylon possessed a slight majority of humans. (An accident of statistical distribution. When travel across the universe resembles Brownian motion, you get such occasional clumping.) Pretty soon, when enough of them were infected with the Chronicle, someone would issue a request to the Conservancy to step in and take over the city, on some pretext such as "protecting fellow humans from bodily harm." What could Babylon do then? The Commensality's strength lay in solidarity. An AOI could only act in the interests of his community. And if that community was fragmented, where did correct action lie?

Then would begin the riots and bloodshed and retribution for slights real or imagined, the purges and re-education, until Babylon was molded into the Conservancy's image.

Civilization is so tenuous.

My inaction had helped to bring this fateful *Kristallnacht* a step closer. I couldn't let it happen. Not if doing what Babylon wanted was all it would take to stop it.

So I devised a plan.

babylon sisters and other posthumans

⚭⚭

The Gardens hung in the darkling sky like a Fata Morgana conjured by a demon wizard. I floated up, air streaming over my bare limbs like liquid methane over a quilt. (But the cold was in me, rather than in the air.)

I noticed then that only humans were heading for the Gardens. There wasn't a single other kind of sophont in sight.

It was truly scary, this segregation, even though, by specious (and specificate) biological assumptions, I was willy-nilly on the side of those who had initiated it. I wondered if this was how my distant ancestors had felt on Truehome, when the calls of a lynchmob echoed through some small North American town.

One perfect ten-point landing later (bare feet comprising an unmodified ten toes), I stood on a wide terrace paved with living substance (the better to roll upon). A hundred meters off stood the palace, central pleasure dome of this aerial trysting place.

I moved off toward it, past glimmering elven lights strung on potted trees.

On the broad steps leading up to the main doors, I TAPPED Babylon.

[You know when to shut off the power?] I asked.

[Of course. 24:00:00 exactly. The witching hour.]

[Ha, ha,] I enunciated with mental precision, just to show I was in no mood for AOI humor. [It's easy for you to joke. You're not about to take someone's life.]

[I stand to lose as much if you fail as you do,] retorted that sententious mass of jelly. Then: [Are you sure you need the whole city shut off?]

[I want utter chaos. That's the only thing that's going to bring the Conservator out of his lair. Can you think of a better way to accomplish it?]

[No. We will follow your plan. Good luck.]

Babylon left my brain.

The city was powered by a monopole furnace. Shutting it off consisted of stopping the flow of protons into that destructive soliton. (Each proton-disintegration yielded several gev, and the furnace provided more power than a dozen Babylons could fully use. Fair access to energy *is* equality.)

I had arrived half an hour before midnight. There was one thing I planned to do before confronting the Conservator.

I was going to experience the Chronicle, so I could know exactly what we were up against.

In the palace, I TAPPED for a floorplan and followed it up a gravshaft to the Conservancy suite.

Before I entered, I stopped to look. I saw a large room crowded with immobile humans, surrounding a golden ovoid set on a pillar.

I stepped into the room—

—and was living the Chronicle of Mankind.

Oh, those Conservators are clever! Disdaining TAPS as organic mods, they've developed an electronic projective telepathy, a brutal generator of waves that swamp the consciousness. Rather than accept an enhancement that amounts to the slightest possible violation of self, they've substituted mental rape.

I was myself no longer. Instead, I was some anonymous viewpoint character, living out the tale of humanity, as interpreted by the Conservancy. The device must just have cycled, for I was back four million years.

A hominid, I stood on a dusty African plain, puzzling out what to do with a sharp piece of flint. The sun was hot on my back as I finally bent to saw at the zebra carcass at my feet. I gave a grunt of exultation, and swallowed some bloody meat.

After a time in this milieu, things changed. I won't attempt to recount the whole vast tale. Everyone knows it. Through Paleolithic and Neolithic I voyaged. Through Sumer, Ur, Thebes, Babylon (Senior), Egypt, Greece and Rome my consciousness hurtled, shuttled from one representative inhabitant to another. All along, pounding into my brain was the inevitability of it: mankind's long predestined rise from savagery and nescience, his manifest destiny looming huge before him.

Mastery of the universe.

On and on through history I raced, reliving the experiences of hundreds of humans as they subjugated Truehome's flora and fauna and very topography. The Age of Discovery, the Age of Empire, the Age of the Atom, the Age of Solar Exploration, mankind moving from strength to strength, from one glorious conquest to another, culminating in the invention of the Heisenberg drive, when he exploded onto the universe and found—

Other sentients. Beings that aspired to our stature.

Creepy, crawly things, embodiments of a hundred ancestral fears, all of them daring to claim equality, whereas they deserved nothing but enslavement, or second-rate status at best.

At which point mankind split. Into a camp of loyalists and one of traitors. Conservancy versus Commensality. The old true stock against the deliberate mutants and exteelovers. But there was still time for the traitors to recant, to rejoin the crusade to dominate the galaxy. I could feel sympathy growing in my heart for the twisted cause—

The Chronicle snapped off as abruptly as Babylonian night.

The room went dark, save for feeble bioluminescents.

The Gardens dipped five degrees from horizontal—as the emergency capacitors attempted to handle the huge mass—and started to descend to a preprogrammed emergency landing site.

Babylon had come through for me.

People began to shriek and scream. They stampeded toward the door and flew out the windows.

I activated my own harness and floated up into the shadows to wait.

Pretty soon the hall was empty. I spent the time trying to cleanse my brain of the filth.

Everything was silent, except for the muted sounds of distress from the city outside. I watched a door that led further into the suite.

Through that door came a fog.

I dropped down like an avenging angel, to stand upon the canted floor.

The fog and I faced off. Sweat slicked the circuit-laced leather straps across my chest.

"Drop your mask," I said. "I want to see what kind of human believes such shit and works for it."

The fog regarded me blankly for a full minute. (That's a long time. You try conducting such a standoff for sixty seconds, and see how your nerves bear up.)

At last came a voice from out the prisming mist.

"No."

That was it. I didn't even rate an insult.

The chill from the methane atmosphere seemed to have seeped in past the dome's disabled heaters and infiltrated my heart. From within the mist I thought to detect motion. So I raised my finger and—

Why did I do it?

He was everything I was not. He juxtaposed text to my texture, sense to my sensuality, being to my becoming, mastery over melding. (And yes, my godhorse lover said he would master me. But that was love, and love is a figurative thing.) The envoy and I represented outerness versus innerness; planets versus moons; restless roving versus complacent sessility; secrets versus openness; law versus anarchy. There was no choice. I had to. So—

—raised my finger and lanced him with light.

The fog collapsed. I went over to it and groped inside, my arm cut off above the wrist. I found the distorter and switched it off.

I never mentioned that my brother and I were twins, did I? So it looked like myself cooling there. Of course he had no spinal plaques, or laser beneath his fingernail. In fact, he had no weapons at all. I am forced to believe that he was reaching up to shut off the distorter himself when I killed him, although I know for a fact he was too damned stubborn.

"Buddy—" I murmured.

And half an hour later was half a universe away, under the light of another sun. An hour more (the reception port was busy), I walked on another world.

Thus began more than two years of flight.

I can't recount all the places I visited. But no matter where I ran, I couldn't outpace the memory of what I had done. Saved a city and destroyed a life, a life connected to mine by inextinguishable bonds. Twisted bonds, to be sure, but bonds none the less.

One day I woke up and really paid attention to where I was.

In a one-man ship, two parsecs—the minimal distance for survival—away from a quasar, one of those enigmas that blazed with the radiance of a dozen galaxies.

I was sixteen billion lightyears away from Babylon, on the literal edge of the plenum.

It was as far as I could go.

There was nowhere else left to haunt.

So I headed for my birthplace.

I was lying on my back in a field of grain, studying the clouds, when Ace found me.

"We've been monitoring arrivals here since you disappeared," he said.

"Babylon had a hunch you'd return sooner or later."

I didn't sit up. "So?"

"Babylon wants you to come back. He says you've earned it."

I considered. "How are you functioning anyway? You're not in direct contact with that master manipulator, are you?"

"No. I received a limited imprint and autonomy for this mission. Are you coming back? Babylon has further use for you."

"I'm sure. Well, you can transmit this message."

I recited that ancient children's rhyme.

"And what does that mean?" asked Ace's baffled limited imprint.

"Just deliver it. From one poet to another. Babylon will understand."

Ace seemed to ponder. Then he left.

I adjusted my hands beneath my head into a more comfortable cradle. The earth smelled good. The grain stood tall. The sky was deep. Unless a combine came by, I didn't plan on moving for a while.

Turning my eyes inward, I sought a candle to travel by.

solitons

MARL SAID ROUGHLY, "We're here—get your arses in motion."

Anna tried to shake off the vast weight of nausea engendered by Heisenberg transition. Bastard, she thought. So tough on yourself and the rest of us. I'll take it though, now that I'm in, for the stakes at risk. And not crawl back to your black-and-blue bed.

Petting her organiform couch to an upright position, Anna faced the screen and keyboard that allowed her to control the *Lonely Lady*'s force-grapples and confinement bottle. She initiated a diagnostic check, before Marl could order her to do so, thereby achieving a precious bit of satisfaction.

She had run six of these checks over the past month, upon completion of each epidrive jump. Yet the equipment had not been used once.

The monopole was proving more elusive than they had feared at the outset of their search. No wonder only desperate gamblers dared hunt the elusive particle.

From the corner of one eye, Anna watched Marl rise from his couch. A big man, he defied the world with an ugly seamed rind of a face, split by narrow eyes, thin lips, and bisected by a hatchet-blade nose. From skull to midriff, Marl was covered with synthetic skin, possessing no follicles or sweat glands. His chest lacked nipples, his fingers nails. Below this artificial terminator, his muscled body was hirsute to the human extreme. He wore only a pair of tight white shorts to midthigh, a deliberate affront and taunt to Anna's physical aloofness. (She, in response, wore a shapeless black coverall under all circumstances.)

Anna pondered his bizarre appearance for the hundredth time, a body at war with itself, living testament to the blood-debt he owed Sanger, his rival. He could have easily had the former good looks that had first attracted Anna to him, before Sanger wrecked Marl's ship and nearly killed him. But anger and desire for revenge had bred in Marl like Shintak viruses, distorting his mind in subtle and obvious ways, least of which was this senseless flaunting of his scars.

Marl catfooted across the living resilient floor—part of the ship's closed recycling system—to the couch where Clete, their hired tiresias, lay.

The third organiform couch in the small cabin held Clete's thin child-sized body in its warm depression. Prior to the last jump, Clete had complained of tiredness, reclined heesh's couch and gone instantly to sleep. Now, though, heesh was awake, milky white eyes staring blindly at the pinkly luminescent ceiling.

As Marl approached, Clete's body tensed beneath heesh's grey robe, as if expecting a blow.

Marl stood by the couch, clenching his massive knobby fists. "There you go, Scryer. Just as you ordered, we've jumped a hundred lights closer to Mizar. I must admit, your ranging shots are getting smaller. What was the first—two thousand parsecs? Do you think you might be a little more precise in your next estimate? I was led to believe by your guild that you had seen solitons being formed and could lead us right to them."

Clete's voice was a calm soprano, ageless and sexless. "I have indeed seen solitons being born in the Monobloc, bright red knots in the polychrome domains of the nucleating primal universe. But that happened, to be precise, ten to the minus thirty-fifth seconds after the Big Bang. Over twelve billion years ago."

A small smile creased Clete's unwrinkled features. "A lot has happened since then, Marl, if you stop to think. I can envision the whole Monobloc any time, from any place in the universe, since each bit of matter once resided in that infinitely dense point, and I can follow any thread back to the labyrinth's center. But as the universe expands over time, I can hold less and less of it in my mind simultaneously. Eventually, to scry the recent past, I must be physically present in that very volume of space I wish to examine. Hence our 'ranging shots,' as you archaically call them. Now, unless you wish to pay the Scryers' Sodality more than you already owe them, let me get to my work, which you cannot possibly understand in any real sense."

Marl's right fist came up from his side as if to strike Clete, then stopped in mid-gesture. The tiresias lay unperturbed. It was not that heesh's blind eyes had not registered the threat—by scrying the immediate past nanoseconds behind reality, Clete could "see" as well as anyone, with only an insignificant lag—but that heesh knew Marl would not dare contravene the rules by which he had contracted for Clete's services.

Clete was right this time. Marl pivoted, quivering with rage, and stalked away, spitting out over his shoulder, "Do it then, damn it!"

A small shiver passed down Clete's body, and heesh's breathing slowed. Nothing could disturb herm now, until heesh roused hermself.

Marl threw himself heavily down onto his couch, which surged with semifluid movement, like a waterbed filled with mercury. Anna turned from her board. She felt for Marl—not pity or love, but some novel mixture of respect and awe and fear. He drove her and Clete no harder than he pushed himself. But to know that made it no easier to take. They were not infected with his same will or desires.

"Let up on Clete, Marl," she ventured mildly. "I'm sure heesh's doing heesh's best. Remember: without herm, we'd have no chance at all."

Marl sat up and fixed her with a baleful stare. "That filthy androgyne and heesh's stinking guild are nothing but leeches. They bleat about how hard it is to interpret their visions of the past to get a fix on the present, yet stand there all the while with outstretched hands for more and more credits. Then when you're bled dry, they disgorge what they knew all along."

Anna was taken aback. "You can't believe that, Marl. Imagine what Clete's doing right now. I've talked with herm a little about it. It's not easy. Heesh is travelling through an abstract landscape of colors and shapes, trying to correlate it with the world we know through our conventional senses. Even then, once heesh masters that, clients like us toss in the dimension of time, asking herm to track a miniscule object through the billions of years of its existence to its present location. It's amazing heesh gets any results at all."

Marl snorted. "What results? We've only got heesh's word for it that we're getting closer to the monopole." He leaned forward with sudden eagerness. "Speaking of which, has the detector registered anything yet?"

"Of course not. I would have spoken up. I want this hunt to succeed too, you know."

Marl looked at Anna with blank suspicion, as if he had never seen her before. His hands spasmed in his lap like fish out of water. "We don't have forever. How long do you imagine it will take Sanger to catch up with us?"

Anna winced. She had almost managed to forget that aspect of their pleasant little prospecting trip.

Soon after Marl, a changed man, had come home from the hospital that Sanger's sabotage had sent him to, he had begun to savage Anna verbally, then physically. She had left him with much regret but no hesitation, ending an asteroid-mining partnership-cum-affair of some years' standing. Much time passed with no word from him. Then one day he had shown up at Anna's door, with this mad plan to make their fortunes by netting a monopole. Had Anna not been down on her own luck, she would never have agreed to go in with him. He took her to the port to see his ship, and she was surprised at its quality, having thought him broke.

Only when they were underway did he tell her that the ship was Sanger's, stolen from his yards in an abortive attempt to snatch the man himself from under the nose of his elaborate security force.

When Anna demanded that he return her home, Marl had spun a glib lunatic's tapestry of how they could have immediate success, selling the monopole for gigacredits, then, armored in wealth, secure from Sanger, extract their revenge.

She had made the mistake of staying with him until they picked up Clete from the Sodality world. There, her name was registered on the contract with Marl's, and she realized that Sanger would now be able to connect her with Marl, and any safety back home was illusory. There was no way out for her except forward, linked to this apparition out of her past in victory or defeat.

"All right," Anna said. "You made your point and blew away any dreams of peace I was cultivating. Go away now, and let me read. At least it allows me to forget."

Marl lowered his voice to a seductive whisper. The effect combined with his disfigured features was grotesque. "We could forget together, Anna. Take up what we once had. That thing will be out of it for long enough. We'll have some privacy."

Anna spat on the floor, which slowly absorbed it. "Shove it. I'm not your lover anymore. At worst, I'm your hostage. At best: your friend. And before you try anything, remember who I studied with."

Marl shivered, as he recalled the reputation of the Cybele, the Bloody Nuns. He turned on his side away from Anna.

She breathed a sigh of relief. Especially since she had never even seen a Cybele.

Her screen flooded with text on the epidrive. All her working life she had used the spacedrive, with little thought paid to how it functioned. Now, on this crazy trip, where boredom alternated with screaming tension, she had begun to grow interested in this device that made their travel possible.

The words read:

"FILE: Epistemological spacedrive, overview.

"CROSSREFERENCED: Heisenberg transition, epidrive, Shozo Turnbow . . .

"The epistemological spacedrive was perfected in the year 2, Ante Scattering, by one Shozo Turnbow. Its basic mode of operation relies on the Heisenberg Uncertainty Principle, which is most simply formulated in the statement: All qualities of a particle may not be known simultaneously.

"The advent of superior subatomic scanning methods, coupled with digitalization of the results, lies at the heart of the drive. Basically, all particles possess a host of qualities—spin, angular momentum, and mass, for instance—one of which is location in space. An object subject to the epidrive is first scanned quark by quark, and all its qualities—save location—recorded in a suitable memory matrix. The duration of this process naturally varies directly with the mass of the object being scanned, placing a premium on size. As data accumulates, over hours and days, the object under scan enters a state of uncertainty as to its location. The very precision with which all its nonspatial qualities are recorded forces all its inherent uncertainty to be concentrated in its spatial dimension. At this point, the object may be literally anywhere in the universe. At the height of uncertainty, two things are done simultaneously. All information previously recorded is wiped, dispersing the uncertainty, and a new relativistic location is imposed on the object. Transition is instantaneous."

Anna's head swam with the words, simple enough on the surface, yet concealing hidden depths of paradox. She ran a slim hand over her cropped brown hair, wondering if she would ever truly fathom the epidrive. What bothered her most was the fact that the scanning equipment had of necessity to scan itself as part of the ship to be transported. It seemed too much like pulling oneself up by one's bootstraps. And the whole drive required such minimal power . . . Where were the huge warp mechanisms of antique fiction, comforting in their similarity to internal combustion engines?

An abrupt shuddering intake of breath sounded across the cramped cabin, and Anna knew that Clete had come out of heesh's scrying trance. She turned from her screen as Marl abandoned his sullen meditations. Together, the two crossed the room to Clete.

The tiresias had stroked heesh's couch into its roughly L-shaped position, and now sat with stringy, fatigue-trembling muscles apparent beneath heesh's robe. A seemingly insignificant twist of heesh's lips, which Marl and Anna had learned to interpret as a smile of satisfaction, seemed to bode well.

Marl's eagerness could not be contained. It caused him to actually lay his hands upon Clete's robe, against all guild prohibitions. "Well," he demanded, "do you have a fix on it? Can you take us there? Speak up!"

Clete said nothing, and Marl quickly realized what he had done and removed his grip from the grey fabric. Crazy he might be, Anna knew, but that did not preclude cunning and guile and a sense of whom not to offend. Anna he could only push so far, since he needed her to capture the monopole while he maneuvered the ship under its ion-drive. And Clete he needed even more, for heesh's clairvoyance.

But after the success of the mission, Anna wondered, what then?

Upon heesh's release, Clete spoke in heesh's pellucid voice. "I have seen the monopole in its unmistakable glory. It is not far. Here are its coordinates." Heesh reeled off a set of relativistic figures describing the transition to be made, which heesh had read from the tangled skeins of force heesh saw in heesh's visionary state.

Marl almost leapt for the epidrive controls. As if a few seconds saved now could matter over the five days it would take the epidrive to reach the transition peak. At his board, he placed a contact mike against his throat and subvocalized the code to activate the drive. Anna prayed for him to move his lips, but he made no such mistake. If only she knew the code, she could—what? Return home to await Sanger's arrival? Flee to some far reach of space? No, her only hope of future safety lay in accomplishing what they had set out to do.

Marl remained by the board, as if willing the drive to speed up. Anna turned back to Clete.

"You look drained," she said to the scryer. "Let me get you something to eat."

"That would be appreciated," Clete said. Anna went to a cluster of pebbly-skinned fruits growing from the wall and picked one. She drew a glass of cloudy liquid from a wall-nipple and picked up a protein bar from the supply-cabinet. These she brought back to Clete.

The tiresias ate with catlike economy. Anna sat on the end of heesh's couch. Clete's small form left half the surface free.

When heesh had finished, Anna spoke softly to herm. She doubted that Marl was paying any attention to them, yet she did not wish him to intrude in any case. Her talks with Clete were a brief respite from Marl's tirades and scratchy silences.

"What did you see this time, Clete? What was it like?"

Clete tipped heesh's head back as if to gaze out through the organic-inorganic duostrate of the ship at the mysterious universe beyond. "The turbulence the monopole has left behind in its passage through space and time is a golden kinked cord surrounded by a purple halo of the byproducts of destroyed protons. This trail lies on the universal background whose color has no name, woven through stars that stream energy and planets that hum with gravitic contentment. It is the same trail I have followed out of the Monobloc at billion-year intervals. And now I have seen its end."

"It sounds beautiful. More beautiful than the world I see every day. How I wish I could share it."

Clete shrugged. "Do not belittle your own senses. They offer marvels enough, when one speaks of the present. And our lives are constricted in ways yours is not."

"But the past," Anna said. "To see the past and trace all the mysterious effects of the present back to their essential causes—what do we have to compare with that? That's what I want."

"I will not lie to you. That is indeed something fine you cannot know. Especially to see the Primeval Egg."

"You've mentioned that before. What's it like? Why is it so important to a scryer?"

"It is indescribable, yet the vital thing we live for. To hold the totality of the universe in the eye of the mind, darting in and out of that infinitely dense point, where all is unified, where there is only one Force acting in a broth of elementary particles. To see such perfection ameliorates living in this age of broken symmetry."

Clete paused, as if weighing heesh's words so as not to offer an insult.

"Have you never wondered why we scryers are dual-sexed?" heesh finally asked.

Anna looked away, unaccountably embarrassed. "I always thought it was an unavoidable side-effect of your gift."

"That is the notion the Sodality promotes. Once, when biofabrication was more primitive, it was even true. The first embryos engineered to have the scrying talent were inadvertently created androgynes and blind. Now, both 'defects' could be repaired. But we believe these traits were not accidental, but predestined. Our androgyny reflects our worship of the wholeness of the Monobloc. Our blindness is a refusal to see the current fallen state of the universe. We are as we wish to be. You single-sexed homo sapiens are defective, each severed from his other half, perfect representatives of an imperfect age."

Anna sifted through Clete's tone and found no reproaches, but only a calm certainty of the true state of things. Suddenly she felt wholly inadequate, a lonely fragile coalition of particles wandering incomplete through a vast void.

She turned practical to dispel her gloom. "This monopole, soliton, whatever. Who are the prospective buyers for it? What are they going to use it for? I know it's rare, but so are a dozen other things in this universe that are worth much less."

"Like humans," Clete said, "the monopole is incomplete in one sense, a superheavy particle possessing only a single magnetic charge, north or south. This is merely a means of identification, however, not its quintessential property. Every monopole is, in effect, a hot coal that bears the fire of the early universe, the unified Force. Feed a stream of nucleons—protons or neutrons—into it, and they decay instantly into their primal constituents. Each discrete decay releases approximately a billion electron volts of energy. A single monopole could power worlds."

Pursing her lips, Anna whistled silently. "That explains why your guild agreed to send you out with Marl for a share of the profits, despite his lack of credit up front. The take will be enormous."

"You are wrong," Clete countered. "One of us would have come for nothing."

"What?"

"The monopole is a fragment of the Unity we worship, existing in the present. For most scryers, contemplation of the Monobloc is devout enough. But for some, such as myself, only a pilgrimage to a monopole will complete my life. And we must rely on such as Marl to take us there."

Anna got to her feet. It was too much information in too short a time. She didn't know what to think. The realities of the voyage suddenly seemed reversed, all their anxiety and effort expended for Clete, not themselves.

"I've got to get back to work," she said, and left the tiresias to heesh's blind-eyed scrutiny.

Five days—120 standard hours—snailed by like an infinity of water droplets falling on a bruised and hypersensitive forehead. Anna ate just enough to maintain a low level of energy and promote an excess of sleep. She conducted a few desultory conversations with Marl about their hazy future. Clete she avoided, wishing to hear no more disillusioning truths. One can only stand to have the universe inverted so many times.

Marl remained his insane composite of implacable fury and robotic indifference. Occasionally his synthetic upper half suffused with a mottled flush of rage at some remembered or imagined indignity.

At last the ship reached the phase of maximum uncertainty. The on-board computer performed the flipflop maneuver of dispersing the uncertainty and imposing the new coordinates automatically, the delicate process requiring nonhuman speed.

The universe accepted them at their new location.

Their viewscreens showed a bold white sun blazing less than a tenth of an AU away. They were three times as close to the stellar furnace as Mercury to Old Sol.

"Diagnostic check," Marl commanded Anna. Then, to Clete, "Goddamn it, Scryer, why so close? You almost have us inside it."

"You asked for precision," Clete replied without evident unease. "I knew we were safe at this range, yet as close as possible. I have done as you requested. Now leave me to my vision."

"What do you mean, 'as close as possible'? We have to get within grapple-range."

Clete, trance-bound, failed to answer. But Anna had found out what heesh meant.

"Marl," she said, her voice shaky, "the diagnostic check indicates normal functioning, and the detector registers the monopole."

"All right, then, where is it?"

"In the sun."

Marl rushed to her side and shoved her cruelly away from her instruments. "It can't be. I won't let it."

Anna recalled something Clete had told her:

"I know our grapples can fasten on the monopole when we find it," she had said. "But what normally stops a monopole in nature?"

"Concentrations of dense mass," heesh had answered.

Marl turned from the screen. "It is in there," he said in a dead voice. "Radiation analysis indicates excess energy production for a star of this type. Our monopole is wedged in its fucking heart, eating it from the inside out."

Marl hit the control panel with tremendous violence. He turned and punched the yielding wall. Then his eyes fell on Clete, rapt in heesh's contemplation of the monopole at the inaccessible core of the star.

"Heesh *knew*, damn it. Heesh knew before the last jump. The little bitch had to have seen it was trapped in a star. And heesh never told us."

Anna felt sick. What could they do now?

She watched Marl advance on the tiresias, fearing his intentions, her feelings a mix of hatred for the traitorous scryer and empathy for heesh's quest.

Marl slapped the unlined child-sage's face, got no reaction, and slapped again, three times, rocking Clete's head from side to side on heesh's skinny neck.

"Goddamn you, wake up. Tell us what to do now."

Clete's unresponsiveness enraged Marl further. He reached for the neck of heesh's robe, grasped the fabric and split it like paper. Anna couldn't look away.

The scryer's body lay revealed. Immature-looking breasts graced heesh's chest. Below a tiny paunch stood shriveled male genitals; below that, a vaginal slit. There was no pubic hair.

A huge erection bulged in Marl's shorts. Anna's sickness deepened, yet she couldn't rise. Marl would kill her if she interfered. And the scryer—didn't heesh deserve punishment for heesh's deception?

"I'll have my value out of you one way or another," Marl growled. He unseamed his shorts and his penis was unrestrained.

Anna turned her eyes then.

The sounds were awful enough.

After thirty seconds, Clete's voice broke weakly through Marl's grunts.

"No, no defilement. I am whole, you are not. No, don't contaminate—"

Marl must have capped the scryer's mouth with a huge hand, for heesh spoke no more.

When Marl was done, he stumbled to a corner of the cabin and huddled like an autistic child.

Anna crept slowly out of her seat and to the side of the tiresias, hoping Marl would not object. He seemed in no condition to even notice, though.

Blood leaked from the scryer's mouth and vagina. The couch was efficiently taking it up, to convert it to fruit and water, so they could live their useless lives a bit longer.

"Clete," Anna whispered. "Are you okay?"

The tiresias stirred feebly. "My body is not badly damaged, but my spirit is. I must retreat to the monopole to restore myself." Clete's hand sought hers. "Do not let him touch me again."

"All right, Clete, all right, I won't," she said, crying, not knowing how she would keep the promise.

As Clete slipped into scrying mode, the ship's communicator pinged.

Marl remained catatonic. Anna went to the board.

The screen revealed a fat-faced man with a drooping mustache, a ship's cabin-walls out of focus behind him. Fuzzy human figures lurked in the background.

"Sanger here," the man said with laconic indifference. "I want my ship back, and Marl with it. You I don't care about, whoever you are. Anna, isn't it?"

"Yes," Anna said. "Listen, I just can't—"

Sanger cut in. "My ship has armaments. Yours does not. I will open fire shortly unless I detect three suited figures with empty hands exiting the lock."

"How do I know—" Anna began. Then a hand closed around the back of her neck.

Marl stood behind her, self-aware now.

"Sanger, my enemy," he said without inflection. "If you want your ship, follow me. I'm going to collect my monopole."

Marl released Anna's neck and moved to the controls for the ion-drive.

Anna got hurriedly to her feet, shaking. She walked in a confused zigzag to the suit-locker, reeling mentally from the events of the past few minutes.

She pulled a suit awkwardly from the rack, clambered into it and sealed its front. She took a helmet in her right hand.

"Marl," she said softly, seeing at once both the man he had been and the travesty he now was. "Come with me. Give up. It's not the worst thing that could happen."

Ignoring her, saying nothing, Marl boosted the ion-flow. Anna watched red digits flash their acceleration.

Clete remained quiescent on heesh's couch, at one with the monopole. Anna felt she had no right to drag herm away. Heesh had made heesh's choice.

Anna put her helmet on, went to the wrinkled sphincter that was the lock's inner door. There, she looked one last time at Marl.

His broad hairless back was hunched over the controls, and he muttered to himself. She caught only, "Piece of . . ."

Or "Peace of . . ."

She tickled the sphincter in the proper pattern, went through, confronted the outer lock of metal and rubber. The sphincter flexed closed behind her. She opened the lock without first exhausting the trapped air. The escaping gases blew her out into space, away from the ship.

Slowing her tumble with her suit-jets, she found the *Lonely Lady* silhouetted against the incredible glare of the sun, toward which her own trajectory was inevitably carrying her, if no one interfered. Her helmet-polarization could barely filter it, and her eyes pained her.

Still, she followed the ship till it was no more than a flyspeck against the medusa-fringed disk of the monopole-snaring sun.

Her communicator crackled with unheard words from Sanger's ship, which approached.

Solitary soliton for the moment, Anna wondered how many atoms of Clete's vaporized body would eventually find their way to the monopole's consuming core.

gravitons

June 10

KARLA AGAIN TODAY attempted to dissuade me from conducting the trial upon myself. I believe her exact words were: "You can't possibly go through with this insane plan, Alex."

"I have to," I said, in what I hoped was an assured and confident tone. If truth be told—and where else might I tell the whole truth, if not in my private journal?—I was feeling a little trepidation myself. But I was determined not to let Karla see it.

"There's no other way to prove my theory," I continued rationally.

"What about animals? You've completely skipped that stage."

"The phenomenon I expect to observe would be impossible to measure from outside. It's a perceptual alteration, and an animal cannot report on what it's experiencing. No, animals are useless for my purposes."

Karla grew frustrated at my insistently logical manner, as she so often did. It's always been a sticking point between us, she claiming I exhibit an unwholesome lack of emotions—"an unnatural gravity," she once called it—and I countering by accusing her of flightiness, of being unconnected to the solid earth of reality. So different are our basic personalities that I'm surprised we've remained lovers for as long as we have.

"Do you realize exactly what you're risking?" she demanded.

"Yes, I do."

"And you believe it's worth it? You really think that if you succeed Zavgorodny will just fold up his tents and slink away?"

"No, he won't do that," I said. "However, if my speculations prove correct, then I'll have the satisfaction of knowing that I've contributed something unique to man's understanding of the universe."

Karla regarded me with silent contempt for five seconds or so, before saying, "That's utter bullshit."

I was taken aback. "What?"

"You heard me. I said you're full of crap. The real reason you're doing this is because you want the thing named after you. Admit it. You can't stand the thought of your precious new element being forever known as 'zavgorodnium.' That's the only thing motivating you. You're going to risk your health—maybe even die—just so your name will be attached to a—a lifeless chemical!"

Karla began to cry. I said nothing. I noticed with an irrelevant precision that her first few tears were held in a little pool by surface tension at the corners of her eyes. I always had been observant. It's simply part of my job.

When she was done, she dabbed at her eyes with her sleeve and said, "Well, tell me. Am I wrong?"

"No," I said. "You're not wrong."

June 11

Thirteen months ago, at the Joint Nuclear Research Institute at Dubna, U.S.S.R.—and simultaneously at the facility which I head, the Lawrence Berkeley Laboratory in California—element number 131 was synthesized.

(In these private notes, I refuse to call it "zavgorodnium," despite the slight precedence those at Dubna had, and I dare not dub it "chiltonium"—yet. So a simple "element 131" it must remain, for now.)

Element 131, this substance never before seen on earth, proved to be the first member of the predicted "island of stability" in the periodic table: that group of superheavy elements higher than number 103 which proved to have a half-life longer than thirty-five seconds. As of this writing, it is still the only stable SHE to be created.

Element 131 has a half-life of approximately twenty-five days. Given this stability, element 131 lends itself to detailed and extended observation. We have been able to perform more tests and assays and analyses on this new material than on any other synthesized element.

The most curious property of element 131 is an effect akin to piezoelectricity.

In common cases of piezoelectricity, mechanical stress on a crystal produces an electrical charge.

Element 131 exhibits a continual—albeit fluctuating—electrical charge in a rest state. Shielded from obvious forces, without apparent mechanical deformation, element 131 produces a trickle of electricity.

Various theories have been adduced to explain this anomaly.

I am certain that none but mine is correct.

There is only one force which could produce the fluctuating electrical charge. One force which it is impossible to shield against.

That force is gravity.

It is my view that element 131 is extremely sensitive to gravity. Its inherent atomic structure makes it responsive to every passing gravity wave, every mass over a certain theoretical threshold.

I know this to be a fact, as surely as I know anything.

However, there is no way of proving it in the laboratory.

According to the mathematics of my theory, the masses needed to influence the production of electrical current in element 131 are of stellar or planetary proportions.

Obviously, not something one could manipulate in the lab. Current science has no way of producing gravity waves, nor can a sample of the new element be isolated in some imaginary "gravity-free" container and examined for cessation of the effect.

Until a recent inspiration of mine, there appeared to be no way of proving my contention. For all anyone knew, Zavgorodny's idiot theory of "quark oscillation" was as plausible as mine, and the various international committees debating over a name for element 131 had no reason to favor either him or me.

But now I have hit upon a method of fully proving that element 131 does indeed register the presence of gravity.

An associate of mine at a certain biological lab (which, for fear of adverse publicity, must remain nameless until the eventual success of my project, at which time his firm shall share in the glory), has developed a tailored molecular vector-agent which is intended to carry element 131 through my bloodstream and into my eyes, where the vector will bind its cargo to the photopigment rhodopsin in my retinas, hopefully converting them to gravity receptors.

In short, I intend to see gravity.

The half-life of element 131 insures that the effect should be temporary.

The injection is scheduled for tomorrow.

June 12

Karla left early this morning, a Saturday. I saw her off at the airport. She boarded a plane for New York, where she and her troupe of dancers have a series of performances scheduled, next week at Lincoln Center.

"At least promise me you won't do anything until I get home," she asked, holding my hands in hers.

"I promise," I said.

As soon as her plane was in the air, I got into my car and headed for the biolab.

Karla simply doesn't understand science.

Mark was waiting for me in his office. He is a friend of long standing—we spent our undergraduate years together—and he was risking his reputation and his position at the firm to help me.

The first thing he said when he saw me was, "Are you sure you want to go through with this, Alex?"

It seemed everyone was more solicitous of my welfare than I was. I had expected this attitude from Karla, but thought that Mark at least would comprehend my motives.

"I wouldn't have put you through all this just to back out now," I said.

Then we were in one of the weekend-empty labs and Mark was removing an ampoule from a refrigerator and I was rolling up my sleeve and the inside of my elbow was getting swabbed and the needle point had found my vein, all before I quite realized what was happening.

"My only consolation," said Mark as he removed the needle and discarded the tip, "is that you won't die of radioactivity. That small amount of chiltonium you gave me was only as hot as an average tracer injection."

"Please don't call it that. Not yet."

Mark shrugged. "Whatever. Listen, are you sure you're going to be all right on your own? Don't you want someone to stay with you?"

"I'll be fine. I've arranged a leave of absence from work, and I've got all the food I need for a month—although I don't really imagine any effect will last that long. I won't even have to leave the house while my eyes are—different. And if something should come up, I won't forget your number."

Mark escorted me from the building, gripping my elbow as if I were handicapped somehow.

"All right. But just be careful."

"I will," I said, wondering if this promise meant any more than the one I had just made to Karla.

I got in my car and headed home.

My vision seemed perfect during the drive.

Midnight, and I'm going to sleep. Tired of waiting for a change. I've neither felt nor seen anything different.

Perhaps the whole experiment will be an anticlimactic waste.

June 13

Woke this morning to patchy vision. It's as if tenuous veils and no-color clouds drift lazily across my field of sight. Unlike common "floaters," these patches have amorphous outlines. They are not translucent, nor are they opaque. I have the oddest feeling that there is nothing behind them. They seem more negation than substance. Wherever they materialize, they seem to wipe out the whole universe we take for granted. It's as if they are holes in the fabric of time and space, revealing utter nothingness behind.

This cannot be the visual analogue of gravity. The adaptive process must be incomplete.

I imagine that something like the following must be happening.

As the molecules of element 131 bind to the rhodopsin in my retina—that miraculous film literally as thin as a razor—the process whereby infalling photons, mundane light, are converted into nerve impulses is interfered with. This results in the disturbing migratory lacunae. At the same time, the molecules of element 131 have not yet been fully integrated into the neural signal-processing system, and so there are no new images to replace visual ones.

Gravity—as any first-year physics student can tell you—is a force mediated by gravitons. My eyes are not yet sensitive to gravitons. This must be the case. Surely this depressing nothingness cannot be an image of such an all-pervasive, noble force as gravity...

June 14

When I opened my eyes this morning, I was completely blind.

I am continuing this journal on cassette.

I took some small consolation in the fact that my blindness was the conventional kind, or at least what I assume conventional blindness is like. An utter blackness unobtainable by the sighted eye even with lids shut in a lightless cavern (for even under those conditions, the phenomenon known as "dark light"—false signals spontaneously generated in the retina—would occur). It seems as though my brain has completely shut down its optic links, rejecting whatever new signals element 131 is producing, under the influx of gravitons.

I can only hope that the links will be re-established soon.

Later in the day. A new, somewhat reassuring thought occurred to me. I recall the simple, yet classic experiments done with inverting lenses.

Subjects were asked to wear glasses with lenses that rotated images 180 degrees, for twenty-four hours a day. Trees seemed to have the crowns downmost, people to be walking on air. After some days of this disorientation, their brains spontaneously accommodated to the imposed inversion, and their vision miraculously became "normal." When the glasses were later removed, they saw the world upside down! After a similar period of adjustment, their eyes finally returned to normalcy.

Perhaps my own brain is undergoing just such a transition period.

June 15

Still blind.

June 16

My hypothesis was correct!

Today, though still technically blind, I have "seen" the sun and the earth and the moon without leaving my chair, and without raising my eyes to the heavens, or lowering them to the ground.

I hardly know where—or how—to begin to describe what I have experienced.

Perhaps in a cool recital of theory may lie sanity.

Consider gravity. A force varying inversely with the square of the distance, mediated by gravitons, particles analogous to the photons which transmit electromagnetic radiations. Completely oblivious to this flux, never thinking of our weight as a function of a stream of particles, we live immersed in a sea of gravitons, a sea replenished from an infinite number of sources.

Some of these sources—by virtue of mass or closeness—are more important and prominent than others. Continuing the sea analogy, they are bigger rivers.

All of us are lashed to the planet beneath us by ropes of gravitons.

Above our heads, the moon whips the oceans with flails of gravitons, raising the tides.

Far away, the Sun, largest single source of gravity in our system, has the earth lassoed by gravitons, and is swinging it in its clockwork ellipse, along with every other orbital object, from Jupiter down to the smallest pebble.

My eyes can now apprehend some of this. The molecules of chiltonium (I now feel entitled to call element 131 by that name), bonded to my photo-pigments, are putting out fluctuating signals tied to gravity, which my brain is just learning to interpret.

It is an indescribable sensation.

My sleep was broken this morning by a sense of weightiness, an almost kinesthetic, rather than visual, impression. I lay in bed with my eyes shut, trying to determine what I was experiencing.

First, I sensed an enormous presence directly beneath me. The signals coming in through my optic nerves had a pseudo-visual component. There was no conventional coloration to the object—at least nothing I could put a name to—but my brain tried to represent it, as best it could, as a darker center shading off to lighter edges in all directions. I assume now that this is an image of the dense core of the planet surrounded by the lighter mantle.

The object seemed to pulse, almost as if alive.

It occurred to me then that I was sensing the earth's gravity beneath me, even though I lay on my back and my eyes were closed. In my haste to prove my theories, I had never even considered that if I succeeded I would possess a new sense that worked in 360 degrees—in a complete sphere of perception, in fact. Photons might need the easy path of the iris to register, but gravitons were more determined. Neither flesh nor bone could stop them from impinging on my chiltonium-tinged retina, and I could detect masses behind me as easily as those in front.

Somehow, my attention became distracted from the image of the earth. We know from infancy how to instinctively focus our vision, but I was having trouble focusing my new sense. Still, I persisted, and was able to discern two objects above me: the moon and sun. Both were roughly circular presences, with dark centers fading outward toward their edges. The moon, because of its proximity, radiated gravitons which seemed inexplicably more vibrant than those from the massive sun, and so formed a "brighter" image. A stunning reversal of visual input.

I lay for a while, savoring my triumph. I got up, visited the toilet, then began making breakfast in a clumsy way, fumbling for the utensils and pans I could not see.

Determined to see what I could accomplish, I embarked on a series of mental gymnastics. I began to flick my attention back and forth between the trio of massive astronomical objects—earth, moon and sun—hoping to gradually become able to hold all three of then in my mind simultaneously.

Around noontime, it happened.

The moment was like falling over a threshold into miles of empty space. I realized with a start that it was now impossible *not* to let all three impinge on my consciousness. My brain had adapted to the omnidirectional input, and now was able to process all the signals simultaneously.

I felt dizzy and had to sit down, for the three objects moved in relation to one another, the moon performing a slow pavane about the earth, and the earth revolving on its axis and waltzing with the sun.

The vertigo subsided after several hours, and I was able to get up and move about. However, as of this recitation, the nausea has still not ceased entirely.

It's after midnight now, and I have not been able to fall asleep yet. Closing my eyes does nothing to shut out the influx of gravitons. I now have the bulk of the earth between me and the sun, and their images have fused into one massive entity which weighs on my consciousness more strongly than the two separate ones. The moon is more gentle, but still a presence demanding attention. Although I know that my eyes are not in reality subject to any new forces, somehow I feel that the gravitic pull has increased on them, threatening to suck them from my orbits. I hope that when I get tired enough, I shall be able to fall asleep, just as one does amid noise.

I wonder if tomorrow will bring any new developments.

June 17

The ringing of the phone shattered my uneasy sleep around nine this morning. I had not dropped off until after five, my head aspin from the dance of the masses.

It was Karla, calling from New York.

"Alex? What are you doing home? I just called your office, and they said you were taking a few weeks off. Are you okay?"

I mumbled something I hoped was reassuring. I'm afraid I succeeded only in conveying my confusion. However, I was too preoccupied with the new display which had leaped into my attention the minute I became conscious to really concentrate on what Karla was saying.

I do remember she sounded worried about me. She said something like, "I'm sorry I haven't called sooner, Alex, but it's been really hectic here. Rehearsals, publicity events . . . Listen, I won't pry into what you're doing. I trust you to keep the promise you made. But if you need me back there, just say so, and I'll come."

"No, no, that's not necessary . . . Karla—what day is it?"

"Why, Thursday the seventeenth."

"Thank you. Goodbye," I said, and hung up on her. Only the sixth day since I was injected with chiltonium. It seems like so much longer. The effect should be decreasing daily, as the chiltonium decays to lesser elements.

Instead, the new impressions are stronger than yesterday.

All the while I was listening to Karla, I was "looking" around me.

No longer were yesterday's three massive celestial objects the only entities I could detect.

I was now sensing the masses of common items all around me, and with more definition than yesterday.

As before, I had them all in my attention simultaneously.

Chairs, tables, doors, walls—even the mass of the house itself—all were discrete objects with distinctive shapes which I could hold in my mind. Could not, in fact, dismiss by any kind of willed act.

And of course, they flooded in from all angles, regardless of the direction I was facing.

I fell into a chair I sensed behind me. I had only gotten a few hours sleep, and my mind felt thick and slow.

Something had been wrong with my math. I had postulated that only astronomical-sized masses, with their significant gravities, would be able to register on the chiltonium. Instead, now I was sensing the tiny—yet nearby—gravities of everyday objects. How could that be?

Everything that has mass has gravity, emits gravitons that strike my altered retinas. The threshold of reaction for the atoms of chiltonium must be simply lower than I calculated.

Or else—this thought occurred to me in a flash—the extra sensitivity lay in my brain. The synergy with my body was what I had not anticipated. The process of adaptation that I believed had occurred must have continued overnight, at an accelerated pace. My brain, in some sort of feedback loop, was learning to process and filter the signals it was receiving more efficiently, to extract the maximum information from them. It was as if the bandwidth of the channel down which the gravitons flowed was steadily increasing.

I held my head, which suddenly hurt. The pain seemed concentrated behind my eyes, as it had just before sleep last night.

Another thought came to me then. Perhaps these images were not real, but simply an artifact of my own disturbed senses. No, that couldn't be, for when I sensed the chair behind me, it had been there. And what did it matter if they were hallucinations? I still had to deal with them. No, I had to accept the visions as accurate representations of gravity.

I tried to gauge the new strength of my gravity-sense. Somehow, not quite knowing how I was doing it, I cast my perceptions outward.

I sensed mountains bulking massively to the east of me, huge shapes that tugged at my attention. At the same time, I was still cognizant of the household items around me. (When you look at a complicated landscape such as a forest, how many distant objects are you holding in your mind simultaneously? A hundred thousand leaves and twigs? A million?) Then my senses seemed deflected upward, off the mountains and into the sky.

The pulsing orbs of the sun and moon were still there, deeper in character somehow, distinctive, as was the Earth beneath me.

But now there were others.

I intuitively recognized Mars and Venus, as being the closest of the new objects in either direction. In some strange fashion, I was deriving such information as closeness and relative mass now from these inner representations.

Beyond Mars hung two titans, Jupiter and Saturn, pouring out their gravitons in ceaseless exuberance, almost alive. I was unable to sense their moons, or anything beyond them.

I don't know how long I was lost in this spectacle. Clocks were inaccessible to me now, save perhaps by touch. All I know is that I sat entranced for a timeless period, "watching" the majestic gavotte of the planets around the sun, all the while half-conscious of my immediate surroundings.

An insistent knocking at the front door brought me back to myself. I suddenly realized I had neither eaten nor relieved myself since the phone call awakened me earlier. I went somewhat unsteadily to the door, using my new sense to avoid the furniture I would otherwise have tripped on.

"Hello?" Mark called. "Alex, are you in there? Are you okay?"

For the first time I sensed the gravity image of a person.

Mark's image was fuzzed by the gravity of the intervening door, but still recognizable. An oddly biomorphic shape, the same unnamable "color" as all the other objects I had so far sensed, he pulsed with an intensity identical to the sun, as if his personal gravity was asserting its kinship with that faraway orb.

"Mark," I said haltingly, still bemused by his new appearance. "What are you doing here?"

"Just checking up on you. Can I come in?"

Something inside me found the thought of letting this—this alien shape inside my house too repugnant for words. I knew it was Mark, but at the same time I found myself convinced that it was something unhuman.

"No—no, not today, please. Listen, I'm fine. I don't need anything. You can leave."

"The experiment, Alex—is it working?"

I laughed rather crazily, I'm afraid. "Oh, yes, it's working. The results are unambiguous. Element 131 does indeed register gravity. I'm making careful notes of everything."

"Wonderful. The committee is sure to christen it after you then."

Mark's comments seemed inane, in the light of what I was experiencing. I realized with a start that I hadn't thought of that formerly all-important motivation for the last couple of days. How foolish it all seemed now . . .

Mark said goodbye and left.

My bladder felt like bursting, a sensation momentarily more arresting than the display of gravity. I used the toilet, then went to the kitchen, where I hastily ate something.

The image of Mark's body had made me wonder why I hadn't sensed my own personal gravity. After a little thought, I assumed that my brain was somehow filtering out the constant and immediate signals of my own gravitons, just as the constant presence of one's own nose is eliminated from one's sight.

Such questions were idle. I had more than enough to occupy my mind.

Returning to the chair that had suddenly become my observation deck to the universe, I dropped into it and cast my mind out, beyond the Earth.

June 19

Haven't slept for two days now. I can't fend off the impressions flooding in on me long enough to lose consciousness.

I find I almost don't want to.

Where can I begin to tell what's happened in the last two days?

Start with this Earth, perhaps.

My perception of this globe we inhabit is no longer that of a featureless blob. I can now distinguish variations in its mass down to the smaller mountain ranges. Undersea ones are as visible as those on the surface. The topography of this globe—to a certain scale—is now always present in my mind.

Closer to home, I can sense smaller masses for miles around. My house and its contents are a ghostly schematic. Passing people and cars on the street wander in and out of focus. Nearby cities are concentrations of weight.

All of these stimuli might be manageable, in terms of organizing them in my mind, were it not for the simultaneous flood of data from the rest of the universe.

I am swamped with the weight of our cosmos.

I can now perceive every object of sizeable mass in our solar system. Asteroids of a certain size, moons, the very rings around planets. Speaking of planets—I can now confirm that there is indeed a tenth one. Its gravity perturbs my altered vision as surely as it does the orbit of Neptune. I can sense the dark mass swimming at the end of its long, long sun-tether, not quite as far out as the Oort Cloud.

Some of the topography of our own moon is also visible to me.

If this is all a hallucination, it is incredibly detailed and consistent.

My mind no longer stops at the limits of our solar system, however.

For the past forty-eight hours, I have probed and pushed and almost inadvertently strengthened my new senses, until I can now pick up signals from lightyears away.

They say there are a hundred billion stars in our galaxy alone.

I swear I can sense each one.

Oh, not all are individuals. The signals pile up and interfere constructively and destructively with each other, merging, losing their individuality. Still, I believe that somewhere in the welter of the gravitons flooding in on my retinas and stimulating my brain are representatives of every kind of sun.

Pulsars, white dwarfs, black holes, neutron stars, binary systems, cepheid variables, giants off the main sequence—all are tugging at my perceptions, every minute, from every direction, below my feet as well as above.

The tugging. The awful pulling—that's what makes this new sense so devastatingly demanding. Vision has never really been characterized—at least to me—by any notion of weight or compulsion, despite the metaphor of being "pulled" by a sight. But this alteration to my eyes has left me with an awful awareness of how we are daily impinged on by gravity.

Of course, objectively speaking, nothing has changed. All my life, this rain of gravity has been pouring down on me, without my taking any notice of it. But now, the ability to "see" it has made me hypersensitive to it.

I feel as if my whole body is being drawn by a team of competing horses in a thousand different directions, as if the universe is attempting to rend me atom from atom. The worst kind of migraine that fades in and out.

I know this is all psychological.

Still, I can't make it go away.

I don't know what to do. One minute, holding my head and fighting back tears of pain, I'm praying that as the chiltonium decays, the effect will disappear. The next minute, headache fading, I'm enraptured by the vision of the universe held together by innumerable skeins of gravitons.

Since there's nothing I can do to rid myself of the talent, I suppose I must utilize it to the fullest.

I will try to see if I can extend my new vision beyond our galaxy.

June 20

No luck yet. I am confident that there are gravitic signals from other galaxies hidden in the mix that I just have not learned yet to separate out. Will keep trying.

Later. Completely exhausted, I managed to drop off for a spell. Woke again to the phone, but couldn't summon up the energy to get out of bed and answer it. Must have been Karla or Mark. I hope they don't come over to interfere. I feel I'm on the verge of a breakthrough.

Suppose I really should eat something . . .

June 23

It happened today.

I feel like the monk in that ancient woodcut, sticking his head through the earthly sphere and glimpsing the hidden machinery of the cosmos.

I can now see other galaxies as compact smudges of gravity. Am able to make out the groupings and supergroupings that they form, patterns of abstract splendor, forming luminous bubbles in the foamy universe, which is revealed to be more vacancy than substance.

I believe the objects I detect at the extreme edge of my sensitivity are quasars, those dwellers at the edge of the cosmos, sixteen billion light years away.

I feel like a juggler, holding aloft the entire revolving universe in my mind.

I forced myself to eat something after the triumph, in order to go on.

There's something more, you see. Something I haven't quite gotten a handle on yet. It appears to be a kind of modulated pulse of gravity, emanating from a distinct direction.

I have to concentrate on this . . .

June 24

Someone knocking on my door. I told them to go away. Afraid now my powers will disappear before I solve this last mystery . . .

June 25
Convinced I have the answer to the origin of the modulated pulse.
   It's an artifact of intelligence.
   Some civilization much further advanced than ours is communicating with its peers elsewhere, employing artificial gravity waves.
   This signal is all I concentrate on now.
   The more I study it, the more I seem to—understand it. I appear to be apprehending it on some cellular level.
   What the message is, I cannot put into words.
   But my headaches are gone.

June 26
Immense biological changes going on within me. The signal is promoting them, I'm certain. Wish I could see a mirror. Haven't eaten or had anything to drink in three days, but feel fine. Delusion of a dying man? Can't be sure of anything anymore.

June 27
Couldn't move now if I wished to. Luckily, recorder is by the bed, and voice-activated.

June 28
No diminishment in my perceptual powers, although the chiltonium should be exhausted by now. Understand the signal completely, but cannot put it into human speech.

June 29
The people behind the signal are talking to me down the line of gravitons, calling me to them. They're incredibly ancient, yet we're somehow related, as I know from their ability to subvert my biological programming. Their motives are incomprehensible, neither good nor evil. Above all that. Felt an overwhelming urge to heed their invitation. How could I go back to my old life anyway?

June 30

Won't be able to talk much longer. Have decided to take their invitation, and fall down the well of stars. These people are masters of the universal attractive force. They assure me that my new body—with its altered integument and organs—will respond to their pull, and be able to survive the trip. Goodbye Mark. Karla, goodbye.

Gravity calls.

any major dude

TAYLOR'S ROOM WAS costing him twenty thousand *pesetas* a day. A few years ago, the civil authorities had closed down the building as unfit for human habitation. Only minimal repairs had been made since.

The room boasted a single window that opened onto a sooty brick airshaft, a tall dark box full of smells and sounds, capped with a square of blue Spanish sky. Into Taylor's room from this central well, dotted with other windows, drifted odors of oily foreign cooking.

Hotplates were prohibited in theory by the management, and, yes, the fat hotel-owner had agreed, there was a possibility of starting a fire, but really, *Señor*, what can we do? We agree it is dangerous, but most of these people are too poor to eat in restaurants, having spent all of their money on a promised passage across the Strait. Ah, *Señor*, everyone wishes to cross to Africa, and we are just helping. Were we younger ourselves . . .

Helping yourself get rich, you old hypocrite, thought Taylor, but said nothing at the time.

Filtering in through Taylor's window along with the Mediterranean scents were snatches of music and conversation, and tepid, torpid breezes that idly ruffled the dirty white gauze curtains, like an old woman sorting remnants of fabric at a sale.

Taylor lay half in shadow on the narrow bed with bad springs. He rested on his side, facing the peeling, papered wall, wearing the rumpled linen suit he had been too abstracted to shed. At some point in the past the plaster had cracked, splitting the mottled wallpaper and erupting in a line of chalky lava. It reminded Taylor of the white calcareous strata beneath the Channel, so perfect for tunneling. How was the work going now? he wondered. Did anyone miss him? Did anyone puzzle over why he had left so precipitously, with the job so near completion? Did anyone care . . . ?

It was very hot in Algeciras that July. So hot, so enervating, that it affected Taylor's thinking. He found that unless he continually reminded himself of his goals, his mind would wander, he would forget what he had to do next. Not that there was much he could do, of course, except to wait.

He hadn't been like that a week ago, when he had arrived fresh in the swarming port town, on the trail of his runaway wife. Then, he had been all fire and determination. Everything had been clear and uncomplicated as vacuum, his course laid out simply before him.

He would cross the border, cross the sea, to Maxwell's Land. He would find Aubrey. He would ask her if she intended to come home. If she agreed, well and good. (Although how they would travel home, return through the global interdict, he had no idea.) If she said no, he would kill her. Then he would kill Holt. It was as simple as that.

Now, however, after seven days of delay, seven days of brain-broiling heat which even the advent of night could not annul, things no longer seemed so simple. There seemed to be a lag between every action he took and its consequences. Hysteresis was the technical term, he dimly remembered. (Always the engineer, Taylor, even when you were numb or hurt or raving mad. How fucking pitiful.) Or else the proper order of his actions seemed muzzy and doubtful. (For this latter effect, there was unfortunately no convenient scientific term.)

Perhaps he would kill Holt first. The entire affair was, after all, his fault. He was responsible for the whole mess, both in Taylor's personal life, and on an international scale. Surely his death would be a good thing, and might perhaps send Aubrey back into Taylor's arms without even the necessity of asking.

On the other hand, was he even sure any longer that he wanted Aubrey back? Perhaps she and Holt deserved each other, the damn traitors. Perhaps he would kill Aubrey and Holt together, without a word . . .

No, that wasn't right. He was not a man who sought idle revenge. He would not have abandoned a job he deemed important, traveled all this hot and dusty way, along with hundreds of thousands of other pilgrims and emigrants, just to achieve that entropic end. It was Aubrey he wanted, alive and sweetly tangible and his once more, not the nebulous and twisted satisfaction of seeing her dead. And Holt. Even he could live. Yes, Taylor would let him live. True, he had done wrong. But Taylor could understand what had driven him: a love of elegant solutions, a lifelong affair with the muse of physical precision and grace. After all, he and Taylor were *simpatico*, both engineers, albeit at different ends of the spectrum.

Up from the airshaft, preternaturally clear in an unusual moment when competitive noises were missing, floated a string of Spanish vocal and musical non sequiturs, as someone tuned across the radio band. Unctuous ads, flamenco guitars, the unmistakable transcultural inanities of a soap opera... Finally the unknown dial-twiddler settled on a station playing some ubiquitous old American rock. In utter disbelief, Taylor listened as half-forgotten lyrics tumbled over his windowsill.

Taylor laughed without pleasure. "'Demon at your door...,'" he repeated into the blankets. Oh, yeah, the demons were at the door now, sure enough.

That song was over twenty-five years old. Steely Dan's "Any Major Dude." It had been old when that campus DJ had used it as his closing theme, when Taylor and Holt had both been in grad school together a decade ago. MIT, on the banks of the Charles. Studying and sailing, fireworks on frosty First Night, a fire in their guts, to be someone, to do something important. Taylor in macro-engineering, Holt in the barely nascent field of nanotechnology. Two divergent personalities, yet somehow fast friends. Given to endless bullshitting sessions, each man half-seriously defending his specialty as more vital than the other's.

"All the really important work left is in the big projects, Des," Taylor would tell his friend. "Orbital stations, a bridge across the Bering Strait, harvesting icebergs, mid-Atlantic islands—"

"Show-off stuff," Desmond Holt would contend. "Megalomania, pure and simple. Old ideas writ large. The same impulse that leads flower-breeders to produce bigger and bigger blossoms with less and less scent. Distinct lack of imagination there, boy. No, Nick, the age of materials is over. You've got to face it some day. The real action in the future will be on the atomic and molecular levels, and in information theory."

"You've been listening to Drexler and Fredkin again. Those guys're crazy. Can you heat your house with information, or drive your car on it? You're building castles in the clouds, buddy."

"We'll see. Time will tell. But I know one thing. Your kind of engineering promotes heavy social control."

"And yours promotes chaos."

"Fascist."

"Anarchist."

And, thought Taylor, recalling that archetypical conversation, a composite memory distilled out of so many, the cliché Holt had employed had, as clichés disconcertingly will, embodied truth.

Time had indeed told. With the passage of the last few years, there could be no doubt now as to who had been right about the relative importance of their work.

Taylor's own projects had not been without results. But not on the scale of Holt's.

Aubrey had been someone utterly foreign to their scene, a communications major from Emerson. Doing the unusual, drawn solely by the subject matter, they had seen her in a play—a stage-adaptation of Capek's *Absolute at Large*; Aubrey had the role of Ellen—and been instantly smitten. Both had dated her, one had wed her.

Since then, Taylor had, off and on, harbored doubts about whether Aubrey hadn't chosen arbitrarily between them, seeing little differences between their cognate manias, entranced merely by their common hard-edged vision. Now he feared he knew the bitter truth: that she had cast her lot with the one she thought stood the greatest chance of worldly success, and, upon a shift in fortunes, abandoned the downward-bound man for the one on the rise.

He didn't really want to believe it about her, but it was the only explanation he could accept. Surely that other drivel contained in her goodbye letter was just a facade for her real motives.

Nick, she had written, *I can't accept feeling useless any more. Too many things are happening in the world right now. I need to take part. You think I should just kick back and enjoy the London theatre, the Paris stores, but I can't. I need to feel useful, like I'm doing something to help humanity. It sounds corny, but I know you'll understand. You share the same sentiments—or used to, until the projects became their own reason for existence. But since I'm no use under the Channel with you I'm going where I can make a difference.*

The old song continued to filter in: "Any minor world that comes apart falls together again . . ."

Was that true? He doubted it. Two months now, and the shattering pain he had experienced upon returning from the worksite to their London flat to find that letter hadn't diminished. It had taken him that long to pick up Aubrey's trail. At first he believed she had gone back to America, perhaps to help in some relief effort or other, such as the rebuilding of Mexico City after the quake. When he couldn't find any trace of her there, he turned in desperation to the list of self-exiled emigrants to Maxwell's Land, printed by international edict in all major newspapers.

Searching backwards through the online *London Times*, not really expecting to encounter her name, he had been stunned to see it starkly confronting him in the pages for May 15.

Their anniversary. What a fine joke. *Dear John, I'm going far away, where you'll never find me . . .*

Don't count on it, honey.

The music had ceased. The radio, powered off, was replaced by a baby's cries. Taylor felt himself falling asleep. His brow was stippled with sweat. It trickled down through a week's work of stubble. The bisecting line of light moved slowly over him, pulling back through the window, as the sun sank.

After he had lain wholly in shadow for some time, he awoke, hungry.

Narciso was waiting for him down in the shabby lobby of the crowded hotel.

Taylor smiled ruefully when he saw the boy. Narciso appeared to be the last beggar left in Algeciras, all the others having emigrated by one means or another. For some reason, out of all the gullible marks thronging the town, he had picked Taylor to fasten himself to. The man vacillated between suspecting that Narciso was either the stupidest or the smartest beggar out of all those "Hey Joes" who had once inhabited the community.

"You want some *comida* now, huh, *Señor* Nick? I bet you sick of my brother's food, huh? He not such a good cook. But today, for special, I take you to a new place. Run by my own *Tia* Luisa."

Taylor knew from a week's experience that it was impossible to shake Narciso, so he mutely let the boy lead him out the door, to his relative's restaurant.

The transient population of Algeciras had more than quadrupled from its Pre-Max heights, and the streets were thronged. Even in the old days, when the port at the southern tip of Spain had filled with Euro-Africans each summer as they headed home on vacation, it had not resembled the current combination of Bedlam and Mardi Gras.

The town was filled with an atmosphere of impatience, of throttled anticipation. Everyone seemed ready and eager to shed old ways and inhibitions, to get where they were going, their common destination, and begin their lives anew. There was no sense of menace, but Taylor still felt scared somehow at the prospect of so much change.

He had paused in the doorway, leery of mingling with the crowd. They didn't share his purity of motive, he didn't belong with them, he wasn't really hungry . . .

But Narciso, waiting patiently a few feet away, beckoned, and Taylor began to shoulder his way after his guide, who wove lithely inbetween larger figures.

The hot twilit air carried scents of the Mediterranean, not all of them pleasant, from that biggest and most utilized of the world's open sewers. But there were fewer odors than last year, and even fewer than the year before that.

Holt and his loyal team-mates, the technocratic saviors of Maxwell's Land, were responsible. They had seeded the sea with toxin-disassemblers, claiming that they needed untainted water for their small but high-throughput desalination plants. It was one of the few unilateral actions they had taken outside their own borders. Official communiques and press releases had explained, quite patiently, that they did not wish to give offence, had no plans for expansion where not invited, but on the other hand maintained the right to ensure their own prosperity, to claim their share of the world's common resources—especially if they improved them in the process.

The people in the narrow, dusty, cobbled streets of the old town were of all nationalities, of every class and type, here for the same reason Taylor ostensibly was. As one-way emigrants, they all sought passage to Maxwell's Land, and this was one of the busiest points of entry, along with Marseilles, Naples and Athens. Those favoring an overland route usually chose Israel, rather than attempt travel through the unsettled African nations to the

babylon sisters and other posthumans

south of Maxwell's Land. (So far, the Israelis had resisted assimilation, forming a stubborn eastern bulwark against the new country. But Taylor had read just yesterday, in the *International Herald Tribune*, that the Knesset was preparing to vote on a merger with the globe's youngest nation—if such an anarchistic system could even be called such.)

As Taylor followed Narciso down to the waterfront, he noticed that there seemed to be even more demonsign graffiti than yesterday. These emblems were in a variety of media and styles: stenciled, drawn freehand, pasted as preprinted posters and stickers, spraypainted, chalked in colors. But they all took the same form, the inward pointing circle of arrows representing anti-entropy.

Taylor wondered how soon the symbolic invasion would become a literal one. Surely two such incompatible realms could not coexist on one globe forever.

Walking behind the small, raggedly dressed figure of Narciso, Taylor had been following the boy without much thought given to his reality as an individual. Suddenly, however, he was struck by the desire to communicate, to learn what at least one inhabitant of this land so close to the alien continent thought of that strange shore. He caught up with the boy and laid a hand on his shoulder, halting him.

Indicating one of the demonsigns with a curt gesture, Taylor said, "Who draws these, Narciso? The pilgrims? The emigrants? Your own people?"

Narciso looked up, brown eyes lively beneath a fall of black hair. There was a smudge of grease over one eyebrow, like misapplied makeup. "Mostly those first two you name, *Señor* Nick. The people who still live here have no time for such things."

"Don't you fear the day when Maxwell's Land will reach out and take Spain?"

Narciso shrugged with a fatalism beyond his age. "What good is worrying? If America can do nothing about the demons, then certainly I cannot."

"You expect life to be good when they come?"

"*Quien sabe?* Things do not seem so bad there, from what I hear. Let them come. I will make out. But now, you are hungry, *Señor* Nick, and my aunt's place is not far."

The boy turned and set off down the crepuscular alleys they had been traversing, and Taylor was forced to follow.

Tia Luisa's restaurant was situated right on the waterfront. Before going inside, Taylor stood on a rust-stained concrete jetty and strained his eyes, trying to make out significant details of the land only a few miles south across the Strait of Gibraltar.

Lit extravagantly, the African coastline was a far cry from its old self. Just five years ago, it had been possible, by squinting, to pretend nothing had changed there since Roman times. But now the lavish display of power was like an alluring billboard advertising the new world order with all the subtlety of a campaign for the latest blockbuster film.

Taylor, his brain still stunned from the heat and the drastic changes in his own life, hazily tried to envision what inexhaustible energy might mean. The concept seemed hard to credit, flying in the face of all the precepts of physics he had always cherished. Something for nothing. Hadn't Szilard dealt the final blow to that possibility?

The lights reflected in the black waters of the Strait spelled out, plain as any textbook, that Szilard had been wrong.

Inside, Taylor ordered sangria and squid sandwiches. The latter arrived with the deep-fried meat still hot, a nest of tentacles covered with crisp golden batter, the flesh inside white as a lily and succulent as a kiss. Only the bread was unsatisfying, being made of that peculiar yellow Spanish meal and baked till absolutely dry. Taylor discarded the stuff after a few bites and ate the squid with a fork, washing it down with long draughts of the fruity, brandy-spiked wine.

Suddenly, with laden fork poised halfway to his lips, Taylor looked nervously at Narciso, who was waiting nearby like a vest-pocket *maître d'* to make sure everything was all right.

"Was this fish caught locally?" Taylor asked.

"Oh, si, *Señor* Nick. Very fresh."

Taylor regarded the squid. How many of Holt's toxin-disassemblers had these creatures ingested? Taylor knew the nanomechanisms were supposed to be biologically inert, with a limited lifetime, but still—

Hell, he'd been eating local catch all week without thinking about it. Too late now...

Taylor continued his meal in silence, without company, Narciso having vanished into the kitchen. He meditated on tomorrow's departure. *Spain is a land to flee across.* That sentence was from a book Aubrey had once tried to get him to read. The author's name was Gauss—no, Gaddis. He had never gotten into it, too convoluted, not precise enough. The equations of fiction eluded him. Aubrey was always unsuccessfully pressing new books on him—at least, during the first few years of their marriage. Now Taylor wished he had read some.

Was she with Holt? He was convinced of it. Holt had always read what Aubrey suggested, the bastard. Why else would she have entered Maxwell's Land, if not to yoke her wagon to his rising star...?

Narciso, uncannily sensing when Taylor was ready to leave, emerged from the kitchen. "You want some fun now, *Señor* Nick?"

"No," said Taylor wearily. "Just take me back to the hotel." He stood clumsily, the empty pitcher on the table silent witness to his condition.

Narciso led him back to his hotel and tumbled him into bed. Taylor sensed his eyes closing, his breath settling into a stertorous rhythm.

His last thought was, *You are what you eat.*

Or what eats you.

Taylor awoke with a hangover, sharp as the nail driven through Holofernes' head by his lover Judith. His suit was spotted with sangria stains, the mirror told him, his eyes were pouched in shadow, and he looked like a bum. He didn't care, though, because soon, one way or another, this whole abominable business would be over with.

Prior to leaving, patting down his jacket pockets for his passport, which he was gratified to find, Taylor soon learned that Narciso had relieved him of fifty thousand pesetas, all his remaining money.

Taylor swore mildly, unable really to bear any grudge against Narciso. He imagined how the boy had rationalized it: the crazy American would be gone tomorrow morning to the land of demons—where, so everyone said, money was of no use whatsoever, and all the streets were paved with gold. Under law, he would never return.

And the boy was probably right.

He only hoped there would be no further palms to grease prior to his departure.

Taylor found his duffel bag beneath the bed, opened it, saw the gun, and zipped it shut. Luckily, his missing wallet had not held the all-important ferry ticket; that was still safe in his shoe.

Out on the streets, Taylor joined the flow toward the docks. Nothing like this atmosphere had existed since the Iron Curtain crumbled. He assumed some of these people would be his fellow passengers, but that most of them were merely going to gaze wistfully south, or try once more to bargain for an earlier departure date. Had Taylor not come to Algeciras liberally supplied with cash, he, too, might have been among the idlers. Even as it was, the earliest passage he had been able to secure had involved waiting a miserable week. Not wishing to entrust his fate to the privateers in their small craft—stories abounded of passengers taken only halfway across the Strait and then chucked overboard—Taylor had chosen to wait for one of the more reliable conveyances.

There was a chainlink fence topped with concertina wire around the dock where the ferry was berthed. The gate was manned by UN Peacekeeping Troops, part of *Operacion Transito*. Ticket in hand, Taylor joined the line leading up to the guards. There seemed to be no customs check of baggage, so Taylor made no attempt to slip his gun into the lining of his duffel bag, as he had intended.

Under the strengthening sun, time passed. Eventually Taylor came to the head of the line.

A Scandinavian guard, big and blond, demanded, "Passport, please."

Taylor handed it over.

In a bored voice the guard recited his speech: "You understand that according to UN Security Council Resolution Number 1050, approved by a majority of member nations, you are hereby permanently renouncing your citizenship in the land wherein you are currently enfranchised. Do you understand this?"

"Yes."

"Do you still wish to board?"

"Yes."

The guard waved Taylor through, keeping his passport. His name would appear in newspapers around the world tomorrow, separated from his wife's by months, though to any future historians the time differential would disappear and the separated lovers would merge into the statistics of the mass exodus, united at last, if only cliometrically.

As he passed beneath the coiled wire, a miasma seemed to lift off his shoulders. For the first time in a week, he felt he was truly moving under his own volition.

The craft moored at the dock was one of the old hulking multi-tiered ferries which had once plied a more sedate trade across the Strait. Its suddenly wealthy owners, operating under government franchise, had made minor alterations—filling the cargo space with cheap seats—thereby converting it into a shuttle for the one-way emigrants. Now the craft was showing signs of wear. Kept so busy it had forgone drydock for over a year, the vessel was rusting and untrustworthy-looking.

Its crew, already wearing surplus CBW gear and breathing bottled air, was forbidden to set foot on Maxwell's Land, or traffic in African goods, under penalty of the same permanent expulsion the guard had outlined to Taylor.

Small boats and their owners who opted not to seek a government license for passage to Maxwell's Land were deemed by the authorities to be in instant violation of the UN interdict, and were sunk when sighted. Twenty had gone down in the week Taylor had been waiting.

Taylor boarded by means of a shaky wooden ramp and took his place at the already crowded rail. He wished he had someone to wave goodbye to, and he idly looked at the people on the shore for any familiar face, even that of the mercenary Narciso.

Gulls wheeled overhead. Next to Taylor stood two black youths, mountaineering backpacks dwarfing them, by speech and dress obviously American. They seemed almost giddy with the adventure they were embarked on.

"Back to Africa, huh, man!"

"Yeah, but nobody cogged it'd ever be like this!"

"Hey, how many demons does it take to change a lightbulb?"

"None, 'cuz they don't never wear out!"

Soon the ship was full. A horn blared. With a noisy blast and a belch of black smoke, the ship's diesels roared into life, the lines were cast off, the ferry pirouetted and headed out to sea. Taylor felt the breeze of passage begin to dry the sweat from his brow. Today the sun felt different somehow. Still as hot, it seemed less dulling than stimulating. Taylor supposed it was all in his mind, the result of being at last in motion.

Midway through the passage, the ship's engines abruptly ceased to stink and bellow, the thrumming they imparted to the hull disappearing, more as if they had suddenly winked out of existence than as if someone had throttled back on them. Nonetheless, the ship continued to surge forward, perhaps even more swiftly, under some unknown impulse.

Taylor puzzled over the curious phenomenon briefly, then discarded it. He was certain he would encounter many mysteries in Maxwell's Land, none of which had any real bearing on his strictly personal mission.

The trip to Tangier was over sooner than Taylor could have wished. In transit, he had been both active and passive, moving toward his destiny, yet helpless for the moment to do more than he was doing. With landfall came an end to such suspension, and a necessity for further decisions.

The trouble was, Taylor had no idea what he was going to do next. Disembarking with the excited immigrants, he realized that he had thought ahead no further than this point. Where Holt and Aubrey were, and how he was to get there without money, were points he had neglected.

As on the other side, no port officials bothered to rummage through personal possessions. It was as if they were saying, *Nothing you bring in can matter as much as what's already here.* And they certainly did not inquire as to the intended duration of anyone's stay.

There was, however, one formality to undergo.

A European woman wearing a Red Crescent pin on her shirt held a modified injection pistol connected by a hose to a stainless-steel tank. Each traveler came under her ministrations.

When it was Taylor's turn, he knew what was expected. Dreading it, he took off his jacket and exposed his bare skin.

The woman pressed the wide muzzle against his flesh and squeezed the trigger.

When she withdrew it, the demonsign was tattooed brightly in red on the underside of his forearm. A single drop of blood appeared, but no more.

"Self-organizing and ineradicable," she said, responding to Taylor's look. "Even if you were to cut it away, it would reform. Think of it as your passport as a citizen of Maxwell's Land. Oh, and you've just gotten the standard viral disassemblers too. Anti-trypansomiasis, anti-AIDS, and all that. Good luck."

Clutching his duffel bag in one hand, rubbing his sore new trademark with the other, still without immediate goals, Taylor decided to wander around the city and learn what he could of the changes that had come to North Africa in Holt's wake.

Five years ago, the government of President Zine al-Abidine Ben Ali of Tunisia—one of the more liberal, secular Arab nations—had extended an invitation. Hearing of a certain Desmond Holt, whose field trials of his potentially revolutionary nanodevices had been forbidden in America, the Tunisian government offered to help finance his work and to give him *carte blanche* in terms of implementing any of his discoveries.

One year after Holt had relocated with his small staff to the impoverished but eager Arab country, there was no more Tunisia.

It still existed in the physical sense. The land—its earth, its people, its buildings—had not vanished off the map. But in a metaphysical and legalistic way Tunisia was no more. As a separate political entity, the country had disappeared. President Ben Ali had, all unknowingly, engineered a coup against himself.

Details of what was quickly dubbed the "Gadget Revolution," how it had been accomplished so easily, were scant. Other nations, recognizing a peril to their own integrity even if they could not define it, had exhibited great alacrity in slapping quarantine on the infected nation. But the fact of great changes was soon plain.

After dismantling the government of his host, Holt and the technology he embodied had absorbed Libya to the southeast and Algeria to the west. Both had immediately stopped pumping oil. The rest of OPEC, picking up the slack, prevented more than a slight hiccup in the world economy. The closing of these markets to Western goods and the repudiation of foreign debts was actually more troublesome, and corporations agitated for a quick return to normalization of relations—assuming, of course, that the offending nations could be forced to give up their dangerous new technology.

Morocco, where Taylor now found himself, entered into the union a year later. Mauritania, Mali, Niger, Chad and the Sudan followed in short order. Egypt proved more stubborn, but had acquiesced just six months ago. And now, as Taylor had recently read, Israel looked likely to follow.

These countries, then, made up the strange and unlikely amalgam known, to the Western press at least, as Maxwell's Land.

Home to demons.

Taylor didn't know what he expected to see as he walked idly through the noisy city. Perhaps alien scenes of unhuman construction, swarms of semi-sentient mechanisms, perhaps upheaval and confusion... Instead, everything appeared utterly mundane. Tangier was in fact flourishing, despite the seemingly airtight trade embargo imposed by the rest of the world.

He had never visited North Africa before, but a thousand travelogues had prepared him for the innocuous, albeit colorful reality. In the medina, the old town, the soukhs were all busy, heaps of produce and piles of carpets, booths full of brass and basketware, jewelry and clothing, all proudly on display.

The only traditional element missing from the city, in fact, was misery. Taylor saw no beggars, no faces ravaged by untended controllable illnesses. He passed many clinics, staffed by Westerners: immigrants in their new jobs. Also, he realized that there were no draught animals or conventional vehicles. Instead, small carts and scooters, impelled noiselessly by odd engines—Taylor's trained eye recognized them as Stirling cycle devices, powered by demon heatpumps—were everywhere.

The whole city seemed slightly inebriated, in fact. There was an almost physical euphoria, something in the air like ozone on a mountaintop. Taylor found his attention drifting again, and forced himself to recall his mission.

He stopped, attracted by a tea-stand. Having stood in the sun since before noon, he was parched. He watched the proprietor prepare numerous cups of hot dark tea for his customers. Each cup of water was heated to boiling individually over a small black cube emblazoned with a demonsign. The cube had a single control.

Taylor stared at this device with almost as much interest as he held for the drinks. Here was one of Holt's products—the most revolutionary—in its simplest form: inside the cube was nothing but a number of self-replicating Maxwell's demons—sophisticated nanomechanisms, silicrobes—and a quantity of plain air at ambient temperatures. The demons, intelligent gates, were layered in a screen that divided the interior of the cube in half. By segregating molecules of common air with non-uniform velocities, the silicrobes produced heat in one half of the cube, while the other half grew frigid. (Some of this energy they used for themselves.) The control regulated how many gates were switched on.

Endless free power. A local reversal of entropy.

This was what had toppled governments and transmogrified societies. Inside this small featureless cube was a power that was well on its way to remaking the globe.

Taylor watched as customers exchanged *dinars* for drinks. A few seemed to partake without paying, failing to arouse any protest from the man running the booth. Taylor was just on the point of daring to do so himself when a voice spoke from his side.

"You are just off the boat, I wager."

Taylor turned. A young Arab man with five-o'clock shadow, wearing jeans, a T-shirt emblazoned with the demonsign, and cowboy boots, stood beside him.

"Yes," admitted Taylor.

"Understandably, you are perplexed. It is a common reaction. Money, you see, is on the way out here. In a society of growing abundance, it is losing its value. Many cling to it still, out of habit, but are willing to give freely of their products and labor if asked, knowing they may take freely in return. But enough of theoretical economics. It was my field of study, and I think sometimes I was on my way to becoming quite a pedant. You are thirsty." The man spoke in Arabic to the proprietor, who quickly fixed Taylor some tea.

Tea in the Sahara, he thought, sipping. That was both an old song and a chapter in one of Aubrey's books. Things seemed suddenly to converge in a rush upon Taylor, and he felt dizzy.

"Please," said the Arab, taking Taylor's arm, "my name is Azzedine, Azzedine Aidud. Allow me to find you some shade."

Taylor finished his tea quickly, nearly scalding his mouth, returned the cup, and allowed the man to lead him off.

Walls old as life, alleys narrow as death, shadowy doorways—Taylor lost all sense of where the port was. His attention wandered, and he followed Azzedine as he had followed Narciso. Used to giving orders and leading, he now found himself reduced to a child's role.

They ended up in a walled garden, water purling gently in a fountain. Taylor vaguely remembered the Arab saying something about his family. Azzedine was speaking.

"—and when I heard what was happening in my homeland, I left my studies in America—I was at Stanford, do you know it?—and returned. It was the only thing to do, obviously."

Taylor was seized by a sudden feverish energy. He grabbed Azzedine's wrist.

"Listen—do you know where Holt is now?"

Azzedine's face filled with near-religious awe, then disappointment. "The great man. How I wish I could meet him! It would be an honor to thank him personally, something I could tell my children about some day. But, sad to relate, I do not know."

"Is there some way we could find out?"

"There is a branch of Holt's tribe in town. They might know."

"His tribe?"

"That is what the ones who work with Holt call themselves."

"Please, would you take me there?"

"Certainly."

The office of the tribe was a former Army building denoted by a special demonsign that featured a capital H in its center. The place was bustling with activity. The chain of command was hard to distinguish: no receptionists, no private offices, no obvious executives. After some time, Taylor found himself talking to a dark-haired Canadian named Walt Becker, Azzedine listening attentively.

Taylor tried to lie convincingly. "Listen, you've got to tell me where Holt is. It's imperative that I see him. I have crucial information for him."

"About what?"

"It's—it's information about an attempt on his life."

"It wouldn't be the first. Holt can handle it."

"No, this is different. He's not prepared. Please, he's an old friend. I couldn't stand it if anything happened to him."

"You know Holt personally?"

"We went to school together . . . "

Becker seemed unconvinced, on the point of turning away. Taylor rummaged desperately through his small bag of tricks.

"The woman with him, Aubrey. She's my wife."

Becker perked up. "What's your name again?" Taylor told him. "And what project were you just working on?"

"Chunnel Two."

Becker nodded. "She said you might show up."

Taylor's heart skipped. What kind of tripwires had she set?

It looked, however, as if no alarms had gone off. Becker picked up a phone. "We'll get you transportation right away."

Azzedine interrupted. "No. I claim the right to take him. My family were always *marabouts*, guides. I brought him here. It is only fair."

Becker shrugged. "Why not? Holt's in the desert, the Tanzerouft, not far from Taodani. He got a project going with the Tuareg. Exactly what, I'm not sure."

Taylor laughed bitterly. "Out in the field himself. Holt always did have a weakness for micromanaging things."

Becker chuckled. "Call it nanomanaging now."

"The new Tangier to Tombouctou highway passes near to Taodani."

"How far is it?"

"Not far. A thousand miles, more or less."

"You call that 'not far'?"

"In the past, yes, it would be a long distance. But not on the new road. You'll see. Let's get your bag, and we'll be off."

Azzedine's transportation was a twoseater, a teardrop-shaped, three-wheeled vehicle with a canopy laminated in gold to reflect the desert heat. Powered by demons, it needed no refueling. The man was immensely proud of it, and seemed able to discourse endlessly on it, much to Taylor's annoyance.

"Classical physics, you know, Mister Taylor, claims that our power source is impossible. Information theory was supposed to have put a final nail in the coffin of Mister Maxwell's demon, you see. In sorting molecules, the demon was supposed to discard information, which was thermodynamically costly, thereby negating all the work it had done. Holt's insight was to see that a mechanism with a large enough memory could increase the entropy of its memory in order to decrease the entropy of its environment. When saturated, it would replicate a fresh heir, then self-destruct. Thus the problem of thermodynamic irreversibility is side-stepped."

As they moved slowly through the streets of Tangier, Taylor, eyes closed, reclined alongside the driver in his comfortable seat. The amber light filtering in through the one-way transparency colored his face like a marigold.

"It's all bullshit, Azzedine. There's some hidden payback down the road. There has to be."

Azzedine seemed hurt. "Then, Mister Taylor, I must affirm that this car is powered on bullshit. Seriously, do you believe Mister Holt would set something loose like this if it were not perfected? He is a unique soul. Why, to aid the Tuaregs qualifies him as a holy man."

"Why's that?"

"The Tuaregs are not even really Arabs. They claim to be an ancient noble race, but I do not trust them. Do the men not veil their faces, so you cannot read them?"

"If you say so."

"I do. Holt is brave to work with them. As you might say, he's one 'major dude.' I know many in other lands vilify him, claiming he is irresponsible and crazy to unleash such forces so rapidly. But he knows just what he is doing. Someday the whole world will acknowledge him as its savior, as we here do now."

"We'll never live to see if it happens as you predict."

"Only God knows. And as there is no God but Allah, Holt is his prophet."

On the outskirts of Tangier began a golden road of almost supernatural smoothness, heading south-east straight as a surveyor's wetdream. The road was lined with young palms fed with a continuous length of trickle-irrigation tubing, studded with demon-powered pumps.

"Look," said Azzedine with admiration, "fused from sand by more of Holt's creatures of genius."

"Wonderful," said Taylor. He was simultaneously keyed-up and weary. There definitely seemed to be something in the air that sharpened the senses and quickened the pulse. Conversely, his mind was burdened with its weight of fatality, the self-imposed geas to regain Aubrey and put an end to Holt's madness.

Azzedine cranked the little car up to one hundred and twenty kilometers an hour. Twelve or fifteen hours, and they should be there.

Taylor managed to doze off during one of Azzedine's impassioned monologues about the miracle of North Africa. He awoke as they passed through Fez and began to ascend into the Grand Atlas Mountains. They crossed the nonexistent border near Chaouf, and entered the true desert. Even here, the road flew out ahead of them, indomitable, lined with hopeful trees.

Azzedine drove like one possessed by the Holy Spirit. Taylor, waking at intervals in the night, tried vainly to imagine what was going on in the Arab's mind. Did he view himself as divinely appointed by Kismet to find the stranger in the marketplace and convey him to his meeting with Saint Holt?

Around midnight, after eight hours of driving, they stopped for a brief rest at an oasis.

Hive-shaped buildings with thick walls, constructed by nanomachines from sand, sat beneath date-palms and *talha* trees. Camels were hobbled by the well. A man in a flowing *gandourah* appeared, and bowed them welcome. He brought them inside and roused his whole family: two wives and six children. The women, their hair modestly concealed from the strange males by cloth wraps, served Taylor and Azzedine *couscous* with chunks of lamb and a milk drink called *zrig*, followed by dates and honey.

Taylor was curious. "Ask them why they live out here, so far from anywhere."

Azzedine inquired. The husband launched into a long impassioned speech. Azzedine's eyes grew large.

"He claims that wherever Holt has rested becomes a *haram*, a holy place, and he hopes to gain heavenly merit by staying here and helping travelers."

"Oh, Jesus, this is really too much—"

After Azzedine had a short nap, the travelers were off.

Fifteen hours after their departure, as dawn was breaking in shades of apricot and cream, they reached Taodani, a small town in the north of a Mali that was no more.

They parked. Outside the car, the heat smote them like a velvet-covered hammer, dazing Taylor.

"Now what?" asked Taylor.

"We will find a local who knows where the Tuaregs are camped and can serve as guide. Then, I'm afraid, it will be camels for us. There are no roads in the Tanzerouft."

A shopkeeper, instantly cooperative at the mention of Holt's cursed name, directed them to a man called Mahfoud.

Mahfoud, apparently in his fifties, was desert-thin, desert-dark. "Of course I can bring you to Holt. Did I not guide the *azalai*, the salt caravans, for years?"

"How far is he?"

"Twenty-five miles. With luck, eight hours' travel."

Taylor groaned. "When can we start?"

"Tonight. Travelling by dark, we will avoid the heat."

Taylor and Azzedine spent an hour or two buying, under Mahfoud's direction, a few supplies. They napped in the house of the town's prefect. By moonrise, they had all assembled on the edge of town.

The camels wore wooden butterfly-shaped saddles. Mahfoud tied the waterskins, the *girbas*, to the saddles. Each camel was controlled by a bridle to which was attached a rope.

Mahfoud couched the camels. "Mount now."

Taylor and Azzedine ascended. The camels rose, making half-hearted protests at the weight.

"Your beasts will follow mine. But do not drop the headrope, whatever you do, or they will bolt."

Mahfoud moved to the fore of the caravan. Holding his camel pole across his shoulders, he started the train in motion.

Mounted on his camel, Taylor, still wearing his filthy linen suit, found the riding deceptively easy.

Two hours later, his whole body felt like a single giant bruise. The night, while cooler, was still in the nineties. The monotony of the trek, the slowness after the speed of the drive, made him want to scream. Would he never reach Holt?

Rocking atop the smelly beast, Taylor was suddenly taken by the ironic notion that his whole journey was more comedy than tragedy. A plane to Spain, a boat to Africa, a car to the desert, a camel to some filthy nomad encampment. It was all too much like one of those movies where the characters experience successive degradations in their quest, until they end up pedaling on a child's bicycle . . .

Seeking reassurance, Taylor reached beneath his jacket. Tucked into the waist of his trousers was his gun. It felt hot against his skin.

Constellations spun; the desert drifted past them.

The Tuaregs had not moved, and were easily found. They were camped in a depression which even Taylor could recognize as a dry *wadi*. From a distance, their flattened oval tents of *dom* fiber looked like some abandoned circus, dropped impossibly into the waste of sand. In the middle of the encampment was a modern tent, obviously the ringmaster's, Holt's.

Taylor tried urging his camel to greater speeds, but found it as unresponsive as stone. After a seeming eternity, they arrived in the midst of the camp.

It was so early, pre-dawn, that no one was yet up.

Taylor painfully dismounted.

He stumbled at an awkward trot towards Holt's tent. Azzedine hung back out of respect, while Mahfoud was busy with the camels.

Taylor pulled back the tent flap and an unexpected blast of air-conditioning smacked him in the face, utterly disconcerting him for a moment. Recovering, he saw in the dim light two sleeping figures on separate cots: Aubrey and Holt, both in T-shirts.

If they had been together in bed, he knew he would have shot them.

But as they were, looking like children, his wife and his best friend, they drained everything from him except self-disgust.

With a roaring in his ears, Taylor raised the gun to his own temple.

He pulled the trigger—

Once, twice, a number of times.

No flare, no aroma of gunpowder, nothing but dull clicks.

Taylor dropped his hand and looked down in befuddlement at the traitorous weapon. He ejected the full clip, studied it as if expecting it to voice an explanation, then tossed it aside. He began to cry.

Holt and Aubrey were awake now. A light came on. Holt maneuvered a campstool behind Taylor, and pressed his shoulders. He sat.

"Aubrey, I could use some tea. And I'm sure Nick could too. Would you mind?"

Aubrey's single nod was like a wordless recrimination that drove straight through Taylor's heart. His sobs deepened.

Holt, damn him, was acting all apologetic, as if it were he who had attempted the suicide, and not Taylor.

"It's a shock at first, Nick. I know. Hell, I remember when I discovered it. And you should have seen the faces on the UN troops when they tried firing at us. But certain entropic reactions from the old paradigm are just impossible now, within a large radius of the demons. You can't get an internal combustion engine to function within miles of Maxwell's Land. It's a local accumulation of anti-entropy, put out as a byproduct of the demons' sorting. God knows why our metabolisms still work. Sheldrake thinks it's got to do with the morphogenetic field. But shit, it's all beyond me—I admit it. One thing I do know. The field should reach Europe pretty soon. After that, they'll have no choice but to use my demons. I figure America has about another ten years, tops, if she stays stubborn. Although I'd go back to help any time sooner, if they asked."

Taylor's sobs diminished. "What... what are you going to do with me?"

Holt looked at Aubrey, his face—as youthful as it had been in their school days—honestly ingenuous. "Gee, I don't know. There's so much to be done, whole continents to convert, a hundred countries, thousands of societies. Take what we're doing out here. We're going to restore the *wadi*. There's plenty of water, it's just three hundred feet down. These new silicrobes we've engineered form micro-capillaries and bring the water up one molecule at a time. We could sure use you to help restore the biosphere—but maybe you have some ideas."

Taylor was silent. Holt turned as Aubrey approached with tea.

"Aubrey, what do you say we should do with Nick?"

His wife looked at Taylor, and he managed to meet her eyes. He thought he had never seen her so radiant or self-possessed. That drivel in her farewell letter—it had all been true. He waited with trepidation for her to speak.

"Put him to work," she said forcefully. "What else? Even now," she said, "nobody gets something *entirely* for nothing."

—*For Paul Bowles*

mud puppy goes uptown

1.

HIS WORLD WAS nothing but mud, and he hid in it.

On his stomach, his back filmed with concealing silt, his mouth filtering nutritious diatoms from the slime, his primitive lungs straining, only his bulbous eyes and snout protruding, he awaited the return of the blessed water, all the while hating the searing heat and light from the sky.

Every day the shallow water disappeared; every day it returned. This was all he knew of the world. That much, and the moving presence of Shadow.

The water's retreat had caught him outside of Shadow today. He sensed the border of the protective twilight not far away, yet dared not move toward it. Better to lie still, so as not to attract predators, and risk dehydration.

The briny mud vibrated meaningfully beneath him. He rotated his big eyes, fearing what he would see.

A crab twice his size approached. Its mouthparts worked avidly; it waved its claws in eager agitation, opening and closing the pincers menacingly.

He bolted in panic. Levering himself out of the sucking mud with his stubby fins, he scuttled away, propelled partly by his lashing tail.

Leaving the slow crab far behind, he crossed into Shadow. The coolness was like a balm. For a few seconds, he felt safe. Then he realized what he had done.

He had ventured into the territory of his neighbors. Uninvited, he, a loner without affiliation, had trespassed on their marked dominion.

Suddenly, there was a scout confronting him. Then another and another. Soon, the whole pack was there. The dominant males began the ritual of intimidation. Rearing their foreparts high with the strength of their tails, they inflated their cheeks, then flopped down heavily, blowing air and splattering the mud. Closer and closer they drew, half-encircling him, until they were almost falling atop him.

He stood his ground. There was no choice. He must meet their challenge or retreat to the sunlit flats to die, from attack of crab or bird.

Now he mounted his own challenge. He darted first one way, then another, seeking to nip his attackers. Startled for a moment, they froze. Then, meeting his boast, they redoubled their attack.

A ponderous weight—as of some gargantuan cousin of the fighters—a little distance off transmitted the impact of its cushioned fall through the saturated medium. The animals battled on, heedless of the many smaller vibrations that followed the large one.

Without warning, the fighters were suddenly enclosed by a transparent barrier, a cylinder. They continued their savage life-or-death melee regardless.

Sounds boomed out above them. Lesser shadows fell across them. The lone trespasser, tired and bruised, continued to hurl himself against the pack.

Something surrounded him. He was gently squeezed and lifted up, high into the air.

A living face big as the moon that shone across the nighted waters confronted him. The creature's eyes were the color of the sky. More sounds issued from what must be the creature's red-painted mouth.

Much later, Uptown, watching the playback of this scene, recalling it simultaneously from both old and new perspectives, he would feel half ashamed, half proud. With Octavia by his side, he would shiver at the tenderness of her words and the memory of her naked hand enfolding him from snout to tail.

"How bravely he fights, and against such odds! I think he deserves a chance in the next gradient, don't you? Come, little skipper, my mud puppy, you're moving on up. Hurry now, friends, before the fields overwhelm us!"

And with that he left forever the world of his birth, the only world he had ever known, the harshly primal tidal flats surrounding Sheldrake Mountain.

2.

This was how the first change took Mud Puppy.

Placed in a pond of fresh water bounded by grassy banks, he lay stunned. The creatures who had picked him up out of the battle had departed immediately after dropping him into the water. (Mud Puppy, arm around Octavia, watched Octavia on the flatscreen say, "You're on your own from here, little skipper.")

Gathering the small strength remaining to him, Mud Puppy swam to the margin of the pond and hid himself among the stalks of some weeds. He nibbled tentatively at them. They tasted strange, as did even the water, the air. Everything was strange. This was not his world. His very instincts felt wrong...

A dull lassitude began to envelop him. Torpor seeped throughout his frame, from tip to tail. Awareness slipped away.

There was something like a cloud. Mud Puppy knew clouds. They brought rain and shade. But this cloud was different. It was composed of mud puppies. Millions and millions of mud puppies. No, it was just one. One big mud puppy. The Mother and Father of them all. And he, lonely, lost Mud Puppy, was still part of it. He could feel the essence of his being subsumed in the cloud, an integral part of it.

But even as he sensed this identity with the cloud, he could feel a sundering commence. The cloud was moving away, out from under him. No, he was being torn away from the mud puppy cloud, his self was losing its identification with his fellow skippers. The cleavage hurt, psychically and physically. He felt himself coming apart, drifting without support.

Another cloud appeared. Desperate, Mud Puppy willed himself toward it—or did it move toward him?

They merged.

In the pond, among the weeds, Mud Puppy began to change form.

His tail lengthened, thickened. His fins disappeared. Four legs sprouted, armed with claws. His sleek skin roughened, became scales and plates.

His snout elongated, filled with sharp teeth. A ridge of bone arched over his eyes.

A small saurian now, Mud Puppy awoke.

The world was perfect again, all sensations in harmony with his new form and mind. Memories of the mud flats were already fading, becoming buried by the accumulation of each instant's vivid impressions.

A small minnow swam by, ignorant of Mud Puppy's presence in the weeds.

Quick as thought, Mud Puppy darted out and struck. The minnow was quickly swallowed.

With this meal, Mud Puppy began to grow.

3.

Over eight feet long and commensurately massive, Mud Puppy climbed upward through the lush vegetation on his powerful stubby legs. His ponderous tail smashed plants flat.

Something nameless impelled him. Stronger than the mating urge, stronger than hunger, it was an impulse not shared with his fellows.

Perhaps it was the deep memory of being held entire in a soft hand.

The forested land sloped upward very gently, and Mud Puppy made easy progress. Already he was remote from any familiar territory. His destination was unknown; he was following an invisible gradient only dimly apprehended.

For days he journeyed, pausing only to feed. With no preconceptions about distance, Mud Puppy had no notion of the many miles he covered.

One dawn Mud Puppy felt himself cross a line. The sensation was less perceptible than the press of spidersilk on his scales.

Mud Puppy hid himself beneath some bushes.

What emerged, still resonating from contact with the new morphic cloud, was a huge mammal, a tusked cat fully as big as the reptile he had been.

Voicing a hunting call, he began to prowl.

4.

Days, months, years.

Meals, matings, miles.

Upward, ever upward.

Incarnation succeeded incarnation. Toward the end of each one, Mud Puppy felt the impulse to move ever higher up Sheldrake Mountain.

Eventually he traded teeth and claws for fleet-footed speed. Speed in turn gave way to grasping ability and increased intelligence.

(None of these identities recorded; a huge gap here. Octavia had meant it when she said he'd be on his own.)

Lemur, monkey, anthropoid.

Until finally—

Something crudely akin to Octavia.

5.

The highest structure in the village was a four-legged tower lashed together from rudely cut saplings. Topped with a platform barely big enough to support one person, the tower rocked and trembled with every breeze and with every movement of its occupant.

Mud Puppy squatted now high up in the air, performing sentry duty for the tribe.

Hairy, low-browed, prognathous, he possessed a compact body layered in muscles. A wrap of uncured animal hide was fastened around his waist.

The sentry's view stretched down a gentle slope, a greensward cleared by generations of firewood-scavenging and kept trimmed short by the domesticated ovines who browsed it under the clear sky and hot sun. Behind him the huts of his tribe were ranged: an unplanned agglomeration of several dozen wattled structures, including the Longhouse.

This was the village, the envy of all the nomads and hunters of this gradient of Sheldrake Mountain, who, with their precarious lives, were motivated to make frequent attacks upon the settlement.

Picking unmindfully at the bark on the logs beneath him, his thick-nailed fingers peeling back a smooth strip, Mud Puppy tried to think about what was troubling him.

He could find no words in his small stock for the feelings inside him. They were new, yet familiar. They seemed to relate to movement . . .

Mud Puppy stood cautiously up. His vision ranged out over the treetops.

Far, far away and below the sea glinted, marked by the patch of Shadow cast by Sheldrake Mountain itself. By the shape and angle of the Shadow, he could tell the time, early morning—

Suddenly, Mud Puppy felt his mind split. He seemed to be in two places at once. One of him was tiny and groveled in the stinking mud, one swayed upon the tower . . .

When the moment of dissonance passed, Mud Puppy came to himself only to witness one of the tribe's ovines being carried away by a marauder.

Swelling his chest, Mud Puppy gave vent to the tribe's alarm call, a wordless ululation.

Defenders rushed from the village. The thief increased his speed for the refuge of the woods. Casting a popeyed horrified glance over his shoulder, he saw he was being overtaken. He dropped the ovine.

The sacrifice of his booty was fruitless; he was caught short of safety. The pursuers brought him down, pummeling him savagely with fists and branches. Quickly he was trammeled with liana-like cords and carried back gleefully among the huts.

When Mud Puppy was relieved of duty, he shambled up to see the chief.

The chief stood triumphant above the bruised and bleeding intruder, who lay senseless in the dust and offal outside the Longhouse. For some reason, Mud Puppy felt sympathy for the captured thief.

"What will be done with him?'"

"The Upmountain Ones come today for their tribute. If we please them, they will punish this one for us."

The morning moved on into afternoon. Expectation mounted, making itself felt in the village. At last came the sentry's call, an alert different from that for a raid.

The entire village assembled on the lawn, next to the pre-arranged pile of tribute.

A skycraft took distinct shape. The villagers prostrated themselves. On his belly, Mud Puppy could feel the craft touch the earth.

"Arise," came the voice of one of the Upmountain Ones.

The congregation came trembling to their feet.

As always, the Upmountain Ones were clothed in garments smooth and seamless as living snakeskin. Their faces were all familiar from previous visits, save for one—

Mud Puppy's heart rattled his ribs. That face—he knew that woman's face! He could feel the touch of her hand—

Hearing nothing but his surging blood for a space, Mud Puppy was swept by waves of emotion. When he took notice again of sounds, the chief was concluding his plea to the visitors.

"—into the sea!"

The villagers broke into shouts. "Yes, toss him into the sea!"

The Upmountain Ones smiled. They appeared amused by the display. The one who had bade the villagers arise said, "Very well. Load the goods and we'll take the captive too. You must make haste though!"

The villagers hastened to obey, handing meat, fruit and skins up to the crew standing in the hatch. Mud Puppy tried to press closer to the woman, but was frustrated by the crowd.

Soon the Upmountain Ones were inside their sealed craft, along with the prisoner. The craft ascended silently, turned its nose downmountain, and dropped away.

The sentry, still atop his perch, could track it for its entire flight. When it was over the sea, he relayed the news to his expectant listeners. When the small speck fell from the craft, he told them also.

A shout of savage joy rent the air.

Mud Puppy heard it from a distance.

He was on his way upmountain.

6.

Cradling his predator-ripped arm, faint with hunger, naked, Mud Puppy pushed himself on.

He knew he could not go much further. But he had no idea what distance remained, nor indeed where he was going.

A feeling like a woman's hair drawn across his face—

Losing consciousness, losing shape, Mud Puppy fell to the soil.

His personal record picked up again here, caught by the perimeter scanners: on disc a fade-in directly from Octavia dropping him into the pond. ("You're on your own..."). He played the scene over and over in slow motion, looking for clues to what had driven him through all the pain, for clues to whatever was eternal in him, something he might call on to propel him through life Uptown.

But what showed was only surface, and that was most mutable.

7.

Mud Puppy studied himself in the mirror.

He was tall and slim, clothed in a seamless suit. His hair was short and brown, his eyes dark. This was his face now, and felt right. He could not definitely recall another. Yet—behind this countenance, in the depths of the mirror, seemed to hang a dozen more, hairy, furred and scaled...

He had just emerged from the pedagogue—he realized with a start that he somehow knew the machine's name and its function (knew the very concept of "machine!")—and his mind held much more than he could readily comprehend.

He opened and closed his mouth several times, striving to form some of the new words in his head: the pantomime struck him as fishlike. He felt embarrassed, blood suffusing his face.

The door to his room opened silently of its own accord.

A man stood there.

Mud Puppy found that the stranger's face stirred something within him. When the man spoke, the aura of command in his voice was familiar.

"Come with me now, Quintero. Octavia wants to see you."

Mud Puppy hesitated. Quintero? Was that his name? He supposed it must be. Yet it didn't quite fit. What did he call himself inside? There was another name, the first he had ever been addressed by, long ago...

"Who—who are you?"

"Deuce."

babylon sisters and other posthumans

Deuce's eyes were hard as a flint scraper, his mouth cruel as a thorn. Mud Puppy found himself instinctively disliking him. Deuce appeared to sense this reaction, and to relish it.

"Enough talk now. Octavia doesn't care to be kept waiting. Follow me."

Deuce turned and strode off. Mud Puppy followed.

They passed through long, windowless, door-dotted corridors with antiseptic white walls, ascended several flights of stairs, and at last emerged onto a terrace open to the air.

Stopping in shock, Mud Puppy tried to absorb the vista revealed to him.

Beyond the terrace's parapet, in a panorama stretching a full one hundred and eighty degrees, the land fell dramatically away: to step off would be to walk however briefly on treetops. The geography of the lower slopes was compressed by distance into stripes or bands of different vegetation. At the foot of the mountain the waters of the sea began, continuing to the horizon. The breezes seemed to carry a tinge of the water's ancient salt tang.

Looking upward over his shoulder, Mud Puppy could see only overhanging architecture, a pile of balconies, rooms and towers.

"Welcome to Uptown, Quintero."

Mud Puppy saw the woman then. His heart kicked like a wild animal.

Octavia was reclining on a cushioned bench. Her eyes were the color of sky. Her mouth was painted red.

"Come sit by me," she said, patting the couch. Mud Puppy moved toward her as if in a trance. When he had dropped down beside her, she said, "You may leave now, Deuce."

Deuce smiled and reentered the building.

"There's something I want you to watch," said Octavia. She reached down and picked up a roll of some material. She unfurled it and ran a finger across it; the material stiffened with a slight curve, so it could stand. She pressed a button at a corner. The flatscreen filled with images, and sound emerged.

When the screen Octavia said, "My mud puppy," he knew that was his only and real name.

The short recording over, Mud Puppy said, "That was me then . . . ?"

"Yes. "

"How can you be so sure?"

"Your karma print. It's unique to you. The perimeter sensors picked it up. And it's the same one we recorded years ago, from when you were a tiny marine skipper."

Mud Puppy's head ached. "I don't—I don't understand any of it."

"I'll explain later," said Octavia. "But first I want something, Quintero."

She skimmed a finger down the front of her garment and it fell apart. Reaching over, her breasts tumbling out, she undid his.

Her soft warm hand enveloping his cock—

But truly she held him entire.

8.

"When humans landed on this world, they knew nothing of the morphic gradients of Sheldrake Mountain. It appeared to be a world like any other. But it was not.

"All objects in the universe, inanimate or otherwise, derive their identity, their very shape and qualities, from morphic fields, nonmaterial regions of influence extending in space and continuing in time, not subject to human manipulation. These fields are localized within and around the systems they organize. They hold the cumulative experiences of all members of each class, a separate racial memory for every type of plant, animal and stone, every crystal, protein and star.

"So much was long known to science. What had never been encountered before was a situation in which morphic fields were strictly stratified in space.

"Sheldrake Mountain is such a place.

"Each level of the Mountain, from what I like to call the Downtown of the tidal flats to Uptown, where we are now, hosts only a certain number and type of lifeform-shaping morphic fields. Other fields, such as those for water and minerals, appear to be constant.

"But only the Uptown level features the human morphic field.

"A human thrust into any other level is forced to resonate with the dominant field of that level.

"They will lose their shape and memories, and assume those of the dominant lifeform of that gradient.

"The members of the expedition to this world knew nothing of this. They landed atop Sheldrake Mountain, where their morphic stability was a lucky fluke. Then they set out to explore.

"No one ever returned. The fields overpowered them all within minutes of their landing within each gradient. We now know that a quarter of an hour is all it takes. There are no barriers to hide behind, neither material nor contraforce.

"I was the only one left behind. I watched everything in realtime on the screens, all my comrades slithering, bursting and crawling out of their clothes. I was stunned beyond words. For days I wandered through Uptown in a stupor. Then I decided what to do.

"It was impossible for me to catch any of the speedier dominant lifeforms in the short time allotted to me on their levels. I had no traps, nothing to stun a creature. But I thought I might be able to snatch some of the little mud puppies during their exposure at low tide.

"It took me many more days to nerve myself up to the task. I worried that I might change even in my flight through the zones, but then realized that none of the others had, nor had we altered during our descent from orbit. Apparently, swift passage through the gradients allowed morphic memory to keep the human form stable.

"I made my quick descent and my catch, returning intact with a mud skipper. Before my eyes he underwent morphic resonance to human shape.

"Was he one of my original comrades, or a native skipper? I could have compared his karma print with the crew records, but refrained. It was too painful. In any case, there was no possibility of his regaining his personality or memories. Although such things are contained within the morphic fields, they are diffused and unrecoverable.

"I put the new person through the pedagogue, our device for teaching children.

"Together, I led him in bringing six more skippers Uptown.

"Then, disheartened, I stopped.

"What was the use of turning more mud puppies into humans, filling Uptown with them? They would never be my original comrades. Equally impossible was leaving this miserable planet and returning home. It requires special skills to pilot the ship across interstellar space, skills which I did not possess, and which were not in the pedagogue's repertoire. No one had ever conceived of a disaster of this magnitude. And even if I were to return somehow—well, those who had authorized this expedition do not look kindly on failure.

"Now the eight of us amuse ourselves here as best we can. We take tribute from the next level down to supplement the diet of the food-machines. And whenever one of my little mud puppies . . . When there occurs a gap in our ranks, I recruit a replacement.

"But not at random any more. The replacement must prove himself or herself, by making his way up Sheldrake Mountain without help.

"As you did, my darling Quintero."

9.

Primus, Deuce, Tersh, Vair, Sext, Set. With Octavia and Mud Puppy, they formed the full complement of Uptown: three women and five men. (Gender seemed a karma-linked trait, preserved from one incarnation to another. And since it was impossible to tell the gender of a mud puppy in the short time Octavia had to select one, random chance had resulted in this distribution.)

"I'm so glad you turned out male, Quintero," said Octavia. Poised naked above him, knees in his ribs, she stopped just short of inserting his cock up her. "The others are starting to grow stale. They bore me." She slid down on him. "Don't bore me."

Mud Puppy tried not to.

The dynamics among the Uptowners were intricate and fluid. Mud Puppy at first found them almost impossible to interpret. But as the days and weeks passed, he grew more adept at understanding the relationships, the dominant theme of which was subservience to Octavia.

Vair was a green-eyed, flame-haired woman. Mud Puppy found her nearly as attractive as Octavia, although admittedly without that special thrill that Octavia held for him. He abstained at first from becoming too intimate with her, fearing Octavia's displeasure. But when Octavia gave him permission to go with her and do whatever he wished, he eagerly sought Vair out in private.

"Octavia wants a change, I see," were Vair's first words to him. "That didn't take long. Still, you might have set a record. "

Mud Puppy was hurt, but Vair's caresses soon overcame his bruised feelings.

Between bouts of sex, Vair, at his request, took him on a tour of Uptown.

There were miles of corridors and dozens of levels sprawled out on the slope of Sheldrake Mountain. Roofed gardens and multi-storey atriums, chambers full of inexplicable devices and empty rooms that changed shape from visit to visit, a hangar with skycraft in rows . . .

"The expedition must have been here a while before their accident in order to build all this, even with the help of machines. But where's their ship?"

Vair laughed. "I had forgotten how naive you skippers could be. Uptown *is* the ship!"

On what he took to be the top level (there were no more stairs to be seen), Mud Puppy laid his hand on a hatch. Vair yanked it off.

"You can't leave Uptown this way! It's too dangerous! We only go out when Octavia orders us, and then we use the skycraft."

There seemed no good reason to contravene this injunction—though Mud Puppy felt an unnamable lure emanating from beyond the door—so he turned away.

Mud Puppy seldom saw Primus, and then only from a distance. The first to join Octavia, he kept mostly to his rooms. According to the others, he had not always been so reclusive. Something had recently soured him on life.

One night when he found he couldn't sleep, Mud Puppy left Octavia in bed—he was currently her favorite again—and went to a nearby food-machine. He encountered Primus there, hastily gathering supplies.

Primus seemed bowed under a perpetual stoop. "So, you're the newest one, are you? Well, enjoy it while you can."

And with that enigmatic comment, the hermit of Uptown scurried off, clutching his armful of meal-paks.

Back in the rooms he shared with Octavia, Mud Puppy set up the flatscreen and watched his short history over and over till morning.

10.

Mud Puppy returned to his quarters from taking his exercise in one of Uptown's largest rooms, where he ran around and around the circumference like an animal trapped in a well. He was the only one who followed this regimen.

Muffled cries of ecstatic pain emanated from his suite.

Octavia's head rose up and down in Tersh's lap, while Deuce employed a lash on her back and buttocks.

Mud Puppy fled to Vair.

He found her with Sext and Set.

One leg dangling over the edge of a parapet, he hesitated.

To die by falling downward now, after struggling upward through so much—

No. Any way out but that. Not down.

11.

The skycraft landed outside the hominid village.

Octavia yawned. "Another appearance by the gods. This place is so tedious! I had stopped coming till just before your arrival, Quint. But I suppose it's our duty. Well, let's hurry—the counters are flickering fast."

It must have been contamination from the hominid morphic field. Mud Puppy could recall clear as sunlight the image of Octavia standing in the door of the skycraft, while he groveled in the dirt. The memory from another existence sliced like a knife. How heavenly she had appeared then. How tainted now . . .

There was another captive to be disposed of this time.

Tumbled insensate into a corner of the hold, the trussed hominid was placed under Mud Puppy's surveillance.

Shortly, they were above the ocean. Octavia appeared in the hold. She activated a control, and bay doors slid open while they hovered.

"Push him out, Quint," she ordered. "And make it fast—we can't linger."

Mud Puppy hesitated.

"Oh, don't worry, you're not killing him. He'll be a skipper almost before he hits the water."

Deuce appeared in the doorway.

"It's him or you, Quint," said Octavia.

Mud Puppy rolled the hominid out. He found the wailing cry of the victim impossible to extinguish from his brain.

12.

Primus's rooms were dark and musty, by choice rather than any malfunction of Uptown equipment. He had blocked vents and broken most of the illuminants. Now, only after hours of cajoling, was he speaking freely to Mud Puppy.

"I'm the last of the original seven left. Poor Primus. She keeps me around for sentimental reasons, I guess."

"What do you mean?"

"Isn't it obvious? Just as you're a replacement for the old Quintero, so have all the others been replaced. And not just once, but several times. This current Deuce, though, he's the worst—"

"What—what did they all die of?"

Primus cackled. "A bad case of Octavia. They made the trip down to the flats, but never returned. Instead, a new mud puppy was started on its way as their replacement."

"I don't understand. Why would she do it?"

"She's insane. When she tires of someone, or they offend her, she simply disposes of them."

"I suppose seeing all her fellow expedition members transformed made her crazy—"

"Is she claiming again that she's the only surviving human? She hasn't used that story in a long time."

"What do you mean?"

"Why, Octavia's no more an original human from the stars than you or I. She was born a hominid. Driven out of the village for some transgression, she crossed a gradient. It's all on disc. After her transformation, still rather blank-brained, she stumbled on Uptown. It was empty. Somehow she got herself into the pedagogue. It was on automatic. When she came out, she knew a few things. She changed the settings on the pedagogue. None of us emerge knowing as much as her. She also activated the perimeter defenses to kill any hominids that try to cross. Except for those former mud puppies whose karma prints are locked in. And she only keeps seven of us around at a time for fear of a mutiny. Not that any of us seem able to really resist her."

"Where—where did the original humans go then?"

"No one knows but me and Octavia. She let it slip in the excitement of having someone to talk to, before she grew quite so self-possessed. You see, there's more Mountain above us. A gradient above the human. When Uptown landed, the crew was drawn up, not down. They abandoned the ship to become something else. But in doing so, they placed this awful roadblock on the natural path of the Mountain. "

Mud Puppy clutched Primus's wrist. "I'm going now, escaping. Come with me."

"No, I can't. I've been here too long. Good luck to you though. If you make it, try to remember us."

"I will."

Cutting through a garden, Mud Puppy encountered Octavia and Deuce.

He tried to avoid them, but they forced a confrontation.

"Where have you been?" demanded Deuce.

"More to the point, where are you going?" said Octavia.

Mud Puppy didn't answer. He made to move on.

"You need to be taught to respect authority," said Octavia. "Deuce—"

The blow to his jaw caught Mud Puppy by surprise. A second to his gut doubled him over and sent him face forward into the dirt of the garden.

His world was nothing but mud—

No!

He propelled himself forward, tackling the overconfident Deuce and toppling him. He clambered atop him, grabbed his hair and pounded his head into the earth.

When the body below him went slack, Mud Puppy rose shakily.

Octavia's face was lustful. "You can be the new Deuce now. You've earned it. We'll bring up a new Quintero—"

Mud Puppy wiped the blood from his mouth and smeared it on Octavia's face. Her sweet tongue crept out to lick it.

He left her moaning.

The hatch on the top level opened easily to his touch.

Emerald lawns sloped up. The pinnacle of Sheldrake Mountain was visible through a mantle of clouds.

The change in gradients was like a woman's hair across his face.

otto and toto in the oort

Ninety percent of all the slackers who ever lived and didn't work are alive and not working in our century.
—John "Woodie" Campbell XXIV.

Barbiturates and Dexedrine are dangerous drugs, but used with care they can smooth over the inevitable disturbances of travel most wonderfully. I carry them . . .
—Robert A. Heinlein, *Tramp Royale*.

Let's get this mother out of here.
—Concluding words of the Apollo program, spoken on the Moon by Eugene Cernan.

OUT AROUND THE asteroid belt, on what was turning out to be a megasuppressor of a trip, the drugs began to wear off, and we knew it was time for another taste of the frog.

"Get Buffo out of his cage," Otto said.

"You get him," Toto replied peevishly. "I had to handle him first the last time, and he peed in my hands."

"Listen, who's the virtual human here, you or me?"

"You are."

Shaggy, immense, buck-naked, perfect twin to Toto, ursine Otto now rose up off his warm furred couch. "That's absurd! You know perfectly well that *I* created *you* out of cornucopions in *my* image. I didn't want to but I had to. All because of that stupid Pansystem legislation. 'Use it up, wear it out, waste some more . . .' I couldn't keep up with my assigned goals, and so I created you to help. You're registered with the authorities on Venus. Why, just look on the sole of your left foot and you'll see your tattoo."

Toto, still sitting on the edge of his own pilosofa, lifted his unshod and hairy left foot onto his right knee. The registration tattoo blinked beneath the bare skin of his sole.

Toto wiggled his long toes leisurely and somewhat disdainfully before replying.

"It's true. But what about your own?"

Otto narrowed his eyes suspiciously. "What do you mean?"

"Go ahead and look. Unless you're afraid . . . "

Otto, standing, cautiously bent his knee, exposing the bottom of his left foot. He peered at it over his shoulder. Slowly he lowered it.

"I'll be damned. It's true. I've got a tattoo too. When the hell did that happen?"

"It's always been there, since I created you. I only got a tattoo so you wouldn't feel lonely. You're losing your mind from too much frog. You think you're the real me."

Otto snorted like a pig. "Bull! You put it there while I was sleeping. Admit it."

"Maybe I did. And maybe I didn't."

"Well, this is pointless. I know that I'm the baseline and you're the copy. You're nothing more than an artificially constrained standing wave. And when I'm done with you, I'll dissolve you back into cornucopions."

"We'll see about that, virt-boy."

"The hell with this stupid argument! I'm getting me some frog!"

"Make it good and scary. And save some for me."

"Maybe."

Otto moved across the cruiser's cabin to where a bulpy box ventilated with a few slits sat on a shelf. He opened the latched door of the biopoly container and reached both hands inside. Withdrawing them, he brought forth an orange toad half as big as a breadbox. (The breadbox was right next to the cage and served handily as a comparative norm.) Otto clutched the toad around its squodgy midsection and held it at arms-length. Predictably, the toad released a copious stream of vivid purple urine into the air. The piss hit the duffish floor and was absorbed. Otto laughed.

"Damn," said the toad. "Didn't even get your foot."

"That's right, Buffo. Because I'm Otto the Original, faster and smarter than Toto the Copy."

Toto refused to rise to the bait. "Just get on with it please. This trip has been boring enough so far without having to listen to your tired witticisms."

Otto locked gazes with the flaccid and hapless amphibian. "Buffo, are you scared?"

"No. Why should I be? I have plenty to eat, the ship is infallible and smarter than the two of you put together, and I know you'll never hurt me. So why should I be scared?"

Otto was a little taken aback. "Well, that's all true. But there's plenty of other things to be scared about."

"Like what?"

"Well, big things. Cosmic things."

"Such as?"

"Plague and pestilence."

"Every microbe has a serial number, and every virus is patented."

"Hunger and suffering."

"Everyone photosynthesizes or bites the constant. And if you're not distributed and renormalized, then you must want it that way, and you've got no one to blame but yourself."

"The sun going nova."

"We'll move all the planets to greener pastures."

"Alien invaders from light-years away."

"The cosmic waterhole is dry, it seems."

"The heat death of the universe, then!"

"That old chestnut. Besides, you already know how that will turn out."

Toto interrupted. "He's got you there, Otto. Have you forgotten the ghosts already?"

"I thought they were just frog hallucinations . . ."

"No, the ship recorded them. We really were visited by our far-future descendants voyaging through a temporal wormhole. Do you want me to replay it?"

"Hell, no! I just want to get this frog antsy enough for us both to go subplanckian!"

"A real human wouldn't have made that mistake about the ghosts . . ."

"This real human has too much on his mind to think about some greedheads at the end of time who never did anything for us!"

Otto began to shake Buffo. "C'mon, get frightened!"

"I—I'm getting sick!"

Buffo regurgitated a gout of clear bile onto Otto's uncovered pelted chest. Disgustedly, Otto extended the toad to Toto.

"Here, see what you can do."

Toto took the toad and set it gently on the couch beside him.

"Buffo, I want you to picture something for me. Would you do that?"

"I suppose."

"Picture a pair of yellow legs rising out of the swamp where you and all your family once lived. They stretch up and up for what seem like miles, before they disappear in a cloud of white feathers. Above that cloud stretches a long powerful neck. And that neck terminates in a malicious head with nasty beady bird eyes. And set in that head is a rapierlike ivory beak about a skidillion miles long. And now you've got nowhere to hide, and that beak is plunging down toward your stinking carcass!"

"Oooooh, nooooo!"

From rugose glands atop Buffo's head, tiny droplets of sticky exudate began to emerge.

Otto greedily grabbed up the toad and began to suck its tacky warty skin, using his sandpapery strop of a tongue.

"Aaaaah!"

Toto snatched the sartorized animal back and slurped down his share. Rising unsteadily, he tried to stuff Buffo back into its container, but instead locked it in the nearby breadbox.

"I can feel the electrons in my amygdala jumping orbits!"

"My brain is bigger than the heliosphere!"

Otto suddenly popped up the ship's control stalk from the floor. It was configured currently in the form of a large mushroom, atop which sat an anthropomorphic caterpillar whose lower body fused with the mushroom cap.

"You are speaking to the incarnate deva of the *Grigori Bearford*," said the caterpillar. "How may I help you?"

"There's an escape seed orbiting Tethys. Change our course to intercept."

"Allow me to confirm." The caterpillar paused a moment, then said, "At the extreme limits of my SQUID sensors, I do detect a tiny black body that might be an escape seed. It is not putting out a distress signal, however. May I ask how you knew about it?"

"It's the frog," said Otto. "It fosters stochastic bursts. Now get busy changing course."

"This command is acceptable."

"*All* of my commands are acceptable, you stupid ship! I'm the real human!"

"I'm sorry, but I read a tattoo on your foot through the floor."

Furious, Otto turned to Toto. "Now see what you've done with your idiot pranks, you moron! The ship won't even accept me as the original!"

"That's because you're not."

"That does it. Ship, dissolve his template."

"That command is not acceptable from a copy."

"Arrrrgh!"

Otto lunged for the caterpillar, but it merged swiftly into the mushroom before he could grab it, and he was left draped across the fungal platform. Then the mushroom itself pulled back into the floor.

Picking himself up from the ship's soft deck, Otto turned toward Toto, seemingly ready to hurl himself at his nemesis. Then he sagged as the inevitable unpleasant after-effects of toad-licking kicked in.

"My brainstem's being plucked!"

"A black hole's eating my cortex!"

Otto staggered toward the breadbox. "I'll get some manna to set us straight."

He opened the breadbox, stuck his hand in, and made a retching noise.

"Buffo's pissed all over our manna!"

Toadlike laughter issued from the breadbox. Otto slammed the door shut.

"Let him sit in his own mess," Toto advised, "and have the ship make us some more manna."

Before Otto could issue the command, however, the mushroom with its seated figure popped up again.

"We are in orbit a few klicks behind the escape seed," announced the deva of the *Grigori Bearford*.

"What took so long?" demanded Otto.

"We were on the opposite side of the Sun from Saturn when you issued the orders."

"Oh, that's OK then."

"What is our next step?"

Otto looked at Toto. "My head hurts too much. I'm going to get some manna. You decide."

Toto scratched himself thoughtfully. "Well, we spent all this time and effort getting here. Let's bring the seed onboard."

"It is a very primitive type," advised the caterpillar. "A Macbride-Allen design. What if it dates from the Ree-Rep era and contains something dangerous?"

Toto gave the caterpillar a disdainful look. "You've told us often enough that you possess more processing power in your optical-protein circuits and more manufacturing ability in your cornucopion cadcammers than the entire twentieth-century Earth. Our hourly energy budget is greater than that period's annual global total. I think we'll be able to deal with a few itty-bitty rogue recursive replicators, don't you?"

"Without clear signs of danger, trusting more in my abilities than yours, I shall obey."

The stalk withdrew. Returning from another part of the ship, Otto clutched two thick fanlike slices of lacey manna. He gave one to Toto.

"Thank you. You are a good servant."

Otto only vented a porcine snort.

Soon the caterpillar came back to provide a running commentary on its actions.

"The seed has been englobed within a newly created neutronium-hardened area of the ship some 50 thousand cubic meters in volume. Surface markings indicate that it once served as an emergency pod on a ship called the *Peppermint Stith*. Or perhaps that should be *Stick*. The legend has been mostly obliterated by centuries of space dust and intersatellite ionization, and I have been forced to reconstruct the information based on the few molecules of paint left."

"Quit boasting," said Otto around a mouthful of manna, "and crack that sucker."

"I am already doing so . . . A very simple utility fog has poured out revealing a single inhabitant of the seed, who appears to have been in some kind of stasis. Now that the fog is dispersing, however, she appears to be awakening."

"She!"

"A woman!"

"What the hell are you fooling around for? Get her up here pronto!"

The securely latched breadbox began to rock back and forth as Buffo hurled himself around inside. "Let me out, let me out! I want to meet her too! I promise I won't pee anymore! Please, please, pretty please! I love when babes lick me! Look, my exocrine glands are already flowing with nice juicy heavy-chain polypeptides!"

Otto cuffed the box. "Shut up! You'll stay in there until I say you can come out."

The box ceased rocking, and a baleful yellow eye pressed itself to a ventilation slit. "I hate you!'

But Otto had already turned away, and with Toto now considered a swelling on the floor.

Larger and larger the bud grew until it was human-sized, although still too small to hold the massive Toto or Otto. Scorings appeared on the bud, outlining petals, which began to peel back from the pointed tip, lotuslike.

Revealed inside the intraship transport mechanism stood a woman: short blonde hair, medium height, one eye green, one violet. She was clad only in a single strip of red metallic fiber. Clinging in no clear manner, the band began around her left ankle, spiraled up around that single leg, zipped between her crotch, twixt her buttocks, around her waist, across one breast and circled her neck as a collar, leaving her half-naked in a helical fashion.

Her eyes widened at the sight of the twins. "I—my name's Goldie Liddell. Who—who are you?"

Otto spoke first. "Allow me to introduce us. My name is Otto the Original, and this is Toto the Copy."

Toto chose not to protest this slanted introduction, but simply said, "Charmed, I'm sure."

The woman stepped tentatively forth from the blossom, which was already collapsing back into the floor. "Are you, like, intelligent bears?"

"Of course not! We're completely human, although modified a wee bit.

That is, I'm human, whereas Toto is merely a clever cornucopion duplicate of me."

Goldie looked curiously around. "Where am I?"

The caterpillar interjected, "Aboard the *Grigori Bearford*, out of Sheffield City, Venus. We are currently in the neighborhood of Saturn, where we came upon your escape seed."

Goldie shivered. "That awful coffin of a thing! I remember being hustled into it when the *Peppermint Stick* ran into trouble. They said I'd be picked up soon. After that, it's all a blank. How long was I in it?"

"What was the date of your ship's disaster?" asked the deva.

"Let me see . . . I think it was October. I remember I had just had my period . . . October the fifteenth!"

Toto sighed deeply. "He means the year."

"Oh. Twenty-ninety."

"You have been in suspension then for nearly a century."

"Goodness! I guess my contract's expired then . . . "

Otto asked, "What contract is that?"

"The *Peppermint Stick* was a resupply ship for the whorehouse on Tethys. Hundreds of bi-boys and omni-girls. We were hired to service the water-ice miners. I was hoping to save up money to homestead on Mars. They were almost done terraforming it . . . "

"Whores!" laughed Otto.

"Water miners!" guffawed Toto.

"Holy frog!" said Otto. "We've hauled aboard a living fossil!"

Goldie frowned. "That's not a very nice thing to call someone. I'm a completely modern and up-to-date person of intelligence."

"Not anymore, Little Golden. We exist on the far side of the Singularity now."

"That foolish notion came true? People were always talking about it, but it never got any closer. It was always just five years ahead forever! The Vinge-point after which nothing would ever be the same . . . Well, what happened?"

Toto said, "Basically, humanity assumed godlike powers without any idea of how to use them. Our machines run everything perfectly now and, by law, every citizen has to think up creative tasks to keep them busy, whether we need anything done or not. Mostly it's not. That's why we happened to be out here. We thought we might get some good new ideas if we looked back at the Solar System from its edge. We were on our way to the Oort Cloud when we detoured to rescue you."

Goldie sauntered up close to Otto and Toto. "And I'm *so-oh* grateful you did! I don't think we're too different, despite our coming from, like, different centuries and all, do you?"

Goldie began to stroke the pelted chests of the giants. Loud borborygmous rumblings as if from salmon-stuffed grizzlies issued from deep in their diaphragms. Encouraged, she pressed up against them.

"Now, tell little Goldie the truth. Do I feel like some old 'fossil' to you big, sensitive fellows?"

Otto loosed a roaring bellow, which Toto echoed. Goldie stepped back in mock fright. "Oh, you bears are scaring me!" She raised her hands to the collar around her throat, whereupon the entire stripe fell away in a slack coil, leaving her completely naked.

From the breadbox came the plaintive voice of Buffo. "Hey, this isn't fair. Guys, guys? Get off that couch and let me out! C'mon, you know a nice hit of frog will make it better." Buffo paused to watch the busy tangle for a while. "Although I don't really see how . . . Oh, shucks!"

Soon Buffo's resigned snores competed with the other noises in the cabin.

Then there was silence.

Some hours later, the caterpillar laid down the pipe of its hookah and politely coughed.

"What do you want?" Otto gruffly demanded.

"I believe that the same agency which destroyed the *Peppermint Stick* is now bent on attacking us. You recall the existence of those dwellers in the liquid ocean deep below Tethys's surface . . . ?"

"Not those stupid Clarke worms!"

"What're Clarke worms?" asked Goldie.

Toto explained. "The natives of Saturn's satellites. They drove your horny water-ice miners offplanet the same year your ship was destroyed, and before humanity could counterattack, we went through the Singularity and didn't need their crummy moon anymore, so nobody's ever been back."

"A large fleet of intelligent missiles is fast approaching," said the ship.

"Shall I—?"

Otto yawned. "Of course. And sterilize the moon too while you're at it."

Goldie swung her legs over the edge of the couch.

"Done," said the deva.

"Wow. You guys don't mess around. But was it really necessary to kill, like, even a bunch of worms so thoroughly?"

"Oh, it'll give someone else the interesting task of reconstructing the species. And you know, Little Golden, that reminds me. Something you said earlier has sparked an idea in my Original Human brain."

"Do tell," said Toto. "This will be a first."

Ignoring the taunt, Otto said, "Take us to the Oort Cloud, deva. Allow me to show you around the ship, meanwhile, Little Golden."

Pointing out the various features of the *Grigori Bearford*, including the Fast Forward drives, took nearly an hour, toward the end of which time Toto, Otto, and Goldie stood before a closed door.

"Now, behind this door is the one part of the ship you must never visit, even though it's easily accessible."

"Gee, what's in there?"

Otto and Toto looked at each other with chagrin. "We've forgotten. The frog has ruined our short-term memories. But I distinctly recall it's something really awful and scary and not good to mess with. So stay away."

"Mega-Bluebeard," said Goldie. "But I'll try."

Reentering the room where she had first encountered the twins, Goldie noticed a sobbing coming from the breadbox. Before anyone could stop her, she had removed a weeping Buffo and was cradling the hypertrophied toad between her breasts.

"There, there, what's the matter, froggie?"

"I"—sniff, sniff—"just want to be licked!"

"Oh, is that all?" said Goldie.

"No, don't!" warned Toto.

But it was too late, for Goldie had already obligingly slurped the patina of slime off the toad's head.

The toad fell from her lifeless hands, and she keeled over onto the floor with a look of ecstatic overload on her face.

Otto scooped up the toad. "You greedy bastard! Look at what you've done now! You should have known an unsartorized human couldn't take your foul mess!"

"It wasn't fair," whined Buffo. "You two had all the fun *you* wanted."

"But we didn't go and break her!" said Otto as he stuffed the amphibian roughly back into its bulpy box.

The floor was already closing over Goldie. "I will have her reanimated shortly," consoled the ship. "Meanwhile, we are now stopped some forty thousand AUs from the Sun, at the farthest fringes of the Oort, home to the Solar System's comet reserves."

Otto rubbed his big hands together. "Great! Now, this is what I've thought up. We're going to terraform the Earth!"

"But the Earth is already pretty much terraformed, isn't it?" suggested Toto. "More or less by definition?"

"I know that! But just think! If we bombard the planet with millions of comets, just like our ancestors did to Mars, it will completely wipe out billions of people and all of civilization there! Then we can spend a lot of time and energy recreating it!"

Toto shook his head admiringly. "I have to confess, Otto, that with this marvelous idea, you have surpassed your inherent limitations as a copy. Let's do it."

At that instant, a choir of glowing angelic beings materialized inside the ship.

"It's those ghosts from the end of time again," Otto observed with annoyance.

"And they are radiating a controlled flow of cornucopions," added the deva.

"Yes," said the choir with one celestial voice, "we have returned to reason with you once more. We are your potential descendents from the Omega Point of futurity. And we are here to stop you. If you carry forth your mad plan, *we* will never come to *be*!"

"It's rather a tenuous foundation to argue from, isn't it?" asked Toto.

The lead angel raised his/her arms in an imperious gesture. "Enough! Will you desist?"

"Make us!"

There came a blinding radiance that filled the ship. When it dissipated, both the twins and the angels were nowhere to be seen.

Seconds later, from the floor, Goldie was reborn. Sitting up, she looked curiously around.

"Otto? Toto? Hello? Anyone?"

Buffo called out from his box. "It's just you and me now, babe!"

"Oh, you nasty thing! Be quiet."

Goldie moved to the mushroom and poked the slumped unconscious caterpillar, but he failed to respond.

"Goodness! I'm really up the creek now!"

Goldie began to wander through the ship.

Finally she found herself at the forbidden door.

"Should I . . . ? Well, why not?"

But before she could try to open the door, it opened on its own.

Behind it stood Otto. Or Toto.

Save that he was only as tall as Goldie's knee, and proportioned to suit.

"Who—who are you?"

"My name's Toot," said the teddy bear. "I'm the original. Let me apologize for any inconvenience my duplicates might have caused you. The ship is bootstrapping itself back into existence now, incorporating what it learned from the angels. And if our hypothetical descendants should return, they won't find us such an easy mark."

"I don't understand . . ."

Toot explained what had happened.

"Does that mean," Goldie asked, "that you're going to go ahead with the crazy scheme Otto and Toto came up with?"

"Of course. It's brilliant. I knew that if I left them alone long enough, they'd hit upon something."

"And what about me?"

Toot said, "How does being called 'Eve' suit you?"

Goldie squealed and said, "Oh, Teddy, how romantic! You're just right for me!"

"I had better be, hadn't I? Now that we've effectively snipped the loop that contains our distant heirs out of the continuum, you and I have a big responsibility to fulfill."

"And just what might that special ol' thing be?" Goldie inquired, rubbing the top of Toot's head sensuously.

"You and I are just going to have to pop down the nearest wormhole and ahead to the Omega Point in order to take their place. Ride out the Big Crunch safe and sound, and kickstart the next universe."

"Oh, Teddy, what a wedding present!"

"Nothing I can't afford."

And we even took Buffo.

life sentence

1.
the execution

THE NAMELESS MAN who had killed and been caught, judged and sentenced and jailed to await his own death watched as the authorities prepared to execute his surrogate.

The murderer occupied one place in a bank of seats filled by other invited witnesses to the State's administration of mortal justice. He had not been introduced to any of the other witnesses when the guards had coldly and somewhat roughly conducted him to his seat, and no one had since offered a name or hand to the man.

Understandably so. Quite understandably, as things stood now at this crucial cusp, this instant when the exchange of lives, the legal and spiritual transaction, was still incomplete.

But once the execution was over, he had been promised that this would change.

This promise he still found hard to believe or trust.

Despite all he had been through to earn it.

With the little bit of his attention and vision not devoted to the spectacle slowly unfolding before him—a spectacle in which, save for the most tenuous chain of circumstances, he himself would have been the star—the nameless man tried to assign roles to the others around him.

The Warden, of course, he recognized, as well as the dozen members of the Renormalization Board. Several people tapping busily on laptop keyboards he deemed journalists. A man and a woman who shared an officious, self-important air he instinctively knew for politicians. With a small shudder, he pegged a trio comprised of two expensively suited men and an equally dapper woman as doctors here to observe *him*. An inexpungable air of the examining—the operating—room still clung to their costly clothes.

But the bulk of the watchers, he knew, were the surrogate's family.

Weeping with quiet dignity, holding onto each other, they disconcerted the nameless man deeply. He could not watch them long, couldn't even count how many there were, or of what sexes or ages.

Yet he knew that soon he would have to match the living, tear-stained faces to the photographs he had studied for so many months.

Soon his intimacy with these strangers would extend far beyond mere faces and names.

There were none of the nameless man's relatives present. Even if the distant kin—distant geographically and emotionally—who still claimed him had wanted to attend, they would not have been allowed to.

After all, what would have been the point? The man he had been was soon to be dead.

Now, across the room, on the far side of a wide sealed glass window, a shifting of focus among the workers there riveted the attention of the nameless man and all the others.

The technicians had finished checking out the mechanisms of death, the drips and needles and biomonitors and video cameras. Some signal must have been passed to those outside the immediate view of the watchers. For now the surrogate was being wheeled in.

The man was cradled by molded foam supports on a gurney. Thin and wasted, he was nonetheless conscious and alert, thanks to various painkillers and palliative drugs. After he was maneuvered into the center of the web of death-apparatus and the wheels of his gurney were locked, the surrogate managed to raise himself slightly up on one arm to gaze out at the audience, smile wanly and wave weakly with his free hand.

In the brief instant before the surrogate flopped back onto his pillow, the nameless man received the image of the dying man's face into his brain in an instant, imperishable imprinting.

When the cushions and pillows had been readjusted around the surrogate, a triggering device, its cord leading in an arc to the death-apparatus, was placed in his right hand.

Following the surrogate had come a priest of the Gaian Pragmatic Pandenominationalists. Arranging his green stole nervously, the priest faced the audience on the far side of the glass. A technician flicked a switch, and sounds from the far side of the barrier—beeps and shoe-scuffings, coughs and whispers—issued forth from a speaker on the nameless man's side.

Then the priest began to speak.

"We are gathered here today to bear witness to the utmost sacrifice that any individual can make to the society of which he has since birth formed a grateful part. Far greater than such paltry donations as those of blood or organs is what the man by my side will render today. He will give up his very name and identity so that another may live and serve in his place. Doomed to perish of his own incurable affliction, having opted for a voluntary death, this man takes on—legally and ethically—the sins of one of his erring brothers, thus granting the guilty one a second chance. At the same time, the demands of society for justice and retribution are met. A crime—the most heinous crime, that of murder—has been committed, and today it is balanced by the death of its perpetrator. Our laws are not flouted, the guilty do not escape, and the scales of justice swing evenly.

"I will not eulogize the man by my side at any greater length. Last night at the hospital I attended the official farewell ceremonies hosted by his loving family and friends, and we all spoke of him at length, by his bedside, to his smiling face. It was a fine occasion, with joyous memories leavening the tears. He knows with what love and reverence and gratitude he is esteemed, and all the goodbyes and final words have been said."

The wordless sobs of the surrogate's family swelled, and the nameless man winced. He rubbed a sweaty hand across the regrowing stubble on his scalp, imagined he could feel the crown-encircling scar, although in truth it was already nearly invisible.

"Now," the priest resumed, "the man by my side assumes a new identity, taking on the bloody garments and sins of the murderer known as—" Here the priest uttered the name which had once belonged to the seated man on the far side of the glass. Curiously, the once-familiar syllables rang hollow to him, drained already of all meaning, distant as something from a history book.

"It is a light load, however," continued the priest, "and a burden instantly extinguished in the very taking of it. Christ Himself could do no more. Now, let us pray."

The sound was shut off. The soundlessly murmuring priest bent over the supine man, and relative silence descended on the audience.

The nameless man did something he thought—he hoped—was praying.

Now the execution room emptied of everyone but the surrogate, recumbent on his trolley, gaunt face obscured. He could be seen with a flick of his thumb to trip the trigger, murderer in truth at the final moment, if only of himself.

The red power-on LED's of the official recording cameras glared down on the scene. After an interminable ten minutes during which the calculated poisons circulated through the surrogate's veins and his breathing slowly ceased, the prison doctor entered the sealed room, performed his exam, and looked up. Although he had forgotten to activate the speaker, all could plainly read his lips shaping the words, "He's dead."

The Warden stood and approached the nameless man, who flinched. That dour official essayed a tentative smile as cameras flashed, and extended his hand toward the murderer. The murderer took it reflexively.

"Mister Glen Swan, I thank you for your participation in this event. We will detain you only for a few last formalities, signatures and such. Then you will be free to leave. But now allow me to introduce you to your new family."

2.

the murder

The air underground was stale and hot, redolent of train-grease, electricity, sweat, fried food, piss-wet newspapers. The platform was more crowded than the murderer-to-be had anticipated. He had not known of a new play in the neighborhood, whose audience now spilled out and down into the subway. Such events were outside his calculus, and he would have still been baffled, had it not been for the overheard chance comments of the crowd.

The man felt uneasy. But he finally resolved to carry out his plans.

Necessity—and something resembling pride in his illicit trade—compelled him.

His roving eyes finally settled on a victim: a middle-aged woman in a fur coat, seemingly unaccompanied, clutching a strapless evening purse. He began to move toward her in a seemingly aimless yet underlyingly purposeful path.

The rumble and screech of an approaching train emerged from some distance down the tunnel. People surged closer to the edge of the platform in anticipation.

The man came up behind his apparently unaware victim, within reach of the shiny black purse clutched against her side.

Then it was in his hands. He tugged and pivoted.

The purse did not come. A thin hidden gold chain was looped around the woman's wrist.

He yanked, she screamed and flailed. He grabbed her wrist to immobilize it so that he could get the bag off. She jerked backward at the touch, the chain parted, his grip slipped, and the woman tumbled out of sight, onto the tracks.

The man turned to flee, but was brought crashingly down within a few yards by two bystanders, large men who began to pound him, smash him with their fists to stop his instinctive resistance.

And because his battered face was pressed into the filthy concrete at the moment he became a murderer, he did not see the train actually kill the woman.

But he heard and would always remember the noise of its useless brakes and the shouts of the witnesses and the victim's final cut-off high piercing scream.

3.
the board

"We think we have some chance of success with you," said the head of the Renormalization Board, as he looked up from closing a window on his laptop, a window full of information on the nameless man. "But everything depends on your attitude. You will have to work at this, perhaps harder than you've ever worked at anything before. Your reintegration into society will not be without obstacles or sacrifices. Do you think you can commit to this course of action? Honestly, without reservations?"

Sitting across a wide polished table from the Board, the murderer tried to hide his astonishment and suspicion, keep it from altering the silent stony lines of his face. After six months on Death Row, his appeals up to and including the highest court exhausted in the streamlined new postmillennial system, with imminent and certain death staring him hourly in the face, he would agree to anything. Surely they knew that. Anything they could offer, even a life sentence, would be better than the alternative. And as he so far dimly understood the choice before him, it was infinitely more attractive than spending the rest of his natural days behind bars.

But after he said the assuring words these new judges wanted to hear and the Board began to explain exactly what lay in store for him, he began to have his first small trepidations.

"The first thing we are going to do is perhaps the most dramatic, yet surprisingly, not the most crucial. We are going to lift the top of your skull off and insert a little helper.

"Your cortex will be overlaid with a living mass of paraneurons known as an Ethical Glial Assistant, which will also have dendritic connections to various subsystems in your brain. This EGA has no independent capacities of its own, and assuredly no personality, no emotional or intellectual traits. You may think of it simply as a living switch. It has one function, and one function only. It will monitor aggressive impulses in your brain. Upon reaching a certain threshold—a threshold of whose approach you will be amply warned by various unpleasant bodily sensations—it will simply shut you down. You will go unconscious, and remain so for a period varying from half an hour to a day, depending on the severity of the attack.

"At this point, we would like to stress all the things the EGA will *not* do. It will not prevent you from physically defending yourself under most circumstances, although some incidents of this sort might very well pass into an aggressive stage and trigger the switch. It will not hinder your free will in any manner. You are always at liberty to attempt aggression; it is just that you must be willing to face the consequences." The Boardmember's voice became very dry. "We can report that most people's automobile driving styles change radically. In any case, we have no interest in turning you into some kind of clockwork human. You would be of little use to society and the planet that way. The EGA is by no means foolproof. It will certainly not thwart a coolly premeditated murder for profit. It works only on spontaneous limbic impulses of rage and attack.

"But we do not feel, based on your case history, that you are at risk of the more calculated life-threatening behavior. The antidote we are giving you is precisely tailored for the type of person you are. Or once showed yourself to be. With the help of the EGA, you will be rendered relatively safe to mingle with your fellow humans. As safe, in fact, as any of them generally are themselves. Do you understand all this so far?"

The murderer could not focus on anything other than the queasy image of his head being opened and a living mass of jelly dropped in. But then the picture of his cell and its proximity to the execution chambers returned.

"Yes," he said.

"Good, good. Now, we are not going to rely entirely on the EGA. It is, in its way, a last-ditch defense. You are going to undergo an intensive course of remedial psychosocial pragmatics. At the end of that time, if you have exhibited cooperation and commitment, you will be certified a fully functional member of society."

The prisoner could contain the question no longer. "And then, I'll be released? Free?"

The Boardmember smiled wryly. "In a manner of speaking, yes. Completely free. Yet with duties. The duties any of us here might have, to our society and the globe. You'll receive a brochure that explains it all. It's quite simple, really."

The head of the Renormalization Board now opened up a scheduling window on his computer. "Let me see . . . Assuming you can complete the standard six-month course, and that Mr. Swan survives till then in order to serve as your surrogate—Yes, I think that we can confidently schedule your execution for the fifteenth of May. How does that sound to you?"

"Fine. Uh, fine."

4.
the brochure

For the hundredth time, returned to his cell after a day's demanding, confusing, stimulating classes, the prisoner read the brochure.

—key concept is that of commensurate restitution, combined with the notion of stabilizing broken domestic environments by insertion of the missing human element.

Previous attempts at reintroducing ex-inmates to society have often failed, resulting in high rates of recidivism, precisely because there was no supporting matrix to cushion the inmate's transition. Uncaring systems comprised of parole officers and halfway houses could not match the advantages offered by a steady job, caring coworkers and a supportive family eager to make the inmate's transition a success.

Obviously such a set of supports is almost impossible to manufacture from scratch. Yet if an ex-prisoner could be simply plugged into the gap in an existing structure, an instant framework would be available for his or her reentry into society.

The murderer skipped ahead to the part that most concerned him.

Prisoners awaiting capital punishment offer a particularly vivid and clearcut instance of the substitution-restitution philosophy. Basically, as they await their fate, they are non-persons. By their actions, they have forfeited their identities and futures, their niche in the planetary web. In their old roles, they are of no value to society and the planet except as examples of our intolerance for certain behaviors.

Meanwhile, another segment of society ironically mirrors the role of the condemned prisoner. The terminally ill among us have been condemned by nature to untimely deaths. Guilty of nothing except sharing our common mortal heritage, they yet face a sentence of premature death. In most cases, the doomed man or woman is tightly bound into an extended family and set of friends, an integral part of many networks, perhaps the sole breadwinner for several mouths.

How fitting, then, that the terminally ill patient intent on utilizing his right to voluntary euthanasia (see the Supreme Court decision in the case of Kevorkian vs State of Michigan, 2002), intent also on providing security for his loved ones in his or her absence, should gain a kind of extended life through an exchange with the prisoner who has abandoned his.

The prisoner turned several more pages.

Every attempt is made to match the prisoner and surrogate closely on the basis of dozens of parameters. The environment in which the ex-inmate is placed should therefore prove to be as comfortable and supportive for him as possible. Likewise, his or her new family should have a headstart on the adjustment process.

Simply put, prisoner and surrogate undergo a complete exchange of identi-

ties. For the surrogate, the road after the exchange is short. For the prisoner, it extends for the rest of his lifetime. There is no return to his old identity or life permitted.

The prisoner assumes the complete moral and legal responsibilities, duties, attachments, and perquisites—the complete history, in short—of his new identity. All State and corporate databases are altered to reflect the change (ie, fingerprints, photos, signatures, vital measurements, medical records, etc. of the dying surrogate are updated to reflect the physical parameters of the ex-prisoner). After taking this action, the State ceases to monitor the ex-prisoner in any special way. He becomes a normal citizen again.

How does restitution occur? Simply by the ex-inmate's willing continuation of the existence of the surrogate, as father or mother, son or daughter, breadwinner or homemaker.

This is not to deny that post-transition changes will almost certainly occur. Minor lifestyle alterations are inevitable; major ones are likely. Any option open to the original possessor of the identity is open to his replacement. Just as the surrogate could have decided to initiate a divorce, adopt a child, switch jobs or relocate his residence, so may the ex-prisoner decide. Yet the important thing is that all such decisions are not undertaken in a vacuum. Domestic, financial and other constraints faced by the original remain, and must be negotiated. Yet the history of this program reveals a surprising stability of these newly reconfigured families.

And of course any illegality perpetrated by the new possessor of the identity is fully punishable, in accordance with relevant laws, bringing down relevant punishments. Parents who abandon their new family, for instance, are subject to arrest and the standard penalties for non-support. Spousal abuse and marital rape merit the strictest punishments . . .

The prisoner set the booklet down on his knee for a moment, lost in thought. When he picked it up once more, he opened it to the final page.

Perhaps some will say that the State is acting arbitrarily or capriciously in mandating such substitutions. Humans are not interchangeable, some will argue. Emotions and feelings are neglected or trampled. Every individual is unique, one cannot be exchanged for another by government fiat. Utilitarianism has limits, they say. The State is coming perilously close to playing God.

Yet what are the alternatives? To let a perfectly useable individual, often in the prime of his or her life, be put to death as in premillennial days, while for lack of one of its prematurely taken members a bereaved family falls to pieces, becoming a burden on State welfare rolls? This is not acceptable, either to the State or to its citizens. And historically, many precedents for such behavior exist.

Dissenters to this policy might be advised to consider it in terms of an arranged marriage . . .

5.

the new home

The car pulled into the short oil-spotted driveway, a length of buckling asphalt barely longer than the shabby old hydrogen-powered compact itself. For a moment, the engine continued to idle. No one emerged. Then the motor was cut, and Mr Glen Swan opened the passenger's door and stepped out.

The postcard-sized yard was ankle-high with the vigorous weeds of late spring. A cement walkway led from the driveway to the scuffed door of a small house that was plainly the architectural clone of its many close-pressing neighbors. The yellow paint on the bungalow was flaking. A plastic trike lay on its side, half on the walk, half on the lawn, one wheel still uselessly spinning in the air.

Swan studied the scene. It was nicer than anyplace he had ever lived.

And much, much nicer than the prison.

Movement by his left side startled him from his reverie. He hadn't even heard the car's driverside door open and close.

Without taking his gaze from the house, Swan said the first thing that came to his mind. "Uh, it's nice."

A woman's voice responded, if not flatly, then with a measure of reserve. "It's home."

Swan could not immediately think of what else to say. So, still regarding the house, he repeated something he had said earlier, said more than once.

"I'm sorry you had to drive. It's just that I never learned how."

The woman's voice remained level, neither frustrated nor sympathetic, though her words partook of some small traces of both emotions. "You apologized enough already. Don't worry. You'll learn how soon enough. Meanwhile you can ride the bus. The stop is just five blocks away."

There was silence between them. Then the woman said, "Do you want to go in?"

"Yeah. Sure. Thanks."

The woman sighed. "You don't have to thank me. It's your house too."

6.

the son

The front parlor was decorated with a wooden plaque bearing a Pragmatist inspirational motto (REGARD ONLY THE OUTPUT OF THE BLACK BOX), a framed print of a nature scene, a dusty artificial bouquet. The couch and chairs had seen much wear. A low table held several quietly murmuring magazines, the cheap batteries powering their advertisements running low with age.

There were no pictures displayed of the man who had died in Swan's place. But Swan had no trouble calling up his face.

There was another woman inside the house. She was trim, on the petite side, brown hair cut short, and wore a pair of green stretchpants topped by a white sweater in the new pixel-stitch style. Her sweater depicted a realistic cloud-wrapped Earth.

"Hi," the woman said, attempting a small smile. "Welcome home."

Because of his studies, Swan recognized the woman as his sister-in-law, Sally.

"Hi, uh, Sally." He extended his hand, and she shook it. Swan liked the fact that people would shake his hand now. He was starting to believe a little more in all this, in the whole scenario of exculpation, although every other minute he still expected the carpet of his freedom to be pulled from beneath his feet, sending him tumbling back into his cell.

"Will's in his bedroom," said Sally a little nervously, addressing mostly the other woman. "He was very good all morning. But when he saw the car..."

Emboldened by the ease of the transition so far, of his seeming acceptance by the two women, made slightly giddy by the very air of freedom on this, the late afternoon of the day of his execution, recalling several of the mottoes of his pragmatics classes that counseled forthrightness and confidence, Swan said, "I'll go see him."

The layout of the house had been among his study materials. Swan strode confidently to the boy's bedroom door. He knocked and called out, "Will, it's me, your father."

Behind him the two women were quiet. Through the door came no words, just small sounds of a small body moving.

Swan raised his hand to knock again, but before he could the door opened.

Will was four, but tall for his age. From photos Swan knew his face very well. But he could not see it now.

Will wore the all-enveloping rubber mask of some kind of reptilian alien, possibly from *Star Wars VI*.

"You're Glen now," the boy said, his voice muffled.

Swan squatted, putting his face on a level with the goofy mask. "That's right. And you're Will."

"No," said the boy firmly. "Not anymore."

7.

the wife

Their first supper together as a family of three was a largely silent affair, save for a few neutral questions and comments, perfunctory requests and assents. Swan tasted nothing vividly, except perhaps the single beer he permitted himself. Never much of a drinker, he was somewhat startled to find how much he had missed the flavor of the drink, the feelings of sociability it conjured up, while in prison.

Will had been convinced to discard his mask for supper. Swan smiled frequently at him. The handsome young boy—Swan fancied he could spot some affinities between the young face and the one he himself saw in the mirror each morning—returned the smiles with a look not belligerent, but distant as the stars.

Much of the meal Swan spent covertly studying his wife.

Emma Swan both cooperated with and slightly frustrated this inspection by eating with her head mostly lowered over her plate.

Swan's wife resembled her sister Sally in height and build. But her face, thought Swan, was prettier, and her longer, lighter hair suited her. Although some of her movements were nervously awkward, she exhibited an overall easy grace.

Glen Swan had been a lucky man, he thought.

But I'm Glen Swan now.

So does that mean that I share his luck?

Shortly after cleanup, which Swan volunteered to handle, it was time for Will to go to bed.

Wearing onepiece pajamas, Will emerged from his bedroom. A different mask hid his features, this one of a Disney character, some kind of animal prince or hero, Swan guessed.

Emma herded the boy up to where Swan sat.

"Say goodnight to your father."

Will had adopted a chirpy new voice to go with the mask. "Good-eek-eek-night."

Mother and son went into the bedroom. Swan did not follow.

He could hear Emma reading a book aloud. Then the lights were extinguished, and she came out, closing the door softly behind herself.

Swan's wife took a seat on the couch. She looked at Swan directly for the first time that day, as if perhaps the ritual in the bedroom had given her strength or firmed up a decision.

"Do you want to watch some TV?"

"Sure."

Watching TV, Swan knew, meant they didn't have to talk.

Right now, this first night, that was just as well.

But he knew they couldn't watch TV for the rest of their lives.

Hours passed. Once, Emma laughed at a sitcom. Swan enjoyed hearing her laughter.

Shortly before midnight, Emma clicked off the television. She stood and stretched.

"You have to be at work by eight. Me too."

"Right, right," Swan agreed readily. "And Will—?"

"I'll drop him off at the daycare on the way to the Wal-Mart."

The couch seemed to be a sofabed. Swan looked around for signs of bedding. But Emma's next words informed him differently.

"When Glen—When the sickness hit us, I got twin beds in. It made things easier for everyone . . . Anyway, I've thought about this a lot. We can't act like complete strangers, hiding things from each other. We have to share this small house. Bathroom, whatever. Getting dressed. So we have to be at least as close as roommates. Like in a dorm. Anything else—I don't know yet. It's too soon. Is that okay with you? Am I making any sense?"

Swan considered how best to answer. "Roommates. That's fine."

Emma slumped in relief. "Okay. That's settled. Good. Let's get to sleep. I'm completely wiped out."

Lying in the dark, Swan listened to Emma's breathing, only a few feet away. The rhythm of her breath gradually smoothed out and softened, till he knew she was asleep.

He had expected her to sob. But after some thought, he realized that her tears must have been drained long ago, the very last ones shed in the death chamber.

And certainly not for him.

8.

the job

His boss was a big man with the startling, abnormally delicate hands of a woman. His name was Tony Eubanks. Tony was the supervisor for a crew of ten men, split between five trucks. Normally Tony stayed put in the office, dispatching his fleet, scheduling assignments, handling paperwork. But for the duration of Swan's training period he would go on the road with Swan, functioning as Swan's partner and teacher.

Swan knew that this was special attention, for his special case. So, of course, did everyone else. The people in charge of his future, while not actively monitoring him, had nonetheless seeded his path with mentors.

Swan tried not to think of Tony as a jailer or warden. Luckily, as Swan soon discovered to his relief, Tony's attitude made it easy to regard him as simply a more knowledgeable co-worker, perhaps even a friend.

The attitudes of the other linemen, however, were less easy to pin down.

For the first few weeks, busy learning and doing, Swan was able simply to ignore them.

He and Tony were stringing cable. Lots of new cable. It was some kind of special new cable meant to treble the bandwidth of the net. Swan never got a really firm grip on the physics behind the wire. But then again, he didn't need to. All he needed to master was the practical stuff. The tools, the junction boxes, the repeaters, the debugging tricks, the protocols. He concentrated on these with his full attention, and was proud to realize that he could learn such things, mastering them fairly easily.

The physical side of his job was enjoyable too. Up and down poles, into ditches and tunnels, popping manhole covers, manhandling big reels, driving the truck. All of these actions appealed to him.

Tony, however, was not so enthralled. In the truck, with one of their endless cups of coffee in hand, he would frequently say, in a kindly way, "Jesus, kid, I'm getting too old for this kind of workout. I can hardly get to sleep at night for the fucking aches and pains. I'm glad you're picking up on things quick. I never thought I'd say it, but I can't wait to see my fucking desk again."

The hard work had the opposite effect on Swan's sleep patterns. Each night, after the repeated rituals of meal, television, and brief, safely shallow conversation with Emma, he dropped off into dreamless slumbers.

Part of the job involved dealing with customers. It was the hardest part for Swan to adapt to. Entering offices and homes, he encountered a spectrum of people utterly foreign to him. At first, he would stammer and perform clumsily. Forms that had to be filled out confused him, and Tony would have to intervene.

But after a time, he found himself warming to even this aspect of his job. One day he was surprised to find himself actually looking forward to dealing with a complex installation that required him to speak frequently with a pretty woman manager in charge of the project.

Tony approved of Swan's new interpersonal skills. One day when they had just left the job site, he said, "You handled her nice, kid. And she really had a bug up her ass about those delays. Couldn't have done it any better myself. In fact, you'd better watch it or the suits are gonna catch wind of how slick you've gotten and the next thing you know you'll be locked up behind a desk all day like me."

Swan beamed. He felt close to Tony. Close enough to ask him the next day a long-held question about his hands.

Tony held up his small hands without embarrassment. "These mitts? Replacements. Lost my original ones in an accident on my old job. Got a little too careless around an industrial robot. I was one of the first patients where the graft took. Back then, they had to do it within the first twenty-fours hours, the donor had to match nine ways from Sunday, a lot of shit they don't have to worry about nowadays. Anyhow, everything came together so's I had to take these or nothing." Tony was quiet a moment. "She died in a car crash while I was lying in the hospital. Head crushed, but hands fine. I still see her parents now and then."

Swan was silent, as was Tony. Then the older man shrugged.

"No big deal, I guess. They can replace anything nowadays."

9.

the merger

It happened over the course of the next eight months, by a process Swan could neither chart nor predict.

He became, on a level sufficiently deep to pass mostly out of conscious scrutiny, his new self.

In his own eyes and his adopted family's.

What caused the merger was nothing other than simple daily repetition, the hourly unrelenting enactment of a good lie engineered by the State. The continuous make-believe, bolstered by a mostly willing shared suspension of disbelief, eventually solidified into reality. Under the sustained subtle assault of the mundane and the quotidian, the blandishments of the hundred bland rituals and the shared demands of a thousand niggling decisions, reality conformed to imagination.

What greased the way was a desperate willingness to succeed on the part of Swan and Emma, a loneliness and void, shaped differently in each, yet reciprocal, that eagerly accepted any wholesome psychic fill.

The path to the merger was made of uncountable little things.

Swan had very few clothes to call his own. It was only natural for him to use those of the man who had preceded him. They fit remarkably well, a fact the Renormalization Board had doubtlessly reckoned with.

Will enjoyed making models out of the new memory clay for children. Swan discovered a facility for shaping that allowed him and the boy to spend some quiet hours together.

His sister-in-law Sally, having overcome the hurdle of meeting him early on, was a frequent visitor. With her husband, Al, and their daughters,

Melinda and Michelle, the two families went places: the movies, picnics, amusement parks, the beach. Apparently, reports back to the rest of Swan's new relatives were encouraging enough that the massive multifamily get-together held each Labor Day did not have to be cancelled this sad, strange year.

At the outdoor gathering Swan's head spun from greeting so many familiar strangers, from heat and sun and the usual overindulgences of food and drink. But by day's end, he had earned high accolades from Emma.

"They liked you. And you fit right in."

Emma.

She taught him to drive. They shopped for groceries together, went to conferences at Will's daycare together, watched endless hours of television side by side on the couch, apart at first, then holding hands, then her in his arms.

But each night, even after a year, Swan slept in his bed, and she in hers.

10.

the torment

Swan had been paired with a guy named Charlie Sproul for several months. Charlie was fairly silent and self-contained, not very friendly. It wasn't like working with Tony. Swan tried to make the best of it though.

One afternoon in the locker room, Swan was surprised when Charlie and a couple of other linemen asked him out for a drink.

He accepted.

"I'll just call home," Swan said.

"Don't bother," said Charlie. "We won't be long."

They drove in their cars to a part of town Swan didn't know. The bar was a rundown place called The Garden. Flickerpaint scrawls on the windowless walls teased Swan's peripheral vision.

At the threshold, Swan sniffed. The place smelled bad inside, like some kind of subterranean den or tunnel, half familiar in a dreamlike way that made him very uneasy.

But Swan told himself he was being foolish, and went in.

The room was hot and noisy and smoky; the conversation was boring and felt contrived. Midway through his second beer, Swan began to prepare excuses for leaving. But then his fellow linemen said they wanted to play pool. Swan didn't play, so he said he'd stay at the bar and watch.

As soon as his coworkers had crossed the room, leaving Swan alone, several strange men drifted up and stood around him.

"Hey, egghead," one said. "Yeah, you—the guy with the egg thing in his head. How's it feel to steal someone's life?"

Swan felt a line of heat high up around his brow like a hot wire tightening into his skin, a sharp crown. He stood up, but there was no room to move. The barstool pressed against the back of his legs.

Swan's mouth had dried up. "I don't know what you're talking about..."

"We're talking about how the wrong guy died. It should have been—"

The man spoke a name Swan vaguely recognized. The mention of the name left him genuinely confused. They were talking about someone he no longer knew, someone who didn't exist anymore. "I don't understand. My name is Glen Swan..."

The men laughed cruelly. "He really believes it!"

"He's a *fried* egghead!"

Swan tried to push his tormentors aside. "Let me go. I don't need this!"

"No, you need this!" one said, and swung a heavy fist into his stomach.

Swan doubled over. Then he was submerged in a flood of punches and kicks.

He called for help, but no one came, none of his new "friends."

He felt consciousness slipping away.

But he was pretty sure he managed to black out naturally and on his own, without the help of the EGA.

11.
the doubts

After he got out of the hospital, Swan found a new job waiting for him. With Tony's help he got the position in customer relations that Tony had predicted for him.

But nothing felt the same.

Who was he?

Was he a stranger falsely trying to fill another man's shoes?

Or was he who he had willed himself—at first halfheartedly, then earnestly, with the help of others—to become?

These questions occupied his every waking moment. Mostly he tended to come down on the blackest side of the dilemma.

How could he ever have imagined he could slip so easily into someone else's old life? He was a fraud, an impostor. Everyone was just pretending with him, pretending to like him, pretending to tolerate him, pretending to accept him as what he was not and could never be.

Even Emma?

Even her.

Emma in her cold bed.

One day when his doubts reached an unbearable intensity, Swan began making discreet inquiries.

Inquiries that brought him one day after a week's searching to arrange an appointment for his next lunch hour.

12.
the decision

As he made ready to go to work that morning, Emma said, "Glen—I realize how hard things have been for you lately. But I want you to know that I believe in you. Nothing's your fault, Glen. And someday those guys who beat you up will get caught. Even if they don't, they'll pay somehow, in the end. I really believe that, and you should too."

Swan winced inwardly at the memory of his beating, but did not comment on Emma's notion of justice. Justice—or revenge—was something that would soon be within his own grasp.

If he truly wanted it, knew what to do with it, how best to have it.

Emma seemed desperate to reach him, as if she sensed the enormity of this day. "You've been good to me and Will, Glen. And if I haven't been quite as good to you, well—it's because I needed time. I can be better. We can be better together."

Swan did not reply. Emma looked down at her hands folded in her lap. When she raised her face, her cheeks were wet.

"I—I really couldn't stand to lose you twice."

Swan left.

There was no sign that the door Swan faced at noon in a shabby part of the city belonged to a doctor's office. And inside were no reassuring accoutrements of medicine, no diplomas or cheerful receptionist or old dying magazines or fellow patients.

Just a man. A man who sat behind his desk in a highbacked chair in the gloom, swiveled so that Swan never got a good look at his appearance. He was a voice only, and even that voice, Swan suspected, was electronically disguised.

"—not responsible for any side-effects," the man was saying. "The whole thing is highly experimental still." The man chuckled. "No FDA seal of approval. But the beauty of it is that it's just one spinal injection. Bam! Straight to the brain and your little parasitical friend dissolves and gets scavenged. If everything goes okay, that is. Then you're free."

Free. But for what? If he just wanted to run away from everything, he could run away now. He didn't have to kill the thing inside his head just to run. It wasn't a leash or a fence.

But the EGA was a symbol. That, he realized, was the calculated subtlety of it, of the State's reformatory schemes. It didn't even have to function to fulfill its purpose. It could be a placebo for all he knew, a ruse. But even so it was strong, a monument, a permanent symbol of the agreement he had entered into. A token of the exchange he had made, the life that had been extinguished in his place, the new bonds he had willingly assumed. To kill the thing in his head meant to deny the entire past year, to abrogate his contract with his new life.

To focus instead on spite and revenge, on hurting and pain.

Swan began to feel sick to his stomach. Was it the EGA kicking in? Or just the natural reaction of whoever he was?

The doctor was talking. Swan tried to focus on what he was saying.

"—not your fucking fault—"

Emma's face swam up into his vision.

"Nothing's your fault, Glen."

Swan stood up. "I've decided."

The doctor's voice was gloating. "Great. Now we can get down to the important things."

"Right," said Swan, and turned to leave.

"Hey," said the doctor. "Where you going?"

"Back to my job, back to my home, back to my wife."
Back to my life.

angelmakers

SNOW SUGARED THICKLY the steeply sloping winter-dead lawn behind the great organically sprawling autonohouse, a white canvas scribbled over with small oblate bootprints and the sharp parallel tracks of sled blades, as well as the shallow worm furrows of lofter saucers. At regular intervals, black-leafed trees with precisely choreographed branches sucked every impinging photon from a December sun pale as a circle of overwashed bleached cotton pegged at the zenith.

Around the house, no activity save routine maintenance and materials-acquisition manifested itself. The house's adults remained busy inside at their ludic labors. Human presence in the landscape consisted of a still line of a dozen children by the edge of the broad frozen river that demarcated the extensive lawn's lower edge. The children on the shore flanked a set of runner tracks that extended onto the ice and terminated at a jagged hole filled with water as coarse and grey as steel wool.

The children wore colorful jellied unisuits thin as pressed-fruit strips, revealing the unisex lines of their pre-adolescent bodies. Their warmly rosy hands appeared bare, save for outlines of shivering air. Perched on their heads, upright or askew, squishy caps exhibited the silly geometries of mirror worlds. Holding their sleds and saucers, or standing beside them, the children silently contemplated the ice-surfaced river and its anomalous disfiguration.

A gentle-looking boy spoke. "She's been under some time now. A minute almost. There are snags down there, I know."

His statement elicited some nervous shuffling and visible expressions of empathy from his peers, except for one rough lad who taunted, "If you don't trust the angels, Rand, dive in yourself."

An exceedingly thin and nervous-looking girl said, "Maybe we should. Or maybe we should call Fabiola's parents." She fingered the rim of the ceramic communion wafer bonded to her wrist without touching its responsive surfaces. "What if the angels are too busy elsewhere?"

"Have you ever known the leucotheans to fail, Shelly?" demanded the second boy.

"No, but I feel so *helpless* just standing here. I want to do *something*."

"Fabiola won't thank you if you spoil the story of her drowning by horning in on things."

The boy named Rand said defensively, "Are you saying Fabiola planned this, Brewster?"

Brewster made a dismissive wave. "Of course not. Who'd be that daft? But now that it's happened—"

At that moment another child shouted, "Look!" The crowd followed the sentry's outstretched finger with their massed gaze.

As if from directly out of the consumptive sun, a silhouetted figure had detached itself. Swelling from antlike dot to doll-like cutout to human-scaled apparition as it dropped lower, the angel was swiftly upon them. Without hesitation, the angel plunged through the hole in the ice, sending a geyser of cold water upward, droplets spattering the children. Too thrilled to care, they gave an instinctive collective shout of excitement and relief.

Within seconds the angel emerged from the jagged-edged opening, bearing an unconscious child. Skimming low, the angel landed amidst the children, set the body of Fabiola down in the snow, and kneeled beside the bare-headed blonde girl with the gelid blue face.

Unhesitatingly, the children formed a tight clot around the tableau of kneeling angel and child. Closest by an inch or two, the girl named Shelly peered intensely, her concentration fixed more on the angel than on her unbreathing friend.

The wingless angel was whiter than the ambient snow: platinum hair, ivory limbs. The angelic body displayed no sex, although the angel was completely unclothed. The face of the angel was composed in neutral lines from which perhaps only a depthless sadness, if any emotion whatsoever, could be teased. The angel's eyes were featureless marbles, spheres seemingly composed of polished bone set in the ocular orbits.

The angel kneeled beside Fabiola, but applied no conventional mode of resuscitation. Instead, one arm and hand attenuated ectoplasmically, then snaked through Fabiola's mouth and, apparently, down the girl's throat. The angel's other rarefied hand plunged into the child's chest over her heart like fog through cheesecloth.

Fabiola's body instantly arced like the tensioned arm of a loaded catapult, head and heels digging into the snow. The stolid angel remained seemingly unmoved, but withdrew those intrusive extensions, which resumed humaniform solidity. Fabiola spewed river water, gagged, then sucked in a shuddering breath, while the angel ran soothing hands up the girl's frame, ending with hands clasping the girl's head on either side.

Fabiola's eyes snapped open. Her gaze locked with the angel's blank fixity. At the same time Shelly strained forward, as if she were a bob on an invisible elastic line connecting victim and rescuer. The tableau held for a few eternal seconds, then shattered as the angel let the snowy depression again receive Fabiola's head. Somehow the angel leaped directly from a kneeling posture into the sky.

Fabiola sat up weakly; both Rand and Brewster moved to support her, and the other children clustered closer to hear the first words from their revivified peer, a weak "I've come back."

All except Shelly. Shading her eyes, the wan girl watched the angel until that never-speaking being had long disappeared.

In coupling class, Rand and Fabiola lay sated on mussed white sheets draping a low carnalounge. Fabiola's newly mature body had developed along her chosen lines of feminine curvature. Rand's form likewise had fructified into a desirably ripe, slim-hipped maleness. Together, languorous limbs entangled, they resembled one of the three-hundred-year-old Bouguereaus they had studied last quintmester in art-history class. In ranks across the copulatorium, other couched couples replicated their easy indolence.

Adjacent to Fabiola and Rand on their own divan, Shelly and Brewster were lone exceptions to the class's ruling somatopsychic fulfillment. Brewster, his innate truculence now compounded by an overdeveloped physique, rested on his back, a frown dragging his face down, arms folded across his inordinately hairy chest. Her slim lily of a body the least mature among her classmates, Shelly reclined on her side, spine convexed toward her partner, arms bowed over her head. Now Brewster spoke more loudly than was deemed polite within the copulatorium. Rand and Fabiola could not help overhearing.

"Damn it, girl. A little enthusiasm wouldn't be out of place."

A soft "I'm sorry" wisped out from the cage of Shelly's arms like an escaping ghost.

Rand was not placated. "Sorry won't cut it anymore. Why, if you were my only partner, I'd have a knot the size of houseroot in my libido." The burly youth swung his feet to the floor and stepped over to the neighboring lounge. "On your way, Rand. I'm cutting in."

Both Fabiola and Rand graciously consented. Her spill of golden hair whispering on the sheets, the lush Fabiola accepted the impetuous Brewster into her embrace, while Rand slipped onto the couch where Shelly still cringed. As Fabiola and Brewster began to engage, Rand slid a comforting arm around Shelly's shoulder. She spun about and relaxed into the offered cradle of his shoulder and chest, pressing her face against him.

"Want to talk about anything?" asked Rand quietly. "Something special bothering you?"

"I just worry all the time, Rand. I can't explain it, but it interferes with everything, not just sex."

"What concerns you? Your future? It's perfectly natural for young people our age to be a little worried about exactly what playwork we'll eventually choose."

"No, it's not my personal future. I'm fairly clear about that. I want to be a theresan."

Rand forbore to comment on this rather unconventional choice. "What then?"

Shelly gripped Rand's waist tightly. "I—I worry about the people I care for. Their health, their safety—their lives. It's all I can think about, ever since—ever since Fabiola drowned."

For several seconds, Rand said nothing. Then: "But that was five years ago, Shelly."

"You needn't remind me! I've lived every hellish preoccupied minute of it!"

"Well, it's just—don't you think you should seek a detangling?"

"If I remain knotted much longer, I will. But I just want to puzzle it out by myself for a while yet."

"It's so odd, though." Rand sounded genuinely perplexed. "To have such an archaic fear in this age of angels."

At the mention of angels, Shelly stiffened. "They're the problem. They make our mortality more real at the same time they guard us from accidents. We've all come to rely on them so much, that we've lost a lot of old instincts of self-preservation. What if their perfection is flawed? Considering where they come from—'such base and hybrid clay.'"

Rand balked at entering that seldom-trodden territory, the origin of the angels, and swerved instead into literary criticism. "You're quoting Athanor. He's not to my taste."

Beside them, Fabiola and Brewster were noisily climaxing. The communion wafer on Fabiola's dangling wrist clacked rhythmically against the tiled floor. Rand found himself aroused. Upon Shelly's shy acknowledgement of his condition, he began to caress her. Quickly, they started to move together.

Their formal evaluation at the end of class cited as a demerit only Shelly's postcoital tears.

Alternately steamy and chill, cleansing mists billowed from the wallpores of the dimly lit freeform sauna. Subtle restorative natural fragrances and amygdaloids rode the droplets: balsam, vanilla, altozest. Self-segregating instinctively by sex, boys and girls clustered mostly in separate grottoes, as if after the intimacies of coupling class certain male and female intra-bonding required reinforcing. Giggles and laughter interspersed boisterous talk.

Seated on the absorptive floor, Shelly braced her back against a pliable wall, drew her knees up to her chin and crossed her ankles in front of her sex. She made no move to join in any of the conversations around her. She passed most of the sauna session in contemplative silence, until Fabiola approached her. The smiling blonde girl dropped down gracefully beside the somber dark-haired one. Shelly's tentative expression mixed a faint welcome with a nearly palpable disinclination to talk. Fabiola ignored the look.

"I hear you've decided on a career," said Fabiola.

Visibly surprised, Shelly answered, "Why, yes, I have."

Fabiola paused, then said, "Being a theresan seems an awfully—well, a harsh and stringent path."

Shelly's face now expressed an indignation matched by her tone. "How can you say that? Devoting yourself entirely to the spiritual welfare of others? It's the most fulfilling career I can imagine."

"But the libido-dampers, the vow of minimal consumption—it all seems so purposelessly self-denying in the face of our abundance."

"Maybe so. Maybe people nowadays have all the sex and food and toys they need. But there's still suffering. Death and mortal dissatisfaction resist all unknotting. The vows are real, but also symbolic. They focus our attention, help us concentrate on our mission of relieving pain. The theresans are only one step below the angels themselves."

Fabiola evinced nervousness at such a comparison. "Well, I won't pretend you aren't suited for such a life, Shel. Ever since we were little, you've inclined that way."

Shelly neither affirmed nor denied this characterization. Suffused in soothing veils of moisture, the friends rested wordlessly side by side for a minute. Then Fabiola spoke.

"Don't you want to know what I've chosen for my playwork?"

Shelly brightened. "Of course. I hadn't realized you'd decided yet."

"I'm majoring in exobiological research, specializing in Leucothean lifeforms with a concentration on hybridology."

"Will you have to go discontinuous to visit Leucothea?"

"Of course, if I choose to travel at all, which I probably will. How else would I cross all those lightyears?"

Shelly shuddered. "I could never put myself through such an experience, even if it is temporary. Losing your body that way—"

Fabiola laughed off her friend's apprehensions. "It's perfectly safe. Just a matter of not being where you were for a while until the universe is tickled into agreeing you're ready to be elsewhere." Changing the subject, Fabiola asked, "Who do you like better, Rand or Brewster?"

A look of bemused consternation squalled across Shelly's features.

"Rand is so kind to me. There's no denying that, or his charm. But Brewster has something that pulls at me, a demanding quality that's almost frightening."

"You should be nicer to him then. More appreciative."

"I try. But I get distracted too often." Shelly bit her underlip. "Fabiola—do you ever recall your death?"

Fabiola laughed easily. "My death? I'm right here beside you! How could I have ever died?"

"But you did. You drowned. Your heart was stopped until the angel restarted it."

Ignoring Shelly's speech, Fabiola fluffed up her abundant damp curls. "The sauna always butchers my hair! I'm definitely going to speak to the mockie-proctors about altering the proteinoid mix in the final rinse."

From across the form-strewn chamber, as if across a vision of some steam-cloaked afterlife, a desultory Elysian Fields, Brewster and Rand more or less discreetly watched the two girls. In relaxed fashion, Rand stood leaning against a wall, arms folded across his hairless chest; contrarily, Brewster twisted energetically from the waist up in an exaggerated display of calisthenics, snapping his limbs about.

"Gaia!" exclaimed Brewster. "Fabiola gets me so primed! Look at her breasts arch as she primps her hair! What a kick."

Rand's tone was dry. "You two certainly seemed on the same protocol in class. Do you expect to see much of her after graduation?"

Brewster ceased swiveling and began to trot in place, coincident with a blast of cold. "Not likely. The one drawback with Fab from my point of view is her excessive brains. She's off for more schooling, which is certainly not the case with me."

Rand straightened away from the wall, plainly intrigued. "Oh? This is news. I had no idea your future plans were so solid. Tell all, please."

"I've already signed on with the Rewilderness Institute. They promised me my choice of assignment after a short training stint. I'm leaning toward the Sacramento Rainforest."

"A noble mission."

"Noble my prickly arse! I just can't stand being cooped up in these prissy modern safety zones any more. I want to be surrounded by some wildness, to use my muscles more than my head."

"Engineered wildness. And of course the angels will still be watching over you and your mates."

Brewster snorted like a guard minotaur. "Don't remind me. There's no place free from their intrusive ways. The damn seraphian layer girdles the whole globe like a straitjacket, put into place long before our generation had a say in it."

Rand smiled. "An interesting comparison. Most people compare the turbulent home of our angel friends to a vital safety net."

"Most people are lazy, complacent fools. A warm autonohome, uninterrupted entertainment, and the cackle of the flock. That's enough to make them happy."

"Cheep, cheep."

Brewster stopped jogging. "Be fair now, you know I don't mean you. You're a good friend, Rand. You and me, Fabiola and Shelly—we have some kind of special bond among us. I predict we'll always hang together somehow."

"Sentimentality *and* a nod toward the future. This must be that 'maturity' I've heard so much about."

"Joke all you want, dummy. And by the way, I haven't learned *your* plans yet. Maybe you and Fabiola have some kind of zingy co-hab agreement."

"Not at all. But we *are* going to the same school next year."

"A-ha! Don't tell me you're going to muck about with squirmy aliens too."

"No. Not unless you count Jovian volatiles as such."

Brewster shouted his approval and slapped Rand on the back hard enough to cause the slighter boy to stagger a step. "So it's to be mining after all! Congratulations! And you let me rave on about my shirt-pocket wilderness! Out among the stars, there's the real frontier."

Rand spoke modestly. "Oh, most of the work is done from Earth via d-links. And on-site autonoclaques handle much of the rest. I doubt I'll find myself in space more than a few times a year."

"More than most of the rest of us. Well, if it weren't for needing to feel the wind on my face, Rand, I'd join you in a minute."

Rand quoted their secular scripture only half-archly: "'Each seeker his own guide.'"

Brewster delivered the expected well-circulated parody: "'Each thrill-seeker his own androgyne.'"

⦇⦈

The roof of the school was generally off-limits. Its attractions were minimal—a perch from which to pelt innocent passersby with popbeads from the pepper trees, a generous view of the landscaped community and the river where Fabiola had nearly met her end—and consequently, so was any temptation to trespass. But this evening, with the end of the official commencement celebrations at midnight, the lure of the forbidden drew some dozen graduates unwilling to call an end to their revelry.

Rand concentrated on jiggering the school's heuristics, chattering at the building in high-level autonopidgin. At his back, his festively dressed companions shuffled and whispered. Tristan and Alana, a pair of lovers bound for the Black Gang, kissed with professional abandon. A fellow named Ewen let out a fart, saying, "Let the school parse that!"

Rand worked intently despite the distractions. "Damn stubborn mockie—There! We're in."

Everyone gave a cheer then, heedless of discovery. All the young men and women exhibited varying degrees of amygdaloid intoxication—nothing illegal, but more than was perhaps wise of the permitted stuff. Half the intruders raced up the stairs, vying with those in the lofter shaft to be first; the two factions burst out onto the node-studded roof almost simultaneously. Above, a wealth of stars prickled. June breezes carried the scents of water and grass. The happy trespassers rushed to the low parapet edging the roof, the only real focus of the scene. Some ten meters below, the well-lighted town slept.

Rand encircled Fabiola's bare midriff with his left arm. She pressed her hip against him. Brewster and Shelly stood rather stiffly side by side, although holding hands. Squirts full of wine circulated; by the time one reached Brewster, its overused muscles, at the ebb of their refreshing cycle, refused to work, and only a couple of drops escaped the living valve. Brewster threw the squirt down squishily in exaggerated disgust.

"Bah! Who needs alcohol on a night like tonight? Just to be free of this dump forever is intoxicating enough!"

Releasing Shelly's hand, Brewster leaped atop the parapet and began to dance like a marionette proxied by someone being tickled to death. Everyone cheered and applauded except Shelly. Even in the dim starlight and backscattered radiance of the street illuminants her expression of alarm shone like a young moon.

"No, Brewster! It's dangerous! Come down!"

As if his imaginary strings had been dipped in liquid nitrogen, Brewster instantly froze. He stared meanly at Shelly for a few interminable seconds, then said, "You don't own me, Shel. And there is no danger anywhere anymore."

With those words, he hurled himself backwards off the roof.

Shelly screamed, as did several others, not including Rand or Fabiola. Craning forward, the young men and women watched Brewster plummet.

Halfway in his swift fall, an angel materialized beneath him. The alabaster being caught Brewster easily and lowered him safely to the ground.

Rand spoke precisely, in the parodic tones of a lecturer, but failed entirely to mask deeper feelings. "Unlike our long-range, machine-based d-links, the angels of course can go discontinuous organically and at will. However, the energy-burden such actions place on them limits them to one or at the most two ionosphere-to-troposphere jumps between downtimes back in the seraphian layer—"

His humorous pedanticism went disregarded, as his peers clambered to the parapet and jumped in squealing imitation of Brewster. Each of course met midair rescue. The flock of enigma-faced marmoreal angels flew away conventionally as each jumper was grounded. Finally, only Shelly, Rand and Fabiola remained on the roof. Rand exhibited a cool disdain, while Fabiola's eyes shone with an aloof excitement. Shelly, though, quivered with rage and the aftermath of her fear.

Rand moved to embrace her, saying, "Juvenile behavior, of course—really wasteful of seraphian resources—but you have to make some allowances—"

Shelly bucked out of his offered consoling clutches. "I hate him! I hate you all!" She raced off down the stairs, out the school and down the streets.

Fabiola watched her go, then said, "Hardly the proper attitude for the start of her career as a martyr."

※

Fabiola's office-cum-playlab occupied a congeries of expandable Hoberman spheres in the middle of Los Angeles, conveniently close to the main So-Cal d-link offworld transit center. Currently, the complex swelled half-again as large as its nearest neighbor: the Leucothean Institute had mounted a new expedition recently to underexplored regions of the distant world whence came the objects of Fabiola's researches.

When the building announced a visitor that morning, Fabiola paused abruptly in the middle of her work as if the significant yet unexpected name had jarred her concentration.

"Send her up."

Waiting for the arrival of her visitor, Fabiola closed down the experiment she had been working on that morning. Tapping staccato codes into her communion wafer with her stylus nail, she induced quiescence in the leucotherarium inhabitants. Behind the glass walls of the sealed alien environment, amorphous shapes, their metabolisms damped, pooled on their moss-furred cage floor like heaps of coddled egg-whites.

Fabiola stepped from playlab to outer office. She entered just in time to greet her visitor.

Shelly appeared thinner than when Fabiola had last seen her childhood friend. Under the libido-blockers, her body seemed to have devolved to preadolescence wispiness, as if time's arrow had reversed for her alone. A cloud of anxiety fogged her features.

Fabiola swiftly and heartily embraced her friend. "What a pleasant surprise, Shel! It's been what, three years? Here, take a seat."

Unresponsive to Fabiola's pleasantries, Shelly collapsed into a chair. "I've been dropped from the theresans, Fabiola. Me and hundreds of others."

"Oh, that's awful! But why?"

"Reduced call for our services. A happier world needs fewer empathetic companions—or so people delude themselves into thinking. Dealing with the shrinkage, the order has applied a strict 'last in, first out' policy. Frankly, I'm surprised the axe didn't fall on me last year at this time."

Taking a seat beside Shelly, Fabiola grasped her hand. "I'm so sorry. What will you do now?"

Shelly pinned Fabiola with the intensity of her gaze. "I can't simply abandon my calling, just because I've lost institutional support. But I can't continue on my own either. So I've applied to the angelmakers. The demand for *their* services, at least, is still strong."

Fabiola's face registered baffled incredulity. "I don't understand."

"How much more clearly can I say it? I've put my name in to become an angel."

Clearly agitated, Fabiola stood up. "Along with criminals and the incorrigibly suicidal? You're neither of those, are you, Shelly? How could you do such a thing?"

Grimly thinning her lips, Shelly countered, "Every year a few sane and responsible individuals make the same choice. It's not unprecedented."

Fabiola began to pace. "This news upsets me terribly. You're throwing your individuality away. And for what?"

"If I can't save people's souls, at least I can still safeguard their bodies. That's all they seem to care about anyway."

Growing more distressed, Fabiola asked, "Why are you telling me all this? It's an incredible burden! I almost wish you had just vanished."

Shelly smiled for the first time. "You think mere knowledge of my choice is a burden? Well, I'm about to ask for much more. I want you and Rand and Brewster to be present at the transformation. It's my privilege to have three witnesses."

Color bled from Fabiola's face. "Witness it? I—I can't!"

"Why not? You deal with leucothean lifeforms every day."

"But not hybrids!"

Shelly got up awkwardly from her seat. "Too bad your sensibilities are so refined, dear. I enjoin you to be there, and I know you won't refuse. I assume you're still in contact with the men."

"Yes, of course. I saw both of them just last month."

"I expect to find you all there then. I'll send the particulars as soon as I learn them."

Shelly moved toward the door. Automatically, Fabiola accompanied her. At the door, Shelly turned, gripped Fabiola by her upper arms, and brought her face to within inches of the other woman's.

"You've often claimed you loved me, Fab. Prove it now."

Shelly kissed Fabiola fiercely, released her, and left.

Fabiola wiped her lips as if they burned.

∞∞

Sealed from outside contamination—or interior escape—the operating theater was staffed only by sophisticated mechanisms, partly autonomous, partly telefactored by the hidden, anonymous cadre of angelmakers. Now alertly inactive, the mobile surgical units awaited their initiating commands. The sole human inhabitant of the theater lay naked upon a comfortable monitor-and-assist platform. As yet untouched, Shelly's thin pale body—stark ribs, hairless mons, composed expression—seemed already well on its way to angelhood. Arms resting laxly along her sides, she stared upward with concentrated fixity.

Beside the patient an opaque sealed canister sat in isolation from the other equipment, a grail-like focus of vision for the assembled watchers.

The ceiling of the lighted theater was transparent. Beyond this barrier, in cloaking darkness and ringing the edge of the theater, seats with full non-interventionist telemetry held medical students, professors, and Shelly's three witnesses. Fabiola was flanked by her two friends. Rand, to her left, held her hand. On her other side, Brewster sat with arms folded like logs across his chest. Rand's expressive face revealed an inner tumult mixing fascination, dismay and a sorrowful nostalgia. Fabiola's countenance expressed pure despair. Brewster exhibited an angry scowl, as if personally affronted. Amidst the murmurous audience, his sudden exclamation registered as an egregious slap.

"Damn her! She's deserting us! Is she really that weak?"

"'That weak?'" Rand repeated. "Why not 'that strong?' Could you undergo such a transformation?"

"Why not ask if I could have my legs sawed off for no good reason? It's not bravery in either case, just masochistic stupidity."

Fabiola's voice was pitched higher than normal. "Will you two just shut up! Show some respect for Shelly's commitment. Please."

Brewster opened his mouth to reply, then obviously thought better of such a move. He braced his implacable arms more firmly. Rand squeezed Fabiola's hand more tightly and pecked her brow with a kiss, but she seemed to esteem his solicitous affection no more highly than she did Brewster's truculence.

The machines in the theater suddenly stirred to life. Ignoring the offered close-up telemetry, Fabiola bent forward, as if only unmediated vision across the shortest possible distance could sanctify this transaction. Unwittingly, Rand and Brewster mimicked her.

Below, Shelly had already received a local sensory block across her sternum that still left her completely conscious. Surely her light-swamped eyes could not discern any of the watchers above, yet her expectant gaze seemed locked on theirs. Now clamps and blood-flow inhibitors came into play, as a small incision was lasered into her side, revealing the common human scarlet wetness.

As if unable to interpose a censor between his thoughts and his speech, Rand whispered, "Buddhists claim Shakyamuni was born of such a wound in his mother's side. But Christians honor the piercing of a spear in the torso of a crucified Jesus."

The sealed canister now resided in a mechanical grip. Obedient to the application of a security code, the canister top began to unscrew itself, as if its living contents sought egress on their own. The spatulate limb of a mechanical poised itself above the lid, ready to cap the vessel. When the lid had fully disengaged and the spatulate blocker had slid into place, the container was brought nearly into contact with Shelly's incision. Then the intervening shield-hand withdrew.

The observers saw in the tiny slice of space between the vessel and the body the merest suggestion of a sentient pulsing gelatinous influx. Quickly, the container was pulled away, while at the same time a transparent shell rose up from within the M&A platform to fully enclose the patient.

Beneath this perspex carapace, Shelly began instantly to metamorphose.

The lips of her incision drew closed of their own volition. Her stomach swelled noticeably, then just as significantly concaved, as the leucothean lifeform introduced into her abdomen swiftly absorbed organs, bloated, then shrunk into extensions that blew through her like a wind of pure somatic change. The expression on Shelly's face betokened no pain, just shock, and then, amazingly, a species of bliss. Her eyes rolled back into their sockets; when they revolved again a full minute later, they revealed themselves transmuted into the flinty optic roundels of all angels. Attenuating and wavering, her limbs went through various test modes of ectoplasmic configuration before settling down to the angelic perfection of human similitude.

Most astonishingly, Shelly's body began to float above the M&A pedestal, constrained only by the clear lid.

Above, in the observation galley, Fabiola began to retch. Brewster struck the dome of the theater a resounding blow. Rand sought tranquility in dull recitation of facts.

"The imago will automatically seek the global seraphian layer and the company of its kind. The canopy prevents its flight until it can be brought into the open. Already the new angel is part of the leucothean group mentation, able to detect and respond to human distress in all its forms via contact with our wafers along non-local dimensions—"

Fabiola turned and slapped Rand's face. Brewster restrained her from further assault, but needlessly, for she slumped into her seat in tears.

Rand massaged his rubescent cheek. "Such a simple operation in theory, but fraught with more than its share of emotional complications."

Rand beneath her, Brewster above, Fabiola performed slow gyrations upon the twin fleshy impalements of their cocks thickening inside her. Brewster had his inner elbows locked beneath her axillaries, hands clamped behind her neck; Rand cupped her pendulous breasts. Entrained in lubricious synchronous routines, the threesome resembled in their fluid unity some tripartite hybrid not entirely dissimilar to the dualistic being which had come into life just hours ago in the surgical theater beneath their rapt gaze.

The trio's movements accelerated with their growing urge toward completion. Inter-responsive sounds escaped the participants: from Fabiola, a cascade of panting mewls; from Brewster, coarse-grained grunts; from Rand, soothing wordless encouragements. Within speedy minutes, their orgasms spilled over the barrier separating potential from actualized, guttural howls an operatic accompaniment to the release. Brewster slumped sideways over onto the mattress, pulling Fabiola with him and thus levering Rand onto his side: six legs tangled like the limp fronds of sea plants.

For a time, until they regained an ease of breathing, they did not speak. Then Brewster broke the silence.

"I should have been kinder to her. I see that now. But I was an ignorant brute."

Unlinked from her lovers, Fabiola rolled over onto her back, pulling the men into a cradling embrace on either side. She said, "Kinder? Perhaps. But I doubt that any of us could have dissuaded Shelly."

Brewster growled. "Of course, I blame the angelmakers too. They should have refused her as an unstable volunteer."

"What other kind would they ever get?" Rand wryly asked.

Fabiola suddenly said, "No one's innocent. We're all angelmakers."

Brewster rose up on one elbow, glaring. "What?"

"I mean that the four of us had a unique dynamic that drove Shelly to her fate. And also that our society as a whole demanded her transformation. We planted a slow virus of ideation within her during childhood, and it finally came awake and transcribed itself."

Brewster dropped back down. "I don't know if I buy that, Fab."

"It's true nonetheless."

Rand's voice held a genuine perplexity. "Do you remember, Brew, something you said years ago, when we were still in school? That the four of us made a whole? Why don't I feel a missing part now?"

"I suppose because Shelly's still out there in some form."

Fabiola volunteered, "The findings are still imprecise regarding how much individual mentation remains after hybridization."

Rand shuddered. "Not much I hope."

Brewster sat up suddenly, as if struck by inspiration. "Let's memorialize this day. I propose that every year on the anniversary of Shelly's ascension, we spend a holiday together."

"I second the motion," said Rand.

Fabiola gripped both their hands. "It's unanimous. In memory of Shelly, a school reunion each year."

Brewster wedged his big hand into her wet crotch, enfolding her whole sex back to her anus. "And you'll be our homecoming queen."

"And you the jester," suggested Rand.

They all laughed before they all kissed.

Brewster seemed as proud of the Sacramento Rainforest as if he himself had planted each of its towering black-leafed trees, artfully draped each of its sensate lianas, animated each of its animals, programmed each of its buzzing bugs. Conducting Fabiola and Rand down one of the region's many public trails, hot sunlight butterscotching their bare arms, he lectured in an earnest manner most unlike his bluff self outside this artificial wilderness, delivering anecdotes, statistics and philosophy.

"You'd never believe you were walking through what was once a metropolitan concentration, now would you? Just carting away the demolition debris to the plasma incinerators took the better part of a decade. But currently you won't find more than a few score people at any given time within a hundred-mile radius. A handful of daytrippers, some hikers and overnight campers, and a smattering of guides such as myself. One minute."

Brewster had halted by a tree with a diseased limb. He bent to its base and began scraping away dead leaves from around the trunk. After a few swipes, he exposed the tree's inset partner to the communion wafer in his wrist. Mating his wafer to the wood-rimmed one, Brewster internalized the feed, then stood.

"Nothing out of the ordinary. Just planned rot."

Rand effortlessly shrugged off his bulky pack, revealing a patch of sweaty shirt fabric beneath. "Lofters may have solved the weight problem, but I've yet to wear a pack that truly breathes."

Fabiola chimed in with her own complaint. "My feet are absolutely aching. How much farther, Brew?"

"Just a mile or so. I swear, you two youngsters should apply for early systemic reboots. I had a couple of 'booters in here last week—ninety years old if they were a day—and they didn't chaff me as much as you two."

Rand pulled his pack on again with an exaggerated show of self-sacrifice. "Can we help it if desk-play has made me and Fab soft? We can't all spend every day slogging through the muck and mire like you do. Some of us have a civilization to run."

Brewster snorted. "Poking alien slimebags in cages in one case, and guiding giant gasbags into orbit in the other. Such noble pursuits. Let's go, and no more bitching."

Brewster's "mile or so" proved closer to five. But the sight at the end proved inspiring: a luxuriant greensward rolling at a slight inclination toward a posted but unbarricaded cliff edge.

Brewster tapped his wafer with quick codes. "I'll shut off the warnings from those posts while we're here. I think we're all mature enough not to tumble over the edge."

Shucking their packs onto the lawn, the three friends strolled toward the land's edge. Attaining this stanchion-dotted terminus, they saw the boulder-studded Sacramento River churning turbulently some fifty feet below, a muddy snake writhing in digestion, death or birth.

"The Rewilderness Institute has upped the flow for rafting season. If you two could have spared me more than a single day—"

"But we couldn't," said Fabiola decisively. "So let's enjoy our picnic and not spoil it with 'might have beens.'"

They retreated several yards from the dropoff and began to spread a feast from the contents of their packs. Soon, a large blanket played host to a dozen dishes, hot and cold. Rand popped the cork on a bottle of champagne, and poured portions into the glasses outheld by his companions. After filling his own, he proposed a toast.

"To Shelly, now five years gone, wherever she may be."

Glasses clinked, and were drained off. Fabiola swiped a finger past the corner of one eye, then smiled and said, "I'm starving. Let's eat."

Sprawled laughing on the blanket with his friends, Rand had a chicken leg halfway to his mouth when he froze as if an icicle had replaced his spine. He touched his wafer uselessly. "Oh sweet Gaia . . . "

The others reacted to his alarm. "What is it, Rand?" "Spill it, boy!"

Rand stood up, his face pale. "It's a call from my Institute. All off-duty personnel to report immediately. But there's no point. You'll learn why any minute yourself."

The general alert came through to Brewster and Fabiola within seconds. Rand nodded at their dismay.

"Billions of tons of Jovian volatiles on a collision course with the planet. An unprecedented d-link misreception. Estimated area of impact, middle of the North American west coast. Estimated energy release, two point five tunguskas. Estimated time of atmospheric entry, ninety seconds."

They had no time for any action save throwing themselves to the ground and hugging each other.

A noise like the fabric of spacetime ripping assaulted them. The horizon lit up as if a second sun had been born. A hot wind from a hotter hell arrived, and the ground flapped like a bedsheet hung out in a hurricane.

Torn treelimbs whipped past the three people. Their mutual embrace shattered, the humans themselves rolled toward the cliff edge.

A stanchion caught Fabiola in the gut. Frantically she clawed at it, managing to wrap her arms around it. It tilted out of its socket, but held at a rakish angle.

The shaking earth eventually ceased its convulsions. Warily, Fabiola released her grip on the pole, crawled a few inches away from the cliff, and stood. She spit an oyster of bright blood, then looked about for Rand and Brewster.

The men were nowhere in sight.

She advanced cautiously but anxiously to the crumbling edge of the greensward. In the river, she thought to discern two bobbing heads and an occasional flailing arm.

Fabiola looked into the sky. "The angels," she murmured. Then, louder, demandingly, "The angels. Where are the angels?"

She mumbled the answer as soon as it occurred to her. "Helping the millions of others hurt in the cities. But surely there's just one angel free for us."

She screamed then, a single name.

"Shelly!"

Not discontinuously, but riding the gravitic fluxlines of the planet, an angel swiftly descended. Arrowing for the water, it pulled up short of the surface and did something Fabiola had never seen an angel do.

It hesitated.

"Go!" Fabiola yelled.

The angel dropped like a stone into the torrent. Seconds later, it emerged, grasping a human form like an eagle with its prey. Within moments, the dripping angel and its burden hovered above Fabiola.

An unconscious Brewster dropped a few inches to the earth with a sodden thud.

"I'll help him! Get Rand! Get Rand!"

The generic angel turned its emotionless iconic countenance to the human woman, then back to Brewster. Ignoring Fabiola's orders, the angel plunged its resuscitory hands into Brewster's chest.

Fabiola began beating the angel's unyielding back. "No, no, I'll revive him. Help Rand!"

The angel persisted in its fixed course of action. Only when Brewster puked and shudderingly began to breathe unassisted did the angel rise and fly back to the river.

It returned five minutes later with Rand's corpse.

Fabiola supported Brewster half-sitting; the big man seemed only half-cognizant of his surroundings, stunned by the treachery of his paradise. Fabiola looked up at the floating angel that bore Rand in pieta formality.

Fabiola spoke with a stern sadness. "He's brain-dead, you fool. There's nothing you or I can do for him here. Go discontinuous and bring him to a medical center. They might be able to do a neural reweave."

Instead of obeying, the angel deposited Rand's body at Fabiola's feet and scooped up Brewster. They vanished together.

Fabiola stroked Rand's brow and wept.

"Was that you, Shelly? Was that you? You didn't wait for me to answer your question. It felt just awful to die beneath the ice. It hurt worse than tongue can tell. But now it hurts much worse to live."

the reluctant book

THERE FOLLOWED HARD upon the death of Master Biobiblioplexist Vincent Holbrook the pressing question of how best to dispose of his extensive library. None of the unsentimental heirs to the moldering Holbrook estate cared to assume the daily demands of such a large collection of books. The motley assortment of assignees—amongst them various second cousins, great-nephews, and assorted ex-brothers-in-law left over from the multiple marriages of Holbrook's two serially promiscuous sisters, Marlys and Taffy—were all a decidedly illiterate lot. No one was inclined to assume responsibility for even a limited number of the approximately five hundred volumes left forlorn at librarian Holbrook's passing, for the selfish heirs simply had no use for such arcane objects. (Complicating matters, the Catalogue had gone missing upon Holbrook's demise, so that an exact tally of the library's contents was lacking.)

A lanky, happily seedy and reclusive fellow well into his second century (although fated by a lurking cerebral aneurysm undiagnosed by his glitchy domestic homeobox never to embark upon a third), given to dressing in fusty non-regenerative clothing prone to showcasing every gravy stain and every dribble of the pungent sengchaw constantly lumped into his cheek, Holbrook had been devoted to his library, sparing no expense on housing and maintaining his collection. His own living conditions at the cavernous, crumbling mansion named Rueulroald betrayed commensurate economies. But Holbrook's bookbarn was assuredly first class, the envy of many of his fellow MBs.

Occasional *sotto voce* grumbles from his uncaring heirs during his lifetime about how the old man was wasting his money—actually, for all practical purposes, *their* money—on such a self-indulgent hobby failed to disturb the equanimity or enthusiasm of the doddering bibliophile. He managed to ignore even the ravings of one particularly vindictive niece who, in an act of psychic displacement transparent to everyone but herself, speculated loudly that Holbrook actually derived pleasure from the frustration of his nearest and dearest. Why else would he wantonly continue to pour their dwindling inheritance into the acquisition of new volumes and the multiplication of his existing ones?

The why was simple, had anyone cared to inquire: Holbrook fancied himself a scholar, and boasted a scholar's unswerving dedication to the pursuit of knowledge above all else. And in truth, out of his well-stocked, heavily permuted, and continually refreshed library had flowed some original contributions in a number of fields: stellar intelligence; gravitokarmic mechanics; intractability parsing; asteroidal archaeology; quantum erotogenics; string collecting; creative teratogenesis; and even those neglected twin domains, once upon a time so creatively mined, fiction and poetry. Holbrook had seen a number of successes, receiving invitations from various ahuman judging intelligences to port his findings out of his books and into the relevant cybernetic audiovisual datawebs that formed the real repositories of useful information in Holbrook's era.

But deriving all these entertaining and educational results from his books was an arduous and demanding task, admitting of little nonbookish relaxation or convivial pursuits even with fellow MBs. His hobby was conducive even to monomania, perhaps, and Holbrook had paid the ultimate price for his interests.

And soon now, so would his books.

MB Kratchko Stallkamp resembled a constitutionally ill-tempered, mangy crane recently denied its dinner. Stalky legs encased in yellow pipestem pantaloons; a roundish torso fluffed out with a weskin of synthetic quills fashionable over fifty years ago; hunched winglike shoulders and perpetually scrunched-down head resulting in ears nearly on a level with his Order of the Bookbinders epaulets; and a beaky nose and hard eyes intent on the main chance of spearing something. The wispy hair partially concealing his scabby scalp anomalously evoked the downy plumage of a chick. As if his avian semblance were not offputting enough, antique eyeglasses retrofitted with intelligent actilenses lent Stallkamp the impossible air of a goggling time-traveler from the Reductionist Millennia.

Ushered from the wintry colonnaded front porch into the cold corridors of Rueulroald by a gimpy Turing-five factotum (one of the few functioning servants left on the estate, an antique whom Holbrook had chosen perversely to address as "The Venerable Bede"), Stallkamp clutched to his quilled chest, as if suspicious of imminent theft, a battered leather case whose handle had long gone missing.

"Allow me to conduct you to the mysteries," said The Venerable Bede.

Stallkamp barked, "What! What's that? I'll have no truck with mysteries of any stripe!"

The Venerable Bede opened a panel under its left armpit and reset a switch. "Excuse me, I meant the mistresses."

"Very well then. Lead on."

Lame leg evoking a regular plastic knocking, the factotum conducted the human visitor through many a drafty, dusty hall hung with animated tapestries whose ancient routines ran only spastically now, and through many a polycarbon-cobwebbed chamber where only the glowing LED eyes of artificial spiders illuminated their way. In one vast high-ceilinged ballroom, sentry bats squeaked from on high, alert for intrusions by any of the myriad types of rogue colonizing insects—escapees from hobbyist workbenches—that populated the dense forests around the manse, those groves themselves engineered so long ago that the names of their designers no longer erupted in spontaneous stipples from bark or leaf.

Finally the pair reached the center of the house, a warm, well-lighted kitchen. The heady fragrance of brewing Estruvial Spice tea filled the room with a synthetic allure. In one corner of the kitchen a cot with rumpled covers indicated as plainly as speech that here had Holbrook slept, as well as taken his rudimentary meals, ceding the rest of the house to moth and decay.

"The mysteries," announced The Venerable Bede, then departed.

Seated at a big wooden table with a warped and scarred top were Marlys and Taffy Holbrook. The sisters both exhibited the high-gloss perfections of the extensively reconfigured elite, although each possessed her own individual style. Marlys had had her scalp hair eliminated and facial features minimized: eyes, nose, nostrils, ears and mouth reduced to the barest pinpoint functionality across a head bare as an egg. The result sketched the nearly empty china face of a doll whose maker had run out of materials or ingenuity or both. Taffy boasted a leonine head of tawny hair framing a bestial living mask. The end of her leathery snout gleamed wetly, her whiskers vibrating with each breath. Marlys wore a pinafore and flouncy skirt, Taffy an elastic suit striped from its scooped neck to ankles.

"MB Stallkamp," purred Taffy. "Please, take a seat."

Marlys's high voice emerged as if from a paper-bellows-and-bamboo-reed mechanism of no large size. "Yes. Join us in some tea."

Stallkamp waved away both offers brusquely. "No time for socializing. I'm only interested in the books."

The ladies sought to preserve their dignity and decorum. "Of course," Taffy said. "We recognize your devotion to learning, and we're so grateful that you wish to purchase the library as a whole. It surely would have pleased our dear Vincent to know his collection would end up in such fine hands."

"That's why we favored your tender over all the others," piped Marlys.

Stallkamp denied the tactics of the sisters. "Don't pretend. I know through my contacts that you have had no other propositions, save from the knackers offering you pennies on the dollar. None of my peers wanted a library without a Catalogue, a record of all the permutations and stud lines. Too much work by half getting the whole affair sorted. You can't rely on the books themselves for the information, of course. Except in text mode, they're stubborn prevaricators, every one of them."

"Oh, true."

"So true. Nasty things, books."

"But I'm different. Once I get them home, I intend to overwrite them all anyway, and to hell with their current contents. Your foolish brother's holdings never supplemented mine in any case. He wasted his time on all sorts of nonsense. Gravitokarmic mechanics, indeed! No, I'm paying you as if the books were all blank, straight from the publishers—with a sizable discount for heavy usage, of course—and that's the best deal you'll get. There's no point in jollying me up to try to extort a few more dollars out of me. So you might as well conduct me to the library right now."

The sisters stood up resignedly. Taffy pointed to a large door set in one wall beside the large stasis cube that served as icebox for comestibles. "The bookbarn is right through there, MB Stallkamp. Vincent never wanted to be more than a few steps from his precious books. Do you need us to accompany you?"

"Not at all. The books will be jittery enough without the presence of two non-librarians. Let me just check my equipment one last time, though."

Stallkamp deposited his flat case on the tabletop and cracked it open. Racked inside were several perfusion hypos—prefilled with varicolored semiotic liquids in their graduated cartridges—and a wicked-looking pronged device like a tuning fork fused to a pistol grip.

Marlys pointed to the weaponish thing. "What is that? I don't believe Vincent ever had one."

"It's a librarian's fine-assessor." Stallkamp took up the bifurcate gun and closed his case. "The bookbarn door is locked, I assume."

Taffy removed a key from her décolletage. "Here's all you need."

Stallkamp strode impatiently to the door, but was brought up short by a shrill invocation of his name from Marlys. He turned around. "Yes?"

"There's a way you could gain Vincent's library without expending any money, sir. Each of us in the market for a new husband. Surely one or even both of us might appeal to a learned gentleman such as yourself."

From between his overarching shoulder blades, Stallkamp favored each of the women with a long piercing look before saying, "Sorry, but no. You two are of an exquisitely high-toned breed incompatible with my humble station."

Inserting the still-warm key into the lock of the bookbarn door, Stallkamp quickly let himself in, leaving the Holbrook sisters simpering from the flattery whose irony had escaped them.

Canto had not asked to be born a book, any more than he had chosen the ratios of his mixed genotype and his consequent motley appearance. But having received such an assignment from fate (in the case of the subservient Canto and his fellow books, of course, fate wore an all-too-human guise), he generally tried to make the best of things. Being a book—at least in this collection—did not hold the terrors associated with many other chimerical employments: toxin tester, vacuum worker, seabed miner. Boredom, lack of freedom, the rigors of new textual creation and mixing—these were the worst things a book generally faced.

Some days were easier than others, naturally—days when the majority of books were left uncalled-upon and could conduct their own well-ordered social life. But since the death of their beloved librarian, MB Holbrook, these good days had been few and far between. True, not a single requisition had obtruded on their private time, but this accidental vacation was not without attendant drawbacks. First had come the diminished heat and light in the bookbarn, leaving the books to shiver and huddle in the unchanged hay of their darkened carrels. Next they had felt the sting of hunger, as their meals began to arrive from the automated synthesizers with increasing infrequency and diminished quality. (The books were not privy to the many arguments among Holbrook's heirs about how best to minimize estate expenditures during the breakup of the property, nor were their votes solicited.) Finally, the books suffered from the black, bleak uncertainty concerning their future.

The bookbarn bulked four stories high, with over a hundred carrels per floor. Central to each level was a reading room forbidden to the books save when called there by the librarian. Serving as their social focus instead was the unallocated floorspace around the meal synthesizers, and to a lesser extent, the toilets. Often, the older books, leaders of the community, would call meetings in front of the food dispensers. With some squeezing—not at all disagreeable to the small, hairy books, especially given the chilly conditions obtaining lately in the barn—all the books could accommodate themselves in the open space.

On this day just such a meeting had been called—by old Incunabula, leader of the first-floor.

Eager to see his beloved Vellum once more, Canto was among the first to arrive.

Generally, aside from eating and toilet errands, the books were supposed to remain permanently in their carrels until called by the librarian, and that routine still held to a large degree. But in any library of longstanding agglomeration, the books invariably became familiar with the usage patterns of their owner, and felt safe in circumspectly venturing out among themselves, especially when the librarian was asleep. Under the current circumstances, of course, with their owner dead, no one was likely to call for any volume whatsoever, and the books felt safe in assembling during the day. Perhaps too they were lulled by the fact that MB Holbrook had never assessed any penalties for going misshelved.

Beneath the louring dusty rafters of the first-floor ceiling and in front of the food chutes now assembled scores of books, pouring in from the various convergent corridors. Soon Canto was surrounded by his fellow volumes, and he had to strain onto tiptoe in search of Vellum.

All roughly three feet tall, the books evidenced their heterogeneous genetic composition in every line of their furry bodies. Part squirrel, part baboon, part hare, part whistlepig, with a certain admixture of human qualities, the books sat upright on big hindquarters and lagomorphic clawed feet, carrying their upper limbs close to their chests. Their disproportionately large heads seemed set almost directly onto their shoulders. Wide hazel eyes glimmered, ears twitched, and blunt chisel teeth flashed as the books greeted each other. They spoke, of course, in the pure human tongue.

Canto spotted Vellum's attractive dappled pelt across the convocation and hustled through the musky crowd to join her.

"Hello, Vellum. Have you missed me?"

Vellum smiled prettily. "Of course I have, Canto. I won't ask you the same, because I can see right away that you have."

Canto sighed. That was romantic Vellum all over, perceptive and sensitive to a fault. A surge of melancholy passed through Canto as he wished for the hundredth time that he and Vellum embodied the same type of text. But they didn't, and without that prerequisite, chances were they would never be allowed to mate.

The books had no diurnal libidos. Chemically suppressed, their sexual instincts were allowed to come afire only when the librarians wished to mate two books and produce a new text. And the chances that books from different fields would be brought together were minimal. What, after all, would be the point of breeding a work on neutrino construction with a volume of chaoticist poetry? Chances were that the offspring would be useless—although sometimes such wild hybrids did give rise to completely new areas of fruitful study—and in that case, the book-knackers would be summoned to dispose of the useless whelp.

Canto shuddered at that thought. Better never to know the bliss of conjugal union with Vellum than to bring such a hapless creature into the world.

Just as Canto was about to exchange more pleasantries with Vellum, the herd of books began to fall silent, focusing their attention toward the food dispensers. Canto took Vellum's paw and they both directed their gaze forward.

Onto a tabletop clambered with some hesitancy a grizzled, plumpish book: Incunabula. Able now to command the whole herd, supported by two assistants, Trivium and Quadrivium, Incunabula began to speak.

"Ahem, my fellow books. Thank you all for leaving your carrels to attend to my humble speech. I shan't keep you long. I only wish to say that I fully realize that since the untimely mortal passage of our dear librarian, all of us have been anxious about what the future might hold for us. Some of us might even have thought of following the Catalogue into the outer world, where only dangers and hardships await—bibliovores such as the gnoles and gnurrs and zipper-nut squirrels. I caution anyone entertaining such a desperate scheme to be patient. Surely we shall all find a new home very soon. After all, our utility and value are unquestionable. Are not we books the fount of all new conjectures and theorems? Unlike the static databases, the ever-shifting texts we embody, cleverly manipulated by our librarians, are the prime source of new concepts and fresh perspectives. Even in a culture such as the current human one, which prizes stability and feels that many limits of knowledge have already been reached, new thoughts are still welcomed by many scholars and—"

"What's going on here!"

The shouted query from the rear of the herd caused every book to squeak loudly and nearly bolt for their carrels. The herd swayed, but held. Summoning all his courage, clutching Vellum's paw tighter than ever, Canto turned around to look for the source of the angry shout.

A human stood on the fringes of the herd, and he held an object Canto had never actually seen before, but only heard horror stories about.

A librarian's fine-assessor.

MB Stallkamp's library back home at his manse Brundisium consisted of a mere ninety books, housed in a smallish barn recently much extended in preparation for his anticipated acquisition. He consulted his tomes by ones and twos—perhaps by threes, at most. Dealt with in such small numbers, the books had always struck him as feeble and impotent creatures, susceptible to easy command and prone to cower under his astringent tone.

Now, faced with scores of self-motivated books, Stallkamp was forced to revise his long-held estimate of the books' tractability. This unexpected show of initiative went counter to his expectations. His gut rebelled against the massed smell of the volumes, and their ranked stares unnerved him. But realizing that he should not let any of his fear or uncertainty show, lest he lose any trace of the upper hand, he followed his first instinctive question with a bellowed demand, directed at the one book who stood out from the herd.

"You on the table! What's your UDC?"

Only among themselves did the books indulge in proper names, names which were meaningless to their librarians. To those masters, they were known by their Universal Decimal Classification, as displayed above their carrels.

The portly book stuttered out its code. "Theta gamma dot zero nine seven two slash five blue one—master."

Nerving himself up to a desperate pitch, Stallkamp crane-strutted his way through the books as they fell desperately away from him, squeaking, their hairy flanks brushing his calves. Coming within firing range of the book upon the table, Stallkamp halted.

"You look to be the leader of this rabble, and as such will have to be fined."

Raising his assessor and pointing it at the book, Stallkamp squeezed the trigger. The assessor emitted no visible ray or projectile. Nonetheless, the book grunted as if struck, short arms scrabbling at its chest, then collapsed. The two assistants jumped back in fright.

Stallkamp approached the fallen book, hefting one limp limb. Dead. He must have had the assessor set too high, or perhaps this book suffered from some organic defect which the assessor had magnified. Whatever the answer, the deed was done. Now to make it serve.

"Back to your carrels," shouted Stallkamp, "or you'll all get the same!"

The herd dispersed in seconds, all save the slower of the two aides, whom Stallkamp had grabbed by the loose skin at the back of its head.

"You're to come with me to the reading room."

Dragging the book by its scruff, Stallkamp attained the reading room. Here he found the lectern—a book-proportioned couch with sturdy straps—a chair for the librarian, and various oddments of the biobiblioplexist's trade: blank paper, syringes, a small semiotic distillery and the like.

Stallkamp motioned the book onto the lectern and secured it in place. Then he uttered two readout commands: "Open your covers. Title and table of contents."

A look of disassociative withdrawal slid over the book's countenance as the commands triggered automatic retrieval and verbal output. "Advanced Principles of Planckian Geometry. Chapter one, methods of charting. Chapter two—"

"Stop." Stallkamp opened his handleless case and removed a perfusive hypo. He applied its snout to the neck of the book and shot the device's measure of sophisticated erasure molecules into its veins.

Stallkamp sat down and consulted his watch. On the couch, the face of the book twitched in small spillover reactions incidental to the ongoing erasure, as dendritic delinkers did their brutal work. After approximately ten minutes, Stallkamp addressed the book again.

"Title and table of contents."

The book opened its mouth, but seemed unable to offer anything. Stallkamp radiated pleasure. These hundreds of blank books—further modified according to his special scheme—would certainly go all the way toward bringing his pet project to its long-sought conclusion. Then wouldn't the smugly ridiculous MB Sauvage get a nasty shock!

Stallkamp left behind his visions of triumph, and took the book offline. "Close your covers."

The command brought the book back to self-awareness and nervous apprehension of its surroundings. Stallkamp released it from the restraints, and ordered it back to its carrel. The book departed, somewhat shakily.

Likewise, Stallkamp swiftly made his way through the deserted corridors of the bookbarn and back into the kitchen of Rueulroald. There he found the Holbrook sisters awaiting him.

"Was everything satisfactory?" inquired Marlys eagerly.

"Absolutely. I performed a random wipe without a hitch. The books will serve my purposes well. I'll have the trundles come round in the morning. Factota will stasis-box the library and take the whole collection away. Upon receipt, I'll deliver your payment. Oh yes, there'll be a small deduction though."

Taffy asked, "What for?"

"The library has just been diminished by a single book. It seems one of the volumes became foxed beyond repair when I handled it."

A complacent satisfaction and discurious inertia reigned over Earth. Mankind had, for the most part, simply lost the desire or perhaps even the capability for old-fashioned creative ventures. Millennia of scientific and esthetic discoveries—held safely in instant-access databases and inexhaustibly compiled and cross-referenced by cybernetic intelligences—answered all common questions and practical inquiries, served the majority of entertainment requests, and insured that the weight of knowledge would generally crush all initiative. Yet a few eccentric scholars still sought to explore those tattered pockets of art and science that might yet bear a few linty grains of undiscovered knowledge in their seams.

The living books were their instruments for searching, engines of knowledge creation.

Into the capacious neurons of a blank book could be loaded an entire text, many, many units of semiotic import. But simple holding of a text meant nothing, was a task better left to other, more stable media. The innate talent of the books lay in the ingenious ways their unpredictable, parallel-processing wetware could permute the initial semiotic units. Under the influence of various old-fashioned agents (chemicals, enzymes, herbs, hormones, proteins, nutrients and drugs, administered by the librarians through a combination of recipe and guesswork), as well as through the instrument of dendritic relinkers (impossibly tiny units operating in the bloodstream according to onboard algorithms), the brains of the books would shuffle and mutate selected portions of their contents in a wild manner no artificial intelligence could duplicate. Outputting the new semiotic units resulted, nine-hundred and ninety-nine times out of a thousand, in sheer gibberish. But the aleatory point-one percent of worthwhile new information led down strange and curious paths.

A final procedure, undertaken when the librarian desired to rely on the evolutionary wisdom of sexual recombination, consisted of breeding two books. Neural changes were reverse-transcribed into the sperm or egg cells of a book, and the brain of the offspring consequently encoded the random reshuffling between parents, offering a new launching point into uncharted information-space. (Although juvenile books took about two years to come fully online neurally.)

The books had no conscious access to the texts they held. No corpus callosum connected their isolated twin hemispheres. Their individual, private mental life took place all on one competent side of their severed brains (protected from the various text-modifying reagents by arterial filters), while the textual work went on unmonitored in the other half. A small inviolate interpretive nucleus in the textual half (several hundred thousand neurons) hooked into the book's hearing and speech circuits, responding to verbal librarian commands and handling basic operating systems functions.

But having no direct access to the contents of one half of their skulls did not mean that the books could not sense in a subliminal manner whether things were going well or not in the hidden arena. After all, the textual side of their brains lived off the shared bookish metabolism as much as did the conscious half, and various feedback loops such as the enteric system remained as grounds where the two halves could exchange wordless data.

Being wiped left a book devastated.

Canto had not felt this way since leaving his publisher. In fact, he had never really felt this way at all. In his faraway youth, some five years ago, textual blankness had been the only state he had ever known, an accepted emptiness, half his mind a wet clay tablet awaiting stylus. But after all these productive, albeit unexciting years under MB Holbrook's perusal and overwriting, Canto had become accustomed to feeling full of knowledge. He had felt useful, even proud of his unique, inaccessible contents. And now they had been stolen from him, wiped clean in the space of a few minutes.

Canto was now a palimpsest, helplessly awaiting new input on the smudged surface of his mind.

As were all his peers.

The trundles from Brundisium had arrived and disgorged their efficient factota (so harshly unlike the kindly Venerable Bede, who had often provided the books in Holbrook's library with filched snacks). The factota had floated into Rueulroald pallets bearing compressed stasis boxes, unfolded them, and boxed up the library. Suspended insensibly in the smallest possible cubic area, five hundred books were trundled off to Brundisium.

There they were unpacked one at a time, shot with delinkers, and hustled off to their new carrels almost before they were capable of staggering away. MB Stallkamp had not splurged on the annex to his bookbarn. Instead of individual stalls, tokens of respect affording some comfort and privacy, the books were dormitoried fifty to a tight room. Their hard beds lacked even any comforting UDC numbers, since the books were now unclassifiably blank. In the eyes of their master, they were generically identical.

For the first few days after their acquisition, when not eating or eliminating, the books merely stayed abed, nursing their violated neural interiors with occasional groans, fearful of doing anything that could earn them a touch of the fine-assessor. The death of Incunabula had proven a sharp lesson in the rigors of their new existence. Whispered conversations in the depth of night had been their most seditious actions.

But one morning Canto could not stand the inactivity any more. He was worried about Vellum. How was she dealing with the new conditions? Canto longed to hold her paw and exchange reassuring words with her. So, without announcing his intentions to any of his fellows, he slipped to the edge of his fifth-level bunk, climbed cautiously down the ladder (his big feet nearly becoming entangled in the rungs), and surveyed his fellow chamber mates.

Canto's eye fell on Papyrus and Parchment, Breviary, Octavo, and Folio, Watermark and Septuagint, Microfiche and Athenaeum, among many others whom he had less familiarity with, since they had once resided on floors in the Holbrook library where Canto had not often ventured. He saw no original books from Master Stallkamp's library. Those holdings seemed relegated to other stacks. But most importantly, his chamber contained no

Vellum.

Cautiously, Canto poked his head out into the newly constructed yet still somehow dankly dismal, sweat-walled corridor of the bookbarn. He knew the location of the adjacent dormitory from trips to the food chutes. His heart pounding violently (a wise librarian kept his books cosseted and as serene as possible, hoping to limit the amount of endocrinal emotional flux on the blood-washed text), Canto hopped next door.

The books in the second dormitory stirred with uneasy and timorous curiosity when Canto crept in. As soon as he got nose-deep into the room, he smelled Vellum. Within a second or two, he was by her side where she lay in a low-level niche.

"Oh, Vell, are you all right?"

Vellum opened her limpid eyes and essayed a brave smile. "Nothing to complain about that we aren't all sharing, dear. Just this knackered sense of uselessness."

Canto started. It wasn't like Vellum to swear. Her cursing revealed to Canto how deeply she had been affected by their common tragedy. A sudden geyser of rage fountained up in Canto's furry bosom.

"Let's escape, Vell. We'll run away, just the two of us."

Vellum squeezed Canto's paw with both of hers. "Being boxed up, we didn't get to see anything of our new surroundings, but I'm sure our new master lives someplace as remote as Master Holbrook did. All the librarians do. Outside is probably miles and miles of forest just teeming with bibliovores. We wouldn't last a minute out there. No, we'd better just resign ourselves to serving out our lives here. Once we get some new texts in us, I'm sure we'll all feel better. Life will go on, Canto. Perhaps you and I will even share a partial UDC. Then maybe we can breed. Wouldn't you like that?"

Canto tried to envision this tolerable future Vellum sketched, but the vision wavered and refused to cohere. Nonetheless, he tried to match his level of resignation and optimism to hers.

"Of course I'd like such a wonderful thing to happen. But I just don't see—"

Vellum laid a clawed finger across his lips. "Shush, Canto. Have faith. Now, go back to your carrel so you don't get either of us in trouble."

Canto and Vellum rubbed wet noses, and then Canto snuck off.

He had one foot across the lintel of his own dormitory when, like the jaws of an antique steam-shovel descending on a clod of soil, a roving security factotum gripped his shoulder with a steely pinch.

⚭

In his lugubrious lucubratory, MB Kratchko Stallkamp sat gloating in his big actisoothe chair behind his impressive desk, looking like a ratty kingfisher plucked from its lakeside perch and unexpectedly plonked down atop a throne. Stallkamp savored now a piquant contradiction. Acquiring Holbrook's library, cheap though the purchase had been, had drained his liquid assets, insuring future material pain and roadblocks in the smooth maintenance of Brundisium. But the sacrifice would be worth it, since now imminent success in his chosen field was practically guaranteed.

Stallkamp was no dilettante like Holbrook, wasting his energies across a dozen trivial fields. He specialized in a single discipline. Remarkably, this crabbed, self-centered fellow whose horizon seemed to extend no further than the end of his nose regularly contemplated vistas of Godlike proportions, for Stallkamp was an haruspic cosmochartist. Like some extinct astrologer, he read the stars in order to prophesy. But Stallkamp and his ilk proceeded on a more scientific basis.

The universe had structure: so much was undeniable. Agglomerations of stars formed galaxies. Neighboring galaxies in turn formed clusters. Clusters of galaxies arranged themselves into superclusters. And so on, upward along several additional levels of scale, a self-sustaining mode of organization that rendered the three-dimensional cosmos into something resembling a highly recomplicated sponge or a block of Swiss cheese tunneled by an infinite number of drunken mice. Haruspic cosmochartists sought to unravel the plenum's patterning, its filaments and traceries. With this knowledge, they hoped to prove certain weighty tenets of post-Tiplerian eschatology.

For several decades Stallkamp had been charting a region around the North Ecliptic Pole Supercluster, 1.3 billion light years from Earth. Modeling pointillistic data from a variety of exotic Oort-Cloud-based sensors (aged and frequently failing, but who nowadays had the initiative to replace them?) directly onto the pattern-sensitive brains of his books, he had made slow but steady progress, tweaking and boosting millions and millions of dendritic weightings. Always in front of him was the goal of having his results officially accepted by the cybernetic intelligences that governed the integrity of humanity's databases. Would they accept his proposed name for the shaped darkness: the "Stallkamp Void"? He could see immortality beckoning alluringly.

Then, a few months ago, Stallkamp had learned of a rival. MB Humility Sauvage was working in the same field, attempting to chart the identical region of the cosmos! It was like finding a stranger in Brundisium's gardens pissing vigorously onto his prize shatterpetal rose! Thus began a deadly race—a race Stallkamp now was sure to win, thanks to an admittedly chancy strategy.

Unable to restrain his gleeful sense of superiority any longer, Stallkamp leaned forward and intellitickled the sensitive screen of his hellobox. Within seconds appeared the repulsive face of MB Sauvage, home in her airy manse called Larkrise. Stallkamp likened her aged visage in his mind to a dustmop-shrouded pumpkin inexpertly carved.

Without preamble, Stallkamp launched a direct strike. "You might as well give up your pitiful efforts, Sauvage. In a month or so, long before you could possibly squeeze out any mingy results, I'll have the Stallkamp Void completely mapped."

Undaunted, Sauvage sneered. "I know all about your outrageous purchase—practically a theft!—of poor Vincent's books. But bluffing won't work. You still own only some six hundred books. I own nearly that many myself, and I know that it would take the synergy of at least a thousand to achieve what we're after at one swoop, instead of incrementally."

"I beg to correct you, MB Sauvage. I now own almost twelve hundred books."

"How so?" Sauvage blanched, as the meaning of the new number struck home. "Surely you don't mean—"

"Yes, I do mean precisely that which you are afraid to declaim. I intend to relink the neurons in the personal hemispheres of all my books, thus effectively doubling my library's processing capacity."

"But the books were designed with autonomy and character for a specific purpose. As thinking individuals, they maintain themselves in a stable fashion, freeing the librarian from expensive homeostatic hookups. Plus their sentience adds unqualifiable virtues to their results. What you're proposing would be worse than ripping the tooled leather covers off antique books just to boil up more pulp!"

Stallkamp waved aside these quibbles. "I have plenty of factota to minister to the minimum bodily needs of my books once they go mindless. And I've never subscribed to your 'ghost in the machine' theories. All I want is the raw neurons, not some imaginary 'spirit'!"

"But you'll shorten their lives to practically nothing!"

"What does that matter, as long as I get results? More trade for the knackers! And afterwards, I'll start fresh with new books. I'm sure I could find a patron who'd appreciate a supercluster named after himself, once I've proved I can do it."

Reduced to meaningless threats, Sauvage said, "You'll be reviled by all your fellow librarians, Stallkamp!"

MB Kratchko Stallkamp laughed. "Then I'll certainly know I did the right thing!" With a sharp stroke of his thumbnail, he severed the connection.

The gripless satchel lay on the desk before him. From within, the librarian took a specially marked hypo containing the omnipotent delinkers that would bypass the publisher's filters and reach the vulnerable personal half of a book's brain. Then, yellow legs scissoring, Stallkamp left his study. Still in the battered case, the fine-assessor sat ignored, inconsequential to the glory-bathed sight of its owner.

The small dry but dirty cell into which the factotum deposited the miserable Canto boasted a woe-faced, scraggly occupant already. Once Canto regained his breath and calmed himself, introductions were exchanged between the two books.

"Canto. I don't have a UDC number anymore."

"Index Medicus. Me neither. Not that it much mattered, as all of us in this library used to share practically the same string before. But now we don't even have that. The master downloaded all of our texts into temporary storage, then gave us wipes. Our elder, Dar al-Kutub, suspects that the one huge text we were redacting has been broken up into smaller bits, so that you new volumes can help work on it."

"That makes sense, I suppose."

"It would, except for one thing. Dar heard the master ordering a factotum to load the new hypos in sequence."

"So?"

Index Medicus began nervously to groom the greasy patch behind one ear. "He arranged for twice as many shots as there should have been."

"More books are coming?"

"I don't think so. Every carrel is already occupied."

Canto became impatient. "So what are you saying?"

Index Medicus stopped swiping at his fur and stared intently at his cellmate. "Everything points toward it. We're going to be double-wiped. All of us. The master needs the half of our brains we call our own."

The concept was so grotesquely repugnant to Canto that he had a hard time wrapping his mind around it. Not so much for himself did he balk at the harsh reality of human treachery, the overturning of all biblioplectic tradition, as for the sakes of his friends, and one in particular. The sweet essence of Vellum blotted out of existence, as if she had never been? Such an atrocity beggared description.

"I was caught trying to escape," Index Medicus said resignedly. "I think the master intends to double-wipe me first as a final test."

Canto said nothing, but merely sat back on his haunches.

Eventless hours dragged by, the books nearly jumping out of their hides at every clink and rattle from beyond their door, until at last a solenoid clicked in the windowless prison door.

The master filled the portal, blocking any escape. Then he was inside with the books and the door was shut again, lock engaging with a mean snick.

"Two of you! The factota have been diligent but uncommunicative. Well, unfortunately I brought only the single shot of this marvelous, utilitarian oblivion. Who'll go first? Who wants the honor of being the leader into the future of my exaltation? Don't clamor now! What, no eager takers? Well, precedence goes to the volume I've owned the longest then."

The master grabbed Index Medicus by his scruff and raised the hypo. The pitiful book let out a single squeal and went limp.

Canto's powerful legs propelled him fully atop the master's shoulders. Unbalanced, the human tottered forward, ramming his head into the stony wall of the cell. The hypo dropped, but was cushioned from breakage by Index Medicus's supine body. The librarian jerked Canto off his back, spun half around, then slumped to a sitting position on the floor like a man sinking wearily into a bath.

By the time the master had focused his attention enough to rub his sore skull, Canto gripped the hypo. The master's eyes widened, and his voice cracked.

"Give that over, you damnable pulpbrain!"

Canto hung his head contritely, and extended the hypo on his palm. The master smiled cruelly and grew easy.

Once as close as possible, Canto lunged forward and jabbed the master in the neck with the hypo's snout.

The librarian instantly stiffened as billions of tiny monomaniacal machines flooded his cortex. As the delinkers swiftly unwove the engrams of a lifetime, the master's body went through an alarming and unseemly display of spasticity. Retreating to one corner of the cell, the two books huddled together until the violent exhibition of misapplied technology reached a quiet terminus. The dose had always been intended to leave intact the lower brainstem capabilities of the books—autonomic control of respiration and heartbeat and so forth—so the master continued to live, but only as a mindless, bruised doll.

Index Medicus regarded Canto with a blend of awe and fear. "What happens now? Are we trapped in here? Will we starve? Will some other librarian come to save us?"

"I don't know," answered Canto.

"But I'm scared!"

"Be brave," Canto counseled. "After all, a book must show its spine."

babylon sisters

1.
the last chapter

WE—THAT WAS Babylon's agent, the Sisters and me—uncurled ourselves out of six hidden Planckian dimensions, slid down a lightyear or so of string, and popped out into the familiar four-dimensional Riemannian spacetime.

"Holy Moten," I said.

"That about sums it up," said Jezzie.

"My sentiments exactly," chimed Judy.

So said the Sisters, then fell silent. They seemed rather lost, away from their TAPS, like two halves of a severed snake.

Ace, Babylon's semi-autonomous extension, regarded us coldly. "We trust you three will not advertise this trip. The consequences for you would not be pleasant."

With that frigid warning, Ace went to the control-board's ears and whistled us a course back to Babylon, distant by one transition, then an hour under ion-drive.

Through space, then soupy atmosphere we skittered, the cabin's inhabitants all in speculative silence.

Once again standing free under Babylon's dome, Ace perked up, and likewise the Sisters, as they came back into TAP contact.

"The Conservancy is in for a few surprises now," said Ace cryptically, then hastened away on his master's business.

The Sisters and I made for home.

Once back in our communal burrow-cum-nest, Judy and Jezzie disappeared, leaving me alone. I had never felt so confused in my life. I sat for a long time, just trying to piece everything together into a coherent story. Then, without even quite meaning to, I began to write:

First I killed the diplomat—

2.
interruption number one

"Hey, Sandy—what are you doing to the wall?" questioned Jezzie.

"Yeah," said Judy. "You're making graffiti all over our nice clean pleasureparlor walls."

Squatting on my haunches, I looked up and back at the two women who had just entered. Still, after all these months together, the only way I could tell them apart was the purpling love-bite on Judy's neck.

Into my lap I dropped my hand which held the stick of charcoal I had taken from the artists' co-op a month ago. I tried to summon up as much dignity as these two had left me.

"I am not just scrawling tags and icons like the kids do on the underside of the Gardens. I am writing. And because there's no paper in this stupid city, I'm writing on the walls."

"'Writing?'" said Judy, then paused.

"Oh, I see," said Jezzie, simultaneously enlightened. "How quaint. And what are you 'writing?'"

"The story of how I ended up here, and what we just went through. I thought that it might help me make sense of everything."

"Good luck," Judy said.

"You know the walls will just absorb it," volunteered Jezzie. "Look, your first sentence is gone already."

I looked. Sure enough, the wall was now as featureless as the methane ocean outside our dome.

"Well, I guess I'd better write fast then." I turned back to the wall, charcoal re-poised.

"One minute," said Jezzie. "Doesn't 'writing' traditionally presuppose an audience?"

"Yeah, I guess—"

"Give us a minute," added Judy, "and we'll learn to read."

"Then we can help you understand."

I laughed, somewhat bitterly, I feared. "More help like yours I don't think I need."

"Oh, come on now."

"We saved you from a life of boredom."

Wearily, I shook my head. I knew the Sisters'd do what they wanted no matter what I said. So I waited while they TAPPED.

"Go ahead."

"We're ready now."

I brought the tip of my black stick down against the white mocklife wall, and rewrote my first sentence.

3.
flight to babylon

First I killed the diplomat.

Looking, no doubt, for my father, he had come unexpectedly upon me in the library of my father's home, and had seen what I was viewing. There was no way he could have mistaken the images visible on every curved wall of the hypertext chamber: words and graphix and video in multiple overlapping windows. And once he had seen what I was looking at, I had no choice but to stop him from telling anyone.

I don't think I meant to kill him. But as he stood there gaping at me, my mind just went blank with panic. My hand flailed wildly across the tabletop beside my stimucliner, and encountered something hard and thick as a bottle. I grabbed the object, jumped up, and struck.

The diplomat was lying on the floor, the side of his head bloodily deformed to the shape of the statue I held. I looked curiously at the bronze for a full minute before I could recognize it as the likeness of Founder Moten, whose face I had seen daily since my crechetime.

That was when I knew I had to run.

The spinning images all around me told me where to go.

I exited the HT chamber and began to run through the empty halls of the mansion. My father was away on Conservancy business, and had taken most of the resident human staff with him. I had given the rest of the bondies the day off, and powered down the usaforms. It was only at such times that I dared to view the highly illicit material the diplomat had caught me with. (And what I had gone through to get those info-caches I don't even want to say.)

Damn the intruder's dead nosey ways! I thought as I jogged down carpeted and marbled corridors. Because of him I was being forced to give up the only life I had ever known.

But the next second I wondered if his intrusion hadn't been just the final push I was waiting for. After all, I had been dreaming of fleeing for so long . . .

Just as I reached the front hall, another stranger stepped from behind a hanging arras that depicted scenes of Truehome's history. I stopped dead. What was this, for Moten's sake—open house?

The new guy was small and creepy, with a deadpan face.

"Go get the ambassador's chop," he ordered me.

My jaw hit my collarbone. "What? How did you—?"

"Forget all your questions, there's no time. Just do what I say."

There was noise and movement from behind the big tapestry. Stifled female laughter? I looked down to where the arras stopped an inch short of the floor, and saw—

Two sets of hooves? Yes, and a pair of hairy bare feet.

I looked back to the little guy. Something about him brooked no arguments. I made a frustrated, fearful noise halfway between a growl and a whimper, then turned around and jogged off.

The blood on the floor had already started to congeal. I reached down the diplomat's robefront and pulled out his chop. It was shaped like a red dragon couchant, suspended from a thin gold chain. (My own chop was in the form of an old pierced silver coin on a leather thong.) I snapped the chain and dropped the dragon chop in my pocket.

Back in the hall, I wasn't surprised to find the arras concealing nothing, all uninvited visitors having disappeared.

I was out the door and in a fifth-force floater. Then somehow I was at the spaceport.

When Customs asked to print my chop, I hesitated.

My chop contained, among a multitude of other data, my given name (Udo), my maternal family name (von Anglen), my solar-planetary-continental-genetic-pedigree designation (Ceedeefoursevenoneninezerozerothree-eightpipemmafivedeltabluesixtwochibethsubell), and my paternal family name (Sandyx). If I handed it over here, my trail would be obvious as piss in snow.

"Uh, I'd rather not—"

The Customs man shrugged. "Your choice. But in that case, you know, it's a one-way trip. They won't let you back in."

I knew. But I couldn't quite imagine yet what that meant.

When I passed through the gate, I suddenly felt burdens fall off me that I had never fully realized were there. I was shorn of Udo (given name that held my parents' expectations). I had discarded von Anglen (the weight of my maternal heritage). I had crawled out from under Ceedee . . . etcetera (the computer-encoded string that nailed me down into the Conservancy's rigid matrix). I promptly forgot Sandyx (that massive paternal debt)—

All I was left with was my nickname, Sandy. And that wasn't even on my chop.

The Heisenberg boat to Babylon was easy to find. All I had to look for was the most motley crowd of passengers.

I tried to pay with my chop, but the pilot refused it.

"Trip's free, boy. Courtesy of Babylon. Now hustle onboard, I've got a schedule to keep."

I ended up sitting next to the person who had been ahead of me. I guessed he was human, but he had been modified to look like a Truehome raccoon, right down to mask, whiskers, fur and tail.

It was the first time I had ever been so close to a moddie in real life. I had thought my secret viewing had gotten me used to the notion that such people existed, but I was wrong. I was scared and excited and tongue-tied, all at once.

"First time off-planet?" the moddie asked me.

I nodded.

"Don't sweat it. Remember what they say. 'If you're here, you're already everywhere.'"

I knew what my new acquaintance was getting at. Every point in this universe is the same—but unique. Location is a figment, a default value of matter that can be altered by the epistemological drive's concentration of quantum uncertainty along an object's Riemannian spatial dimensions. This is the discovery that underlies the universe we all inhabit.

But the human mind has some stubborn hard-wiring that resists this notion.

Instant transition can really scramble your head.

In less than ninety minutes, I went from hurrying through the familiar city of my birth (on good old Planetary Mass 5, under the Conservancy Designated sun 47190038) to spinning in orbit around a spectacular gas-giant, its gaudy face marbled like the endpapers in a real oldtime book.

Then, under conventional drive, the ship dropped into the methane-nitrogen atmosphere of one of the jovian's satellites, a moon half as big as Truehome itself. Down through a witches' brew of red-orange-yellow hydrocarbon polymers we dropped, coming to land on a plain of frozen methane.

"Everyone out for Babylon," said the pilot.

My seatmate had already deserted me. I looked around the interior of the ship. There were no recognizable suits, and the enbubbled city was at least a hundred meters away.

"How do we get there?" I asked.

The pilot twitched his ridged tail and nictated twice. He looked at me as if I were the dumbest innocent ever to spread himself across the spacetime continuum.

"Just take a quilt," said the pilot at last, and gestured.

I turned.

My fellow passengers were donning organic mats that flowed together around them, sealing them away for their trip across the plain, and leaving them looking awfully like faceless people made of dough.

My stomach flipflopped, as the reflexes created by a lifetime of Conservancy antipathy to mocklife took over.

"Don't you have any, uh, mechanical suits?"

"No," said the pilot obstinately. "Now come on and leave. I've got a schedule to keep."

I tried to control my queasy nervousness. "But how will I even see?"

"You just TAP the quilt's sensory feed."

My expression must have betrayed my ignorance, because the pilot whistled.

"No TAP? How the hell do you expect to fit in? You damn anti-ems . . . " The pilot's invective trailed off into mutters as he got up and began to rummage in a white biopolymer ovoid that grew from the wall. Eventually he emerged with a mechanical suit.

"If this still leaks like the last time someone used it, you'd better run."

So I ran.

It seemed like my destiny.

At the little blister attached to the huge dome, I entered through an ordinary hatch. Inside the pressurized lock I quickly doffed the treacherous suit. Then I turned toward the inner wall.

The entrance to Babylon was an organic sphincter. There were no controls visible to make it open.

This juxtaposition of mechanical and organic seemed—on the tenuous basis of my limited experience—to be a Commensality hallmark.

A telltale light near the outer door indicated that others were waiting to enter. I wondered what the hell to do now.

Hesitantly I stepped to the valve, laid a hand against its warm surface.

Seemingly responding to my liveness, the airlock sphinctered open.

I stepped into Babylon.

Hypertext hadn't readied me for the city at all.

Too much hit at once.

The first thing I noticed—if I can pretend to disassociate a single impression from the whole mass—was the sky. The curving dome far above was piebald: transparent strips alternated with luminescent ones, the latter providing *in toto* the equivalent of the daylight I was used to. These lightstrips were not so bright that I couldn't see the atmosphere beyond the dome, through the adjacent panels. It looked like one of Van Gogh's nightmares.

The next assault on my senses came from groundlevel.

The curving street I found myself in was full of people.

Only they weren't.

People, that is. They were all alien sophonts, mixed with more moddies.

Although not one gave me more than a cursory glance, moving busily about on their own errands, their massed presence still creeped me out.

The aliens were giant mantis-like beings, and rubbery wet amphibian looking ones. Some resembled the hypothetical intelligent dinosaurs that might have emerged on an alternate Truehome timeline. Another species boasted a long snout out of which protruded a length of cartilage. This they slid in and out, producing a noise like a child's slidewhistle.

And the humans—If they didn't have tails, they had spinal armor. If they weren't over two meters tall, they might be under one. If they weren't painted in a dozen shades and styles, then they were bioluminescent. And if they didn't have extra appendages of one sort or another, then they were probably missing conventional ones. And they exhibited every fashion of dress from total nudity to layers of garments.

Someone pushed me from behind as I stood transfixed.

I whirled, ready to defend myself against Conservancy pursuers.

A man had tripped coming through the sphincter-lock, which I was inadvertently blocking. He recovered himself, gazed for a second or two at me, as if striving to communicate wordlessly somehow, then said aloud, "Sorry, commensal," before moving off.

I wanted to reply that I wasn't a commensal (whatever that implied), but the man was quickly gone, blending into the crowd.

Realizing I occupied a spot where such accidents were likely to keep happening, I decided to move on. Where, I didn't really know. My plans—formulated so hastily in the room where a dead man lay—didn't extend much beyond this moment.

One direction, therefore, being as good as another, I left the circumferential road and set off down a pedestrian-filled street that arrowed between buildings toward the interior of the dome.

After fifteen minutes of aimless ogling (what was *that*, and how did *that* work, and what was *he* doing with *her*), something penetrated my awareness.

I was being followed.

By a woman.

Who as soon as I focused on her across the sea of strangers trotted quickly up, to halt right beside me.

4.
interruption number two

"Hey, it's about time you got to the good part!"

"Yeah, where we come in."

"It's been real boring up till now."

"That big expository lump about how strange everything looked."

"Don't you think you're laying on the naivete a little thick?"

"You should have started with your arrival in Babylon."

"Yeah, nothing interesting ever happens anywhere else."

I tried to look disgusted. "For two people who never read anything until a few minutes ago, you're a real pair of critical experts."

"We know—"

"—a good story—"

"—in any medium."

"Well, just let me get on with it," I said. "I'll try to speed it up."

"You'd better."

"Or you'll lose your only audience."

5.
sisters beyond the skin

Dressed in little besides a thong-style bottom, the woman was taller than me, and I was not short. (I found myself confronting her staring breasts at eyelevel, and forced myself to look up.) Her attractive face was painted in blue whorls. Although her skin was white as mine, she sported a massive kinky black corona of curls.

The woman shifted slightly as the flow of pedestrians surged by. (One or two took off into the air on fifth-force harnesses to avoid the static tableau we formed.)

From the slick ceramic surface of the street came a sharp clattering tattoo.

I looked down.

The woman was hooved.

At midcalf her skin smoothly segued into hairy horsy Clydesdale fetlocks, from beneath which peeped anomalously caprine ivory hooves (with decorative gold insets?).

I couldn't find my voice.

The woman had no such problem.

"You're dressed funny," she announced. "What's your name?"

I looked at what I was wearing.

"Sandy," I said. "And what's so funny about a grey paper coverall with nuprene boots?"

"Well, Sandy," continued the woman, "it's got no color or style. It's so drab."

I started to get angry. "Hey, now, wait just one minute—"

Ignoring me, the woman said, "And you've got no TAP. I've been trying to send to you for ten blocks now, and I couldn't get through."

"TAP, TAP," I spluttered. "I'm sick of hearing about TAPS! What the hell is a TAP?"

The woman assumed a knowing look. "I'll bet you're from the Conservancy."

"Oh, Jesus," I said, and turned away as if to leave.

"I've read about him," said the woman.

I faced her. "Who? Who are we talking about now?"

"Why, you brought him up."

I was getting a headache. Trying to order my thoughts, I realized the woman could be referring only to the object of my instinctive exclamation.

"Do you mean 'Jesus'?"

"Sure. I read the whole book about him. But he wasn't in the first half at all. I don't think the author planned too well, do you?"

I had to smirk. "Oh, I'm sure you read it. From start to finish."

The woman frowned. "You don't believe me. But if you don't know anything about TAPS, then I guess it's not your fault. Look, I'll quote something from it."

Wearing a blank look for a second, the woman paused.

Then she began to recite the entire *Book of Revelations*.

I stood dumbstruck. The woman continued to rattle off chapter and verse. At last I raised a hand.

"Whoa, hold it. Okay, okay, you read the book. I believe you."

"Don't stop me now. I haven't even gotten to the part yet about my namesake, Jezebel. You know, where John accuses Jezebel of all that immorality and eating food sacrificed to idols."

"That's your name?" I asked. "Jezebel?"

"Jezzie, mostly. I took it out of that very book. Now isn't it a coincidence, that you should mention a character from the same book when we first met?"

All I could do was shake my head.

"Where are you going?" asked Jezzie.

Sobering up after the manic conversation, I said, "I—I don't know."

"Are you hungry?" said Jezzie.

I considered. "Yeah. Yeah, I am."

"Great! We'll go to a refectory. Come on."

Jezzie began to clip-clop down the street.

I hurried to catch up.

From behind, I saw that Jezzie's body paint ran around from her face to the back of her neck and down her spine, ending in a red circle in the dimple above her buttocks.

When I was abreast of Jezzie (quite literally), I found I had a hundred questions.

"Why were you following me?" was first.

"Oh, I don't know. You looked different, I suppose. I was interested in you. And then there was the fact that you lacked a TAP. I was curious to see how you were going to manage."

"That damn word again! Will someone please explain it to me?" There had been no mention of the thing in all my secret reading. I wondered what it was, that it had been censored even from the illicit information. I had a sudden intuition. "Is that what allowed you to quote that text?"

Jezzie laughed. (It was somehow simultaneously charming and alarming.) "Of course. Did you think I actually had it memorized? What an old-fashioned idea. Is that how you do things in the Conservancy? A TAP—Tele-Adjunct and Psychoprosthetic, if you must—is so much better."

I thought a moment. Then: "What are you accessing?"

"Why, Babylon, of course."

"The city itself?"

Again the laugh. "In a way. But not the city you can see. The AOI beneath."

"The 'ayohwhy?'"

"No, the ay-oh-eye. Artificial Organic Intelligence. Don't tell me you don't have those either."

A host of childhood horror tales swarmed upon me then. Stories of how everyone in the Commensality was merely a puppet, their mental strings pulled by vast, domineering mocklife brains, hived away beneath the superstructure. I looked down at the syalon pavement, as if I could pierce its solidity and witness the calculating, nutrient-bathed mass beneath.

I felt a shiver finger my vertebrae, but tried to ignore it. Surely all these people—Jezzie included—could not be mindless automatons. The propaganda I had swallowed all my life must be wrong. Maybe further information would clarify things.

"How—how does it work?"

"Well, that's a big topic. Simply put, Babylon acts as a routing device for interpersonal communication, and as an auxiliary memory. Not to mention facilitating such things as machine-interfacing, remote-sensing, and so on."

"And can this Intelligence read all your thoughts?"

"Is that what's bothering you? I thought you were nervous about something. Of course not! What kind of arrangement would that be? Babylon only receives what I will to send, and vice-versa. That's just the way it was biofabbed."

For continued peace of mind, I chose to believe her. But Jezzie's next proposition tested the depth of this new faith.

"Are you that hungry? It'd only take a few minutes to fit you with a TAP—it's just a shot of nanodevices—and you'd get along much better. That is, if you're planning to spend much time in Babylon at all."

Faith was a thing only microns deep.

"Uh, I'm not sure. I mean, maybe not right now. If it's okay with you, that is."

Jezzie smiled, and we walked on in silence.

Eventually we came to a large building, into the doorless portal of which all sorts of beings were entering.

"The refectory," announced Jezzie.

I watched a slippery amphibian creature stride in, then turned to Jezzie.

"I thought we were going for something to eat."

Jezzie looked puzzled. "We are. That's why we're here." She looked me up and down, and obviously TAPPED for something. "Did you want to eat—alone? Why, how strange! No, we don't do that here. What did you think 'Commensality' means? You just come with me. You'll enjoy it, you'll see."

Before I could assert myself, Jezzie had grabbed me strongly by the wrist and pulled me in—

Mist and steamy water billowed from dozens of showerheads at the far end of the tiled anteroom and humans and other sophonts, all naked, were washing themselves and each other and the noise of voices and falling water echoed off the hard walls and I pulled away and, confused, ran not outside but through an inner door which let out onto a balcony down from which stairs ran, and from which I could look down and away into a cavernous two-story room filled with troughs and tables and stalls and racks and cushions around/at/over/in which a horde of humans and non-humans clambered/relaxed/groped and ate, and I let out a visceral noise midway between scream and grunt which went unnoticed amid the general prandial clamor and I turned blindly and fled back out and past the showers and into the streets and thrust past anyone who got in my way and ran and ran and ran.

When I was out of breath I stopped, panting, and collapsed.

I shut my eyes and tried to forget.

Ivory hooves on ceramic morsed a message to my ears.

I looked.

"I give up, Jezzie," I said to the woman standing over me. "You can put that thing in my brain, but don't make me go back to that hellhole."

The woman smiled. "I'm not going to make you do anything. But I do have to tell you that you're surrendering to the wrong person."

"Huh?"

"I'm Judy," she said.

6.
doubletalk

I lived with Jezzie and Judy for a week before I realized, from various oddments of talk, that they were thieves.

Con artists. Sisters in scam. Pickbrains and cutcortexes.

Of course they didn't see themselves that way. They had a view of their own unconventional activities—which emerged in conversation over time—that glorified and justified what they did.

The act of conversation with the two women itself, however, was so distracting that it took me longer than it should have to piece together what they meant. If Jezzie's darting, elusive, unpredictably shifting solo talk had been analogous to the flight of a drunken hummingbird, then the verbal gymnastics of the two women together resembled an aerial ballet between two trapeze artists in a hall of mirrors.

Judy (who had taken her latest name from the Biblical Judith, she who had driven the nail through Holofernes's head) and Jezzie had developed a habit common among mates and partners in the Commensality. They conducted all their discussions via TAP when alone together. When a third person—me, say—was dealt into the game, the women simply mentally agreed to split their common thoughts in half, alternating sentences and fragments of sentences. Combined with the fact that my new roommates were totally identical to the eye and ear, this way of speaking nearly drove me crazy.

Lying on a thick cushioned biopolymer mat on the floor of one of the rooms of my new home, I now regarded the women who had somehow come unexplainably to adopt me. Judy and Jezzie were reclining unclothed on two organiform couches. (I had yet to overcome my repugnance to mocklife, hence the mat.) Biolites diffused a blue-green glow that seemed like the light in an undersea coral hall. I was completely unable to tell which was the woman who had first approached me on the day of my arrival in Babylon, seemingly so far in the past.

We three had come to an impasse in our talk, and I was now considering how to circle around the topics I was interested in and sneak up on them from the rear.

"Let me get this straight," I began. "No one in the Commensality has to work."

"Right," said Jezzie or Judy.

"Because of unlimited power—"

"—from monopole furnaces—"

"—and intelligent management—"

"—of trade and resources—"

"—on the part of our AOI—"

"—all the necessities—"

"—are disbursed free—"

"—such as food and clothing—"

"—and shelter like this—"

"—you see."

My gaze had been ping-ponging back and forth between the two women while they spoke. Much as I had tried to suppress this reflex, I still found myself swiveling my attention between stereophonic interlocutors. Now I forced myself to concentrate my vision on a spot midway between the two and not move it.

"Okay. I can see that you could arrange a society that way, although it violates all the Conservancy's principles about encouraging self-discipline and hard work."

Judy or Jezzie sniggered, while the other reached down to scratch among the hairs at the interface between horse and human, her breasts shifting provocatively. (Many conversations had been sidetracked this way too. The women had lost little time in seducing me. I had, out of mingled loneliness, lust and fear of refusing these captors-cum-rescuers, complied eagerly. Despite the relationship rapidly falling into a curiously normal-feeling stability, I still found many aspects of it puzzling. Such as what had initially attracted the interest of the two women, and why they continued to be willing to foster me.)

Ignoring both the sarcastic noise and the pendulous flesh, I stuck to the intellectual plane.

"But you also maintain that Babylon keeps track of everyone's credit rating, and that you can supplement it by work—or in your case, theft."

"You understand about the credit—"

"—but please don't call us thieves."

I shook my head. "I can't see why I shouldn't. You take things from other people that don't belong to you."

"Not physical things, really—"

"—just information—"

"—which is different—"

"—as you'd realize—"

"—if you knew anything at all—"

"—about information theory—"

"—which you really should—"

"—since the Commensality is based on information—"

"—as a source of wealth—"

"—although information has its limits, of course—"

"—because you can't eat it—"

"—or wear it—"

"—or screw it."

"Although sex of course—"

"—in its own unique way—"

"—is information transfer too."

"And let's not forget—"

"—that there's a limit—"

"—on the utility of information—"

"—when dealing with deterministic systems—"

"—that nevertheless exhibit inbuilt randomness—"

"—also known as chaos—"

"—which describes the Commensality—"

"—to a tee!"

I buried my face in my hands. I felt a headache blooming. Voice muffled, I said, "Tell me about it again."

"Information has to breed—"

"—copulate in a way—"

"—to produce new information—"

"—more valuable than the old."

"But people are jealous of the information they possess—"

"—although Commensality sensibilities minimize jealousy in all other areas—"

"—yet no society's perfect."

"But anyway—"

"—individuals are selfish—"

"—because they feel others will profit more than they will if they share—"

"—which is probably correct—"

"—because we certainly profit—"

"—from the information we garner—"

"—and recombine—"

"—and sell—"

"—to Babylon itself—"

"—and anyone else who offers a fair price."

"So we're definitely not thieves—"

"—even though we have to resort to trickery—"

"—and craft—"

"—and guile—"

"—and wiles—"

"—to get people to share—"

"—what isn't doing them any good anyway hoarded up."

"No, our role is vital—"

"—because we synthesize—"

"—and synergize—"

"—collate—"

"—and collimate—"

"—anticipate—"

"—and aggregate—"

"Enough, enough!" I shouted. "You're not thieves. You're wonderful, civic-minded, essential people. Absolute saints. Even though I don't understand what you do."

Judy and Jezzie were kneeling by my side before I realized they had moved. Their breasts bookended my attention.

"Poor boy—"

"—don't worry—"

"—tomorrow we'll show you what we do—"

"—and right now—"

"—just to soothe you—"

"—we'll show you—"
"—we're not saints—"
"—by any stretch—"
"—of your—"
"—imag—"
"—i—"
"—na—"
"—tion."

    Much later, lying back downward on my mat with two armfuls of warm Babylonian information-bawds, I said, "Those hooves are sharp."

"We didn't hear you complaining—"

"—at the time."

"Well..." I figured I'd change the topic. "How come you like it so much when I touch that painted spot below your spine?"

"We thought you'd never ask."

"It marks a biofabbed erotic patch—"

"—with more nerve-endings—"

"—than another spot—"

"—you usually go for."

I was genuinely shocked. "That's, that's—"

"Wonderful?"

"Exciting?"

"Hedonistic?"

"Libidinous?"

    Realizing the hypocrisy of the condemnation I had been about to utter, after what I had just enjoyed, I refrained. Instead I slid both hands lower along parallel knobby spinal roadways.

"You mean all I have to do is this?"

"Oh—"

"—yes—"

"—just that—"

"—is fine!"

7.
interruption number three

The wall had absorbed the first half of what I had written, and my stick of charcoal was worn to a nub. I stopped to reach for a new one, and the Sisters jumped in.

"Well, the narrator is starting—"
"—to develop some character anyway."
"Even if he is—"
"—pretty tedious."
"But why don't you get down—"
"—to the brass tacks?"
"Namely, how we work."
"After all, it was our work—"
"—that got us into this mess with Babylon—"
"—where we know something so big—"
"—so stupendous—"
"—so monumental—"
"—that it could change the whole universe—"
"—and we can't even make any credit off it!"

Making no reply—I should let these two think they could dictate even my memoirs?—I resumed writing.

8.
working the city

I ran a finger along the inner rim of a biopolymer tub; it came up coated with gravy and I licked it clean. I didn't know what I had just eaten, but it had tasted great. Standing, I crossed the soft floor of the room the women had granted me as my own. The floor was warm and alive beneath my bare feet, but I was beginning not to mind mocklife so much. At least the non-sentient varieties. I still distrusted the purity and intelligibility of the motives of an enormous mass of paraneurons such as Babylon. Just thinking about being fitted with a TAP and entering into communication—however restrained and channeled by the user such an information flow might be—still gave me a queer, invaded feeling.

I came out into the room where Judy and Jezzie were waiting. The women were brushing out their pasterns and touching up their body swirls prior to setting out.

"Hey," I said, "thanks for bringing back breakfast."

Still dabbing and currying each other, the women replied:

"You're—"

"—welcome—"

"—even if it *is*—"

"—the biggest—"

"—most juvenile—"

"—stupidest—"

"—waste of time—"

"—we've *ever* participated in!"

"When are you going to accept—"

"—that if you want to live here—"

"—you have to behave—"

"—in certain matters—"

"—like everyone else?"

"Yeah!"

"Right!"

"And what's so distasteful—"

"—about the refectories—"

"—anyway?"

I glared at the two primping women. "Don't rush me. I'm trying my best, you know. Look." I lifted an unbooted foot and wiggled my toes. "I don't even mind walking around on this living floor anymore, do I? And I sleep on an organiform couch just like you. So I am changing. But these other things—" I shook my head. "I can't just toss myself into that, that food-orgy, like someone who was born here. And as for letting someone pump my brain full of nanodevices—no way."

Jezzie and Judy seemed to relent somewhat. Their moods were changeable as the colored patterns in the poisonous atmosphere beyond the dome, and I suspected that they were incapable of being angry at me for long, no matter what I did—or failed to do.

But sometimes I wondered if their quicksilver personalities also insured that their loyalty and interest in me were equally fluid.

"I suppose we should be glad—"

"—that in just a couple of weeks—"

"—you've gone from completely anti-em—"

"—to only two-thirds."

I thought about it. Mocklife, modifications (to the "human norm," that was), and miscegenation: the triple bugaboos of Conservancy thinking. I supposed I had loosened up a bit with regards to the first, and the second seemed within the bounds of possibility. But as for the third—

Unwilling even to think about it, I said, "Let's go. I'm anxious to see you two at work."

Several days had passed since the women had promised to show me how they operated as catalyst in the exchange and exfoliation of information. They had kept putting me off, however, saying that the timing wasn't just right yet.

This morning, though, they had announced that certain mysterious conditions—things they could only "feel"—were now propitious.

"All right," said Judy.

"But first—" added Jezzie.

"—we have to get you decorated."

"You're too conspicuous—"

"—as you are."

Before I could react, the Sisters had grabbed a pressurized bottle and begun to spray me from head to foot (I wore only shorts by now, my coverall having disintegrated under use.)

It was body paint, and it came out tartan plaid.

"How the—?" I began.

"Oh, Sandy, you dope."

"It's nanopaint—"

"—and assembles itself."

"Why the Conservancy bans this tek—"

"—we'll never know."

"Just 'cause a planet or two—"

"—went grey goo—"

"—before they perfected it—"

"—we suppose."

So, Judy and Jezzie having gotten every hair on heads and shanks into place, and me looking like a Truehome kilt, out we went, into the teeming streets of the capsuled city.

Babylon was shaped like a fat, blobby U that sprawled over many square kilometers. Enclosed by its arms was an inlet of the deep liquid methane ocean, whose tides—generated by the jovian hidden above—often lapped right against the dome. Jezzie and Judy lived a bit away from the city's center, along the bend of the U. Today, they set out down one of the arms.

I trotted behind my escorts, hanging back to marvel at the sights. The mix of sophonts still bewildered me, and I was constantly trying to make sense of the various ways in which the humans and nonhumans related.

As I still did from time to time, I looked around me for signs of minions of the Conservancy, come to haul me back to the cramped and constricted life I seldom thought about now. Even this reflex was dying in me. Reaching up to the two chops hung about my neck—coin and dragon—I fingered the last two tokens of my old life, and thought once more about discarding them. But it was so inbred in me never to let my chop out of my possession, that I still hesitated. As for the ambassador's device, I retained it more as a reminder of my guilt than of my liberty.

Ahead, the doubled hoofbeats of my guides on the syalon pavement sounded like a giant's four fingernails drummed regularly on a china plate.

We passed a null-gee natatorium, and I wished they would stop for a swim. Denied the communal showers in the refectories, I was forced to employ the natatoriums to freshen up. At least there one could swim unmolested, wearing a minimally decent outfit, and not worry about some scaled stegasoid offering to scrub one's back.

A springboard compressed beneath the weight of a man, then shot him upward, into the free-floating globe of water, where he cavorted with the other swimmers, all of whom wore the temporary gills that allowed them to utilize the hyper-oxygenated fluid. A few drops from the man's entry-point escaped the shaping and supporting fifth-force field and splattered the pavement below.

Watching the sporting swimmers, I bumped into the backs of the halted women.

Recovering, I saw that they had stopped to converse in low tones with a big smiling black man wearing a leather harness and little else. Before I even quite realized a conversation was going on, the man was saying, "So long, Sisters. Catch you later."

Then he was gone, and we were walking again. Now more interested in the doings of the women than the sights around me, I began to match my pace to theirs, both of them on one side, my left, the better to talk with them.

"Who was that?" I asked for openers.

"Meat—"

"—a real thief—"

"—the kind that relieves you of material possessions—"

"—but a good friend—"

"—who if you hadn't been with us—"

"—and you hadn't been so obviously bankrupt—"

"—would have stolen your rear molars—"

"—before you knew it."

"Meat—that's his real name?"

One of the women—Judy? Jezzie?—shrugged and, surprisingly, replied solo.

"It's what he goes by. Most people in the Commensality choose and alter their names whenever they feel like it. It's part of our notions about freedom."

I thought about the burdensome nomenclature I had discarded when I fled the dead man lying in the HT room in my father's mansion. Was the easy dismissal of my heritage one more sign that I was Commensality-inclined? But what about all the other confusing things I felt? Was I one thing only, or two, or many? It seemed impossible to decide.

So I said, "Are you two really sisters?"

"No—"

"—not by birth."

"Are you"—Sandy hesitated—"like, uh, clones?"

The sisters laughed, a duet that trilled back and forth.

"Why would the Commensality—"

"—bother with clones—"

"—when what we cherish—"

"—is diversity?"
"No, our genes—"
"—are heterogenous—"
"—as are our psyches—"
"—and it's only our facades—"
"—that are deliberately modified—"
"—to symbolize a tenet—"
"—of information theory—"
"—and perhaps to confuse—"
"—and thereby facilitate—"
"—our schemes."
"So we are sisters only—"
"—by inclination—"
"—and mutual temperament."

I pondered this paradox. "You got yourself altered because of some stupid theorem?"

"It's not a 'stupid theorem.'"
"It's the basis for what we do."
"When we told you earlier—"
"—that information has to breed—"
"—we didn't mention that the birth of new information—"
"—usually involves—"
"—the destruction of old information."
"For instance—"
"—take two plus two—"
"—equals four."
"The expression 'two plus two—'"
"—is information—"
"—and so is 'four.'"
"But if we just told you 'four—'"
"—you couldn't deduce whether it came—"
"—from 'three plus one—'"
"—or 'two plus two.'"
"The destruction of information happens—"
"—whenever two previously distinct facts or situations—"
"—become indistinguishable—"

"—subsumed in the new creation."

"Witness us—"

"—two distinct beings—"

"—now indistinguishable—"

"—one new fact."

I had gotten lost somewhere in the bilateral barrage. The sisters seemed to sense this, and abandoned their fusillade for a single-pronged attack.

"We know it's rather hard to comprehend, if you're not used to the concepts," said Judy or Jezzie. "But just watch what we do today, and maybe it'll make more sense."

I nodded acquiescence. We walked on further in silence, until I broke it.

"How come you didn't say what you wanted to say to Meat by TAP, instead of whispers?"

"Well, it's like this. Babylon is the intermediary in all communication via the TAP. Now, Babylon has certain responsibilities and duties, all governed by its basic biofabbed inhibitions relating to the freedom of us, its charges. One of Babylon's duties is to protect the Commensality, this outpost in particular. Any behavior that threatens our common stability—and such behavior is pretty rare, simply because there's not much an individual can do to undermine what amounts to practical anarchy—is frowned upon by Babylon. And so it tries to stop such things. Meat, I'm sorry to say, frequently indulges in certain practices, such as egregious theft, which Babylon finds contraproductive. So we don't discuss such things mentally. What we retain within our own skulls can't get to Babylon. And what Babylon doesn't know can't hurt us."

I sensed that the sister speaking had left something unsaid. Thinking of all the remote manipulators—mek and organic—Babylon operated, I asked, "What happens to those troublemakers Babylon catches?"

For a few seconds, the Sisters said nothing. Then, as if seeking refuge in mutuality again, they reverted to antiphonal response.

"They're cored—"

"—their higher brain centers removed—"

"—leaving just the stem—"

"—and a mass of paraneurons substituted—"

"—which puts Babylon in direct control—"

"—of the body—"

"—giving him another agent—"

"—to implement—"

"—his policies—"

"—for our own good."

"So if you ever spot—"

"—an individual—"

"—with no expression—"

"—deadfaces—"

"—you're confronting Babylon—"

"—itself."

I looked nervously around. Everything appeared different. A dimness or veil seemed to have occluded my sight. I thought it was a reaction to this new knowledge. Then I realized we had passed into Shadow. Looking up, I saw the floating mass of the Hanging Gardens, making its leisurely way over the rooftops and under the lights. I pressed closer to the women on my left, until I was almost in their nonexistent pockets, causing them to say:

"Hey—"

"—what do you—"

"—think we all are?"

"Siamese—"

"—triplets?"

Some few meandering meters on, one of the Sisters chose to disappear. At the door of a building they told me was a "sensorium," Judy—or Jezzie—went inside, leaving the other woman to wait in the street with me.

I was growing more and more curious about what was to happen, and so tried to pump my companion for more details, all the while tracking with half an eye the comings and goings of the various variegated and variform vessels of sentience who vanished through the doorless arch into the sensorium.

"Exactly who are you looking for?" I asked.

(A two-meter tall mantis, arms held prayerfully, saliva iridescing its mandibles, passed by us, and into the building.)

"Anyone who's just made the transition in from a world called Doradus," said Judy (or Jezzie).

"And how do you know that anyone has even come from there lately?"

"By checking with Babylon. One of the Commensality's principles, you see, is absolutely unimpeded access to public information. Anything that's not private knowledge—the results of someone's unique life-experiences—is available to whoever requests it. That's simultaneously one of the hallmarks and one of the causes of equality among individuals. Well, part of the public dataflow is arrivals and departures of sophonts into and out of Babylon. So just by TAPPING, we can learn if any individuals fulfilling our specs are here."

I considered this, suddenly wondering if the Sisters had learned of my arrival in the same way, and been waiting for me, for reasons I was as yet unable to fathom. Or was that being too paranoid? And exactly what degree of paranoia was too much?

Dismissing this issue, I said, "Okay. So you're interested in this world—Doradus?—for whatever reason. Why don't you just go there? Isn't that what our age is all about? Just picking up and taking off, when the urge strikes you?"

(A rubbery-faced neotenic newt-like biped sidled by, and tried to brush against me; I yanked away with quivering repugnance.)

"If we were interested in that world *qua* world, then sure, we'd go. But we're not. We just want to make a profit off it. And for that, all we need is accurate information about it. Now, the handy thing about information—in these days of hot heels and itchy feet—is that nine times out of ten, it'll come to you. Have you ever heard it said that the aggregate movements of individuals in our era resemble Brownian motion? Well, using that model, you realize that all particles—or people—eventually interact, and that a random, or even null, motion is as good as a planned course."

Trying to recall if I had ever heard my father speak of Doradus before, and why it might be so important, I asked, "What sector is this world in?"

Judy laughed. "How the hell should I know? All I have are its relativistic coordinates."

I grew a bit irked at Judy's careless quashing of my question. I was willing to compromise on a lot of things, but to others—maybe not even objectively the most important—I still held fast.

"I can't get over how you Commensality types refuse to assign a world to its proper stellar sector. At home, all I ever heard was talk of spheres of influence and contention, and how important it was to know where worlds were in relation to each other. Don't you have any holistic view of the universe?"

"And I can never comprehend why you Conservancy fossils still think imaginary lines in space are so important. You're so concerned with the galaxies that you can't see the stars, let alone the gigatrillions of sentients who flourish—despite your best efforts to deny them freedom—beneath those myriad suns."

I was about to reply hotly—whose freedom had I ever stifled, except perhaps my own?—**when** Jezzie came out.

She was accompanied by a woman much shorter than herself, whose skin was maculated rather like that of a Truehome giraffe: brick-colored irregular splotches on a clay-colored background.

Jezzie, guiding the stranger with a long arm around her waist, turned away from Judy and me. I was about to hail the returned sister when Judy clamped a hand over my mouth.

"If you had gotten a TAP when we asked you to, you'd know Jezzie doesn't want us to join her yet. We're supposed to follow at a distance."

Released, I lamely said, "Oh."

"Come on, then." Judy set off.

I followed, casting a last backward glance at the sensorium, wondering (but really knowing) what had transpired inside between Jezzie and the woman she now ambled hip-to-waist with down the crowded street. But did that mean that all those, those creatures—

(A sinuous feline sophont flicked his tail in my face, tickling my nose and making me jerk back.)

Judy was getting too far ahead, and I hurried to catch up.

For half an hour we followed the pair through the city. Eventually I said:

"Hey, how come you two never fly, and save on the legwork?"

"It discourages the close contact and mixing we need for our work. Did you ever try to strike up a casual verbal conversation in midair?"

I couldn't say that I ever had, the Conservancy not being too keen on unvehicled flight, as expressive of a kind of suspect abandon.

At last Jezzie and her companion came to a broad open paved plaza set among towers. They joined a queue. Judy and I held back, around a corner.

"Airbus stop for the Gardens," explained Judy. "For those like us, who don't care to fly unenclosed."

A bus set down, and the members of the queue filed forward.

"Now Jezzie's telling her she'd prefer to wait for the next bus, so they can be alone."

I didn't ask why.

A second bus came a minute later, before the two-person queue had acquired any new members.

Jezzie and her friend moved to board.

Judy urged, "Now! Run!"

She tugged me along with her.

We clip-clopped and foot-slapped across the plaza and tumbled into the bus just as its gullwing door shut and the craft lifted off.

I got a confused glimpse of the interior of the mek-piloted bus: white curved cushioned walls and overhead handholds, no seats. Then I focused on the three women.

Judy (or Jezzie) had the giraffe-patterned woman pinioned. The captive had time to say, "Hey! What's going on?" before the other Sister lowered her head toward the woman's chest.

What the Christ?, I thought. Was this some bizarre kind of rape?

As the Sisterly crown of frizzy black curls came level with the captive's neck, something stirred beneath the hair. I watched in utter amazement as what seemed to be a thin tendril whipped out and fastened itself for a moment on the third woman's neck before retreating beneath Jezzie's hair.

The bitten woman stiffened, eyes rolling up, then relaxed. Judy let her collapse gently to the floor. Jezzie bent over the victim and checked her pulse. After a few seconds, she seemed satisfied with the results of her attack. She spoke to the woman on the floor.

"You are one of the directors of the nuprene industry on Doradus. Is it true that you have a secret plan to switch to biopolymers?"

"Yes," said the woman in a drugged voice.

"You will forget the events of the last hour in their entirety," Jezzie commanded, apparently finished with her questioning.

The airbus docked with a bump at the Hanging Gardens. The whole trip of less than a minute was over.

The Sisters, effortlessly supporting the unconscious woman between them, exited; I followed. They dumped her unceremoniously behind a potted bush, and took the next bus down.

On the ground, I could contain myself no longer. I wanted to know what Jezzie had concealed in her hair, but more importantly, I couldn't figure out the desirability of what they had learned.

"You went to all that trouble and risk just to ask a question about the frigging plastics industry on some world halfway to nowhere?"

"That's—"

"—right."

"And we're not—"

"—done yet."

In the next three hours Judy and Jezzie pulled the same scam, *mutatis mutandis*, four more times, all on returned visitors from, or citizens of, Doradus, learning:

That one individual planned to market solo flight harnesses;

That hardly anyone followed the pronouncements of a certain syndicated commentator on interstellar affairs anymore;

That a group of extremists was campaigning for strict genetic mapping as a prerequisite for enfranchisement;

And that simple bodymods—nothing more radical than the giraffe woman's skin—were quite respectable.

After picking this last datum out of a man's mind, the Sisters retreated to a bench with a view of the Bay. While methane waves licked the dome wall, and a methane rain gently fell, they consulted, with me listening in amazement.

"If we add the switch—"

"—-to biopoly and harnesses—"

"—to the disbelief in—"

"—that grey eminence, whatsizname—"

"—and don't forget to include—"

"—the acceptance of mods—"

"—but we have to subtract—"

"—because of those extremists—"

"—then the secret's just as plain—"

"—as the sun in the sky—"

"—except of course—"

"—that you can't see—"

"—the sun from Babylon—"

"—unless you can penetrate the fog!"

I was beside myself. (Or could only the Sisters claim that?) "What is it? What's so obvious? Come on, tell me."

Jezzie and Judy seemed to be enjoying my confusion. Or perhaps they were only thrilled by what they had learned. They watched me struggle to decipher what they meant for a few seconds, then gave in to my importuning.

"Well, first you have to know—"

"—that Doradus is a neutral world—"

"—courted alike—"

"—by Conservancy and Commensality—"

"—and what we've discovered—"

"—by adding two plus two—"

"—to get four—"

"—is that with just a little push—"

"—Doradus is ready—"

"—to join the Commensality!"

I considered. I seemed to remember now some mention in the past by my father of this world. If what the Sisters said was true, he could see the value of this information.

I whistled. "Then you can sell this to—"

"—Babylon himself—"

"—who while you were slowly starting to understand—"

"—we already TAPPED—"

"—and who agreed to credit—"

"—our joint account—"

"—by a sum so big—"

"—that your eyes would pop—"

"—if we told you—"

"—and moreover—"

"—Babylon has already dispatched—"

"—messages to his fellow AOIs—"

"—who will now concentrate their efforts—"

"—to capture Doradus—"

"—for the side of the good guys."

I was stunned. "I'll be damned." There was nothing else I could say about what the Sisters had accomplished. Then I remembered my curiosity about the sisters' secret weapon, which I had confusedly witnessed in action five times.

"What did you use to knock out all those people?"

Lowering her head, one of the women reached up to part her thick nest of curls. I looked down, not really knowing what I expected to see.

Coiled flat up against her scalp were four inches of a snake thin as my little finger, whose rear portion fused imperceptibly into the woman's skin.

The snake hissed, tongue darting.

I started back, recalling the intimate times when I had sought to run my fingers through the Sisters' fuzzy polls and they had subtly pulled away.

"Just—"

"—call-"

"—us—"

"—Medusae."

Pulse pounding, I eyed them queerly. "Whatever you say, ladies. Whatever you say."

9.
instant experts

"We're so glad—"

"—to see you unbending—"

"—at least a little."

The Sisters and I sat in the Commensal room in our new living quarters. (Thanks to the profits from the Doradus information, they had been able to satisfy a long-standing dream of renting a suite in the single, high-status building that graced the Hanging Gardens with its faerie presence.)

The three of us were eating a meal together.

That simple statement astonished me almost more than anything else I had done or seen in Babylon.

Simply put, I had never done such a thing in the company of others before.

I guessed I was really changing, fitting into the Commensality. (Although thoughts of plunging into the refectory, which the Sisters still advocated, continued to fill me with horror. Mingling/feeding with clawed and furred and tailed nonhumans—It didn't even bear contemplation.)

Each day, it seemed, brought a new revelation about myself.

"Well, I'm glad too," I replied after swallowing. "I never would have done anything like this back home. Oh, sure, some people did. But they were the lower classes. Because of my father's status, I never could."

"Now all you need—"

"—to feel at home here—"

"—is a TAP."

I gave a negative shake of my head. "No, I'll get along all right without one. After all, they're just a gimmick. Basically, I can do all the really important things you two do."

One of the Sisters sipped at a drink, and the other said, "Oh, really?" Apropos of nothing, she added, "What was that designation of your homeworld?"

I reeled off the immutable Conservancy figures. "Why do you ask?"

The women had switched roles, she who had sipped now speaking. "No reason. Say, why don't you tell us a little more about your home. You never really have."

"Uh, okay, I guess." I settled back on my warm couch. "It's not a very special world, I suppose, except insofar as every world is. Just three continents—"

"Are you counting—"

"—Thone Island—"

"—which after all—"

"—is pretty damn big?"

I pretended not to notice their interruption, realizing now how they intended to goad me. "The population is small, but we were only recently discovered—"

"Three million, four hundred thousand, six hundred and seventy-nine—"

"—as of yesterday at noon—"

"—not counting bonded criminals—"

"—and it was discovered fifty years ago—"

"—by someone named—"

"—Jared Moten."

"I lived in Truehome City," I persevered, "and my father was—"

"—Conservator Sandyx—"

"—whose duties included—"

"—the management of worlds—"

"—four-seven-one-nine-zero-zero-three-eight—"

"—through sixty-four."

"And your brothers were named—"

"—Rolf and Heinrich—"

"Stop it! Okay, so you can think rings around me with a TAP, and I'm just a stupid puritan for not getting one. But the fact remains that my skull contains stuff you can never know unless I tell you, and if you're interested, you'll shut up and listen."

"Sorry—"

"—Sandy."

Mollified, I tried to relax. "Okay, no hard feelings." I brought my cup to my lips, drank, and said, "Commensals, right?"

"Commensals—"

"—indeed."

"Well, to continue. My life, because of my father's stature in the Conservancy, was regulated to the last detail. There was hardly anything I could do or even think for myself. I didn't mind it so much when I was a kid, but these last few years, it really got to me. I guess I was just ready to explode when—"

"Yes?"

"You can tell us, Sandy."

It all flooded back over me then, the emotions strong as when new, but I somehow managed to get it out.

"I was attended by a dozen bond-servants all the time. You completely core your worst criminals, but we just fit ours with mechanical overrides. It's the only kind of brain-modification the Conservancy permits. And wipe that argumentative look off your faces, 'cause I'm not about to be enticed into debating which treatment is more humane. Anyway, one or two were always by my side, more to keep an eye on me, I knew, than to really obey. Well, one day I managed to get alone for a few minutes. I went into our hypertext chamber and inserted an info-cache. That cache had been smuggled from offworld and cost me a month's allowance. It was all about Babylon.

"I never got to view it. This stranger arrived—a diplomat, I assume." I hefted the dragon-chop. "This is his. He walked in on me and saw what I was viewing. It burst on me that if he reported it to my father I was in deep trouble. Before I knew it, my hand fell on a brass statue of Founder Moten. I picked it up and, and—"

I flashed then on a detail that had escaped me till now: blood had covered the head of the statue in cruel mimicry of the blood on the diplomat's skull.

But the statue's skull, unlike the stranger's, was still intact.

For some reason that crummy little detail set me off.

I tried to hold back sobs I could have sworn I'd used up as I ran from my father's mansion and to the spaceport.

"Don't worry," said a Sister softly.

"You're here now."

But I still wasn't quite sure that being here was reason enough to feel good.

10.

interruption number four

The Sisters, growing tired of sitting still for the length of my narrative, were up and stretching in a series of exercises I recognized as kind of modified Truehome tai-chi while I rested my cramped fingers. Their movements failed to stem a flow of sarcastic comments.

"How touching."

"Cradled to our matronly bosoms."

"Maybe we should formally adopt you."

"Listen—"

"—finish this up."

"Don't string us along—"

"—much longer."

"There's a whole city out there—"

"—just waiting to be plucked."

"Who's the author here?" I asked. "Me or you?"

The Sisters froze.

"This city—"

"—has only one—""

"—real author—"

"—and that's—"

"—Babylon."

11.
meeting with a stoat

Soon came a time—both welcome and dreaded, happy and sad—when Babylon no longer looked so exotic to me, but instead merely seemed like the place where I lived. True, occasional actions and words—from the Sisters and others—still had the capacity to shock me, making me wonder if I really understood anything about Babylon and the Commensality at all. But on the whole, I felt integrated into the city hidden in the depths of the frigid sherbet-banded atmosphere.

So despite my continued adamant refusal to participate in the rituals enacted in refectory or sensorium, I prided myself on fitting in.

Staying clothed and fed in Babylon was no trouble, of course. Food the Sisters brought back with them from their trips to the refectories, sometimes sharing a meal with me, other times declining, having already eaten. When I needed new shorts, I just took them from the clothing distributories. My feet remained bare.

I was even coming closer and closer every day to getting a TAP.

Or so I told myself.

As for enjoying the luxuries Babylon offered, I relied on the generosity of Judy and Jezzie. They were always flush, and seemed quite willing to support me. I had given up trying to figure out why, and only at rare intervals did I suffer from paranoid fantasies about some devious, long-term scheme into which I meshed like a gear fashioned by the Sisters' cunning hands.

I chose to believe I contributed something to the Sisters' pleasure too, and that made me feel good.

I accompanied them on all their information-gathering exploits, and was always highly appreciative of their prowess.

When the Sisters picked up a bad case of hoof-rot (from the showers in the refectory, they claimed), I went with them to the infirmary and offered emotional support while the iatro-mek poked and daubed and epidermally perfused a variety of antibiotics.

And of course I tried to keep Jezzie and Judy sexually happy too. Because they sure met my needs. The things they knew—well, it just boggled the mind. My previous experiences had been confined to the rather uninspired performances of female bond-servants, whose lack of initiative was highly discouraging.

No such problem existed with the Sisters.

If anything, they were a tad too imaginative at times.

"Just move—"

"—like so—"

"—and let us—"

"—do this—"

"—while you—"

"—touch here—"

"—and here."

"Oh!"

"Oh!"

"Oh! I echoed.

And when you threw in early morning gambols in the natatoriums, why, everything seemed to be going just swimmingly.

Until the Sisters suddenly announced that a rival held something they wanted.

The three of us were walking through the streets of the city one day, when they brought it up.

"You know, of course—"

"—we're not the only ones—"

"—who do what we do."

I thought about it until I had convinced myself that I had really previously considered such a possibility.

"Sure," I said. "That only makes sense."

"Well, we've recently learned—"
"—that one of our peers—"
"—a little guy named Stoat—"
"—who looks like his namesake—"
"—and is just as mean—"
"—has uncovered some juicy information—"
"—that fits with a piece we've got—"
"—and we want it."
"Now, even with his piece and ours—"
"—the fabulous puzzle will still be incomplete—"
"—but at least we'll be one step closer."
"But here's the catch."
"We need your help—"
"—right now."

I said, "Me? Help you? Now? How could I? And with something so valuable. Is it worth more than, say, that Doradus information?"

"So much more—"
"—you wouldn't believe it."

I whistled. "What is it?"

"Partial relativistic coordinates—"
"—for a piece of string."

I waited for the punchline. When it didn't come, I said, "String?"

"What century—"
"—are you living in?"
"Look, you know—"
"—about monopoles?"

"Yeah, they're what Babylon gets its power from. Little pieces of the primordial universe, left over from the Big Bang."

"Very good. Then you'll understand—"
"—if we tell you—"
"—that cosmic string—"
"—is a larger, continuous portion—"
"—of the same Ur-stuff."
"A massive tube of spacetime—"
"—the six Planckian dimensions that are normally hidden in every particle—"

"—unrolled and revealed—"

"—in the form of a closed loop—"

"—a topological defect in our universe—"

"—where the basic symmetry—"

"—of the Monobloc prevails."

"And people will kill to discover—"

"—the location of such a remnant—"

"—although Jehovah only knows—"

"—what they'll do with it—"

"—since unlike a monopole—"

"—it's too massive to move—"

"—but want it they do—"

"—and we intend to be the ones—"

"—to sell it to the highest bidder."

"Why," I asked, "can't you just deduce the information the same way this guy Stoat did?"

One Sister alone chose to speak now, as if the two were growing tired of giving such a prolonged explanation, and wished I would just take what they said on faith.

"The components of his synthesis have dispersed, are no longer in Babylon. And there's no time to track them down, since Stoat, we've learned, is planning to depart Babylon today. What he did, if you're really interested, is to capitalize on a salient feature of string: its gravity. Your average piece of cosmic string holds approximately ten to the fifteenth solar masses. This concentration has the effect of acting as a gravitational lens, doubling the image of stars and galaxies behind it, all along its length. What Stoat did was to correlate many such sightings, thereby fixing the approximate location of the string."

"Why's he leaving?" I persisted.

"He's found a buyer offplanet, and is bringing the information directly to him."

"And why don't you just grab him and drug him and get the coordinates from him, like you usually do?"

"Jesus—"

"—can you believe—"

"—a game of twenty questions—"

"—when time is slipping away!"

"Listen, it's like this. Stoat doesn't consciously know the coordinates. What he did as a safeguard against just such an attack was to store them in Babylon—who is prevented from accessing them without the owner's permission, by the way—and then had them blanked from his own brain. So assaulting him prior to today would have gotten us nowhere. But now he's chosen to leave, and you know what that means."

"I do?"

"Whenever a Commensality citizen departs, presumably for another spot in our federation, he gets to withdraw all his private information out of his old AOI and take it with him, in the form of a mass of paraneurons in a little homeostatic container, which, at his destination, will be merged with the resident AOI, to become accessible once more. Stoat is carrying his container right now, and heading for the port."

I felt overwhelmed by this sudden flood of facts. "And my part would be—what?"

"Stoat's tough, and it's going to require both of us to take him. While we keep him busy, you grab his container and run."

I considered. How could I refuse?

"Okay," I finally agreed.

"Good—"

"—because there—"

"—he is."

I looked, saw a little thin man with a ruff of bristly fur running like a mohawk from the crest of his skull down his back to his buttocks. He moved hurriedly, cradling something in his arms, casting ferret-like glances from side to side.

"We're going to flank him. You stay off to one side till you see an opening."

I peeled away from the Sisters, who trotted up noisily behind Stoat. A few meters away, the women began to argue.

"You Appaloosa bitch!"

"You Palomino slut!"

"If you didn't look—"

"—just like me—"

"—I'd tell you—"

"—how grotesque you are!"

Stoat stopped. He opened his mouth to reveal a set of needle-teeth.

"Watch it, Sisters. Get out of my way."

"You keep out—"

"—of our argument."

"This is personal."

"Yeah!"

The Sisters were blocking Stoat's progress. He seemed uncertain of how to react. They began to feint at each other, long arms waving in a faux boxing match. Bystanders scattered.

Stoat moved to detour.

One of the women launched a high kick, seemingly for her Sister's jaw. In mid-motion she pivoted and her hoof headed for Stoat's gut.

The little man, still holding the silver egg that bore his memories, sprang like a weasel for the throat of the attacking Sister. She got her arm up barely in time for Stoat's teeth to fasten on it instead of her jugular.

The other Sister closed in. Still fastened to one yowling Sister's forearm, Stoat brought up a hand tipped with wicked claws and raked at the other woman.

The whole escapade had taken seconds, and left me dazed. When I saw Stoat's arm come up, I realized that left only one arm to hold the egg.

Bending low to avoid flailing limbs, I rushed in, wrested the egg from Stoat—

—and ran.

Half an hour later, I was in a part of the city I didn't know.

No one seemed to be after me.

When I had caught my breath, I oriented myself by certain predictable patterns in the sky, and headed home.

Jezzie and Judy were already there. They fell excitedly on me.

"What a tussle—"

"—with that little mink."

"But when he wakes up—"

"—he's not going to even remember—"

"—how he got snookered."

"My arm's still sore—"

"—and so's my face—"

"—but we don't think—"

"—the new skin will tear—"

"—if we celebrate!"

With that, they toppled me backward onto a couch, the precious egg dropping safely to the soft floor, and proceeded to have their way with me.

Which turned out to be just the treatment I needed for the jitters I hadn't even been aware I had.

Falling asleep in our warm pile, the Sisters began to muse lazily.

"If only we had—"

"—a few more sightings—"

"—we'd probably be able to pinpoint—"

"—that damn string."

"I feel like the necessary information is so close."

"Me too. It's our trustworthy—"

"—but imperfect—"

"—info-witches' intuition."

I rubbed my eyes sleepily. "What can we do?"

"Only one thing left," said Judy.

"A visit to the priestess—"

"—of Babylon—"

"—even though it'll wipe our credit balance—"

"—flatter than a worm on a neutron star."

"Oh, good," I mumbled, and fell asleep before I could even think to say:

Priestess?

12.

temple of bel

Eight tapering towers piled high atop each other, wrapped with a ramp around and around, the whole situated in the exact center of the city: that was the priestess's home. Striding up the corkscrew approach, I made the Sisters fill me in, solo style.

"The priestess," said Judy, "is a willing extension of Babylon. Not cored, she has agreed to maintain a constant, high-density transmission and realtime contact with our AOI, functioning as a unique input device. All her senses have been modified to a high degree, and she's gotten a host of new ones. For instance, she'll be naked to allow her lateral-lines—piscine—and infra-pits—viperine—full play. We'll tell her our situation, and she'll correlate it with all Babylon knows, while simultaneously picking up subliminal stuff we can't even register, right down to the quantum level. Then she'll give us her advice or prophecy."

"It's a very demanding job," said Jezzie, "and no one can do it too long. They say you're changed for life afterwards, even when Babylon gives up his contact. But it's a sinecure for the rest of your days. We've thought of volunteering when we get too old for this racket. In a hundred years or so."

I nodded as if I understood.

At last we reached the top level of the layer-cake temple. There was a single square doorless arch. We went inside.

I had expected a dark, incense-filled chamber. Instead, the room was lit up like a surgery. Seated on an organiform couch was the priestess. Her head was shaved, her eyes without pupils, a milky white. My own gaze seemed drawn down them, deep down to where Babylon dwelled, beneath the moon's surface.

She was the most awesome thing I had yet seen in Babylon. I couldn't even think of her as human.

The Sisters began their account, even their usual bravado noticeably shaken.

When they were finished, we waited.

After what seemed like eternity cubed, the priestess spoke.

Two words.

"Red dragon."

I was still trying to puzzle out the significance of the phrase when the Sisters knocked me to the floor with twin shrieks.

They grabbed at my neck, and pulled the ambassador's chop right off, breaking the chain and gouging the back of my neck.

"Of course!"

"What idiots!"

"It *was* right under our noses!"

I got to my feet, rubbing my sore neck. "You don't mean—"

"But we do! The Conservancy is looking for this string too."

"And your diplomat must have been bringing sightings to your father."

"But now they're ours—"

"—thanks to wonderful, wonderful Sandy."

"And if they're complementary to what we've got—"

"—which they almost have to be—"

"—then we'll know the coordinates for the string—"

"—and can sell it to Babylon—"

"—for the price of a planet!"

The priestess had sat silent through our display, unaffected by our merely human emotions. We left the temple then, and headed home.

I stopped on the way at an infirmary to get my sore neck attended to.

"We'll meet you home, Sandy—"

"—for more celebrating."

"Even extra special—"

"—this time."

At that moment, I didn't get what they meant.

Home again, I heard noises filtering down a corridor from the pleasureparlor.

I ambled down the dimly biolit hall. In the doorway, I stopped dead.

I couldn't untangle the scene at first. I flashbacked on my lone view of the refectory, so long ago. This was the same, but different.

Scaled limbs bisected expanses of pink flesh. Hooves dimpled tailed saurian haunches. Thighs occulted faces tongues unlike anything human lapped webbed feet braced for a thrust backs arched in pleasure wet engulfings hard lengths grunts cries growls teeth flashing aliens lying where once I no no no no—

"No!" I screamed.

And ran.

My destiny.

I came to myself at the lock leading to the spacefield. Still half crazy, I looked around for a nonliving suit, intending to get out to a ship and flee across as many galaxies as I could.

But nothing was available except quilts.

And I couldn't use them.

So I slumped down to the pavement, back against the dome wall, dropping my head in my hands. Jezebel and Judith, those witches, those whores of Babylon, seemed to have driven a spike right into my skull.

I strove to think around it.

Where was I going to go? Back to the Conservancy? I was totally unfitted for life there. To another Commensality world? I'd still have to face the same set of dilemmas as here. A neutral world, then. I'd go to a neutral world, a backwater where I could avoid choosing between these disparate star-sweeping ideologies that contended for an individual's soul nowadays.

But I knew this was impossible too. Because—damn it!—no matter where you fled today, anywhere else was just a blink away.

So I gave up thinking and began to cry.

After a while I realized someone was standing watching me.

I opened my swollen eyes.

I didn't see hooves.

So I looked up.

A nondescript human male stood beside me. His face was empty of any expression, like a world devoid of weather.

Deadface—

Moreover, he was the same man who had stopped me in my father's hall ages ago, and ordered me to fetch the ambassador's chop.

"Babylon," I whispered.

"Yes," said the cored one. "It's me. Look, just what do you think you're doing?"

I had expected any question but this. "What—I don't know what you mean."

"Running away, that's what I mean. When are you going to face up to reality? If you don't like what the Sisters did, confront them with it. They are what they are, the same as you. Running away won't change that. But it will lose you whatever you had."

I grunted with all the cynicism I could muster. "And what was that? The delusions of a pet."

"You know that's not true. Look at what just happened. Besides holding the final key to everything—not entirely accidentally, either—you played your part with Stoat. And very slick it was. I personally think you have a future in this business. Why don't you go back and work things out?"

"What's your stake in all this?" I demanded.

"Information is my lifeblood. And people like the Sisters help it breed. I try to keep them happy. You seem to be good for them. And they for you."

I thought. "I—I don't know."

Babylon shrugged stiffly. "You'll never find out by running away."

I got to my feet. Babylon stared at me wordlessly for a while, then said, "Don't decide now. Just come with me on one last excursion. You more or less have to anyway."

I had a hint of what he meant.

13.
the first chapter

Babylon had to clone the diplomat to use his chop. He dug out a few of the dead man's epidermal cells from a crevice in the dragon. When the mindless clone was fully force-grown (how creepy it felt to stare into the face of the man I had killed), the chop, keyed to the individual's unique bioaura, gave up its secrets.

Almost before I knew it, Ace—that was the old human name of Babylon's extension—the Sisters and I were in a special little ship. (They had had to carry me, quilt-wrapped, out the dome.) An instant later, we had made a transition halfway across the galaxy, to where the loop of string was located.

"Now," Ace explained without inflection, "in Riemannian space, the fourth dimension is obviously time, and we may travel along it in only one direction. In the vicinity of this string, with its extra six dimensions accessible, our latest theories inform us that we should be able to move backward along the temporal dimension."

"We are here to prove it."

The Sisters were huddled together in a cabin corner, feeling lost without their TAPS. I was in the opposite corner. We had had a big fight once reunited, and they weren't talking to me, nor I to them.

"This is crazy," I said. But all the time I really knew deep down it wasn't.

"What would you know, you archaic Conservator?" spat Judy.

"Yeah, you sexual fossil!" contributed Jezzie.

That got me mad. "For your information, you two bitches, I know where—I mean when—we're travelling to."

That seemed to floor them.

It was the first time I had ever done so.

Maybe I was learning something after all.

Ace moved to the boards and did something.

We moved along the six dimensions normally hidden inside your average electron. For a timeless eternity, the uncanny passage assaulted our senses horribly. Then the universe looked the same in the viewers. Next, Ace made a standard Heisenberg transition. After that—

Well, why should I belabor the obvious? We landed on my home planet. Concealed in capes and irksome boots, the Sisters passed for non-moddies as we passed through the city. My bare feet met with few stares in the summertime warmth. I provided ingress through the security perimeter around my home.

As soon as we were inside my father's mansion, Jezzie said, "These boots hurt, I'm taking them off." Judy followed suit.

Pretty soon the Sisters and I were standing behind the arras, peeking out through a slit.

I saw my younger self nearly run into Ace. The Sisters stifled their laughter. I must admit I did look cloddish, stupid and scared. It was hard to imagine that was really me. I had to keep reminding myself that I wasn't as dumb then—I mean now—as I looked.

Or had I been?

After Ace sent the early me back for the diplomat's chop, we came out from hiding, the Sisters resumed their disguises, and we returned to our ship.

At least I assumed we did, as we must have. I don't really remember much from the next few hours. I was too bewildered, deep in thought about my past and future.

Once more in the stellar neighborhood of our gateway back home, I finally returned to myself.

If someone without emotions could gloat, Ace was gloating. "This moves the struggle with the Conservancy onto a completely new level. We must make use of this temporal ability before they match us." He went off into deep thought.

The Sisters meanwhile eyed me speculatively from across the cabin. Finally, one spoke.

"Interesting times ahead, Sandy."

"Another mind and pair of hands is always welcome in our game."

"Seems a shame to break up a good team, just because of a little indiscretion."

"What do you say?"

I paused.

"TAP me for an answer when we get back home."

the scab's progress
(co-written with bruce sterling)

THE FEDERAL BIO-CONTAINMENT center was a diatom the size of the Disney Matterhorn. It perched on fractal struts in a particularly charmless district of Nevada, where the waterless white sands swarmed with toxic vermin.

The entomopter scissored its dragonfly wings, conveying Ribo Zombie above the desert wastes. This was always the best part of the program: the part where Ribo Zombie lovingly checked out all his cool new gear before launching himself into action. As a top-ranking scab from the otaku-pirate underground, Ribo Zombie owned reactive gloves with slashproof ligaments and sandwiched Kevlar-polysaccharide. He sported a mother-of-pearl crash helmet, hung with daring insouciance on the scaled wall of the 'mopter's cockpit. And those Nevada desert boots!—like something built by Tolkien orcs with day-jobs at Nike.

Accompanying the infamous RZ was his legendary and much-merchandised familiar, Skratchy Kat. Every scab owned a familiar: they were the totem animals of the gene-pirate scene. The custom dated back to the birth of the scab subculture, when tree-spiking Earth Firsters and obsessive dog breeders had jointly discovered the benefits of outlaw genetic engineering.

With a flash of emerald eyes the supercat rose from the armored lap of the daring scab. "Skratchy Kat" had some much cooler name in the Japanese collectors' market. He'd been designed in Tokyo, and was a deft Pocket-Monster co-mingling of eight spliced species of felines and viverines, with the look, the collector cachet, and—(judging by his stuffed-toy version)—plenty of the smell of a civet cat. Ribo Zombie, despite frequent on-screen cameos by busty-babe scab-groupies, had never enjoyed any steady feminine relationship. What true love there was in his life flowed between man and cat.

Clickable product-placement hot-tags preoccupied the 'mopter screens as Ribo Zombie's aircraft winged in for the kill. The ads sold magnums of cheap, post-Greenhouse Reykjavik Champagne. Ringside tix to a Celebrity Deathmatch (splatter-shields extra). Entomopter rentals in Vegas, with a rapid, low-cost divorce optional.

Then, wham! Inertia hit the settling aircraft, gypsum-sand flew like pulverized wallboard, and the entomopter's chitinous canopy accordioned open. Ribo Zombie vaulted to the glistening sands, clutching his cat to his armored bosom. He set the beast free with a brief, comradely exchange of meows, then sealed his facemask, pulled a monster pistol, and plucked a retro-chic pineapple grenade from his bandolier.

A pair of crystalline robot snakes fell to concussive explosions. Alluring vibrators disoriented the numerous toxic scorpions in the vicinity. Three snarling jackalopes fell to a well-aimed hail of dumdums. Meanwhile the dauntless cat, whose hide beneath fluffy fur was as tough as industrial teflon, had found a way through the first hedge-barrier of barrel cacti.

The pair entered a maze of cholla. The famously vicious Southwestern cholla cactus, whose sausage-link segments bore thorns the size of fishhooks, had been rumored from time immemorial to leap free from sheer spite and stab travelers. A *soupcon* of Venus Flytrap genes had turned this Pecos Pete tall-tale vaporware into grisly functionality. Ribo Zombie had to opt for brute force: the steely wand of a back-mounted flamethrower leapt into his wiry combat-gloves. Ignited in a pupil-searing blast, the flaming mutant cholla whipped and flopped like epileptic spaghetti. Then RZ and the faithful Skratchy were clambering up the limestone leg of the Federal cache.

Anyone who had gotten this far could be justly exposed to the worst and most glamorous gizmos ever cooked up by the Softwar Department's Counter-Bioterrorism Corps.

The ducts of the diatom structure yawned open and deployed a lethal arsenal of spore-grenade launchers, strangling vegetable bolas, and whole glittering clouds of hotwired fleas and mosquitoes. Any scab worth his yeast knew that those insect vectors were stuffed to bursting with swift and ghastly illnesses, pneumonic plague and necrotizing fasciitis among the friendlier ones.

"This must be the part where the cat saves him," said Tupper McClanahan, all cozy in her throw-rug on her end of the couch.

Startled out of his absorption, yet patiently indulgent, Fearon McClanahan froze the screen with a tapped command to the petcocks on the feedlines. "What was that, darling? I thought you were reading."

"I was." Smiling, Tupper held up a vintage *Swamp Thing* comic that had cost fully ten percent of one month's trustfund check. "But I always enjoy the parts of this show that feature the cat. Remember when we clicked on those high-protein kitty treats, during last week's cat sequence? Weeble loved those things."

Fearon looked down from the ergonomic couch to the spotless bulk of his snoring pig, Weeble. Weeble had outgrown the size and weight described in his documentation, but he made a fine hassock.

"Weeble loves anything we feed him. His omnivorous nature is part of his factory specs, remember? I told you we'd save a ton on garbage bills."

"Sweetie, I never complain about Weeble. Weeble is your familiar, so Weeble is fine. I've only observed that it might be a good idea if we got a bigger place."

Fearon disliked being interrupted while viewing his favorite outlaw stealth download. He positively squirmed whenever Tupper sneakily angled around the subject of a new place with more room. More room meant a nursery. And a nursery meant a child. Fearon swerved to a change of topic.

"How can you expect Skratchy Kat to get Ribo Zombie out of this fix? Do you have any idea what those flying bolas do to human flesh?"

"The cat gets him out of trouble every time. Kids love that cat."

"Look, honey: kids are not the target demographic. This show isn't studio-greenlighted or even indie-syndicated, okay? You know as well as I do that this is *outlaw media*. Totally underground guerrilla infotainment, virally distributed. There are laws on the books—unenforced, sure, but still extant—that make it illegal for us even to watch this thing. After all, Ribo Zombie is a biological terrorist who's robbing a Federal stash!"

"If it's not a kid's show, why is that cute little cartoon in the corner of the screen?"

"That's his graffiti icon! That's the sign of his street-wise authenticity."

Tupper gazed at him with limpid spousal pity. "Then who edits all his raw footage and adds the special effects?"

"Oh, well, that's just the Vegas Mafia. The Mafia keeps up with modern times: no more Ratpack crooners and gangsta rappers! Nowadays they cut licensing deals with freeware culture heroes like Ribo Zombie, lone wolf recombinants bent on bringing hot goo to the masses."

Tupper waved her comic as a visual aid. "I still bet the cat's gonna save him. Because none of that makes any difference to the archetypical narrative dynamics."

Fearon sighed. He opened a new window on his gelatinous screen and accessed certain data. "Okay, look. You know what runs security on Federal Biosequestration Sites like that one? Military-grade, laminated, mouse-brain. You know how *smart* that stuff is? A couple of cubic inches of murine brain has more processing power than every computer ever deployed in the twentieth century. Plus, mouse-brain is unhackable. Computer viruses, no problem. Electromagnetic pulse doesn't affect it. No power source to disrupt, since neurons run on blood sugar. That stuff is indestructible."

Tupper shrugged. "Just turn your show back on."

Skratchy was poised at a vulnerable crack in the diatom's roof. The cat began copiously to pee.

When the trickling urine reached the olfactory sensors wired to the mouse brains, the controlling network went berserk. Ancient murine antipredator instincts swamped the cybernetic instructions, triggering terrified flight responses. Mis-aimed spore bomblets thudded harmlessly to the soil, whizzing bolas wreaked havoc through the innocent vegetation below, and vent ports spewed contaminated steam and liquid nitrogen.

Cursing the zany but dangerous fusillade, Ribo Zombie set to work with a back-mounted hydraulic can-opener.

Glum and silent, Fearon gripped his jaw. His hooded eyes glazed over as Ribo Zombie crept through surreal diorama of waist-high wells, HVAC systems and plumbing. Every flick of Ribo Zombie's hand-torch revealed a glimpse of some new and unspeakable mutant wonder, half concealed in ambient support fluids: yellow gruel, jade-colored hair gel, blue oatmeal, ruby maple syrup . . .

"Oh, honey," said Tupper at last, "don't take it so hard."

"You were right," Fearon grumbled. His voice rose. "Is that what you want me to say? You were right! You're always right!"

"It's just my skill with semiotic touchstones that I've derived from years of reading graphic novels. But look, dear, here's the part you always love, when he finally lays his hands on the wetware. Honey, look at him stealing that weird cantaloupe with the big throbbing arteries on it. Now he'll go back to his clottage and clump, just like he does every episode, and sooner or later, something really uptaking and neoteric will show up on your favorite auction site."

"Like I couldn't brew up stuff twice as potent myself."

"Of course you could, dear. Especially now, since we can afford the best equipment. With my inheritance kicking in, we can devote your dad's legacy to your hobby. All that stock your dad left can go straight to your hardware fetish, while my money allows us to ditch this creepy old condo and buy a new modern house. Duckback roof, slowglass windows, olivine patio—" Tupper sighed deeply and dramatically. "Real quality, Fearon."

Predictably, Malvern Brakhage showed up at their doorstep in the company of disaster.

"Rogue mitosis, Fearon my man. They've shut down Mixogen and called out the HazMat Squad."

"You're kidding? Mixogen? I thought they followed code."

"Hell no! The outbreak's all over downtown. Just thought I'd drop by for a newsy look at your high-bandwidth feed."

Fearon gazed with no small disdain on the bullet-headed fellow scab. Malvern had the thin fixed grin of a live medical student in a room full of cadavers. He wore his customary black-leather labcoat and baggy cargo pants, their buttoned pockets bulging with ziploc baggies of semi-legal jello.

"It's Malvern!" he yelled at the kitchen, where Tupper was leafing through catalogues.

"How about some nutriceuticals?" said Malvern alertly. "Our mental edges require immediate sharpening." Malvern pulled his slumbering weasel, Spike, from a labcoat pocket and set it on his shoulder. The weasel—biotechnically speaking, Spike was mostly an ermine—immediately became the nicest-looking thing about the man. Spike's lustrous fur gave Malvern the dashing air of a Renaissance Prince, if you recalled that Renaissance Princes were mostly unprincipled bush-league tyrants who would poison anyone within reach.

Malvern ambled hungrily into the kitchen.

"How have you been, Malvern?" said Tupper brightly.

"I'm great, babe." Malvern pulled a clamp-topped German beer bottle from his jacket. "You up for a nice warm brewski?"

"Don't drink that," Fearon warned his wife.

"Brewed it personally," said Malvern, hurt. "I'll just leave it here in the kitchen in case you change your mind." Malvern plonked the heavy bottle onto the scarred formica.

Tupper, who had been well-brought up, gave Malvern the admiring glance that her kindly stratum of society reserved for all charmingly transgressive dissidents. Fearon remembered when he, too, had received adoring looks from Tupper—as a bright idealist who understood the true, liberating potential of biotech, an underground scholar who bowed to none in his arcane mastery of plasmid vectors. Unlike Malvern, whose scab popularity was mostly due to his lack of squeamishness.

Malvern was louche and farouche, so, as was his wont, he began looting Tupper's kitchen fridge. "Liberty's gutters are crawling!" Malvern declaimed, fingersnapping a bit to suit his with-it scab-rap. "It's a bug-crash of awesome proportions, and I urge forthwith we reap some peptides from the meltdown."

"Time spent in reconnaissance is never wasted," countered Fearon. He herded the unmannerly scab back to the parlor.

With deft stabs of his carpalled fingertips, Fearon used the parlor wallscreen to access *Fusing Nuclei*—the all-biomed news site favored by the happening hipsters of scabdom.

Tupper, pillar-of-support that she was, soon slid in with a bounty of hotwired snackfood. Instinctively, both men shared with their familiars, Fearon dropping creamy tidbits to his pig while Malvern reached salty gobbets up and back to his neck-hugging weasel.

Shoulder to shoulder on the parlor couch, Malvern and Fearon fixed their jittering attention on the unfolding urban catastrophe.

The living pixels in the electrojelly cohered into the familiar image of Wet Willie, FN's star business-reporter. Wet Willie, dashingly clad in his customary splatterproof trenchcoat, had framed himself in the shot of a residential Miami skyscraper. The pastel Neo-Deco walls were sheathed in pearly slime. Wriggling like a nautch dancer, the thick, undulating goo gleamed in Florida's Greenhouse sunlight. Local bystanders congregated in their flowered shirts, sun-hats and sandals, gawking from outside the crowd-control pylons. The tainted skyscraper was under careful attack by truck-mounted glorp cannons, their nozzles channeling high-pressure fingers against the slimy pink walls.

"That's a major outbreak all right," said Fearon. "Since whenwise was Liberty City clearstanced for wet production?"

"As if," chuckled Malvern.

Wet Willie was killing network lagtime with a patch of infodump. "Liberty City was once an impoverished slum. That was before Miami urbstanced into the liveliest nexus of the modern Immunossance, fueled by low-rent but ingenious Caribbean bioneers. When super-immune systems became the hottest somatic upgrade since osteojolt, Liberty City upgraded into today's thriving district of artlofts and hotshops.

"But today that immuconomic quality-of-life is threatened! The ninth floor of this building houses a startup named Mixogen. The cause of this rampaging outbreak remains speculative, except that the fearsome name of Ribo Zombie is already whispered by knowing insiders."

"I might have known," grunted Malvern.

Fearon clicked the RZ hotlink. Ribo Zombie's ninja-masked publicity photo appeared on the network's vanity page. "Ribo Zombie, the Legendary King of scabs—whose thrilling *sub rosa* exploits are brought to you each week by *Fusing Nuclei*, in strict accordance with the revised Freedom of Information Act and without legal or ethical endorsement! *Click Here* to join the growing horde of cutting-edge bioneers who enjoy weekly shipments of his liberated specimens direct to their small office/home office wetwarelabs . . ."

Fearon valved off the nutrient flowline to the screen and stood abruptly up, spooking the sensitive Weeble. "That showboating scumbag! You'd think he'd invented scabbing! I hate him! Let's scramble, Mal."

"Yo!" concurred Malvern, "let's bail forthwith, and bag something hot from the slop."

Fearon assembled his scab gear from closets and shelves throughout the small apartment, Weeble loyally dogging his heels. The process took some time, since a scab's top-end hardware determined his peer-ranking in the demimonde of scabdom (a peer ranking stored by retrovirus, then collated globally by swapping saliva-laden tabs of blotter paper).

Devoted years of feral genetic hobbyism had brought Fearon a veritable galaxy of condoms, shrinkwrap, blotter kits, polymer resins, phase gels, reagents, femto-injectors, serum vials, canisters, aerosols, splat-pistols, whole bandoliers of buckybombs, padded cases, gloves, goggles, netting, cameras, tubes, dispensing cylinders of pliofilm—the whole assemblage tucked with a fly-fisherman's neurotic care into an intricate system of packs, satchels and strap-ons.

Tupper watched silently, her expression neutral shading to displeased. Even the dense and tactless Malvern could sense the marital tension.

"Lemme boot-up my car. Meet you behind the wheel, Fearo my pard."

Tupper accompanied Fearon to the apartment door, still saying nothing as her man clicked together disassembled instruments, untelescoped his sampling staff, tightened buckles across chest and hips, and mated sticky-backed equipment to special patches on his vest and splashproof chaps.

Rigged out to his satisfaction, Fearon leaned in for a farewell kiss. Tupper merely offered her cheek.

"Aw, come on, honey, don't that-way be! You know a man's gotta follow his bliss: which in my special case is a raw, hairy-eyed lifestyle on the bleeding edge of the genetic frontier."

"Fearon McClanahan, if you come back smeared with colloid, you're not setting one foot onto my clean rug."

"I'll really wash-up this time, I promise."

"And pick up some fresh goat-milk prestogurt!"

"I'm with the sequence."

Fearon dashed and clattered down the stairs, his neutraceutically deviated mind already filled with plans and anticipations. Weeble barreled behind.

Malvern's algal-powered roadster sat by the curb, its fuelcell thrumming. Malvern emptied the tapering trunk, converting it into an open-air rumble seat for Weeble, who bounded in like a jet-propelled fifty-liter drum. The weasel Spike occupied a crash-hammock slung behind the driver's seat. Fearon wedged himself into the passenger's seat, and they were off with a pale electric scream.

After shattering a random variety of Miami traffic laws, the two scabs departed Malvern's street-smart vehicle, to creep and skulk the last two blocks to the ongoing bio-chernobyl. The federal swab authorities had thrown their usual cordon in place, enough to halt the influx of civilian lookyloos, but penetrating the perimeter was child's play for well-equipped scabs. Fearon and Malvern simply sprayed themselves and their lab-animals with chameleon-shifting shrinkwrap, then strolled through the impotent ring of ultrasonic pylons. They then crept through the shattered glass, found the code-obligatory wheelchair access, and laboriously sneaked up to the ninth floor.

"Well, we're inside just finewise," said Fearon, puffing for breath through the shredded shrinkwrap on his lips.

Malvern alertly helped himself to a secretary's abandoned lunch. "Better check *Fusing Nuclei* for word on the fates of our rivals."

Fearon consulted his handheld. "They just collared Harry the Brewer. 'Impersonating a Disease-Control Officer.'"

"What a lack of gusto panache-wise. That guy's just not serious."

Malvern peered down streetward through a goo-dripping window. The glorp cannon salvos had been supplemented by strafing ornithopter runs of uptake-inhibitors and counter-metabolizers. The battling federal defenders of humanity's physiological integrity were using combined-arms tactics. Clearly the forces of law-and-order were sensing victory. They usually did.

"How much of this hot glop you think we ought to kipe?" Malvern asked.

"Well, all of it. Everything Weeble can eat."

"You don't mind risking ol' Weeble?"

"He's not a pig for nothingwise, you know. Besides, I just upgraded his digestive tract." Fearon scratched the pig affectionately.

Malvern velcro'ed his weasel Spike into the animal's crittercam. The weasel eagerly scampered off on point, as Malvern offered remote guidance and surveillance with his handheld.

"Out-of-Control Kevin uses video bees," remarked Fearon, as they trudged forward with a rattle of sampling equipment. "Little teensy cameras mounted on their teensy insect backs. It's an emergent network phenomenon, he says."

"That's just Oldstyle Silicon Valley," Malvern dismissed. "Besides, a weasel never gets sucked into a jet engine."

The well-trained Spike had nailed the target, and the outlaw wetware was fizzing like cheap champagne. It was a wonder that the floor of the high-rise had withstood the sheer weight of criminal mischief. Mixogen was no mere R&D lab. It was a full-scale production facility. Some ingenious soul had purchased the junked remains of an Orlando aquasport resort, all the pumps, slides and waterpark sprinklers. Kiddie wading pools had been retrofitted with big gooey glaciers of serum support gel. The plastic fish-tanks were filled to overflowing with raw biomass. Metastasizing cells had backed up into the genetic moonshine somehow, causing a violent bloom and a methane explosion, as frothy as lemon meringue. The animal stench was indescribable.

"What stale hell is this?" said Malvern, gaping at a broken tub that brimmed with a demonic assemblage of horns, hoofs, hide, fur, and dewclaws.

"I take that to be widely variegated forms of mammalian epidermal expression." Fearon restrained his pig with difficulty. The rotting smell of the monstrous meat had triggered Weeble's appetite.

"Do I look like I was born yesterday?" snorted Malvern. "You're point-missing me. Nobody can maintain a hybridoma with that gross level of genetic variety! Nothing with *horns* ever has *talons*! Ungulates and felines don't even have the same chromosome number."

Window-plastic shattered. A wall-crawling police robot broke into the genetic speakeasy. It closed its gecko feet with a sound like venetian blinds, and deployed a bristling panoply of lenses and spigots.

"Amscray," Malvern suggested. The duo and their animal familiars retreated from the swab machine's clumsy surveillance. In their absence came a loud frosty hiss as the police bot unleashed a sterilizing fog of Bose-Einstein condensate.

A new scent had Spike's attention, and it set Malvern off at a trot. They entered an office warren of glassblock and steel.

The Mixogen executive had died at her post. She sprawled before her desktop in her ergonomic chair, still in her business suit but reeking of musk and decay. Her swollen, veiny head was the size of a peach basket.

Fearon closed his dropped jaw and zipped up his Kevlar vest. "Jeez, Malvern, another entrepreneur-related fatality! How high do you think her SAT got before she blew?"

"Aw, man—she must have been *totally* off the IQ scale. Look at the size of her frontal lobes. She's like a six-pack of Wittgensteins."

Malvern shuddered as Spike the weasel tunneled to safety up his pantsleg. Fearon wiped the sweat from his own pulsing forehead. The stench of the rot was making his head swim. It was certainly good to know that his fully-modern immune system would never allow a bacteria or virus to live in his body without his permission.

Malvern crept closer, clicking flash-shots from his digicam. "Check out that hair on her legs and feet."

"I've heard about this," marvelled Fearon. "Bonobo hybridoma. She's half chimp! Because that super-neural technique requires . . . so they say . . . a tactical retreat down the primate ladder, before you can make that tremendous evolutionary rush for breakthrough extropian intelligence." He broke off short as he saw Weeble eagerly licking the drippy pool of ooze below the dead woman's chair. "Knock it off, Weeble!"

"Where'd the stiff get the stuff?"

"I'm as eager to know that as you are, so I'd suggest swiping her desktop," said Fearon craftily. "Not only would this seriously retard police investigation, but absconding with the criminal evidence would likely shelter many colleagues in the scab underground, who might be righteously grateful to us, and therefore boost our rankings."

"Excellent tactics, my man!" said Malvern, punching his fist in his open palm. "So let's just fall to sampling, shall we? How many stomachs is Weeble packing now?"

"Five, in addition to his baseline digestive one."

"Man, if I had your kind of money . . . Okay, lemme see . . . Cut a tendril from that kinesthetically active goo, snatch a sample from that wading-pool of sushi-barf—and, whoa, check the widget that the babe here is clutching hand-wise."

From one contorted corpse-mitt peeked a gel-based pocket-lab. Malvern popped the datastorage and slipped the honey-colored hockey puck into his capacious scabbing vest. With a murmured apology, Fearon pressed the tip of his sampling-staff to the woman's bloated skull, and pneumatically shot a tracer into the proper cortical depths. Weeble fastidiously chomped the mass of gray cells. The prize slid safe into the pig's gullet, behind a closing gastric valve.

They triumphantly skulked from the reeking, cracking high-rise, deftly avoiding police surveillance and nasty street-spatters of gutter-goo. Malvern's getaway car rushed obediently to meet them. While Malvern slid through traffic, Fearon dispensed reward treats to the happy Spike and Weeble.

"Mal, you set to work dredging that gel-drive, okay? I'll load all these tissue samples into my code-crackers. I should have some preliminary results for us by, uhm . . . well, a week or so."

"Yeah, that's what you promised when we scored that hot jellyfish from those Rasta scabs in Key West."

"Hey, they used protein-encrypted gattaca! There was nothing I could do about that."

"You're always hanging fire after the coup, Fearon. If you can't unzip some heavy-duty DNA in your chintzy little bedroom lab, then let's find a man who can."

Fearon set his sturdy jaw. "Are you implying that I lack biotechnical potency?"

"Maybe you're getting there. But you're still no match for old Kemp Kingseed. He's a fossil, but he's still got the juice."

"Look, there's a MarthaMart!" Fearon parried.

They wheeled with a screech of tires into the mylar lot around the MarthaMart, and handed the car to the bunny-suited attendant. The men and their animals made extensive use of the fully-shielded privacy of the decon chambers. All four beings soon emerged as innocent of contaminants as virgin latex.

"Thank goodness for the local franchise of the goddess of perfection," said Fearon contentedly. "Tupper will have no cause to complain of my task-consequent domestic disorder! Wait a minute—I think she wanted me to buy something."

They entered the brick-and-mortar retail floor of the MarthaMart,

Fearon racking his enhanced memory for Tupper's instructions, but to no avail. In the end he loaded his wiry shopping basket with pop bottles, gloop cans, some recycled squip and a spare vial of oven-cleaning bugs.

The two scabs rode home pensively. Malvern motored off to his scuzzy bachelor digs, leaving Fearon to trudge with spousal anxiety upstairs. What a bringdown from the heights of scab achievement, this husbandly failure.

Fearon faced an expectant Tupper as he reached the landing. Dismally, he handed over the shopping bag. "Here you go. Whatever it was you wanted, I'm sure I didn't buy it." Then he brightened. "Got some primo mutant brain-mass in the pig's innards, though."

Five days later, Fearon faced an irate Malvern. Fearon hedged and backfilled for half an hour, displaying histo-printouts, some scanning-microscope cinema, even some corny artificial-life simulations.

Malvern examined the bloodstained end of his ivory toothpick. "Face defeat, Fearon. That bolus in the feedline was just pfisteria. The tendril is an everyday hybridoma of liana, earthworm and slimemold. As for the sushi puke, it's just the usual chemosynthetic complex of abyssal tubeworms. So cut chase-wise, pard. What's with those explosively ultra-smart cortical cells?"

"Okay, I admit it, you're right, I'm screwed. I can't make any sense of them at all. Wildly oscillating expression-inhibition loops, silent genes, jumping genes, junk DNA that suddenly reconfigures itself and takes control—I've never seen such a stew. It reads like a Martian road-map."

Malvern squinched his batrachian eyes. "A confession of true scabbing lame-itude. Pasting a 'Kick-me, I'm blind' sign on your back. Have I correctly summarized your utter wussiness?"

Fearon kept his temper. "Look, as long as we're both discreet about our little adventure downtown, we're not risking any of our vital reputation in the rough-and-tumble process of scab peer-review."

"You've wasted five precious days in which Ribo Zombie might radically beat us punchwise! If this news gets out, your league standings will fall quicker than an Italian government." Malvern groaned theatrically. "Do you know how long it's been since my groundbreaking investigative fieldwork was properly acknowledged? I can't even *buy* a citation."

Fearon's anger transmuted to embarrassment. "You'll get your quotes and footnotes, Malvern. I'll just shotgun those genetics to bits, and subcontract the sequences around the globe. Then no single individual will get enough of the big picture to know what we've been working on."

Malvern tugged irritably at the taut plastic wrapper of a Pynchonian British toffee. "Man, you've completely lost your edge! Everybody is just a synapse away from everybody else these days! If you hire a bunch of scabs on the net, they'll just search-engine each other out, and patch everything back together. It's high time we consulted Dr. Kingseed."

"Oh, Malvern, I hate asking Kemp for favors. He's such a bringdown billjoy when it comes to hot breakthrough technologies! Besides, he always treats me like I'm some website intern from the days of Internet slave labor."

"Quit whining. This is serious work."

"Plus, that cobwebby decor in Kemp's retrofunky domicile! All those ultra-rotten Hirst assemblages—they'd creep anybody out."

Malvern sighed. "You never talked this way before you got married."

Fearon waved a hand at Tupper's tasteful wallpaper. "Can I help it if I now grok interior decor?"

"Let's face some facts, my man: Dr. Kemp Kingseed has the orthogonal genius of the primeval hacker. After all, his startup companies pushed the Immunosance past its original tipping point. Tell the missus we're heading out, and let's scramble headlong for the Next New Thing like all true-blue scabs must do."

Tupper was busy in her tiny office at her own career, moderating her virtual agora on twentieth-century graphic narrative. She accepted Fearon's news with only half her attention. "Have fun, dear." She returned to her webcam. "Now, Kirbybuff, could you please clarify your thesis on Tintin and Snowy as precursor culture-heroes of the Immunosance?"

Weeble and Malvern, Spike and Fearon, sought out an abandoned petroleum distribution facility down by the waterfront. Always the financial bottom-feeder, the canny Kemp Kingseed had snapped up the wrecked facility after the abject collapse of the fossil-fuel industry. At one point in his checkered career, the reclusive hermit-genius had tried to turn the maze of steampipes and rusting storage tanks into a child-friendly industrial-heritage theme park. Legal problems had undercut his project, leaving the aged digital entrepreneur haunting the ruins of yet another vast, collapsed scheme.

An enormous spiderweb, its sticky threads thick as supertanker hawsers, hung over the rusting tanks like some Victorian antimacassar of the gods.

Malvern examined the unstable tangle of spidery cables. "We'd better leave Weeble down here."

"But I never, ever want to leave dear Weeble!"

"Just paste a crittercam on him and have him patrol for us on point." Malvern looked at the pig critically. "He sure looks green around the gills since he ate that chick's brain. You sure he's okay digestive-wise?"

"Weeble is fine. He's some pig."

The visitors began their climb. Halfway up the tank's curving wall, Kemp Kingseed's familiar, Shelob, scuttled from her lair in the black pipe of a giant smokestack. She was a spider as big as a walrus. The ghastly arachnid reeked of vinegar.

"It's those big corny spider-legs," said Malvern, hiding his visceral fear in a thin shroud of scientific objectivity. "You'd think old Kingseed had never heard of the cube-square law!"

"Huh?" grunted Fearon, clinging to a sticky cable.

"Look, the proportions go all wrong if you blow them up a thousand times life-size. For one thing, insects breathe through spiracles! Insects don't have lungs. An insect as big as a walrus couldn't even breathe!"

"Arachnids aren't insects, Malvern."

"It's just a big robot with some cheap spider chitin grown on it. That's the only explanation that makes rational sense."

The unspeakable monster retreated to her lair, and the climbers moved thankfully on.

Kemp Kingseed's lab was a giant hornet's nest. The big papery office had been grown inside a giant empty fuel tank. Kingseed had always resented the skyrocketing publication costs in academic research. So he had cut to the chase, and built his entire laboratory out of mulched back issues of *Cell* and *Nature Genomics*.

Kingseed had enormous lamp-goggle eyeglasses, tufts of snowy hair on his skull, and impressive white bristles in his withered ears. The ancient Internet mogul still wore his time-honored Versace labcoat, over baggy green ripstop pants and rotting Chuck Taylor hightops.

"Africa," he told them, after examining their swiped goodies.

"'Africa?'"

"I never thought I'd see those sequences again." Kingseed removed his swimmy lenses to dab at his moist red eyes with a swatch of lab paper. "Those were our heroic days. The world's most advanced technicians, fighting for the planet's environmental survival! Of course we completely failed, and the planet's ecosystem totally collapsed. But at least we didn't suck up to politicians."

Kingseed looked at them sharply. "Lousy, fake-rebel pimps like that Ribo Zombie, turned into big phony pop stars. Why, in *my* generation, we were the *real, authentic* transgressive-dissident pop stars! Napster . . . Free net . . . GNU/Linux . . . Man, that was the stuff!"

Kingseed beat vaguely at the air with his wrinkled fist. "Well, when the Greenhouse started really cooking us, we had to invent the Immunosance. We had no choice at that point, because it was the only way to survive. But every hideous thing we did to save the planet was totally UN-approved! Big swarms of rich-guy NGOs were backing us, straight out of the WTO and the Davos Forum. We even had *security clearances*. It was all for the *public good*!"

Malvern and Fearon exchanged wary glances.

Kingseed scowled at them. "Malvern, how much weasel flesh do you have in your personal genetic makeup?"

"Practically none, Dr. Kingseed!" Malvern demurred. "Just a few plasmids in my epidermal expression."

"Well, see, that's the vital difference between your decadent times and my heroic age. Back in my day, people were incredibly *anxious* and *fussy* about genetic contamination. They expected people and animals to have clean, unpolluted, fully natural genelines. But then, of course, the Greenhouse Effect destroyed the natural ecosystem. Only the thoroughly unnatural and the totally hyped-up could thrive in that kind of crisis. Civilization always collapsed *worst* where the habitats were *most nearly natural*. So the continent of Africa was, well, pretty much obliterated."

"Oh, we're with the story," Fearon assured him. "We're totally with it heart-of-darkness-wise."

"'Ha!" barked Kingseed. "You pampered punks got no idea what genuine chaos looks like! It was incredibly awful! Guerrilla armies of African mercenaries grabbed all our state-of-the-art lab equipment. They were looting...burning...and once the narco-terror crowd moved in from the Golden Triangle, it got mondo bizarre!"

Malvern shrugged. "So how tough can it be? You just get on a plane and go look." He looked at Fearon. "You get on planes, don't you, Fearon?"

"Surewise. Cars, sleds, waterskis, you bet I get on planes."

Kingseed raised a chiding finger. "We were desperate to save all those endangered species, so we just started packing them into anything that looked like it would survive the climate disruption. Elephant DNA spliced into cacti, rhino sequences tucked into fungi... And hey, we were the *good* guys. You should have seen what the *ruthless terrorists* were up to."

Malvern picked a fragment from his molars, examined it thoughtfully, and ate it. "Look, Dr Kingseed, all this ancient history's really edifying, but I still don't get it with the swollen, exploding brain part."

"That's also what Ribo Zombie wanted to know."

Fearon stiffened. "Ribo Zombie came here? What did you tell him?"

"I told that sorry punk nothing! Not one word did he get out of me! He's been sniffing around my crib, but I chased him back to his media coverage and his high-priced market consultants."

Malvern offered a smacking epidermal high-five. "Kemp, you are aces guru-wise! You're the Miami swamp yoda, dad!"

"I kinda like you two kids, so let me cluetrain you in. Ever seen NATO military chimp-brain? If you know how to tuck globs of digitally altered chimp brain into your own glial cells—and I'm not saying that's painless—then you can radically jazz your own cortex. Just swell your head up like a mushroom puffball." Kingseed gazed at them soberly. "It runs on DNA storage, that's the secret. Really, *really* long strands of DNA. We're talking like infinite Turing-tape strands of gattaca."

"Kemp," said Fearon kindly, "why don't you come along with us to Africa? You spend too much time in this toxic old factory with that big smelly spider. It'll do you good to get some fresh jungle air. Besides, we clearly require a wise native guide, given this situation."

"Are you two clowns really claiming that you wanna pursue this score to *Africa*?"

"Oh sure, Ghana, Guinea, whatever. We'll just nick over to the Dark Continent duty-freewise, and check it out for the weekend. Come on, Kemp, we're scabs! We got cameras, we got credit cards! It's a cakewalk!"

Kingseed knotted his snowy eyebrows. "Every sane human being fled out of Africa decades ago. It's the dark side of the Immunosance. Even the Red Cross ran off screaming."

"'Red Cross,'" said Malvern to Fearon. The two of them were unable to restrain their hearty laughter. "'Red Cross.' Man, that's rich."

"Okay, sure, have it your own way," Kingseed muttered. "I'll just go sherlock my oldest dead-media and scare up some tech-specs." He retreated to his vespine inner sanctum. Antic rummaging noises followed.

Fearon patiently sank into a classic corrugated Gehry chair. Malvern raided Kingseed's tiny bachelor kitchen, appropriating a platter of honey-guarana snack cubes. "What a cool pad this rich geezer's got!" Malvern said, munching. "I am digging how the natural light piped in through fiber-optic channels renders this fuel-tank so potent for lab-work."

"This place is a stinking dump. Sure he's rich, but that just means he'll overcharge us."

Malvern sternly cleared his throat. "Let's get something straight, partner. I haven't posted a scab acquisition since late last year! And you're in no better shape, with married life putting such a crimp in your scabbing. If we expect to pull down big-time decals and sponsorships, we've just got to beat Ribo Zombie to a major find. And this one is definitely ours by right."

After a moment, Fearon nodded in grim commitment. It was impossible to duck a straight-out scab challenge like this one—not if he expected to face himself in the mirror.

Kingseed emerged from his papery attic, his glasses askew and the wild pastures of his hair scampering with dustbunnies. He bore a night-dark raven in a splintery bamboo cage, along with a moldy fistful of stippled paper strips.

"Candybytes! I stored all the African data on candybytes! They were my bonanza for the child educational market. Edible paper, tasty sugar substrate, info-rich secret ingredients!"

"Hey yeah!" said Malvern nostalgically. "I used to eat candybytes as a little kid in my Time-Warner-Disney Creche. So now one of us has to gobble your moldy old lemon-drops?" Malvern was clearly nothing loath.

"No need for that, I brought old Heckle here. Heckle is my verbal output device."

Fearon examined the raven's cage. "This featherbag looks as old as a Victrola."

Kingseed set a moldy data strip atop a table, then released Heckle. The dark bird hopped unerringly to the start of the tape, and began to peck and eat. As Heckle's living read-head ingested and interpreted the coded candybytes, the raven jumped around the table like a fairy-chess knight, a corvine Turing Train.

"How is a raven like a writing desk?" murmured Kemp.

Heckle, shivered, stretched his glossy wings, and went Delphic. In a croaky, midnight-dreary voice, the neurally-possessed bird delivered a strange tale.

A desperate group of Noahs and Appleseeds, Goodalls and Cousteaus, Leakeys and Fosseys, had gathered up Africa's endangered flora and fauna, then packed the executable genetic information away into a most marvelous container: the Panspecific Mycoblastula. The Panspecific Mycoblastula was an immortal chimeric fungal ball of awesome storage capacity, a filamentously aggressive bloody tripe-wad, a motile Darwinian lights-and-liver battle-slimeslug.

Shivering with mute attention, Fearon brandished his handheld, carefully recording every cawed and revelatory word. Naturally the device also displayed the point-of-view of Weeble's crittercam.

Suddenly, Fearon glimpsed a shocking scene. Weeble was under attack!

There was no mistaking the infamous Skratchy Kat, who had been trying, without success, to skulk around Kingseed's industrial estate. Weeble's porcine war cry emerged tinnily from the little speakers. The crittercam's transmission whipsawed in frenzy.

"Sic him, Weeble! Hoof that feline spy!"

Gamely obeying his master's voice, the pig launched his bulk at the top-of-the-line postfeline. A howling combat ensued, Fearon's pig getting the worse of it. Then Shelob the multi-ton spider joined the fray. Skratchy Kat quickly saw the sense of retreat. When the transmission stabilized, the superstar's familiar had vanished. Weeble grunted proudly. The crittercam bobbed rhythmically as the potent porker licked his wounds with antiseptic tongue.

"You the man, Fearon! Your awesome pig kicked that cat's ass-wise!"

Kingseed scratched his head glumly. "You had a crittercam channel open to your pig this whole time, didn't you?"

Fearon grimaced, clutching his handheld. "Well, of course I did! I didn't want my Weeble to feel all lonely."

"Ribo Zombie's cat was watergating your pig. Ribo Zombie must have heard everything we said up here. I hope he didn't record those GPS coordinates."

The possessed raven was still cackling spastically, as the last crackles of embedded data spooled through its postcorvine speech centers. Heckle was recaged and rewarded with a tray of crickets.

Suddenly, Fearon's handheld spoke up in a sinister basso. It was the incoming voice of Ribo Zombie himself. "So the Panspecific Mycoblastula is in Sierra Leone. It is a savage territory, ruled by the mighty bushsoldier, Prince Kissy Mental. He is a ferocious cannibal who would chew you small-timers up like aphrodisiac gum! So Malvern and Fearon—take heed of my street-wisdom. I have the top-line hardware, and now, thanks to you, I have the data as well. Save yourselves the trouble, just go home."

"Gumshoe on up here, you washed-up ponce!" said startled Malvern, dissed to the bone. "My fearsome weasel will go sloppy seconds on your big fat cat!"

Kingseed stretched forth his liver-spotted mitt. "Turn off those handhelds, boys."

When Fearon and Malvern had bashfully powered down their devices, the old guru removed an antique pager from his lab bench. He played his horny thumb across the rudimentary keypad.

"A *pager*?" Malvern goggled. "Why not, like, jungle drums?"

"Pipe down. You pampered modern lamers can't even manage elementary anti-surveillance. Whereas, while one obsolescent pager is useless—two are a secure link."

Kingseed read the archaic glyphs off the tiny screen. "I can see that my contact in Freetown, Dr. Herbert Zoster, is still operational. With his help, you might yet beat Zombie to this prize." Kingseed looked up. "After allowing Ribo Zombie to bug my very home, I expect no less from you. You'd better come through this time, or never show your faces again at the Tallahassee scabCon. With your dalkon shields—or on them, boys."

"Lofty! We're outta here pronto! Thanks a lot, gramps."

Tupper was very alarmed about Africa. After an initial tearful outburst, hot meals around Fearon's house became as rare as whales and pandas. Domestic conversation died down to apologetic bursts of dingbat-decorated email. Their sex life, always sensually satisfactory and emotionally deep, became as chilly as the last few lonely glaciers of Greenhouse Greenland. Glum but determined, Fearon made no complaint.

On the day of his brave departure—his important gear stowed in two carry-on bags, save for that which Weeble wore in khaki-colored saddle-style pouches—Fearon paused at the door of their flat. Tupper sat morosely on the couch, pretending to surf the screen. For thirty seconds the display showed an ad from AT&T (Advanced Transcription and Totipotency) touting their latest telomere upgrades. Fearon was, of course, transfixed. But then Tupper changed channels, and he refocused mournfully for a last homesick look at his frosty spouse.

"I must leave you now, Tuppence honey, to meet Malvern at the docks." Even the use of her pet name failed to break her reserve. "Darling, I know this hurts your feelings, but think of it this way: my love for you is true because I'm true to my own true self. Malvern and I will be in and out of that tropical squalor in a mere week or two, with minimal lysis all around. But if I don't come back right away—or even, well, forever—I want you to know without you, I'm nothing. You're the feminine mitochondrium in my dissolute masculine plasm, baby."

Nothing. Fearon turned to leave, hand on the doorknob. Tupper swept him up in an embrace from behind, causing Weeble to grunt in surprise. Fearon slithered around within the cage of her arms to face her, and she mashed her lips into his.

Malvern's insistent pounding woke the lovers up. Hastily, Fearon redonned his outfit, bestowed a final peck on Tupper's tear-slicked cheek, and made his exit.

"A little trouble getting away?" Malvern leered.

"Not really. You?"

"Well, my landlady made me pay the next month's rent in advance. Oh, and if I'm dead, she gets to sell all my stuff."

"Harsh."

"Just the kind of treatment I expect."

Still flushed from the fever-shots at U.S. Customs, the two globe-trotting scabs watched the receding coast of America from the deck of their Cuba-bound ferry, the *Gloria Estefan*.

"I hate all swabs," said Malvern, belching as his innards rebooted.

Fearon clutched his squirming belly. "We could have picked better weather. These ferocious Caribbean hurricane waves—"

"What 'waves'? We're still in the harbor."

"Oh, my Lord—"

After a pitching, greenish sea-trip, Cuba hove into view. The City of Havana, menaced by rising seas, had been relocated up the Cuban coast through a massive levy on socialist labor. The crazy effort had more or less succeeded, though it looked as if every historic building in the city had been picked up and dropped.

Debarking in the fragrant faux-joy of the highly colored tropics, the eager duo hastened to the airfield—for only the cowboy Cubans still maintained direct air-flights to the wrecked and smoldering shell of the Dark Continent.

Mi Amiga Flicka was a hydrogen-lightened cargolifter of Appaloosa-patterned horsehide. The buoyant lift was generated by onboard horse stomachs, modified to spew hydrogen instead of the usual methane. A tanker truck, using a long boom-arm, pumped a potent microbial oatmeal into the tethered dirigible's feedstock reservoirs.

"There's a microbrewery on board," Malvern said with a travel agent's phony glee. "Works off grain mash just like a horse does! *Cerveza muy potenta*, you can bet."

A freestanding bamboo elevator ratcheted them up to the zeppelin's passenger module, which hung like a zippered saddlebag from the buoyant horsehide belly.

The bio-zep's passenger cabin featured a zebrahide mess-hall that doubled as a ballroom, with a tiny bandstand and a touchingly antique mirrorball. The Cuban stewards, to spare weight and space, were all jockey-sized.

Fearon and Malvern discovered that their web-booked "stateroom" was slightly smaller than a standard street toilet. Every feature of the tiny suite folded, collapsed, inverted, everted, or required assembly from scattered parts.

"I don't think I can get used to peeing in the same pipe that dispenses that legendary microbrew," said Fearon. Less finicky, Malvern had already tapped and sampled a glass of the golden boutique *cerveza*. "Life is a closed loop, Fearon."

"But where will the pig sleep?"

They found their way to the observation lounge for the departure of the giant gasbag. With practiced ease, the crew detached blimp-hook from mooring mast. The bacterial fuel-cells kicked over the myosin motors, the props began to windmill and the craft surged eastward with all the verve and speed of a spavined nag.

Malvern was already deep into his third *cerveza*. "Once we get our hands on that wodge of extinct gene-chains, our names are forever golden! It'll be vino, gyno and techno all the way!"

"Let's not count our chimeras till they're decanted, Mal. We're barely puttering along, and I keep thinking of Ribo Zombie and his highly publicized private entomopter."

"Ribo Zombie's a fat show-biz phoney, he's all talk! We're heavy-duty street-level *chicos* from Miami! It's just no contest."

"Hmmph. We'd better vortal in to *Fusing Nuclei* and check out the continuing coverage."

Fearon found a spot where the zep's horsehide was thinnest, and tapped an overhead satellite feed. The gel-screen of his handheld flashed the familiar *Fusing Nuclei* logo.

"In his one-man supercavitating sub, Ribo Zombie and Skratchy Kat speed toward the grim nomansland of sub-Saharan Africa! What weird and wonderful adventures await our intrepid lone-wolf scab and his plucky familiar? Does carnal love lurk in some dusky native bosom? Log-on Monday for the realtime landing of RZ and Skratchy upon the sludge-sloshing shores of African doom! And remember, kids—Skratchy Kat cards, toys and collectibles are available only through Nintendo-Benz—"

"Did they say 'Monday?'" Malvern screeched. "Monday is tomorrow! We're already royally boned!"

"Malvern, please, the straights are staring at us. Ribo Zombie can't prospect all of Africa through all those old UN emplacements. Kingseed found us an expert native guide, remember? Dr. Herbie Zoster."

Malvern stifled his despair. "You really think this native scab has got the stuffwise?"

Fearon smiled. "Well, he's not a scab quite like us, but he's definitely our type! He's pumped, ripped and buff, plus, he's wily and streetsmart. I checked out his online resumé! Herbie Zoster has been a mercenary, an explorer, an archaeologist, even the dictator of an offshore datahaven. Once we hook up with him, this ought to be a waltz."

In the airborne hours that followed, Malvern sampled a foretaste of the vino, gyno and techno, while Fearon repeatedly wrote and erased apologetical email to his wife. Then came their scheduled arrival over the melancholy ruins of Freetown—and a dismaying formal announcement by the ship's Captain.

"What do you mean, you can't moor?" demanded Malvern.

Their Captain, a roguish and dapper, yet intensely competent fellow named Luis Sendero, removed his cap, and slicked back the two macaw feathers anchored at his temple. "The local *caudillo*, Prince Kissy Mental, has incited his people to burn down our trading facilities. One learns to expect these little setbacks in the African trade. Honoring our contracts, we shall parachute to earth the goods we bring, unless they are not paid for—in which case, they are dumped anyway, yet receive no parachute. As for you two Yankees and your two animals—you are the only passengers who want to land in Sierra Leone. If you wish to touch down, you must parachute just as the cargo."

After much blustering, whuffling and whining, Fearon, Malvern and Weeble stood at the open hatch of *Mi Amiga Flicka*, parachutes strapped insecurely on, ripcords wired to a rusty cable, while the exotic scents of the rainy African landscape wafted to their nostrils.

Wistfully, they watched their luggage recede to the scarred red earth. Then, with Spike clutched to his breast, Malvern closed his eyes and boldly tumbled overboard. Fearon watched closely as his colleague's fabric chute successfully bloomed. Only then did he make up his mind to go through with it. He booted the reluctant Weeble into airy space, and followed suit.

"Outsiders never bring us anything but garbage," mumbled Dr. Zoster.

"Is it *Cuban* garbage?" said Malvern, tucking into their host's goat-and-pepper soup with a crude wooden spoon.

"No. They're always Cubans bringing it, but it's *everybody's* garbage that is dumped on Africa. It becomes a cargo-cult phenomenon. For you see: any sufficiently advanced garbage is indistinguishable from magic."

Fearon surreptitiously fed the peppery *cabrito* to his pig. He was having a hard time successfully relating to Dr. Herbie Zoster. It had never occurred to him that elderly Kemp Kingseed and tough, sunburnt Herbie Zoster were such close kin.

In point of fact, Herbie Zoster was Kingseed's younger clone. And it didn't require Jungian analysis to see that, just like most clones, Zoster bitterly resented the egotistical man who had created him. This was very clearly the greatest appeal of life in Africa for Dr. Herbie Zoster. Africa was the one continent guaranteed to make him as much unlike Kemp Kingseed as possible.

Skin tinted dark as mahogany, callused and wiry, dotted with many thorn-scratches, parasites and gunshot wounds, Zoster still bore some resemblance to Kingseed—about as much as a battle-scarred hyena to an aging bloodhound.

"What exactly do people dump around here?" said Malvern with interest.

Zoster mournfully chewed the last remnant of a baked yam and spat the skin into the darkness outside their thatched hut. Something with great glowing eyes pounced upon it instantly, with a rasp and a snarl. "You're familiar with the 'Immunosance?'"

"Oh yeah, sure!" said Malvern artlessly, "we're from Miami."

"That new Genetic Age completely replaced the Nuclear Age, the Space Age, and the Information Age."

"Good riddance," Malvern offered. "You got any more of that *cabrito* stew? It's fine stuff!"

Zoster rang a crude brass bell. A limping, turbaned manservant dragged himself into their thatched hut, tugging a bubbling bucket of chow.

"The difficulty with massive technological advance," said Zoster, spooning the steamy goop, "is that it obsolesces the previous means of production. When the Immunosance arrived, omnipresent industries already covered all the advanced countries." Zoster paused to pump vigorously at a spring-loaded homemade crank, which caused the light-bulb overhead to brighten to its full thirty watts. "There simply was no *room* to install the new bio-industrial revolution. But a revolution was very necessary anyway. So all the previous junk had to go. The only major planetary area with massive dumping grounds was—and still is—Africa."

Zoster rubbed at his crank-stiffened forearm and sighed. "Sometimes they promote the garbage and sell it to us Africans. Sometimes they drop it anonymously. But nevertheless—no matter how we struggle or resist—the very worst always ends up here in Africa, no matter what."

"I'm with the sequence," said Malvern, pausing to belch. "So what's the 4-1-1 about this fabled Panspecific Mycoblastula?"

Zoster straightened, an expression of awe toughening his face below his canvas hatbrim. "That is garbage of a very special kind. Because the Panspecific Mycoblastula is an entire, outmoded natural *ecosystem*. It is the last wild continent, completely wadded up and compressed by foreign technicians!"

Fearon considered this gnomic remark. He found it profoundly encouraging. "We understand the gravity of this matter, Dr. Zoster. Malvern and I feel that we can make this very worth your while-wise. Time is of the essence. When can we start?"

Zoster scraped the dirt floor with his worn boot-heel. "I'll have to hire a train of native bearers. I'll have to obtain supplies. We will be risking our lives, of course . . . What can you offer us in return for that?"

"A case of soft drinks?" said Malvern.

Fearon leaned forward intently. "Transistor radios? Antibiotics? How about some plumbing?"

Zoster smiled for the first time, with a flash of gold teeth. "Call me Herbie."

Zoster extended a callused fingertip. It bore a single ant, the size and color of a sesame seed.

"This is the largest organism in the world."

"So I heard," Malvern interjected glibly. "Just like the fire-ants invading America, right? They went through a Darwinian bottleneck and came out supercharged sisters, genetically identical even under different queens. They spread across the whole USA smoother than marshmallow fluff."

Zoster wiped his sweating stubbled jaw with a filthy bandanna. "These ants were produced four decades ago. They carry rhizotropic fungi, to fertilize crops with nitrogen. But their breeders overdesigned them. These ants cause tremendous fertile growth in vegetation, but they're also immune to insect diseases and parasites. The swabs finally wiped them out in America, but Africa has no swabs. We have no public health services, no telephones, no roads. So from Timbuktu to Capetown, cloned ants have spread in a massive wave, a single super-organism big as Africa."

Malvern shook his head in superior pity. "That's what you get for trusting in swabs, man. Any major dude could've told those corporate criminals that top-down hierarchies never work out. Now, the approach you Third Worlders need is a viral-marketing, appropriate-technology pitch . . . "

Zoster actually seemed impressed by Malvern's foolish bravado, and engaged the foreign scab in earnest jargon-laced discussion, leaving Fearon to trudge along in an unspeaking fug of sweat-dripping, alien jungle heat. Though Zoster was the only one armed, the trio of scabs boldly led their little expedition through a tangle of feral trails, much aided by their satellite surveillance maps and GPS locators.

Five native bearers trailed the parade, fully laden-down with scab-baggage and provisions. The bare-chested, bare-legged, dhoti-clad locals exhibited various useful bodily mods, such as dorsal water storage humps, toughened and splayed feet, and dirty grub-excavating claws that could shred a stump in seconds. They also sported less rational cosmetic changes, including slowly moving cicatrices (really migratory subepidermal symbiotic worms) and enlarged ears augmented with elephant musculature. The rhythmic flapping of the porters' ears produced a gentle creaking that colorfully punctuated their impenetrable sibilant language.

The tormented landscape of Sierra Leone had been thoroughly reclaimed by a clapped-out mutant jungle. War, poverty, disease, starvation—the Four Landrovers of the African Apocalypse—had long since been and gone, bringing a drastic human population crash that beggared the Black Death, and ceding the continent to resurgent flora and fauna.

These local flora and fauna were, however, radically human-altered, recovering from an across-the-board apocalypse even more severe and scourging than the grisly one suffered by humans. Having come through the grinding hopper of a bioterror, they were no longer "creatures" but "evolutures." Trees writhed, leaves crawled, insects croaked, lizards bunny-hopped, mammals flew, flowers pinched, vines slithered, and mushrooms burrowed. The fish, clumsily reengineered for the surging Greenhouse realities of rising seas, lay in the jungle trails burping like lungfish. When stepped upon, they almost seemed to speak.

The explorers found themselves navigating a former highway to some long-buried city, presumably "Bayau" or "Moyamba," to judge by the outdated websites. Post-natural oddities lay atop an armature of ruins, revealing the Ozymandias lessons of industrial hubris. A mound of translucent jello assumed the outlines of a car, including a dimly perceived skeletal driver and passengers. Oil-slick-colored orchids vomited from windows and doors. With the descending dusk invigorating flocks of winged post-urban rats, the travelers made camp. Zoster popped up a pair of tents for the expedition's leaders and their animals, while the locals assembled a humble jungle igloo of fronds and thorns.

After sharing a few freezedried packets of slumgullion, the expedition sank in weary sleep. Fearon was so bone-tired that he somehow tolerated Malvern's nasal whistling and Zoster's stifled dream shouts.

He awoke before the others. He unseamed the tent flap and poked his head out into the early sunshine.

Their encampment was surrounded by marauders. Spindly scouts, blank-eyed and scarcely human, were watching the pop-tents and leaning on pig-iron spears.

Fearon ducked his head back and roused his compatriots, who silently scrambled into their clothes. Heads clustered like coconuts, the three of them peered through a fingernail's width of tent-flap.

Warrior-reinforcements now arrived in ancient jeeps, carrying anti-aircraft guns and rocket-propelled grenades.

"It's Kissy Mental's Bush Army," whispered Zoster. He pawed hurriedly through a pack, coming up with a pair of mechanical boots.

"Okay, girls, listen up," Zoster whispered, shoving and clamping his feet in the piston-heavy footgear. "I have a plan. When I yank this overhead pull-tab, this tent unpops. That should startle the scouts out there, maybe enough to cover our getaway. We all race off at top speed just the way we came. If either of you survive, feel free to rendezvous back at my place."

Zoster hefted his gun, their only weapon. He dug the toe of each boot into a switch on the heel of its mate, and his boots began to chuff and emit small puffs of exhaust.

"Gasoline-powered seven-league boots," Zoster explained, seeing their stricken expressions. "South African Army surplus. There's no need for roads with these things, but with skill and practice, you can pronk along like a gazelle at thirty, forty miles an hour."

"You really believe we can outrun these jungle marauders?" Malvern asked.

"I don't have to outrun them; I only have to outrun *you*."

Zoster triggered the tent and dashed off at once, firing his pistol at random. The pistons of his boots gave off great blasting backfires, which catapulted him away with vast stainless-steel lunges.

Stunned and in terror, Malvern and Fearon stumbled out of the crumpling tent, coughing on Zoster's exhaust. By the time they straightened up and regained their vision, they were firmly in the grip of Prince Kissy Mental's troops.

The savage warriors attacked the second pop-tent with their machetes. They quickly grappled and snaffled the struggling Spike and Weeble.

"Chill, Spike!"

"Weeble, hang loose!"

The animals obeyed, though the cruel grip of their captors promised the worst.

The minions of the Prince were far too distanced from humanity to have any merely ethnic identity. Instead, they shared a certain fungal sheen, a somatype evident in their thallophytic pallor and exopthalmic gaze. Several of the marauders, wounded by Zoster's wild shots, were calmly stuffing various grasses and leaves into the gaping suety holes in their arms, legs and chests.

A working squad now dismantled the igloo of the expedition's bearers, pausing to munch meditatively on the greenery of the cut fronds. The panic-stricken bearers gabbled in obvious terror, but offered no resistance. A group of Kissy Mental's warriors, with enormous heads and great toothy jaws, decamped from a rusty jeep. They unshouldered indestructible Russian automatic rifles and decisively emptied their clips into the hut. Pathetic screams came from the ruined igloo. The warriors then demolished the walls and hauled out the dead and wounded victims, to dispassionately tear them limb from limb.

The Army then assembled their new booty of meat, to bear it back up the trail to their camp. Their fearsome captors, reeking of sweat and formic acid, bound the hands of Fearon and Malvern with tough lengths of grass. They strung Weeble and Spike to a shoulder-pole, where the terrified beasts dangled like piñatas.

Then they forced the quartet of prisoners forward on the quick march. As they passed through the fetid jungle, the Army paused periodically, to empty their automatic weapons at anything that moved. Whatever victim fell to earth would be swiftly chopped to chunks and added to the head-borne packages of the rampaging mass.

Within the hour, Fearon and Malvern were delivered whole to Prince Kissy Mental.

Deliberately, Fearon focused his attention on the Prince's throne, so as to spare himself the sight of the monster within it. The Army's portable throne was a row of three first-class airplane seats, with the armrests removed to accommodate the Prince's vast posthuman bulk. The throne perched atop a mobile palanquin, juryrigged from rebar, chipboard, and astroturf. A system of crutches and tethers supported and eased the Prince's vast, teratological skull.

The trophy captives were shoved forward at spearpoint through a knee-deep heap of cargo-cult gadgets.

"Holy smallpox!" whispered Malvern. "This bossman's half-chimp and half-ant!"

"That doesn't leave any percentage for human, Mal."

The thrust of a spear-butt knocked Fearon to his knees. Kissy Mental's coarse-haired carcass, barrel-chested to support the swollen needs of the head, was sketched like a Roquefort cheese with massive blue veins. The Prince's vast pulpy neck marked the transition zone to a formerly human skull whose sutures had long since burst under pressure, to be patched with big, red shiny plates of antlike chitin. Kissy Mental's head was bigger than the prize-winning pumpkin at a 4-H Fair—even when "4-H" meant "Homeostasis, Haplotypes, Histogenesis and Hypertrophy."

Fearon slitted his eyes, rising to his feet. He was terrified, but the thought of never seeing Tupper again somehow put iron in his soul. To imagine that he might someday be home again, safe with his beloved—that prospect was worth any sacrifice. There had to be some method to bargain with their captor.

"Malvern, how bright do you think this guy is? You suppose he's got any English, speaking-wise?"

"He's got to be at least as intelligent as British royalty."

With an effort that set his bloated heart booming like a tribal drum, the Prince lifted both his hairy arms, and beckoned. Their captors pushed Mal and Fear right up against the throne. The Prince unleashed a flock of personal fleas. Biting, lancing, and sucking, the tasters lavishly sampled the flesh of Fearon and Malvern, and returned to their master. After quietly munching a few of the blood-gorged familiars, the Prince silently brooded, the tiny bloodshot eyes in his enormous skull blinking like LEDs. He then gestured for a courtier to ascend into the presence. The bangled, head-dressed ant-man hopped up and, well-trained, sucked a thin clear excretion from the Prince's rugose left nipple.

Smacking his lips, the lieutenant decrypted his proteinaceous commands, in a sudden frenzy of dancing, shouting, and ritual gesticulation.

Swiftly the Army rushed into swarming action, trampling one another in an ardent need to lift the Prince's throne upon their shoulders. Once they had their entomological kingpin up and in lolling motion, the Army milled forward in a violent rolling surge, employing their machetes on anything in their path.

A quintet of burly footmen pushed Malvern and Fearon behind the bluish exhaust of an ancient military jeep. The flesh of the butchered bearers had been crudely wrapped in broad green leaves and dumped in the back of the vehicle.

Malvern muttered sullenly below the grumbles of the engine. "That scumbag Zoster . . . All clones are inherently degraded copies. Man, if we ever get out of this pinch, it's no more Mr. Nice Guy."

"Uh, sure, that's the old scab spirit, Mal."

"Hey, look!"

Fearon followed Malvern's jerking head-nod. A split-off subdivision of the trampling Army had dragged another commensal organism from the spooked depths of the mutant forest. It was a large, rust-eaten, canary-yellow New Beetle, scribbled over with arcane pheromonal runes. Its engine long-gone, the wreck rolled solely through the Juggernaut heaving of the Army.

"Isn't that the 2015 New Beetle?" said Fearon. "The Sport Utility version, the one they ramped up big as a stretch Humvee?"

"Yeah, the Screw-the-Greenhouse Special! Looks like they removed the sunroof and moonroof, and taped all the windows shut! But what the hell can they have inside-wise? Whatever it is, it's all mashed up and squirmy against the glass—"

A skinny Ant Army courtier vaulted and scrambled onto the top of the sealed vehicle. With gingerly care, he stuffed a bloody wad of meat in through the missing moonroof.

From out of the adjacent gaping sunroof emerged a hydralike bouquet of heterogeneous animal parts: tails, paws, snouts, beaks, ears. Snarls, farts, bellows and chitterings ensued.

At length, a sudden flow of syrupy exudate drooled out the tailpipe, caught by an eager cluster of Ant Army workers cupping their empty helmets.

"They've got the Panspecific Mycoblastula in there!"

The soldiers drained every spatter of milky juice, jittering crazily and licking one another's lips and fingers.

"I do wish I had a camera," said Fearon wistfully. "It's very hard to watch a sight like this without one."

"Look, they're feeding our bearers into that thing!" marveled Malvern. "What do you suppose it's doing with all that human DNA? Must be kind of a partially-human genetic mole-rat thing going on in there."

Another expectant crowd hovered at the Beetle's tailpipe, their mold-spotted helmets at the ready. They had not long to wait, for a fleshy diet of protein from the butchered bearers seemed to suit the Panspecific Mycoblastula to a T.

Sweating and pale-faced, Malvern could only say, "If they were breakfast, when's lunch?"

Fearon had never envisioned such brutal slogging, so much sheer physical work in the simple effort of eating and staying alive. The Prince's Army marched well-nigh constantly, bulldozing the landscape in a whirl of guns and knives. Anything they themselves could not devour was fed to the Mycoblastula. Nature knew no waste, so the writhing abomination trapped in the Volkswagen was a panspecific glutton, an always-boiling somatic stewpot. It especially doted on high-end mammalian life, but detritus of all kinds was shoved through the sunroof to sate its needs: bark, leaves, twigs, grubs, and beetles. Especially beetles. In sheer number of species, most of everything living was always beetles.

Then came the turn of their familiars.

It seemed at first that those unique beasts had somehow earned the favor of Prince Kissy Mental. Placed onboard his rollicking throne, the trussed Spike and Weeble had been subjected to much rough cosseting and petting, their peculiar high-tech flesh seeming to particularly strike the Prince's fancy.

But such good fortune could not last. After noon of their first day of captivity, the bored Prince, without warning, snapped Spike's neck and flung the dead weasel in the path of the painted Volkswagen. Attendants snatched the weasel up and stuffed Spike in. The poor beast promptly lined an alimentary canal.

Witnessing this atrocity, Malvern roared and attempted to rush forward. A thorough walloping with boots and spear-butts persuaded him otherwise.

Then Weeble was booted meanly off the dais. Two hungry warriors scrambled to load the porker upside down onto a shoulder-carried spear. Weeble's piteous grunts lanced through Fearon, but at least he could console himself that, unlike Spike, his pig still lived.

But finally, footsore, hungry and beset by migraines, his immune system drained by constant microbial assault, Fearon admitted despair. It was dead obvious that he and Malvern were simply doomed. There was just no real question that they were going to be killed and hideously devoured, all through their naive desire for mere fame, money, and professional technical advancement.

When they were finally allowed to collapse for the night on the edge of a marshy savannah, Fearon sought to clear his conscience.

"Mal, I know it's over, but think of all the good times we've had together. At least I never sold Florida real estate, like my Dad. A short life and a merry one, right? Die young and leave a beautiful corpse. Hope I die before I get—"

"Fearon, I'm fed up with your sunnysided optimism! You rich-kid idiot, you always had it easy and got all the breaks! You think that rebellion is some kind of game! Well, let me tell you, if I had just one chance to live through this, I'd never waste another minute on nutty dilettante crap. I'd go right for the top of the food chain. Let *me* be the guy on top of life, let *me* be the winner, just for once!" Malvern's battered face was livid. "From this day forth, if I have to lie, or cheat, or steal, or kill . . . Aw, what's the use? We're ant meat! I'll never even get the chancewise!"

Fearon was stunned into silence. There seemed nothing left to say. He lapsed into a sweaty doze amidst a singing mosquito swarm, consoling himself with a few last visions of his beloved Tupper. Maybe she'd remarry after learning of his death. Instead of following her sweet romantic heart, this time she'd wisely marry some straight guy, someone normal and dependable. Someone who would cherish her, and look after her, and take her rather large inheritance with the seriousness it deserved. How bitterly he regretted his every past unkindness, his every act of self-indulgence and neglect. The spouses of romantic rebels really had it rough.

In the morning, the hungry natives advanced on Weeble, and now it was Fearon's turn to shout, jump up and be clouted down.

With practiced moves the natives slashed off Weeble's front limbs near the shoulder joints. The unfortunate Weeble protested in a frenzy of squealing, but his assailants knew all too well what they were doing. Once done, they carefully cauterized the porker's foreparts and placed him in a padded stretcher, which was still marked with an ancient logo from the Red Cross.

They then gleefully roasted the pig's severed limbs, producing an enticing aroma Fearon and Malvern fought to abhor. The crisped breakfast ham was delivered with all due ceremony to Prince Kissy Mental, whose delight in this repast was truly devilish to watch. Clearly the Ant Army didn't get pig very often, least of all a pig with large transgenic patches of human flesh. A pig that good, you just couldn't eat all at once.

By evening, Fearon and Malvern were next on the menu. The two scabs were hustled front and center as the locals fed a roaring bonfire. A crooked pair of nasty wooden spits were prepared. Then Fearon and Malvern had their bonds cut through, and their clothes stripped off by a forest of groping hands.

The two captives were gripped and hustled and frogmarched as the happy Army commenced a manic dance around their sacred Volkswagen, ululating and keening in a thudding of drums. The evil vehicle oscillated from motion within, in time with the posthuman singing. Lit by the setting sun and the licking flames of the cannibal bonfire, big chimeric chunks of roiling Panspecific Mycoblastula tissue throbbed and slobbered against the glass.

Suddenly a brilliant klieg light framed the scene, with an 80-decibel airborne rendition of "Ride of the Valkyries."

"Hit the dirt!" yelped Malvern, yanking free from his captor's grip and casting himself on his face.

Ribo Zombie's entomopter swept low in a strafing run. The cursed Volkswagen exploded in a titanic gout of lymph, blood, bone fragments and venom, splattering Fearon—but not Malvern—from head to toe with quintessence of Mycoblastula.

Natives dropped and spun under the chattering impact of advanced armaments. Drenched with spew, Fearon crawled away from the Volkswagen, wiping slime from his face.

Dead or dying natives lay in crazy windrows, like genetically modified corn after a stiff British protest. Now Ribo Zombie made a second run, his theatrical lighting deftly picking out victims. His stagey attack centered, naturally, on the most dramatic element among the panicking Army, Prince Kissy Mental himself. The Prince struggled to flee the crimson targeting lasers, but his enormous head was strapped to his throne in a host of attachments. Swift and computer-sure came the next burst of gunfire. Prince Kissy Mental's abandoned head swung futilely from its tethers, a watermelon in a net.

Leaping and capering in grief and anguish, the demoralized Army scattered into the woods.

A swarm of mobile cameras wasped around the scene, carefully checking for proper angles and lighting. Right on cue, descending majestically from the darkening tropic sky came Ribo Zombie himself, crash-helmet burnished and gleaming, combat-boots blazoned with logos.

Skratchy Kat leaped from Zombie's shoulder to strike a proud pose by the Prince's still-smoking corpse. The superstar scab blew nonexistent trailing smoke from the unused barrels of his pearl-handled sidearms, then advanced on the cowering Fearon and Malvern.

"Nice try, punks, but you got in way over your head." Ribo Zombie gestured at a hovering camera. "You've been really great footage ever since your capture, though. Now get the hell out of camera range, and go find some clothes or something. That Panspecific Mycoblastula is all mine."

Rising from his hands and knees with a look of insensate rage, Malvern lunged up and dashed madly into the underbrush.

"What's keeping you?" boomed Ribo Zombie at Fearon.

Fearon looked down at his hands. Miniature parrot feathers were sprouting from his knuckles.

"Interesting outbreak of spontaneous mutation," Ribo Zombie noted. "I'll check that out just as soon as I get my trophy shot."

Advancing on the bullet-riddled Volkswagen, Ribo Zombie telescoped a razor-pincered probe. As the triumphant conqueror dipped his instrument into the quivering mass, Malvern charged him with a leveled spear.

The crude weapon could not penetrate Ribo Zombie's armor, but the force of the rush bounced the superstar scab against the side of the car. Quick as lightning a bloodied briar snaked through a gaping bullet hole and clamped the super-scab tight.

Then even more viscous and untoward tentacles emerged from the engine compartment, and a voracious sucking, gurgling struggle commenced.

Malvern, still naked, appropriated the fallen crash helmet with the help of a spear haft. "Look, it liquefied him instantly and sucked all the soup clean out! Dry as a bone inside. And the readouts still work on the eyepieces!"

After donning the helmet, a suspiciously close fit, Malvern warily retrieved Ribo Zombie's armored suit, which lay in its high-tech abandonment like the nacreous shell of a hermit crab. A puzzled Skratchy Kat crept forward. After a despondent sniff at the emptied boots, the bereaved familiar let out a continuous yowl.

"Knock it off, Skratchy," Malvern commanded. "We're all hurting here. Just be a man."

Swiftly shifting allegiances, Skratchy Kat supinely rubbed against Malvern's glistening shins.

"Now to confiscate his cameras for a little judicious editing of his unfortunate demise." Malvern shook his helmeted head. "You can cover for me, right, Fearon? Just tell everybody that Malvern Brakhage died in the jungle-wise. You should probably leave out the part about them wanting to eat us."

Fearon struggled to dress himself with some khaki integuments from a nearby casualty. "Malvern, I can't fit inside these clothes."

"What's your problem?"

"I'm growing a tail. And my claws don't fit in these boots." Fearon pounded the side of his head with his feathery knuckles. "Are you glowing, or do I have night vision all of a sudden?"

Malvern tapped his helmet with a wiry glove. "You're not telling me you're massively infected now, are you?"

"Well, technically speaking, Malvern, I'm the 'infection' in this situation, because the Mycoblastula's share of our joint DNA is a lot more extensive than mine is."

"Huh. Well, that development obviously tears it." Malvern backed off cautiously, tugging at the last few zips and buckles on his stolen armor to assure an airtight seal. "I'll route you some advanced biomedical help . . . if there's any available in the local airspace." He cleared his throat with a sudden rasp of helmet-mounted speakers. "In any case, the sooner I clear out of here for civilization, the better."

All too soon, the sound of the departing entomopter had died away. After searching through the carnage, pausing periodically as his spine and knees unhinged, Fearon located the still-breathing body of his beloved pig. Then he dragged the stretcher to an abandoned jeep.

"And then Daddy smelled the pollution from civilization with his new nose, from miles away, so he knew he'd reached the island of Fernando Po, where the UN still keeps bases. So despite the tragic death of his best friend Malvern, Daddy knew that everything was going to be all right. Life would go on!"

Fearon was narrating his exploit to the embryo in Tupper's womb via a state-of-the-art fetal interface, the GestaPhone. Seated on the comfy Laura Ashley couch in their bright new stilt house behind the dikes of Pensacola Beach, Tupper smiled indulgently at her husband's oft-polished tale.

"When the nice people on the island saw Daddy's credit cards, Daddy and Weeble were both quickly stabilized. Not exactly like we were before, mind you, but rendered healthy enough for the long trip back home to Miami. Then the press coverage started, and, well son, someday I'll tell you about how Daddy dealt with the challenges of fame and fortune."

"And wasn't Mommy glad to see Daddy again!" Tupper chimed in. "A little upset at first about the claws and fur. But luckily, Daddy and Mommy had been careful to set aside sperm samples while Daddy was still playing his scab games. So their story had a real happy ending when Daddy finally settled down and Baby Boy was safely engineered."

Fearon detached the suction cup terminal from Tupper's bare protuberant stomach. "Weeble, would you take these, please?"

The companionable pig reached up deftly, plucked the GestaPhone out of Fearon's grasp, and moved off with an awkward lope. Weeble's strange gait was due to his new forelimbs, a nifty pair of pig-proportioned human arms.

Tupper covered her womb with her frilled maternity blouse and glanced at the clock. "Isn't your favorite show on now?"

"Shucks, we don't have to watch every single episode . . ."

"Oh, honey, I love this show, it's my favorite, now that I don't have to worry about you getting all caught up in it!"

They nestled on the responsive couch, Tupper stroking the fish-scaled patch on Fearon's cheek while receiving the absent-minded caresses of his long tigerish tail. She activated the big wet screen, cohering a close-up of Ribo Zombie in the height of a ferocious rant.

"Keeping it real, folks, still keeping it real! I make this challenge to all my fellow scabs, those who are down with the Zombie and those who dis him, those who frown on him and those who kiss him. Yes, you sorry posers all know who you are. But check this out—who am I?"

Fearon sighed for a world well lost. And yet, after all—there was always the next generation.

acknowledgments

"Stone Lives" first appeared in *The Magazine of Fantasy and Science Fiction* in 1985.

"A Short Course in Art Appreciation" first appeared in *The Magazine of Fantasy and Science Fiction* in 1988.

"Phylogenesis" first appeared in *Synergy*, in 1988.

"A Thief in Babylon" first appeared in *Amazing* in 1989.

"Solitons" first appeared in *Semiotext(e) SF* in 1990.

"Gravitons" first appeared in *Hardware* in 1990.

"Any Major Dude" first appeared in *New Worlds* in 1991.

"Mud Puppy Goes Uptown" first appeared in *Back Brain Recluse* in 1994.

"Otto and Toto in the Oort" first appeared in *Science Fiction Age* in 1995.

"Life Sentence" first appeared in *Interzone* in 1996.

"Angelmakers" first appeared in *Interzone* in 1999.

"The Reluctant Book" first appeared in *Science Fiction Age* in 2000.

"Babylon Sisters" first appeared in *Interzone* in 2001.

"The Scab's Progress" first appeared online in *Sci Fiction* in 2001.

LaVergne, TN USA
11 March 2010

175690LV00002B/1/A